THE BOOK
OF COLD CASES

TITLES BY SIMONE ST. JAMES

THE BOOK OF COLD CASES

SIMONE ST. JAMES

BERKLEY | NEW YORK

BERKLEY
An imprint of Penguin Random House LLC

Copyright © 2022 by Simone Seguin
Penguin Random House supports copyright. Copyright fuels creativity, encourages diverse voices, promotes free speech, and creates a vibrant culture. Thank you for buying an authorized edition of this book and for complying with copyright laws by not reproducing, scanning, or distributing any part of it in any form without permission. You are supporting writers and allowing Penguin Random House to continue to publish books for every reader.

BERKLEY and the BERKLEY & B colophon are
registered trademarks of Penguin Random House LLC.

ISBN 9780440000211

Printed in the United States of America

Book design by Elke Sigal

For my mother, who didn't get to read this one.

PART I

PART I

CHAPTER ONE

Claire Lake, Oregon

The Greer mansion sat high on a hill, overlooking the town and the ocean. To get to it from downtown, you had to leave the pretty shops and the creaking seaside piers and drive a road that wound upward, toward the cliffs. You passed the heart of Claire Lake, the part of town where the locals lived and the tourists didn't usually go. You passed a grid of shops and low apartment blocks, local diners and hair salons. On the outskirts of town, you passed newer developments, built between the foot of the cliffs and the flat land on the edge of the inland lake that gave the town its name.

The land was too wet and rocky to keep building, so the newer developments tapered off into woods and two-lane roads. Along the west edge of the lake were homes built in the seventies, squat shapes in brown brick and cream siding, the gardens neatly kept for over forty years by people who had never moved away. Past those houses, around the other edges of the lake, there was nothing but back roads, used only by hikers, hunters, fishermen, and teenage kids looking for trouble. In the seventies, the houses along the lake were for the up-and-coming ones, the people with good jobs. Everyone else lived in town. And if you were rich, you lived on the hill.

The road climbed on the north side of the lake. The houses were set far apart here for privacy, and the roads were kept narrow and uneven, as if trying to keep outsiders away. The wealthy had come to Claire Lake in the twenties, when the town was first created, looking for a place that was scenic, secluded, and cheap to build big houses. They brought their money from Portland and California and settled in. Some of the houses sat empty after the stock market crash, but they filled up again during the boom after World War II. The people who lived here called the neighborhood Arlen Heights.

The Greer mansion was one of the original houses in Arlen Heights. It was an ugly Frankenstein of a house even when it was built—a pseudo-Victorian style of slanted roofs and spires, though the walls were of butter yellow brick. And when Julian Greer bought it in 1950 with his newly inherited pharmaceutical fortune, he made it worse. He remodeled the lower floor to be more modern, with straight lines and dark brown wood. He also put in a bank of windows along the back wall to open up the house's dark, gloomy interior. The windows looked out to the house's back lawn and its drop-off to the ocean beyond.

The effect was supposed to be sweeping, breathtaking, but like most of Julian's life, it didn't work out as planned. The windows fogged, and the view was bleak. The lawn was flat and dead, and the ocean beyond the cliff was choppy and cold. Julian had done the renovations in hopes of pleasing his new wife, Mariana, but instead the relentless view from the windows unsettled her, and she kept the curtains closed. She decorated the rest of the house dutifully but listlessly, which was a harbinger of their marriage. Something about the Greer mansion stifled laughter and killed happiness. It might sound dramatic, but anyone who had lived there knew it was true.

By 1975, both Julian and Mariana were dead, Julian with his blood all over the kitchen floor, Mariana in the twisted wreck of a car crash. The house watched all of it happen, indifferent.

Tonight it was raining, a cold, hard downpour that came in from the ocean. Arlen Heights was quiet, and the Greer mansion was dark. The rain spattered hard on the panes of glass, tracing lines down the large windows overlooking the lawn. The dark skeletons of the trees on either side of the house bowed back and forth in the wind, the branches scraping the roof. Drops pocked the empty driveway. The house was still and silent, stoic under the wind and the water.

On the lawn, something moved across the surface of the grass. The touch of a footprint. Inside the house, one of the cupboard doors opened in the dark kitchen, groaning softly into the silence.

In a bedroom window a shape appeared, shadowy and indistinct. The blur, perhaps, of a face. A handprint touched the bedroom window, the palm pressing into the glass. For a second, it was there, pale and white, though there was no one to see.

The wind groaned in the eaves. The handprint faded. The figure moved back into the darkness. And the house was still once more.

CHAPTER TWO

September 2017

SHEA

The day before I met Beth Greer was a Tuesday, with a gray sky overhead and a thin drizzle that wet my face and beaded in my hair as I waited at the bus stop. It was unseasonably warm, and the concrete gave off that rainy scent it sometimes has, rising up from beneath my ballet flats. There was a man standing next to me, wearing an overcoat and scrolling through his phone with an exhausted look on his face. On my other side was a worried-looking woman who was frantically texting. I closed my eyes, inhaling the scent of the rain laced with a thread of cologne from the man next to me, overlaid with gasoline and diesel fumes from the street. This was my life.

It wasn't a bad one. I was twenty-nine and divorced. I lived in a small complex of low-rise condos on a tangle of curved streets with the aspirational name of Saddle Estates. In my mind I called it Singles

Estates, because it was almost exclusively populated with romantic failures like me, people who needed somewhere to live when they sold off their married house and took their half of the money. The man in the overcoat was divorced, guaranteed, and I'd bet money the woman was texting a kid who was in school while spending a court-designated week with his father.

My divorce was still new. I had no kids. My place was small, smelled of paint, and only contained the bare necessities of furniture. But it wasn't the worst life I could have. I'd known since I was nine that I was lucky to have any life at all.

On the bus, I pulled out my phone, put my earbuds in my ears, and played the audiobook I was in the middle of listening to. A thriller: a woman in danger, most of the characters possibly lying, everything not quite as it seemed. A twist somewhere near the end that would either shock me or wouldn't. There were dozens of books just like it, hundreds maybe, and they were the soundtrack of my life. The woman's voice in my earbuds told me about death, murder, deep family secrets, people who shouldn't be trusted, lies that cost lives. But a novel always ends, the lies come to the surface, and the deaths are explained. Maybe one of the bad characters gets away with something— that's fashionable right now—but you are still left with a sense that things are balanced, that dark things come to light, and that the bad person will, at least, most likely be miserable.

It was dark comfort, but it was still comfort. I knew my own tally by heart: My would-be killer had been in prison for nineteen years, seven months, and twenty-six days. His parole hearing was in six months.

Work was a doctor's office in downtown Claire Lake. I was a re-ceptionist, taking calls, filing charts, making appointments. As I came through the door, I pulled the earbuds from my ears and gave my coworkers a smile, shaking off all of the darkness and death.

"Busy day," Karen, the other receptionist, said, glancing at me, then away again. "We open in twenty."

We weren't bosom friends, my coworkers and I, even though I had worked here for five years. The other women here were married with kids, which meant we had nothing much in common since my divorce. I hadn't talked to any of them about the divorce, except to say it had happened. And I couldn't add to the conversations about daycares and swimming programs. The doctors didn't socialize with any of us—they came and went, expecting the mechanism of the office to work without much of their input.

I took off my jacket and put on my navy blue scrub top, shoving my phone and purse under the desk. I could probably make friends here if I tried. I was attractive enough, with long dark hair that I kept tied back, an oval face, and dark eyes. At the same time, I didn't have the kind of good looks that threaten other women. I was standoffish—I knew that. It was an inescapable part of my personality, a tendency I couldn't turn off no matter how much therapy I did. I didn't like people too close, and I was terrible at small talk. My therapists called it a defense mechanism; I only knew it was me, like my height or the shape of my chin.

But my lack of gregariousness wasn't the only reason my coworkers gave me a wide berth. Though they didn't say anything to me, a rumor had gotten out in my first week; they all knew who I was, what I had escaped. And they all knew what I did in the evenings, the side project that consumed all of my off-hours. My obsession, really.

They probably all thought it wasn't healthy.

But I've always believed that murder is the healthiest obsession of all.

"Don't tell me," my sister, Esther, said on the phone. "You're hibernating again."

"I'm fine," I said. It was after work, and I was at my local grocery store, the Safeway in the plaza within walking distance to Singles Estates. I put cereal in my cart as I shoulder-pinned the phone to my ear. "I'm grabbing some groceries and going home."

"I told you to come over for dinner. Will and I want to see you."

"It's raining."

"This is Claire Lake. It's always raining."

I looked at a carton of almond milk, wondering what it tasted like. "I know you worry about me, but I'm fine. I just have work to do."

"You already have a job. The website isn't paid work."

"It pays enough."

My big sister sighed, and the sound gave me a twinge of sadness. I really did want to see her, along with her husband, Will, a lawyer who I liked quite a lot. Esther was one of the only people who really mattered to me, and even though she gave me grief, I knew she tried hard to understand me. She'd had her own guilt and trauma over what had happened to me. She had her own reasons to be paranoid—to hibernate, as she put it. The difference was, Esther *didn't* hibernate. She had a husband and a house and a good job, a career.

"Just tell me you're trying," Esther said. "Trying to get out, trying to do something, trying to meet new people."

"Sure," I said. "Today I met a man who has a hernia and a woman who would only say she has a 'uterus problem.'" I put the almond milk down. "I'm not sure what a 'uterus problem' is, and I don't think I'm curious."

"If you wanted to know, you could look in her file and find out."

"I never look in patients' files," I told her. "You know that. I answer phones and deal with appointment times, not diagnoses. Looking in a patient file could get me fired."

"You make no sense, Shea. You won't look at patients' medical files, but you'll talk about murders and dead bodies on the internet."

I paused, unpinning my phone from my shoulder. "Okay, that's actually a good point. I get that. But does it mean that in order to be consistent, I should be more nosy or less?"

"It means you live too much inside your own head, overthinking everything," Esther said. "It means you need to meet people who aren't patients, real people who aren't murder victims on a page. Make friends. Find a man to date."

"Not yet for the dating thing," I told her. "Maybe soon."

"The divorce was a year ago."

"Eleven months." I dodged a woman coming the opposite way up my aisle, then moved around a couple pondering the cracker selection. "I'm not opposed to finding someone. It's dating itself that freaks me out. I mean, you meet a stranger, and that's it? He could be anyone, hiding anything."

"Shea."

"Do you know how many serial killers dated lonely women in their everyday lives? Some divorcée who just wants companionship from a nice man? She thinks she's won the dating lottery, and meanwhile he's out there on a Sunday afternoon, dumping bodies. And now we're supposed to use internet apps, where someone's picture might not even be real. People are lying about their *faces*."

"Okay, okay. No dating apps. No dating at all yet. I get it. But make some friends, Shea. Join a book club or a bowling league or something."

My cart was full. I paused by the plate glass windows at the front of the store, letting my gaze travel over the parking lot. "I'll think about it."

"That means no," Esther said.

"It means I'll think about it." The parking lot looked like any normal parking lot during after-work hours, with cars pulling in and out. I watched for a moment, letting my eyes scan the cars and the people. An old habit. I couldn't have told you what I was looking for, only that I'd know it when I saw it. "Thanks, sis. I'll talk to you later."

I bought my groceries and put them in the cloth bags I'd brought with me. I slung the bags over my shoulders and started the walk home in the rain, my coat hood pulled up over my head, my feet trying to avoid the puddles. The walk toward Singles Estates took me down a busy road, with cars rushing by me, splashing water and giv-ing me a face full of fumes. Not the most pleasant walk in the world, but I put my earbuds in and put one foot in front of the other. Esther had long ago given up on telling me to get a car. It would never happen.

Besides, I got home before nightfall, so I didn't have to walk alone in the dark. I called that a win.

CHAPTER THREE

September 2017

SHEA

At home in my little condo, I changed into dry clothes, made myself a tuna salad sandwich, and powered up my laptop.

Despite the stress, the gnawing uncertainty, the expense, and—yes—the heartbreak, this was the upside of getting divorced: I had the freedom to sit in my underfurnished living room in pajama pants and a T-shirt, eating mayonnaise-drenched tuna and working uninterrupted for the rest of my evening. The project I was working on, the obsession of my off-hours, was my website, the Book of Cold Cases.

It wasn't an actual book. It was a collection of posts and articles written by me about unsolved crimes, the famous and the not so famous. The site included a private message board where people as obsessed as I was could post their theories or the new facts they'd found. I'd started the site nearly a decade ago as a personal blog, a place where

I could post in near obscurity about the things that fascinated me. But over the years, it had started to take on a life of its own, and now the site had nearly two thousand members, all of whom paid a small yearly fee. I sold ads on the site sometimes, too. The money wasn't nearly enough to live on, but it was enough for me to pay for upgraded servers, occasional professional webmaster work, and—most importantly—research help.

I logged on and scrolled through the new messages on the message board. There was a lively conversation going on about the disappearance of a little girl in Tennessee, and another one about a woman in Michigan who claimed she was abducted but could provide no evidence of it. Someone had revived an old thread about the Zodiac Killer because of a recent podcast they'd heard, and someone else had posted a link to a new theory about the JonBenét Ramsey case. I read through everything and added my own comments, looking out for messages that were inflammatory or insulting. Even in a closed group, the internet was the perfect place for people who wanted to call each other names, and it required constant moderation. People could get as angry about a twenty-year-old murder as they could about modern-day politics.

When I was finished, I clicked over to the article I was currently working on, about a woman in Connecticut who had left her house and disappeared, leaving her two-year-old daughter alone in her playpen. Security footage showed her walking past a mall three miles away, but how had she gotten there, and why? She'd left her car in the driveway. Cell phone records showed a single phone call from the woman's phone to 911 four hours after she disappeared. The call had disconnected as soon as the operator answered. Did that mean the woman was still alive then, trying to call for help? Or had someone else used her phone? These were the kinds of questions that could send me straight down the rabbit hole for days on end.

I picked up my phone and called Michael De Vos, the private

detective who worked for me sometimes. Being a layperson had its limits when you wrote crime stories, and Michael was a help when I needed expert analysis. He used to be a cop in the Claire Lake PD. He picked up right away.

"Shea. You're home?" he said. Michael knew a lot about my paranoia, though he didn't know the reason. He didn't seem to find it strange; he often checked that I was home safe when we talked.

"I made it," I said. "Where are you?" Michael was usually somewhere interesting. As a private detective, he lived the kind of life that would be way too much for my anxiety to handle.

"Right now I'm in a parked car," he said, "waiting for someone. Where I've been since noon."

He did, in fact, sound bored. "Waiting for who?"

"You know that's classified."

I felt myself smiling. Everything Michael did was classified, according to him. At least the interesting stuff was. "If you're doing a boring stakeout," I said, "then you had time to read the article I sent."

"I did." I heard him sip something. I pictured him in a car parked at the side of a road somewhere, the misty rain dripping down the windows. Maybe he was waiting for a cheating spouse or an embezzler. In my mind, the car was a big, boxy seventies thing, even though it was 2017. Michael gave off that old-school vibe.

Not that he was old. As far as I knew, he was somewhere in the second half of his thirties, with dark brown hair and brown eyes. Good-looking, most women would think. Women who weren't closed off like me. I'd only ever seen a photograph of him, which he'd sent me early on; we'd never met in person.

I wasn't very good with meeting strange men in person.

"What did you think?" I asked him.

"If you want to know what I think about the article, it was excellent. If you want to know what I think about the case, then the husband did it. With the father's help."

"There's no evidence," I said.

"When they find her, there will be. Because she's definitely dead."

Something inside me that had been coiled tight loosened for the first time all day. I loved Esther, but she didn't really get me. Our parents lived in Florida, and they definitely didn't get me. My coworkers didn't get me. My ex-husband didn't get me.

Michael got me. I didn't know how or why. He just did.

No one in my life wanted to talk about this stuff except him.

"What about the mall footage?" I asked him.

"Inconclusive. My guess is it isn't her. The killers caught a lucky break with that."

"The husband and the father working together is unusual."

"Unusual, but not unheard of. It's going to be difficult for them to maintain. One of them will probably make a deal, giving up the other one."

"But the husband, really? Everyone says they were a loving couple."

"Everyone always says that, and everyone is always wrong."

"You're a cynic," I said, scrolling through the article again, looking for typos. "That's a good quality to have."

"My ex-wife would not agree."

I paused. He hadn't mentioned an ex-wife before; we didn't usually get personal. "Then she can call my ex-husband," I said, trying it out. "It sounds like they have a lot in common."

"They'd probably get along just fine." He paused. "I think I see some movement. I have to go. Put the article up. It's good."

"Thank you," I said. "Good luck."

When we hung up, I put my phone down and did a circuit of my place, checking that the doors were locked, the windows fastened. Singles Estates had a security guard at the entrance to the complex, but that didn't mean much to me. Anyone on foot who was determined to get in could find a way. I was on the third floor—no way was

I taking a ground-floor apartment—and I had a security system just in case. Locks on the windows, no fire escape, no easy-to-pop screens. One of the few things I missed about marriage was the everyday presence of a man in the house, keeping the bad things away without even knowing it.

But I didn't have that anymore, so I had to be careful.

Everything was in place. When I was finished, I sat down in front of my computer again. I tapped it awake and logged in to the Book of Cold Cases. And I started tonight's journey into the darkness.

CHAPTER FOUR

September 2017

SHEA

I was tired at work the next day, because I'd stayed up later than I should have, working on the Book of Cold Cases. The bus had been ten minutes late, I'd dropped my bus pass, and I'd gotten to work out of sorts. I was on autopilot.

Our office was in downtown Claire Lake, and our patients were mostly rich, or at least well-to-do—Claire Lake on the whole was well-to-do, a town of chic kitchen specialty stores and French bistros laid out along the ocean shore. The spectacle I saw from the safety behind my Plexiglas was never that of people digging their nails in for survival, doing their best to get through every day. Instead it was often the foibles of the rich, the ones who had the money to make their aches and pains go away.

For a few minutes, I thought the woman who walked in might be someone famous. Her face was familiar in a way I couldn't quite place. She was an actress, maybe, one who had been on TV several decades ago. She was tall and stately, likely over sixty. Her skin was nearly flawless, with creases around the eyes and the mouth to give her character. Her hair was fashionably cut, with long bangs sweeping to her eyebrows and layers falling to her shoulders in light and dark shades of gray. She wore a black turtleneck sweater and sleek black pants under a trench coat. To me, the glamour wafting off her was worthy of Isabella Rossellini or Helen Mirren, though the woman seemed unaware of it. She looked distracted, and after slipping her ID beneath the Plexiglas to Karen, she took a seat, pulled out a pair of stylish reading glasses, and started reading a dog-eared novel.

"What?" Karen said to me as she wheeled her office chair back to the shelf and looked for the woman's file.

"I know her from somewhere," I said. There was a brief lull in which the phone wasn't ringing, and I sipped my coffee and tried to be discreet as I looked at the woman again. She flipped a page in her book, oblivious. I couldn't read the title from here, but I could see a cover of deep blue with slashes of jarring yellow lettering, which meant a thriller like the ones I read.

"She doesn't look familiar to me," Karen said. "Maybe she was a teacher of yours? A neighbor?"

I shook my head, studying the woman's face, still trying to place it. There was something about her cheekbones, the line of her mouth. She was beautiful, for sure, and had likely been even more so when young. I'd never had a teacher who looked like that. She had to be an actress, yet that didn't seem right.

"A singer?" I said, trying to jar my memory. "A politician?"

Karen shrugged, uninterested. "I don't follow music or politics. If it bothers you, Google her." She glanced down at the file she was holding. "Elizabeth Greer."

I went still, the breath going out of me. "What?"

"That's her name, Elizabeth Greer." Karen squinted at me, frowning. "What? Is she famous? Should I try and get an autograph?"

I put my hands on the desk. My fingers were tingling, my cheeks going numb. "No," I said. "No, you don't want her autograph."

"Whatever," Karen said. The phone rang, and she turned away to answer it.

Elizabeth Greer, I thought, glancing at the woman again. *Beth Greer.* She sat reading her book, unaware I was staring.

Of course I knew her face. I'd seen dozens of photos of her, news footage. I'd put photos of her on my own website. I hadn't recognized her because the photos on my site were from forty years ago, and no one had a photo of what she looked like now.

The woman sitting twenty feet away from me, reading a book, was Beth Greer.

And in 1977, she'd been Claire Lake's most famous murderer.

In October of 1977, a man named Thomas Armstrong left work at six o'clock at night and got in his car. He left downtown Claire Lake and drove toward his house at the edge of the lake, taking the smaller roads out of town. He never got home. At seven thirty, his car was found, the lights on and the engine still running as Armstrong lay dead on the side of the road.

Armstrong was a family man, with a wife, two children, no criminal ties, and no debts. It appeared that he'd pulled over on his way home, possibly to help someone who needed aid. He was shot twice in the face, one bullet piercing his brain and killing him instantly. Next to him was left a note written in a woman's hand that said: *Am I bitter or am I sweet? Ladies can be either. Publish this or there will be more.*

Murders were rare in Claire Lake, so there was no question the case would receive front-page press. But the note put the local police in a quandary. Keep the note quiet and don't encourage a possible copycat? Or give the killer what she wanted? There didn't seem to be a right answer. Finally, they handed the note to the press, who immediately dubbed the murderer the Lady Killer.

No one could understand it. Had a woman really shot a strange man point-blank in the face, like the Zodiac Killer or the Son of Sam?

Thomas Armstrong had no enemies. No one could think of anyone who would have wanted to murder him; he seemed to be an everyday husband and father on his way home from work. No one could see a reason why he was targeted. But there he was, dead by the side of the road, the lenses of his glasses smashed and a note in a woman's hand left by his body.

And then things got worse.

Four days after Armstrong's murder, family man Paul Veerhoever left work to go home. He, too, pulled over to the side of the road on the outskirts of town, where he was shot twice—one bullet hitting his jaw and one his right temple. This time a witness walking his dog heard the shot and came out of the trees to find a woman get in a car and drive away. She had red hair and she was wearing a trench coat.

Next to Veerhoever's body was a note in the same hand as the first one: *Catch me!*

The town panicked. No one in Claire Lake had ever seen crimes so violent, so brutal, so random. WHO IS THE LADY KILLER? was the headline from the *Claire Lake Daily*. The next day, in the *Claire Lake Free Press*: POLICE WARN CLAIRE LAKE RESIDENTS TO "STAY SAFE AFTER DARK." People—men especially—were warned not to pull over and help anyone on the road. The news wires picked it up, and within days the case had gone statewide, with reporters from Portland and Eugene coming to town to cover it.

It was a great story: two innocent, upstanding husbands and fathers, gunned down execution-style in cold blood. A dark predator on the streets of a quiet seaside town, apparently hunting for victims. The victims, in this case, were men, and the cold-blooded killer was quite possibly a woman.

The witness to the second murder identified the woman he saw as Beth Greer.

In 1977, Beth was twenty-three, beautiful, and rich. Her family lived in a mansion in the city's wealthiest neighborhood, Arlen Heights. Her father had died in 1973, shot during a home invasion that was never solved, and her mother had died in a car accident two years later, leaving Beth alone in the house with an inheritance of millions. Beth had red hair, and she owned a trench coat. She also owned a car like the one the witness had seen. She said she'd been home at the time of both murders, drinking alone.

Beth was photographed coming out of the Claire Lake police station after an interview, looking beautiful and cold and carefree. No one liked her; her neighbors said she was standoffish, and she tended to have unsavory people at her house. Her car was seized and her mansion searched, but no evidence was found. No one could come up with a reason for a rich girl with no problems to start killing random men. But *someone* had. And Beth Greer sold papers.

The Portland papers ran a story with a photo of Beth Greer laughing, looking beautiful and sexy. It was a photo from a year before, but no one cared. They ran it with the headline IS SHE THE FEMALE ZODIAC KILLER? Then the *New York Times* picked up the story, though the photo it ran was more recent and the headline was subdued: MURDERS BY APPARENT FEMALE KILLER BAFFLE OREGON POLICE. The article said: "local socialite Beth Greer has been identified as a person of interest," and Beth Greer became the most famous murder suspect in America.

The woman who had sold all of those papers was sitting in my waiting room right now, quietly reading a book.

I remembered the photos of her from 1977—Beth was sleek and gorgeous, her body in tight-fitting seventies tops and high-waisted pants, her long red hair cascading over her shoulders and down her back. She had big, dark, perfectly even eyes that were hypnotic and somehow sexual. Even as she was being led from jail to the courthouse and back, wearing an ill-fitting jumpsuit, she looked like a movie star.

My fingertips were numb as I moved files around, as I typed patient information on my computer and answered emails. Beth Greer glanced at her watch briefly, then turned another page. They had arrested her as the Lady Killer and taken her to trial, which had been covered in a nationwide spectacle. She was acquitted, but that didn't stop the headlines: HAS A DEADLY FEMALE KILLER GONE FREE?

No one knew the answer. I'd written an article about the Lady Killer case for the Book of Cold Cases, and all I'd found was an endless spiral of speculation. There were so many details, so many what-ifs. So many questions. Why those two men? Had they known Beth? Was she a young woman grieving her parents' tragic deaths or a seething psychopath with a sexy body? Did the notes even mean anything, and if so, what? Why had the state gone to trial with no murder weapon and no forensic evidence? If the killer wasn't Beth Greer, why had the killings stopped when she was arrested? The killer had written *Catch me!* Had they caught her? Was Beth an innocent victim or a femme fatale?

I'd spent five weeks writing the article for my website, and three times I'd taken the bus to Arlen Heights so I could walk past the Greer mansion. I'd found Beth's birth certificate, her DMV records, her property taxes. I'd read the local newspaper coverage and compared it with the national coverage, including articles in *Newsweek*. I'd read every rumor—there were hundreds—and every wild conspiracy theory. I'd looked at every photo of her, including the baby and childhood pictures I could find. I'd even tracked down a pirated copy of the 1981 TV movie made about the case, starring Jaclyn Smith, and bought a ripped DVD that cost me $300 because the movie wasn't available digitally. I'd dug up every scrap, searching for answers, just like so many others before me. I'd been obsessed. I still was. And Beth Greer was at the center of it, in all her unreadable complexity.

I glanced up through the Plexiglas and watched her absently scratch her temple. She was still beautiful, there was no doubt of that. Still fascinating, at least to me.

No one else in the room noticed her. For most people, the Lady Killer murders were ancient history, a curious footnote, if they had heard of them at all. The frightened fall of 1977 was a long-ago memory or a rumor of a time before you were born. After the trial and the sensational acquittal, Beth had dropped out of the public eye. Information about her over the past forty years was thin, though I knew she hadn't married or had kids, that she still lived in the mansion, presumably all alone. Whether she was innocent or guilty, there were no more Lady Killer murders. The story seemed to be over.

Beth crossed one leg over the other, turning the pages of her novel.

I wondered if the book was about murder.

"Miss Greer?" One of the nurses poked her head out the door from the exam rooms. Beth put her book away and stood. I looked at her and saw the young woman who had been photographed being led to and from the courthouse, the acquitted prisoner standing next to her attorney, wearing a red shawl and red lipstick. I saw a woman, and I also saw the biggest mystery in the history of Claire Lake.

No one watched as she crossed the waiting room. No one except me.

CHAPTER FIVE

September 2017

SHEA

"I'm taking my lunch break," I said.

It was early for lunch, but Karen shrugged. I was entitled, and the sooner I went, the sooner I could come back and relieve her. I pulled my purse from under the desk and grabbed my coat.

Beth Greer had taken forty-five minutes for her appointment. Then she'd walked through the waiting room, disappearing into the elevator without a backward glance. I couldn't have said what possessed me to follow her, but I had the impulse not to let her out of my sight.

The rain had let up today, the sky a chalky gray-blue, the wind carrying the scent of ocean. On the street, people sat at the outdoor cafés or window-shopped, taking pictures of the houseboats on the water. Claire Lake had a neighborhood of citizens who lived on their

boats, docked in the marina. They had walkways and window plant-
ers, garden gnomes and pinwheel birds, like any other home. In some
past decade, the city had made the houseboats legal residences, and
subsequent attempts to change the zoning had failed. Now it was one
of Claire Lake's tourist attractions, a pretty spot for people to stroll
and enjoy their fancy take-out coffee. People came here to stay in the
B&Bs, stroll the tidy, cobblestoned streets, and get away from the
bigger, more crowded cities.

Beth didn't head toward the marina. Instead she turned a corner
down a side street. I followed at a safe distance, under cover of the
downtown crowd. Beth turned another corner, then another. Then I
lost her.

I stood next to a small, shaded park and turned in a circle, wondering which way she'd gone. Then a voice came from the park: "Why
are you following me?"

It was Beth. She was sitting on a park bench under the canopy of
trees, watching me. She wore sunglasses, the big kind that covered
half her face, even though it was a cloudy day. Behind her was a statue
of a man getting out of a boat—some Oregon explorer. Beth's purse
was on the bench next to her, and she had one knee crossed over the
other. She watched me, waiting politely for an answer.

"I'm sorry," I said. "I know who you are." That sounded vaguely
threatening, so I hurried to add, "I'm a crime writer."

Beth looked me up and down, taking in my scrub top. "You don't
look like a crime writer."

"I do it in my off-hours. I run a website." I shook my head. "I'm
sorry. My name is Shea Collins."

Beth Greer tilted her head, watching me.

When I was researching my article on the Lady Killer case, I'd
found a video on YouTube of Beth right before her arrest. She was
getting out of her car and walking up the lane to the Greer mansion.
The reporter—a man in a belted trench coat and plaid wide-legged

pants, straight from 1977 central casting—had caught Beth as she pulled up and opened the car door. The reporter must have gotten a scoop, because there were no other reporters there. It was raining, and Beth was wearing a trench coat, too. It was an uncanny image, that of a woman in red hair and a trench coat, just like the witness to the second murder had reported seeing.

Beth Greer looked like she could have been walking the Paris runway any time in the twenty-first century.

"Miss Greer!" the reporter had shouted as he followed her, waving his wired microphone. "Miss Greer! Do you have anything to say about the murder accusations against you? Are you the Lady Killer?"

Beth slammed her car door and put her hands in her pockets. She looked at the reporter and leaned toward the microphone. "I'm just a girl who minds her own business," she said. Her tone was cold and without inflection, almost robotic.

In 1977, everyone thought that Beth Greer's lack of emotion about being put on trial for murder made her unfeeling, almost unnatural, like a witch. Watching the clip in 2017, I heard in her voice a woman who was sick to death of everything, a woman who had lived through the trauma of her parents' deaths and was living through a media frenzy, a woman who knew that nothing she said or did would ever matter. It wasn't that she was unfeeling. It was that she'd stopped caring, stopped being afraid.

I'm just a girl who minds her own business. That woman was looking at me now. The same woman who had possibly shot two men in cold blood and left taunting notes for the police.

"So you want to write about me. Is that it?" Now that I heard her voice, it was unmistakable. It was the same voice from the video. "You're not the first person to ask."

"I already wrote about you." People were passing me on the sidewalk, so I stepped forward, toward Beth, hoping I wasn't spooking her. Or spooking her more than I already had.

"Then what do you want?" Beth asked me. Not a hostile question. A curious one.

What did I want? I knew the answer to that. I could feel the blood pulsing in my veins, and my thoughts were mercury-quick, as if I were high. "I want to interview you," I said. I had one shot at Beth Greer—maybe the only shot in my life. "I want to hear what really happened. I want to hear it from you." I paused. "I want to know what it was like to be you. Back then. And what it's like to be you now."

"You're asking a lot," Beth said.

"I know." I supposed I wasn't a girl who minded her own business. I dug in my purse, looking for a business card—I'd had some printed once, when I had felt the urge to be more official. Now I couldn't find any.

I found a flyer instead—one I had found shoved in my condo mailbox, that I'd put in my purse and forgotten. It advertised a local Thai place. I found a pen and wrote the URL of my website on it. Beneath that, I wrote my phone number.

I handed Beth the Thai menu, my cheeks heating. "I swear I'm a professional," I said.

Beth didn't look convinced, but she took the menu. She didn't throw it in my face or tell me to mind my own business. She read what I had written, then folded the flyer and tucked it in her own purse. "I'll think about it," she said.

"Thank you."

She waited a second, then waved a hand. "Go back to work, Shea."

I stood rooted. I couldn't move until I knew. "Are you going to think about it, or are you going to throw it away?" I asked her. "Just tell me, so I'm not jumping every time the phone rings. This is the biggest thing that's ever happened to me. It's hard to explain."

She took her sunglasses off. She had aged forty years, but she still had the eyes of the woman in the YouTube video. "You're really serious, aren't you? Are you writing a book or something?"

"No," I said, because I wasn't. I had no idea how to write a book or get it published. It wasn't something that had even crossed my mind. "But, yes, I'm serious."

"All right, I'll be honest," Beth said. "I've been asked for a lot of interviews. I've been offered money. I've never been interested. But you're not like anyone who has ever asked me."

I was silent. Was that good or bad? Did it matter?

"So, yes, I'll consider it," Beth continued. "Despite how gauche your pitch was—or perhaps because of it—I'll think it over. Does that satisfy you?"

"Yes," I said. "Thank you."

"You're welcome. Go back before they fire you."

I turned and walked back to the office, my mind racing. I didn't see a single thing in front of me. I forgot that I hadn't actually had lunch. I'd have to eat the crackers and cheese I'd stuffed in my purse this morning.

At my desk, my gaze moved to the stack of patient files on the trolley that had been wheeled between me and Karen. One of those files was Beth Greer's.

Was she ill? Was that why she was considering my offer? A sort of deathbed confession?

I could find out. It would be easy.

My gaze traveled up to the sign on the wall above the locked filing cabinets. A REMINDER TO EVERY EMPLOYEE: PATIENT FILES ARE CONFIDENTIAL!

If I were caught reading Beth's file, I'd be fired.

For a second, I was still tempted. But I'd never broken a rule like that. I stood up, picked up the stack of files, and began to put them away.

CHAPTER SIX

September 2017

SHEA

"Well, you didn't get served with a restraining order," Michael said over the phone. "That's something, at least."

I was at home, putting my single-serve piece of lasagna in the oven, the phone crooked between my ear and my shoulder. "I talked to an older lady in a public park," I protested. "It was perfectly innocent."

"'Innocent' is a curious choice of words when you're talking about Beth Greer."

I closed the oven door and straightened, catching the tone in his voice. "You think she did it? Are you familiar with the case?"

"Everyone in Claire Lake is familiar with the Lady Killer case. And I spent five years in the Claire Lake PD. Cops are especially opinionated when it comes to that case. Her acquittal left egg on their faces and two unsolved murders that have never been closed."

The fact that Michael was a former cop was one of the reasons I'd hired him. I'd wondered why he wasn't a cop anymore, but it seemed like a personal thing to ask. "So you think she did it," I said.

"I think that Beth Greer was indicted for murder," he said. "And, yes, sometimes indictments are wrong. But most of the time, they happen for a reason."

"There wasn't any forensic evidence." This was my favorite topic; I could talk about it for hours. "As in literally none. No hairs, no fibers, no blood, no DNA."

"You're forgetting that the bullets matched the gun that killed Beth's father."

"But they never found that gun. And Beth was nineteen when her father was killed. You think a nineteen-year-old girl shot her father and made it look like a robbery?"

"Shea, there was a witness to Veerhoever's murder."

"One who only briefly saw her in the dark, and admitted on the stand that he'd been drinking that night. The handwriting on the notes didn't match Beth's. And no matter how many times they interviewed Beth, they never got a confession or a single slipup in her story."

"Which just means she was very, very good."

"Oh, come on. Cops do the best they can—I know that. But they aren't infallible."

"I'll admit that the evidence at trial wasn't as strong as it could have been. And Beth Greer had the best lawyer money could buy. But, Shea, I've met sociopaths in my line of work. The smart ones are experts at deception. They can make people believe anything; it's what they do. Manipulation is how they get through life, because they don't know any other way. They can lie as easy as breathing, and they're convincing because they almost believe it themselves. People like that can trap you, and they're dangerous. You read and write about these cases, but I've seen them firsthand."

I thought about my would-be killer, who was sitting in a cell somewhere, likely counting down the days to his parole hearing. I had received a letter from the Department of Corrections, inviting me to come to the hearing and give a victim impact statement. I had buried the letter under a pile of mail, unable to even look at it. "I've met terrible people firsthand, too," I said. "I may not have been a cop like you, but I've met them."

"Okay," Michael said. "I'm just asking you to be careful. In every interaction, Beth Greer is going to try and keep the upper hand. She's already got you breathless in anticipation, waiting for her to decide. She's been asked for interviews dozens of times, maybe even hundreds, in the past forty years. Why do you think she chose you?"

That stung, but he was right. I wasn't an author or a reporter or an investigator. I was no one. Why would Beth Greer choose no one? "I guess if she agrees, I'll ask her," I said.

"She knows you want information, so she's going to give some things and withhold others. She's going to meet with you on her terms. She's going to lead you where she wants you to go."

Logically, I knew he had a point. I wrote about sociopaths and psychopaths almost every night; I had a layman's understanding of how they worked, like any normal woman who had a first edition of *Small Sacrifices* on her bookshelf. I knew that even though Beth was a woman over sixty, there was no guarantee that she wasn't dangerous. The problem was that I wasn't completely convinced she was a killer in the first place.

"If Beth were a man," Michael said, "you would never have approached her."

I laughed, even though his insight was as sharp as always. "I can't even approach you, and I've been working with you for over a year."

"I'm not a serial killer," he said.

"See, that's exactly what a serial killer would say."

"A fair point. Do you want to run my fingerprints and DNA? I can probably arrange something."

The oven timer beeped, and I turned it off. "That's what a serial killer would say, too," I said. "Make a grandiose promise he can't keep, because it sounds so convincing."

"All right. I'm offended, but at least you're thinking the way I want you to think when it comes to Beth Greer."

I promised him I would be careful, and I hung up. But as I pulled my lonely dinner out of the oven, listening to the wind splatter rain against my windows—as I prepared for yet another lonely night in the darkness—I admitted to myself that anywhere Beth Greer led me, I was more than willing to go.

The call came at one in the morning. I had just drifted off when the phone rang on my nightstand. It was a number I didn't recognize.

My heart in my throat—a one a.m. call had to mean Esther or my parents were dead—I answered it. I recognized the voice on the other end immediately.

"It's Beth."

I sat up. "Beth?"

"I've been reading your website," she said, ignoring the fact that she'd woken me up. "I've been reading what you wrote about me."

I rubbed my face in the darkness. When I wrote the article, I'd never imagined it being read by the real Beth Greer. "What did you think?" I asked.

"You got some things right and some things wrong. You didn't talk to Detective Black. Or to Ransom."

Detective Joshua Black had worked the Lady Killer case. Ransom Wells had been Beth's attorney. Both were still alive, and both were still in Claire Lake. "I tried. Neither of them would talk to me."

"They will when I tell them to," Beth said. Her voice carried the perfect confidence of a woman born rich and beautiful, who even now was used to people doing what she wanted.

"Wait a minute," I said. "Are you telling me you'll get me access to both of them?"

"Yes, because I'm going to grant your interview," Beth said. "We'll start on Sunday. Be at the mansion at ten. I don't cook, I don't make coffee, and I don't have servants, so bring your own shit." There was a *click*. She had hung up.

I stared into the darkness, the dead phone against my ear.

It was happening.

I was going to talk to Beth Greer.

CHAPTER SEVEN

September 2017

BETH

Beth Greer hung up the phone and put it on the bed next to her. Then she stared into the darkness.

She was in the master bedroom of the Greer mansion. Forty-five years ago, this had been her parents' bedroom. This very bed had been their actual bed. Beth had never replaced it. That was strange, she knew. The bed was old now, with a musty smell. The blankets were gray from hundreds of washes. On the nightstand was her father's ashtray, huge and heavy glass, and on the dresser was a jar of her mother's cold cream, nearly fifty years old now, long dried out and desiccated. At least Beth's pajamas were her own, fine silk ones that were the best money could buy. They were kept in a dresser drawer atop her mother's old nightgowns.

Beth drew her knees up to her chest, hugged them. She hadn't taken a sleeping pill tonight; she'd been on the internet on her laptop, reading Shea Collins's article about her, and she'd lost track of time. Now it was late, too late. She could take a pill now, but she'd still hear the noises before she dropped to sleep.

It was best to take the pill before the noises started, so you didn't hear them at all.

Something moved in the hallway outside. It was a soft sound, and Beth's fingers squeezed the blanket, a reflex. She was used to the fear—she'd been living with it for so long. Decade after decade. For as long as she could remember, really. All the way back. She didn't know what a life without fear would look like. Beth knew the contours of fear intimately, its shifting shapes, its taste and its smell.

You're not leaving.

You're not talking.

Those were the rules. But she was about to break the second one, wasn't she? She was going to talk—to Shea Collins, who had read so much about her. Who knew everything and nothing at all.

There was a footstep in the hall outside the room, and a dragging sound. Beth closed her eyes, even though it made no difference in the pitch-blackness. She had turned the lock on the bedroom door. She had. She remembered doing it, remembered the cool feel of the latch against her fingers. Or was she remembering last night? Or the night before?

The pills were on the nightstand, but she couldn't take one now. Not until she was sure about the door. Because if the door was un-locked, she didn't want to be asleep when the thing outside came in.

So she waited, listening.

The dragging sound came again, and then there was the soft *click* of a doorknob, followed by the *creak* of a door. That was the bathroom down the hall. The dragging again, the *click*, the *creak*. That was Beth's teenage bedroom. One by one, each door was being tried, opened. Then the next. Then the next. Until it came to the door of the master bedroom, at the very end of the hall.

Beth knew she should get up, run to the door, and make sure it was locked. But it was too late now. She couldn't make herself move.

The dragging sound came closer now. Then the *click*. The doorknob to the master bedroom, being tried. Moving one way, then the other.

Beth closed her eyes.

You're not leaving.

You're not talking.

But things were changing. The fever of madness was about to break after all this time, and it was going to be messy. People would get hurt. That was what happened when you were touched by madness. You got hurt.

Beth knew all about madness.

Click. Click.

The doorknob turned one way, then the other. Then one way again. Then the other.

It didn't open, because the door was locked.

Beth lunged for the bottle of pills on the nightstand as a voice rose in the hallway. A wail of despair, rising up and up. Then weeping.

"Please," the voice said. "Please."

It isn't real, Beth told herself as she dry-swallowed the pill. *She's been dead for so long. It isn't real.*

"Please," the voice wailed in the hall. Something jerked the doorknob hard, the *click* loud, but the lock held.

Beth Greer pushed the covers down and slid under them. None of this was real. The pill would kick in, and all of this would be gone in the morning, like a dream.

She closed her eyes and waited for sleep as outside in the hall, her mother wept and wept.

CHAPTER EIGHT

October 1977

BETH

The man sitting across from her put a cassette in the tape recorder on the desk and pressed the button. "It's the twentieth of October, 1977," he said as the tape turned. "My name is Detective Joshua Black, Claire Lake Police. Present are Detective Melvin Washington of the Oregon State Police and Elizabeth Greer. We are in the Claire Lake Police Department interview room. Miss Greer, do you agree to this interview being recorded?"

Beth kept her hands still in her lap. "Yes, I do."

"Please state your age for the record."

"I'm twenty-three."

"And you are here voluntarily and are not under arrest. Is that correct?"

"That's correct."

Detective Black paused for a second, then nodded. He was in his early thirties, with thick brown hair worn just long enough to curl. She recognized him from the newspapers, especially the photo in the paper the morning after the first murder. It was taken from across the road from the murder scene and showed a car parked at the side of the road, a body under a sheet on the ground near it. Standing next to the car, wearing a dark coat, frowning at the ground, had been this man, who was sitting across from her now. She'd recognized him when he came to the door with his partner and asked her to come to the station. He was good-looking and clean-shaven, unlike his partner, Detective Washington, who stood leaning against the wall behind him, glaring at her from behind his heavy mustache.

Beth crossed her arms over the buttons of her blouse. It was cold in here, and she'd already noticed Washington giving her the once-over.

"Okay," Detective Black said. "Miss Greer—"

"My name is Beth."

He blinked, then said, "Okay, then, let's get started. Can you tell us your whereabouts on the evening of October fifteenth, five days ago?"

"I was home."

"Take your time and think. Are you certain?"

"Yes, I'm certain."

"Are you sure about that?" This was Washington, his gaze fixed on her. His fingers drummed impatiently on the leg of his pants for a second, then stopped. "What were you doing, exactly?"

Beth tried not to flinch. "I was drinking," she said.

"Alone?"

"I don't know." She was messing this up, her nerves scrambling her thoughts, making her doubt herself. "Yes, I was alone. I was drinking."

Washington's eyes narrowed in disapproval. Beth was used to that look. Everyone gave it to her—strangers, grocery store clerks, the neighbors in Arlen Heights that she had the misfortune to cross paths with. It was a look that said, *You're twenty-three and one of the wealthiest people in town, you have everything, and all you do is drink and party. You ought to be ashamed.* No one cared that her parents were dead, that rich didn't mean happy. No one cared that she lay awake nights, alone in the Greer mansion, imagining noises in the hallway and wondering what was real. The alcohol made all of those feelings go away, at least for a while. Beth was numb to that look, just like she was numb to everything else in her life.

"Miss Greer," the handsome cop said, and even though his voice was gentle and understanding, the numbness fell away for a second. It was replaced with fear, toxic and wrenching, so consuming that Beth felt like screaming. This wasn't a nightmare she was going to wake up from. These were the police, and this was real. She was here all alone.

She looked at Detective Black, waiting for him to say something, unable to speak while she wrestled with the fear.

"You need to think very carefully," Detective Black said. "I know you say you had a few drinks, that things are fuzzy." He ignored the derisive snort from his partner. "But you need to think back very carefully to where you were that night, whether you were with anyone. Whether anyone saw you. Think hard."

Suddenly she could see the whole scene like a photograph: Black sitting at the table wearing a dark brown suit and navy tie, Washington standing against the wall in his shirtsleeves, his striped tie loosened half an inch. It smelled like cigarette smoke in here, though no one was smoking right now. She saw the tape recorder, the bleached lighting, the scratched table. The pen that Black held in his hand, hovering over the notepad on the table as he waited for her to speak. And her, sitting with her arms crossed. She was wearing a deep green blouse and high-waisted jeans, high-heeled zip-up ankle boots on her feet. She had her red hair in a ponytail and gold hoops in her ears.

Every cop had watched her as she followed Black and Washington through the station to the interview room. The place had gone silent, conversations hushing in waves. Beth looked like a rich girl, she knew. She *was* a rich girl. Not the kind of girl who gets hauled into a police station. Rich didn't mean happy, but no one cared about that, least of all the cops who looked at her and saw the girl who would turn them down if they talked to her in a bar. The girl who would laugh at them if they tried to sleep with her. The girl who might have shot two good family men in the face just for something to do.

If she'd done that, she must be crazy. Did they all think she was crazy?

"What about last night?" Detective Black asked, polite and persistent. "Do you remember where you were last night?"

Yes, this was real. Definitely real. She felt the same squeeze of panic she'd felt when she'd seen the aftermath of her father's dead body on the kitchen floor, the blood everywhere. He'd been taken away by then, but she'd had the feeling that this was really happening, that it wasn't going to stop, that she couldn't just close the book or turn off the TV and walk away. That this was the beginning of something bad.

"I was home last night," she said, because it was important. She had to be clear. She couldn't tell the truth. She couldn't.

Another man had been murdered last night. It was all over the papers.

Detective Washington stood forward from the wall he was leaning on. His hand slipped into his pocket and pulled out a pack of cigarettes. "Do you own a black 1966 Buick?" he asked, his voice harsh.

They knew the answer already. They must have known before they came to her door. "Yes, it's one of my cars." She had three. That was how rich she was. It was enraging. She could see it in his eyes.

"Did you drive it on October fifteenth?"

"No."

"You just said you were drinking and you don't remember."

"I would know if I drove it." She'd remember getting in the car, turning the key in the ignition, even if she was drunk. She'd done drunken joyrides before, and she never completely forgot them, no matter how much she'd had. Besides, the morning after the murder the Buick had been parked neatly in the garage alongside the other cars. No way she'd be able to do that while so drunk she had no memory.

It was the same this morning. She'd parked the Buick like she always did last night. She definitely remembered that.

"Perhaps you wouldn't know. Perhaps you drove it and don't remember," Detective Black said. He really sounded quite sorry that she was here at all, that he was bothering her with this. Along with his good looks, this was probably a tactic that worked on every female murder suspect. She had the thought before she remembered that Claire Lake didn't have any other murders she could think of, let alone any female suspects. Just these murders. And her.

Washington flipped the cigarette pack open, and Black looked at his partner. Just a brief, dark glance, and Washington put the cigarettes away again. There was a mottled flush on his face as he did it—but he did it. Black turned back to Beth and waited for an answer.

"I was home," she said.

"Did you know Thomas Armstrong?"

"No."

"Did you know Paul Veerhoever?"

"No."

Washington took another step forward. Now he was standing next to his partner, looming over Beth, still angry because his partner had forbidden him to smoke. "Do you own a gun?" he asked.

"No."

"A man walking his dog heard the shots," Detective Washington said. "He saw a car that resembled a Buick driving down Claire Lake Road away from the murder. There was a woman driving."

Icy sweat was trickling down her back. "That wasn't me," she said.

"Claire Lake Road doesn't get much traffic," Detective Black said. "The woman had long hair and a trench coat. He believes her hair was red. He identified a photo of you."

The fear broke then, like a fever. It reached a certain pressure point, and then it just stopped. It was replaced by anger, the cold rage that seemed too big for her body to contain, too big for her mind. She'd always had a temper, though she rarely let it off its leash. She said the words again, trying not to spit them at him: "That wasn't me."

"Except you don't know that, because you claim you can't remember." Detective Washington's tone was tight and harsh. "You were too drunk, or so you say. So how do you *know* it wasn't you?"

She looked up at him and met his eyes. The anger broke loose, and for a second she thought about how stupid he was. How he had no idea what he was dealing with, and now he was in the way. The words came out of her, cold with fury: "It wasn't me, you idiot. I wasn't in that fucking car."

There was a second of stunned silence from both men. Panic, they could deal with; trembling fear, they were used to. They even expected lying and clumsy attempts to dodge questions. But anger was something they didn't expect. It burned pure inside her, like fire fed with oxygen. She knew she should put it out, but instead she held Detective Washington's gaze and she let it burn.

He looked back at her with shocked disgust, as if she were a zoo animal who had pissed on the floor. Anger *and* profanity. She should have stayed quiet.

But the anger was loose now, and she couldn't find it in herself to be sorry.

Detective Black cleared his throat and took over again. "Mr. Armstrong and Mr. Veerhoever were shot with .22-caliber bullets. And I know this is confusing to you, because normally we wouldn't question a nice young lady like yourself about something like this. Normally, you'd be the last person we'd think of."

Beth held still, waiting. In the silence of the room, she could hear the whirring of the tape recorder.

Detective Black continued. "Your father died in 1973 in a home invasion. He was shot in the kitchen of your house while he was home alone. He was killed with a .22-caliber weapon. We're going to pull the ballistics report from those bullets and compare it to these bullets. Do you understand?"

This wasn't happening.

Oh, yes, it was.

"Perhaps there's something you'd like to tell us," Detective Black said.

"There's nothing I want to tell you," she said.

A lie, maybe. Part of her wanted to tell him what her life was like. That being drunk kept the ghosts away most of the time, but not all of the time. That the fear ate away at her sometimes, and so did the anger. That she had moments when she wasn't sure what was real and what wasn't.

But she wasn't going to talk. Not about her father's death. Not about anything. Some things needed to stay buried.

Some things *had* to stay buried.

"Did you know Thomas Armstrong?" Washington asked her again.

"No," she said through numb lips.

"Did you know Paul Veerhoever?"

"No."

"Were you seeing either of them?"

"No."

"Were the notes from you?"

"No." Now the anger had drained, and she was exhausted. She

needed a drink. She stood up. "I'm not answering any more questions. I'm leaving."

They let her go—Washington with anger, Black with resignation. She felt the eyes on her as she walked through the station. The conversations quieted again. One cop gave a low whistle. She was almost at the front doors when someone said, "You'll be back, sweetheart. Next time will be worse."

She walked outside and paused on the station steps, inhaling the air infused with the smell of the ocean. Getting her equilibrium back now that she wasn't in that stuffy room anymore, looking at those two men.

It was starting.

Maybe she wouldn't survive it.

Maybe she deserved it.

She headed toward her car to go home.

CHAPTER NINE

September 2017

SHEA

There was a photo taken of Beth on October 20, 1977, the day after Paul Veerhoever's murder. Beth was exiting the Claire Lake police station after being interviewed by the cops. They hadn't arrested her yet—that would come later, when the police were more certain they had a case they could win.

Beth was wearing a dark green blouse tied in a knot at her waist and high-waisted jeans, her hair tied back in a ponytail, gold hoop earrings in her ears. She was alone. Beth's face was turned as she caught sight of the camera, and in that fleeting moment her eyes were narrowed, the top lids drooping down over the irises, the pupils inky black. She looked beautiful and sexy, and at the same time she looked hard. She looked like a murderess.

Beth wasn't arrested that day, but when that photo ran in the *Claire Lake Daily*, the town made up its mind. That woman—that uncaring, unfeeling woman—was guilty. Everywhere Beth went between the murders and the arrest, she was photographed.

That first photo was the one I pulled up on Saturday morning as I drank my coffee and got out the notes I'd kept from my research on the Lady Killer case. I looked at Beth's face again, comparing it to the woman I'd talked to in the park. There was no doubt that even though she was beautiful, Beth Greer was not a sweet, innocent victim. There was a steeliness to her that people had found hard to reconcile in a twenty-three-year-old, and that steeliness was still there today. The woman I'd met in the park hadn't been flustered or even angry to find me following her. She'd simply turned the tables on me until I answered her questions.

I've met sociopaths in my line of work, Michael had said. *The smart ones are experts at deception.*

Beth Greer, as far as I knew, had never been diagnosed as a sociopath. She had never been examined by a psychiatrist at all.

Sociopaths were good liars because they were empty of true human emotion. They knew how to mimic it, but they did so because they never felt it. Anger, grief, fear, empathy—the research suggested that a true sociopath couldn't feel any of them.

When Ransom Wells, Beth's lawyer, was asked about Beth in an interview in 1989, his only comment was, "I know pure evil when I see it."

I clicked open my browser and played the video clip of Beth getting out of her car in the rain. For the hundredth time, the reporter in the plaid pants and trench coat pursued her, microphone in hand. For the hundredth time, Beth put her hands in the pockets of her coat and faced him.

"I'm just a girl who minds her own business," she said.

Was she just tired?

Or deep down, was she trying not to smile?

When I looked out my window after my morning of research, there was a man I didn't recognize reading in a car in the parking lot. The weather was unsettled, the last of summer giving in to the chill of fall, and clouds moved quickly past the sun, making its dim light dapple on and off. The man was in the small lot nearest my building, sitting in a black Jeep SUV. His face was obscured by a baseball cap. The car was off, and he was reading a book.

I wanted to mind my own business, but who sits and reads a book in a parked car? Parents waiting to pick their kids up from school, maybe. That was all I could think of. If he just wanted to read his book, there was a clearing with a park bench twenty feet away. I waited a minute, then two, then five, but the man didn't leave.

Jesus, Shea. I heard my sister Esther's voice in my head. *You just answered your own question. He's waiting to pick someone up. It's Saturday morning, and people are living their lives. Mind your own business.*

I knew I should. But in my mind's eye, I still saw a car pull up next to me as I walked home from school, the tires crunching gently in the snow as the window rolled down. I heard a voice say, *Hi there, are you cold?* I heard my mother's voice say, *Always be polite to grown-ups, Shea.*

That had been a lie—the worst lie I'd ever been told, that children should always be polite to adults. It was a lie that haunted me to this day. I picked up my phone and raised it, thinking to take a picture of the man, his car, and his license plate. Just in case.

As my finger hovered over the button, I heard Esther's voice again, so calm and rational. *Shea, have you seen your therapist lately?*

I hadn't. The last time was just before the divorce, over a year ago. Despite the fact that I had "lingering trauma issues," as my therapist called them, she felt that I'd made tremendous progress. I was off the medication—her idea. At the time I quit, I had a stable career and a stable marriage, and was living a productive life. *You can put this in the past, Shea,* my therapist had said. *You're already doing it. It isn't easy, but people do it all the time.*

So I stopped going. A month later, my husband, Van, moved out. He had a new girlfriend now. The thought of that made me feel nothing.

Hi there, are you cold?

Now I lived alone, and a woman alone could never be too careful. I snapped the photo and put my phone away.

When I left to pick up food for lunch, I smelled smoke. I opened the door of the stairwell to find a woman quickly putting a cigarette out. She was my neighbor from across the hall. We'd met once, briefly, on the day she moved in.

"Sorry," she said sheepishly. "I'm trying to quit. I felt like if I snuck one in the stairwell it wouldn't count, you know?"

"It's okay," I said, though it wasn't. I didn't have the heart to give her any grief. She was wearing stretched-out yoga pants and a tee, her graying brown hair scraped back into a ponytail. It was the uniform of the recently broken up, yet for some reason she had taken the trouble to put on mascara and line her eyes with dark, precise eyeliner. I'd been in that place, spinning hopelessly between *I should do something* and *I don't care.*

"It's Alison, right?" I said.

She nodded. "And you're Shea." We both smiled. "I won't smoke anymore, I promise. It's just been a hard week."

"I get it." I took a chance. "Your hard week doesn't have to do with the man sitting in his car in the parking lot, does it?"

She looked surprised, then dismayed. "Is he still there?" She dropped her gaze to the floor. "Yeah, that's my ex. We made plans, but then we had a fight and I changed my mind. Now he's here and he says he's waiting for me to come to my senses." She looked back up at me. "Don't tell me you're divorced, too."

"I am."

She gave an awkward laugh. "You're too pretty to be divorced."

It was an odd comment, but again, I understood. She was feeling self-conscious about her yoga pants, her messy hair. I wasn't looking very glamorous myself—I had on jeans, a tee, a fitted cargo jacket, my long hair in its ponytail, almost no makeup—but I was further along this rough road than she was.

"My ex thinks his new girlfriend is prettier," I said, even though I had no resentment that Van had moved on. I watched Alison's shoulders relax a little, the crinkles around her eyes ease as she nodded.

"Fuck him, then," she said.

I nodded. What was the difference, I wondered, between a sociopath and someone who does everyday lying to make other people feel better? "Definitely," I said. "And don't come to your senses."

She looked surprised. "You think?"

"I think."

"He says he misses me, but when we were together I annoyed him like crazy. He never wanted me around. He practically packed my things. So why does he miss me now?"

Van had tried a let's-try-again line two weeks after he left. I was surprised at first, but then I remembered how much he hated shopping and cooking, which he'd left to me. He had probably starved for those first two weeks. "Splitting up is hard," I said to Alison, "but if it's the right thing to do, then it's worth it."

She stared at the extinguished cigarette in her hand, as if wishing she could relight it. "He says he wants the cat. He barely noticed we had a cat, so I took it with me when I left, because he wouldn't get fed otherwise. The cat, I mean." She frowned. "Now he says he wants to discuss the cat. What does that mean? Who wants to talk to someone so badly that they discuss a cat they don't care about? Still, I could just give him the cat and he might go away. What do you think I should do?"

I thought it over. I thought about what it would be like to be married to someone who sat in a parking lot, reading a book, waiting for you to come to your senses, and give him what he wanted, whether he'd ever said he wanted it or not. I'd rather be single until I died.

I shrugged. "Don't go back," I said, "and don't give him the cat, either. That's my advice. But then again, I haven't seen my therapist in a long time."

She looked shocked at that, and then she nodded. By the time I got in the elevator, I heard her door close without another word.

CHAPTER TEN

September 2017

SHEA

On Sunday, the sky was dark and lowering, the air damp. The salt smell blowing in from the ocean was getting stronger as I took the bus to Beth Greer's neighborhood. Arlen Heights was built on a slope that rose above the marina downtown, ending on a bluff overlooking the water. The wind was sharper here, but the view was beautiful, a vista of the town below and the vast and empty Pacific.

My parents had never been rich; my father worked for an auto parts company, and my mother was a substitute teacher. During my childhood, we lived in one of the small houses in Claire Lake, away from the piers and the tourists. As a child, I walked every day through my quiet neighborhood to my school, past well-tended shrubbery and a park with a baseball diamond. Lots of people think that nothing bad ever happens in a place like that, but it isn't true.

Arlen Heights was different. The houses were spread out, set far back from the winding streets, which were kept narrow and rough on purpose, as if that made the place more real. I saw one elderly man with a dog, a woman doing a brisk walk, and no one else as the bus pulled up to the stop. As it drove away, the silence descended.

I shifted my messenger bag and walked down the street toward the Greer mansion. I pulled my phone out and texted Michael.

I'm on my way to the interview. She isn't going to kill me, right?

Unlikely, he replied. *But I can track your phone if it makes you feel better.*

I thought about it. I had a lot of rules about meeting strangers, but this was Beth Greer. *It's fine*, I texted back. *She isn't Ted Bundy. I think. Besides, I have a confession. If Beth Greer murders me, I don't think it's the worst way to go.*

His humor, as always, was equally grim. *At least you'll make the history books. I'll make sure of it.*

My fingers hovered over the screen. I had something else to say, but I wasn't sure what it was. Did I want him to tell me I wasn't crazy? I already knew there was plenty wrong with me. Maybe I wanted to tell him the truth about me. Maybe I just longed to hear someone say, *You're trying. You're doing the best you can.* Or maybe I really did want him to reassure me that Beth wasn't going to kill me.

She'd been acquitted, after all. But her own lawyer had said of her: *I know pure evil when I see it.*

I was breaking every one of my careful rules. I was going to an accused murderer's house alone. For someone who lived like I did, this was the height of insanity. And I was looking to Michael, a complete stranger, for reassurance. Statistically, it was Michael who was more likely to be Ted Bundy, not Beth.

This is why you don't have any friends, I thought. *Or any actual dates.*

I had Xanax in my purse, but I didn't take it. I wanted to be sharp. The Xanax was a gesture from my doctor when I had a series of anxiety attacks after the divorce. *Sometimes just knowing you have it lowers the anxiety*, she'd said. Just knowing I had pills did not, in fact, lower my anxiety, but I carried them with me anyway, in case the theory started working.

I turned up the drive to the Greer mansion, taking in the sight. Something about this house always fascinated me. It was half pseudo-Victorian, half midcentury, an unlikely mix of peaked gables with yellow brick, brown wood, and glass. It was ugly—very, very ugly—but it drew the eye, moving your gaze over one line and then another, as if every time you looked it created itself anew. Julian Greer, Beth's father, had bought this house and remodeled it. He'd also died in the kitchen, shot by an unknown robber in his home.

The lawn was slightly unkempt, as if it hadn't been tended in a while. Shading the house was a heavy overhang of mature trees, their branches brushing the rooftop and the windows. There was a single car in the driveway—an expensive Lexus—and no other sign of life. The silence seemed to envelop me as I knocked on the front door.

Beth answered immediately. She was wearing cream linen pants and a dark brown blouse that was tailored at her narrow waist. For a second, her slim figure and the seventies color combination threw me back in time, until I saw her gray hair with her reading glasses pushed back into it. She looked me up and down. "Come in," she said.

I followed her inside. We walked through a tidy foyer to a living room, an open space that took up much of the lower level of the house. I paused, taking in the decor in surprise.

I felt like I'd stepped into an old photo album. The room was large, with floor-to-ceiling windows—now covered with curtains—lining the back wall. A sectional sofa in burnt orange and two matching chairs were arranged around a coffee table. The entire room was a throwback from forty years ago: an olive green knotted rug on the hardwood floor, the sectional low and flat with overstuffed arms, the coffee table made of heavy wood with angled legs. A bookshelf lined one wall, and I glimpsed vintage author names: Leon Uris, Sidney Sheldon, Alex Haley, Jacqueline Susann. There were ashtrays on the end tables, though they had no ashes in them and the room didn't smell of smoke. The lamps had ceramic bases and triangular shades that were genteelly yellow with age. On a shelf behind the sofa was a ceramic mermaid with red lips and blue eyeshadow, her nipples coyly hidden by seashells. Next to her was a ceramic shepherdess with a crinolined dress and a crook in her hand, her bonnet flopping over her forehead.

There were people right this minute who would pay thousands of dollars to get a vintage look like this; the Greer mansion was the real thing. It was clean and tidy, but nothing here had been replaced since before I was born.

"I suppose we need some light," Beth said, walking to the back wall. The curtains were cream with a dark brown diamond pattern, another vintage look that exactly matched Beth's outfit. For a moment, it was a weird portrait of a midcentury Miss Havisham.

I looked down to see a stack of magazines on the credenza next to the door. The top one was an issue of *Life* from October 1977. The month of the Lady Killer murders.

There was the swish of curtains, light filled the room, and I caught my breath. The windows looked over a vista of flat lawn, slightly overgrown like out front. It was an empty square, framed on either side by dark trees, and past the end of the yard the land dropped away sharply, leaving only the dark, bruised sky and emptiness. It looked like a cliff over the edge of the world.

"I hate the view," Beth said matter-of-factly, "but it's better than the darkness with the curtains closed. If you want a drink, you can go find something in the kitchen."

"I'm okay," I managed, pulling my gaze away from the view. If you walked out onto that lawn, I guessed, you'd be able to see over the edge to the ocean, but you couldn't see that far from here. Just lawn and sky. I watched Beth pick up a glass of something with clinking ice cubes and take a sip.

"You don't have a car," she said as she took a seat on the sofa.

She must have seen that I hadn't parked in the driveway. "I don't drive," I said.

She narrowed her eyes a little—my tone was harsher than I'd intended—but she let it slide. "Let's do this," she said, picking up the glass again. "How do we start?"

I sat in one of the chairs, a little far from her. Neither of us was ready to get close yet. "Is that alcohol?" I asked, maybe because the car question had cut close to the bone. Most people assumed I didn't drive because I had DUIs that had led to my license being revoked, which wasn't true. It had happened so often it made me angry. I wanted Beth to be as unnerved as I was.

Beth's smile had very little humor as she answered my question. "Not today. Not for eight years now. If you'd asked me in '09, you would have a different answer. And in '97 and '84. That's the first scoop for your article, I suppose: Beth Greer has been an on-and-off drunk since 1974 or so. She keeps kicking it, then backsliding, then kicking it again."

"That's tough," I said. "I'm sorry."

She shrugged. "Third time's a charm. Before we start, I should tell you that I looked you up."

I was opening my messenger bag, but I stopped. "Pardon?"

"I had to know that you're who you say you are. Which, it seems, you are. The name you gave me is real, and you've worked for that doctor's office for five years. I had to make sure you were legitimate before I let you into my house."

It was almost funny. I was worried about being alone with Beth, but it had never occurred to me that she'd worry about being alone with me.

"What else did you find?" I asked, thinking about what had happened when I was nine. The Incident, I called it. My name hadn't made the news, as far as I knew.

Beth put her drink down. "Not very much. I let you in. If I'm never seen again, then I guess I took my chances." She looked at my face. "That's what you were thinking about me, wasn't it? That I might kill you?"

"You were acquitted," I said.

To my surprise, she laughed. Her laugh had bitterness in it, but it also had real humor, and for a second I saw the young woman who had captivated the media for a few months in 1977. Whether she was a killer or not, Beth Greer had charisma that was hypnotic to experience in person.

"You don't quite think I'm innocent, do you?" Beth said.

What was I supposed to say? I had to tell her the truth. Our entire interview was about the truth. "I have a lot of questions," I said. "I've read so much about this case, and I keep feeling like I can only see a piece of it."

"Then you're as perceptive as I thought you were," Beth said. "The first thing you need to remember is that if there was anything true spoken at that trial, I can't think of what it is. That trial was all rumors and lies. Did you know they thought I was sleeping with Ransom?"

"I read that," I said. Ransom Wells, Beth's lawyer, was older than her and a married man, but that didn't mean much. "I never believed it."

Beth leaned back on the sofa. She was in control of her emotions, but her expression was hard. "There were rumors I was fucking *everyone*," she said. "In 1977, if you had tits and an ass, you were a piece of meat. And if you got mad about it, everyone thought it was funny. I was a dirty joke—to the cops, to the media, to the judge. The only time they took me seriously was when they thought I might blow their brains out. That was the only time I had them scared."

I stared at her. I couldn't summon a single word. My blood hummed in my veins, and sweat prickled the back of my neck, harsh yet somehow pleasant. Beth Greer was telling me the truth. It was amazing, and it was terrifying. This—*this* was what I wanted. This was what made the rest of my life pale into nothingness. This was a high I didn't think any drug could match.

"Tell me more," I said.

Beth picked up her drink, the ice cubes clinking some more. "Why don't you drive?" she asked instead of answering. "You're not a drunk like me, so that's not the reason. Tell me the real one."

I wasn't going to tell her. It was my automatic reaction to never tell anyone. Esther knew; so did my parents. My therapists, of course. My ex-husband had only heard the story once after we'd dated six months, and then never again. No one else had heard it, at least from me. So when the words came, I surprised myself.

"I was nine," I said. "I was walking home from school. A man pulled up in his car and asked if I was cold. He said I needed to get in. He said my parents were waiting for me." I kept my eyes on Beth, watching me. "I got in. After a few minutes, I realized something was wrong. I asked to get out, and when he said no, I begged. He hit me. I started struggling, screaming. He tried to pin me down and make me be quiet, but he was driving at the same time. When he was distracted and the car slowed, I opened the door and jumped out and ran. I told my parents, and eventually the police found him and arrested him. He went to prison." I took a breath. "He's been put away, but it doesn't matter. He gets out in a few months, and I don't drive. I don't feel safe in cars since that day. I hate them."

There was a roaring inside my skull, like someone had opened the hatch of a spaceship. A presence and an absence at the same time. Everything and nothing at once.

It was my biggest secret, the thing I never talked about. Ever. I had just told my biggest secret to Beth Greer.

I couldn't read her expression. It didn't crumple into pity, which was what I'd dreaded. If anything, she looked thoughtful, with no emotion at all. In that moment, she had the face of a woman who just minded her own business, and I had the crazy thought that sometimes it was a relief to be friends with someone who didn't have any emotions.

"Is that the end of the story?" she asked.

Cold sweat broke out on my hands, and my stomach turned. For a second, I thought I might throw up. "Yes," I said. "That's the end of the story."

I wondered if she knew I was lying.

Who was I kidding? Of course she knew.

CHAPTER ELEVEN

September 2017

SHEA

"Okay," I said, pulling out my cell phone and turning on the recorder. "Let's talk about the Lady Killer murders."

"Let's," Beth said, her tone dry.

I looked at her. "I don't suppose there's any point in me asking you if you committed them or not?"

She didn't blink. In the merciless light from the windows, her high cheekbones and large eyes were especially striking. "You'll form your own conclusions," she said. "Everyone does."

I looked around at the old-fashioned figurines, the expensive dark wood paneling, the now-vintage print of a racing horse on the wall. "You were living in this house when it happened," I said. "Alone."

Beth waited. She had a talent for stillness.

"Your parents had died, and you'd been on your own for two years," I said.

"Is there a question in there?"

"Didn't you hate it?" I asked. "Living in this house?" It was oppressive in here. Beautiful in a way, but oppressive. Like the house of someone who's died. Everywhere you turned, you could see the windows with their cold, bleak view, and even with the light coming in I found myself wishing Beth would close the curtains again. "Your mother must have decorated this place," I reasoned. "You were living with your mother's decorations after she died. You're still living with them."

I looked back to Beth to see her watching me from her seat on the sofa, her expression unreadable. "No one has ever asked me that before," she said. "Did I do it? That's all anyone wants to know."

"I just can't imagine it," I said. "Living in my parents' house after they were gone. After all that tragedy. Why didn't you move?"

Her gaze shifted to the windows. "It's such an easy thing to say. Just pack up and leave. I've said it to myself a thousand times. But some places hold you so that you can't get free. They squeeze you like a fist." She turned back to me, something quietly stark behind her eyes. "Sometimes you just get stuck. For years, even. Like you and your silly car phobia."

I opened my mouth to get defensive: *My phobia isn't silly.* But I stopped myself, sensing a trap. Was this misdirection? If so, from what?

I cleared my throat. "I suppose it would be hard to leave the house your parents lived in."

Beth seemed almost amused at that, though I didn't know why. "Are your parents dead?" she asked.

I shook my head. "No, they're in Florida."

The ghost of a smile touched the corner of her mouth. "Should I bother making a joke about how that's the same thing?"

"I don't think you need to."

"Then I'll refrain."

She was charming. Really charming. According to everything I'd read, sociopaths often were. I had to remember that. "What was it like for you at that time?" I asked her. "After your parents' deaths, and before the murders?"

"I was numb," Beth said. "I was nineteen when my father died, twenty-one when my mother died. In 1977, you didn't go to therapy or grief counseling. I was a legal adult and I'd inherited a lot of money, so everyone assumed I must be just fine. There was no one to look out for me, and I didn't know how to look out for myself. There were some people my age that I knew, people my parents would have hated. They started showing up, or maybe I invited them—I don't remember. They'd come here, and we'd drink. Or I'd go to a party and we'd drink. There was no one to stop me, and it never crossed my mind to stop myself. I just knew I didn't want to be sober."

"The papers portrayed it like you were partying without any guilt," I said.

"Of course they did. I told you, I had tits and an ass, so I wasn't a real person. A girl who had lost her parents couldn't possibly be spiraling, unable to cope. Easier to write that she's a slut. It sells more papers. The cops, too—they all thought the fact that I drank and partied meant I was evil. If I were a man, they would have had sympathy. They probably would have joined me."

"Even Detective Black?" I asked. Detective Joshua Black had been one of the two main investigators on the Lady Killer case, and he'd gone on to be a detective for thirty more years. I'd seen dozens of photos of him from that time: young, dark-haired, suits with wide lapels and wide striped ties, a serious frown on his face every time he saw a camera. Frankly, he had been kind of hot. I knew he still lived in Claire Lake, though he was now retired. His partner on the Lady Killer case, Detective Melvin Washington, had died in 1980. I'd never had any luck getting an interview with Detective Black or getting any copies of the Lady Killer case file. According to the Claire Lake PD, the case was still open, which meant the files weren't public.

"Black was a cop," Beth said. "He still is, even though he pretends he's retired. He's always been too nosy for his own good."

"I think cops are supposed to be nosy," I said, thinking of Michael.

"It's different when it's directed at you," Beth said. "When you're sitting in a cold room in a police station with a bunch of men asking you about your sex life. I didn't even *have* a sex life to speak of, as a matter of fact. I know the story goes that everyone was screwing like crazy in the seventies, but I had to be careful. I was terrified of ending up like my mother."

"What does that mean?" I asked. I knew almost nothing about Beth's mother. "Why were you scared of ending up like your mother?"

Beth raised her glass and drained it. Maybe I was imagining things, but I thought she was stalling for time, maybe because she regretted she'd said that. "My mother never wanted to get married," she said at last. "But it was the fifties, and my grandparents were rich. They expected her to marry well. She met my father, and that was that. More of a business deal than anything else. And a year later, she had me. She was trapped."

I watched Beth's face. The pain etched on it was buried deep, but I thought it was real. I also thought she didn't want to talk about this anymore.

"Where's your bathroom?" I asked, just to get a breather for both of us.

"Down the hall to the right." Beth looked up, and her gaze moved past me, to something over my shoulder. Her eyes were unbearably bleak for a moment, and I wondered what she was thinking.

Then she broke the gaze, looked at me, and held up her glass. "Get me a drink in the kitchen while you're up, if you don't mind. Grapefruit juice and soda, with ice."

That voice—her I'm-rich, people-do-what-I-say voice—it should have annoyed me. But instead it didn't occur to me to question her. I took the glass from her hand and stood.

Beth's gaze moved past me again, and I had the uncanny feeling that someone was behind me. But I turned and no one was there. There was just the heavy furniture, the cold light from the windows, the old print on the wall next to the doorway to the corridor. I walked down the hall.

The bathroom had a beige tile floor and a heavy sink, the taps inlaid with turquoise. It was spotlessly clean, not a hint of clutter. I glanced at myself in the mirror, also framed with turquoise. I didn't look any different than I normally did. I was tempted to open the medicine cabinet behind the mirror and snoop through it, but I didn't. I dried my hands and left the bathroom, wandering to the kitchen.

This was also unchanged from the late seventies, though like the bathroom it was perfectly clean. The cupboards were pale blue, and the counters were dark brown. The laminate floor was cream. The windows over the sink looked to the side of the house, which was crowded with trees. From here you couldn't see that end-of-the-world view, or the ocean, or the road. Just thick trees, as if you were isolated in the woods somewhere. I put the glass down on the counter and realized that this was where Beth's father had been murdered, where a maid had found his body when she came to clean the house.

My spine went cold, and behind me I heard a noise.

A squeak, and then rushing. Water. Someone had turned on a tap.

Maybe Beth was in the bathroom, though I hadn't heard her get up and follow me. I stepped back to the kitchen entrance and looked down the hall.

The bathroom door was open, the sound of the running water coming from inside. I walked into the hall and looked. The water *was* running in the bathroom sink, both taps turned on. But there was no one there.

"Beth?" I said.

"Are you getting my drink?" Beth's voice came from the living room.

I hadn't turned those taps on, and neither had she.

Steeling myself, I walked briskly into the bathroom, turned the taps off, and went back to the kitchen. I opened the fridge, poured Beth's grapefruit juice. Added soda, then opened the freezer and added ice. There was almost no food in the fridge except for a few take-out containers and premade meals. No wine or other alcohol, either. The fridge must have been on some ultrahigh setting, because I was struck with an icy blast that I imagined I could even feel on my back. My fingers were so cold they were clumsy, though I moved as fast as I could, my stomach turning uneasily as I put everything in Beth's glass.

I finished with the drink, closed the freezer, picked up the glass, and turned around. Then I stood still, my breath in my throat.

All of the cupboards behind my back were open. Four doors above the kitchen counter that hadn't been open when I walked in. Four more doors on the lower level beneath the counter. They had all swung open to the same precise degree, the doors aligned like soldiers. The entire room was silent, and nothing moved.

It wasn't Beth. It wasn't me. It wasn't anyone.

A cold draft hit me again, this time a breeze. As if a window had been left open somewhere. But why would the air be so cold? It wasn't that cold outside. And yet the wind was so distinct I felt it lift the tendrils of hair that weren't tied back in my ponytail.

In the bathroom, the taps turned on again. I stood frozen, holding the drink forgotten in my hand, listening to that sound as my heart hammered in my chest. For a second, I felt like I had gone back in time to the seventies, to the house's heyday. I would walk out of this kitchen and find a different world, one filled with Jell-O salads and *The Waltons* on TV.

Except the Greer mansion wasn't a house of rosy brown and orange nostalgia. A man had been murdered here. Right where I was standing.

I put the drink on the counter and walked to the bathroom again, my feet moving mechanically. I almost expected to see Beth in there—except a teenage Beth, slim and youthful, wearing a T-shirt and jeans with embroidery on the pockets, her hair long down her back. But just like before, there was no one there.

I put my hand on the tap, and blood splashed into the bowl of the sink. It mixed with the water, red and rancid, swirling down the drain. I jerked my hand away. I wasn't bleeding. Yet the blood still ran, as if someone were dumping it into the water, or rinsing bloody hands. The cold air hit the back of my neck, along with a rotten metallic smell, and I nearly gagged.

In one quick motion, I twisted the taps off. Then I went back to the kitchen, grabbed the drink with a numb hand, and walked back to the living room. Beth was still on the sofa, waiting. She looked at me curiously. "Are you all right?"

"Sure," I said, trying not to think about what I'd just seen. The living room was stuffy, with no sign of a breeze. I handed Beth her drink. "This house . . ."

"It's horrible, I know." Beth took the glass and put it next to her. "Let's continue. What else did you want to ask me?"

My phone was still sitting on the table. I hadn't stopped the recording when I left the room. I picked it up and saw that it was paused. "Did you stop this?" I asked her.

"No," Beth said. Her expression was calm as she looked at me. "You look pale, Shea. What's the matter?"

CHAPTER TWELVE

October 1977

BETH

The Greer mansion, Beth thought, must be worth a lot of money. Her father had spared no expense when he'd renovated the place. Her mother had bought expensive furniture and decor. It was supposed to be the nicest, most beautiful house in the city.

Beth figured she should probably burn it down.

All of Arlen Heights was oppressive and gloomy this morning, the rain coming down on the carefully untended streets. The interview with the police detectives had been the day before. Since then, Beth had been driving, spending endless hours behind the wheel of her car. Searching, searching. She'd barely slept, and even though she was sober, she still had a headache behind her eyes that felt a lot like a hangover. She didn't want to go home.

Just keep control, Beth. You can handle this. Just keep control.

She'd finally decided to come home and try to sleep. She felt jumpy and wild, unable to sit still, but when the Greer mansion came in sight, a chill descended. There was a car in her driveway, a big sixties Chevy, floating like a freighter. She'd know that car anywhere. And parked on the street in front of the house was a van she didn't recognize. As she pulled into the driveway behind the Chevy, a man got out of the van, carrying a microphone. He was followed by another man with a camera on his shoulder.

Now she wasn't jumpy anymore. Now she was just angry.

It was cold, her anger. Her parents' anger had always burned hot, especially when they shouted at each other. Then they'd both storm out of the house, leaving Beth alone, and everything would go cold and silent. Beth had learned early which one she preferred. Which one kept her calm and served her purposes when she needed it instead of making her surrender control.

"Miss Greer!" The reporter was coming up the drive as she opened her car door and got out. The cameraman hurried behind him, only able to go so far before he ran out of cable. "Miss Greer!" the reporter shouted. "Do you have anything to say about the murder accusations against you? Are you the Lady Killer?"

Beth closed the car door behind her. She shoved her hands in her pockets, because she couldn't think of anything else to do with them. Part of her thought that if she left her hands free, she'd slap the man across the face, right there on camera. It was the same anger she'd felt during the police interview, but this time she kept her foot on its neck by sheer force of will as it struggled to get free.

The camera was pointed at her, a large bulky thing that was snarled with cables and a huge lens. The reporter had his microphone pointed at her face. Beth savored the feeling of her anger, the cold in her bones. She leaned toward the microphone and said, "I'm just a girl who minds her own business."

Then she turned away and walked up the drive where the camera couldn't follow her. She circled the house to the backyard, where she knew Ransom would be.

He wouldn't be in the house. He had never said as much, but Ransom Wells hated this house as much as Beth did. Beth walked past the dripping trees to the open lawn that led to the cliff over the sea. It was a view of flat green grass and churning, dark blue ocean far away off the shore, birds wheeling in the sky overhead. She shivered. The rain was letting up, but it was always cold back here, no matter what time of year it was.

Standing on the lawn was a man well over six feet tall, with big shoulders and a big body to match his height. His hair and beard were salt-and-pepper, though he was only in his thirties. He was wearing a suit and an overcoat. He seemed oblivious to the rain, like most of the lifetime residents of Claire Lake. He looked exactly the same as the last time she saw him, after her mother died two years ago.

At that time, he'd told her she was hiring him whether she wanted to or not.

I don't need a lawyer, she'd replied.

And he'd said: *You're young, you're beautiful, and as of now you're alone and very rich. My dear, you need a lawyer more than anything.*

"Ransom," she said now, approaching him across the grass. "What are you doing here?"

He didn't reply until she was standing next to him. "This is a beautiful view," he said. "Your father always loved it."

Beth waited. Ransom had a newspaper, now damp, folded under one arm. She tucked a windblown lock of hair behind her ear as the anger she'd felt for the reporter drained away. When Ransom had something to say, there was no power on earth that would make him say it faster.

Finally, Ransom spoke again. "I first met your father when he called me up to make an impaired driving charge go away. Did you know that? Not the most illustrious meeting." His brows drew together as he looked at the ocean. He wasn't a handsome man, exactly, but he was hard to look away from. "I didn't think I'd like him, but I did. I got him off the drunk driving charge, because I'm good and that's the way the world works. I've been sorry for his loss every day since he died. Literally every day. I'm as puzzled by that as you are."

Beth swallowed and looked at the trees. Her father had been complicated—unhappy, sometimes angry. In his own way, as trapped as her mother was. For a long time, during the years of alcohol-fueled fights and lonely Christmases, she had hated him. Part of her still did.

But she had loved him, too. She had wished, with the stupid wistfulness of a daughter, that she could have been the one to make him happy. But she wasn't. She could never be. Fixing her father hadn't been possible.

She turned back to see Ransom looking at her. He'd been her father's lawyer, and then her mother's, and now hers. He was as familiar to her as a tool she used every day. She knew he had a wife who left him frequently—he always got her back—and three kids. He liked steak and loathed cigarettes, claiming the smell made him sick. She hadn't seen him in two years, but she knew all of those things were still true.

"You need a lawyer," he said.

"No, I don't."

He took the newspaper from under his arm and handed it to her.

Reluctantly, Beth took it and opened it. It was this morning's *Claire Lake Daily*, spattered with rain and hot off the press, and the headline read DO POLICE HAVE A SUSPECT IN THE "LADY KILLER" MURDERS? Beneath it was a photo of Beth leaving the police station after the interview yesterday. She'd been surprised by the man standing outside with a camera, and he'd caught her looking pale and hard, hostility in her eyes. Even Beth looked at that photo and could easily see a murderer. A trick of the light, the random angle of her face, the surprise and anger mixed in her features, and she looked guilty as hell.

She'd probably looked guilty as hell on camera just now, too. It all added more fuel to the fire.

Beth stared at the words in the headline again. They threatened to blur and jumble in front of her face. Things were moving now, going faster, as if sliding downhill. None of it was under her control.

"Do you have anything to say to me, Beth?" Ransom asked, cutting through her haze of anger and panic.

"They think I did it," Beth said, because she couldn't tell Ransom the truth. He already knew some of it; he'd been the family lawyer for too long not to know the buried secrets. But there were other secrets that were too dangerous for even Ransom to know. "The police, I mean. They think I killed those men."

"And yet they didn't arrest you," Ransom pointed out calmly. "That means they're still fishing. They'll pressure you as much as they can while they build their case. They're hoping you give in, get scared, start weeping or cracking. They're looking for vulnerable spots. Something tells me they're looking in vain."

Beth folded the paper, unable to stare at the words anymore, the photo of her murderous face. Everyone thought she had it together. Well, she may as well play the part. "I didn't tell them anything because I don't know anything."

Ransom tutted. "You shouldn't have talked to them without me. Always call your lawyer first, Beth. But it's no matter. I'll have whatever you said discredited so thoroughly no one will even be sure you said it in the first place. What can you tell me about the cops? Are we dealing with any level of competence?"

It hadn't occurred to Beth that she would gain her own information from that interview. Maybe she should start thinking like a criminal. "Yes," she said. "They're both competent. Black is younger, but he has more authority somehow. He wouldn't let the other one smoke during the interview."

"Competent and righteous. A deadly combination. I'll keep it in mind."

"I don't need you." She didn't need anyone. She couldn't. Even now, with everything going to hell.

Ransom was unfazed. "Yes, you do. Where were you on the nights of the murders?"

"Home."

"Was anyone with you?"

Beth shook her head.

"You were out just now, when I got here."

"I was driving around."

"Alone?"

"Yes." She'd been searching. But she wasn't going to tell Ransom that.

"We'll work on it," he said. "What to tell them. What to say. When to shut up, which is most of the time. Tell me everything they asked you, everything you said. Everything they told you."

She did. She remembered every word so easily. It was the only thing she had thought about since she walked out of the police station.

Ransom listened, then gave his judgment: "It could be worse, and it could be better. You have me now. How much money do you have left of your parents' inheritance?"

"Just about all of it."

"Good, because I'll need a retainer." As if there was never a question of hiring anyone other than him. Because in all honesty, there wasn't. "You can swim through this, Beth. But it's a sensational case, and like it or not, you're a sensational young woman. This is going to get ugly."

"I know." Two years. Two years she'd been doing—what? Drinking, spending time with the wrong people. Sleeping with her eyes open, thinking that after her mother's death nothing in her life could get worse. Thinking that the worst of it was over.

All of this was her fault.

Her life, as she knew it, was over. There was some relief in that, because she hadn't liked her life much. But what was waiting for her was not going to be any better.

"Did you tell the police about your mother?" Ransom asked. "About her history?"

The words gave her chills. It had been years since this topic had come up. "No, of course not."

"I thought things were settled," Ransom said, looking out over the ocean, "but perhaps I was wrong. I can make some inquiries."

"Don't bother," Beth said.

Ransom looked pained, but he nodded. Years of history passed between them, unspoken.

Do you think I'm a murderer? Beth wanted to ask him. A moment of weakness. Just one moment. *Say it. Say that you don't think I killed those men. Please.*

But he didn't say that, and instead of asking, she said, "I can handle it."

Ransom took the newspaper from her and put it back under his arm. "I'll never understand why Mariana made the choices she did. They must have seemed like the only choices possible to her, I suppose. Still, now she's gone, and we have to deal with the fallout." He glanced at Beth. "I'll be honest. Because of all the times in your life, now is the time for honesty. Could I believe that you did it? That you killed those men, just by looking at you? Yes, I can believe it. Easily. It's a good thing I can believe it, because I'm going to look at all the same angles as someone who thinks you're guilty. And you're going to get a fair trial."

The wind stung Beth's face, crawled down her neck. She looked at the ocean.

"Julian died in that house," Ransom said. "There are times I look at it and I can still see him, standing in a hallway or coming out the front door. I can still see Mariana, too. If I believed in ghosts, which I don't, I'd believe that those two are still in that house, which is why I can't bear to go in there. I'd rather stand out here in the rain. But it doesn't change the fact that they're dead and their daughter is still alive. It doesn't change the fact that I'm not going to let the jackals eat you, Beth."

Beth swallowed. "Get me out of this," she told him. "Not just for me. Get me out of this so I can lay the ghosts to rest."

Ransom paused, and then he nodded. "Fine," he said. "I intend to try."

CHAPTER THIRTEEN

SHEA

"Telekinesis," I said.

"What?" Michael's tone was thick with disbelief.

"Telekinesis," I said again. "The ability of a person to move physical objects with their mind. According to the research, it can sometimes be deliberate and sometimes subconscious, brought on by extreme emotion or stress. Some people have even reported telekinetic powers during sleep, when they're completely unaware of it. The person is asleep, and they're still making things move."

Michael cleared his throat. I was on the bus, but it was nearly empty and I was sitting at the back, where no one could hear my crazy ranting. "Shea, you're trying to tell me that Beth Greer isn't only a serial murderer, she's also a psychic?"

"I'm saying it's a *possibility*," I replied. "That's all. I looked up the research, and—"

"What research? The entire theory is a load of bullshit."

Of course that's what Michael would think. He was a cop. Deep down, I thought it was bullshit, too—I'd never believed in psychics, ghosts, demonic possessions, or any of it. But still. "I saw what I saw," I said. "The taps turned on by themselves, and the cupboard doors opened." Telekinesis wouldn't explain the blood I'd seen in the sink, which I hadn't told Michael about. But there had to be an explanation for that. There *had* to be.

"It's an old house," Michael said. "The pipes in my apartment make weird moaning noises at night, but that's all it is. Pipes."

So Michael lived in an apartment. I hadn't known that. Ever since he'd mentioned a divorce, I'd wondered if he lived in an apartment or if he still lived in their house, if they had one. "This wasn't pipes," I said. "This was taps being *turned on*."

"Well, it wasn't telekinesis, either," Michael said. "Maybe Beth was trying to distract you."

I blinked in shock as the bus turned a corner, heading for downtown. "You think Beth rigged some kind of deliberate setup?"

"Why not? It's her house. She's had forty years to put in any switches or levers that she wants. You're dealing with a liar, Shea. Please remember that."

I closed my eyes, feeling two distinct sides of myself at war. On the one hand, I absolutely did not believe in ghosts or the supernatural. It was regular, everyday earthly evil that kept me up at night.

But on the other hand, to believe it was a fun-house trick was to believe that Beth Greer had some strange, psychopathic wish to deceive me. And—I could admit it to myself—I didn't want to believe that.

I didn't want to believe she was a liar, and I didn't want to believe she was a serial killer. Which was exactly what Beth wanted.

"I can go over there and check it out, if you like," Michael said.

"No."

"Are you saying no because you don't want to ask for help from a man?"

"That isn't it." That was kind of it. "Beth and I have only just started talking. If I bring someone over to dismantle her house, looking for levers, she'll stop talking to me."

"Of course," Michael said. "The carrot and the stick. That works entirely in her favor."

Once again, I pictured Michael as an old-school gumshoe, sitting on a park bench somewhere, trying to look casual as he followed a subject. He was holding a newspaper in front of his face, watching from behind it. A turtleneck—I definitely pictured him in a turtleneck. Dark brown, with a blazer over it. The picture was so vivid it felt real. "Beth has held up her end of the bargain so far," I argued. "I'm on my way to interview Detective Joshua Black right now."

"At least I don't have to worry about you when you're with him," Michael said. "I envy you, to be honest. Black is a legend in the Claire Lake PD. He's been retired for years, but they still talk about him. He's put countless thieves and rapists away, worked every big murder Claire Lake has ever seen. His work on the Sherry Haines murder was practically a textbook on how to catch a killer."

My body went cold and my head went light. There was a thready pulsing sound in my ears. I held the phone, silent.

"Shea?" Michael said. "Are you there?"

"Yes," I managed. "He worked . . . He worked that case? I didn't know."

"Sure, he worked it," Michael said. "We don't have a big detective force in Claire Lake, and we don't have that many murders. Especially child murders. You sound strange. Are you all right?"

"I'm fine." I looked out the window, saw the piers and the water. "This is my stop. I have to go."

I screwed that up, I thought as I got off the bus and inhaled the cold, salty smell of the ocean. Michael probably thought I was crazy. Then again, he thought that already. I had to forget about it and get a grip for this interview with Joshua Black.

Black's address was one of the houseboats on the downtown piers. I walked along the grid of wooden slats, following the signs with twee names like Ocean Lane and Saltwater Avenue. Black's boat was trim and tidily kept, though the decorations weren't overly fussy. A single man's dwelling.

I knocked on the door, and he answered right away. Though Black was over seventy now, he looked a lot like the handsome man I'd seen in photos. He had the same cheekbones and dark eyes, but his hair was white. Still, his face had changed somewhat. It was thinner, the roundness of his young man's features gone. The effect was just as pleasing, but in a different way.

I looked at him and tried to remember if I recognized him, if Detective Black's was one of the many faces I'd seen after I'd escaped the car when I was nine. If he'd worked the case, been the lead, then I must have been brought to talk to him at some point. But everything was a terrified blur, and there were so many strangers' faces in the days and weeks that followed the abduction—police, doctors, psychologists, social workers. I'd sat numbly and told my story over and over, gotten in the car with my parents and gone to office after office. I hadn't known who anyone was, and I hadn't asked many questions. I had only wanted all of it to be over.

But it was almost certain that Detective Black and I had met twenty years ago, that he'd been one of the people to interview me and have me tell my story. It was certain that he knew my name, because I hadn't changed it. Maybe he'd forgotten; it was a long time ago. But when I looked in his eyes, I knew he hadn't forgotten at all.

"Shea Collins?" He held out his hand, and I shook it. "It's nice to see you again."

My throat was tight, my tongue clumsy and dry in my mouth. "I don't remember you," I said, the words spilling out of me. "Not specifically."

"I didn't think you would," he said. Then he stepped back. "Come in."

The inside of the houseboat was small and neat, a bachelor's space. There was a sofa and a TV, a coffee table that likely served as a dining table. There was a galley kitchen to the left and a partition with, presumably, a bedroom behind it. From the window over the kitchen sink, I could see nothing but water.

"Have a seat," Black said, indicating the sofa. I sat down, realizing that I was obeying because I thought of him as a cop. The cop who had worked—had solved—the Sherry Haines case. The man who, at some point, had interviewed me. I pressed my palms together between my knees.

"Can I get you anything?" Black asked, walking to the galley kitchen.

"No, thank you."

"We'll get something out of the way first," he said in the easy manner of a man who has conducted hundreds of interviews with strangers, most of them hostile, as he poured water into his glass. "I remember you from the Sherry Haines case, but we're not here to talk about that today."

"No," I managed.

"I understand. You want to talk about the Lady Killer case. You asked for an interview before, I think. A year or so ago."

I nodded. "I'm a blogger. Not as my day job. As my hobby." I stopped talking, realizing that for once I was with someone who didn't need an explanation about why I liked true crime. If anyone would understand, it was Detective Joshua Black.

Black turned around, the glass in his hand. "I recognized your name when you made the first request," he said frankly, "but I make it a policy never to talk about that case with anyone. This time, though, I got a personal request from Beth to meet with you, and I was too curious to turn it down."

This part had me completely baffled. "You have a relationship with Beth," I said, and it didn't come out as a question.

Detective Black leaned against his tiny kitchen counter. "We live in the same town," he said. "We've both lived here all our lives. Claire Lake isn't a very big place."

"So even though you investigated her and testified at her murder trial, the two of you are friends."

He laughed, though the sound had little humor in it. Instead I heard layers of complexity I didn't understand. "We aren't friends." He gestured at the view out the kitchen window. "Did you know that these houseboats were originally put here by Claire Lake's homeless people?"

I blinked. "Pardon?"

"Hard to believe, isn't it?" He smiled. "In the early 1960s, the city wanted to put up single-family houses by the lake. They were going to tear down public housing in order to do it, and evict everyone in the neighborhood. No one stopped them, so the city evicted over two hundred people, all of whom had to find somewhere else to live. Some wise soul realized that he could buy a boat that was headed for the junkyard for much cheaper than a house, and also that the city's zoning laws technically allowed for residential boats off the piers. So a lot of the evicted people, who were now homeless, bought up old boats, anchored them, and lived in them instead."

"I'll bet the city was pleased," I said.

Black smiled again. "The city was livid, but there was nothing they could do. The zoning laws were on the books. Since then, this area has gentrified so much that only artsy types and retirees like me live here. But the first boats were owned by the poor rabble, the people who had nowhere else to go." He shook his head. "I guess you're not interested in my Claire Lake history lesson."

"It's interesting," I said, which was true. I pulled out my phone. "Is it okay if I record this conversation?"

Detective Black looked amused. "So I'm on the other side of the recording this time. Okay, I give my permission."

I put the phone down, hoping it would pick up the conversation with Black, standing a few feet away. I didn't want to ask him to sit down in his own house, and I didn't want to stand up and crowd him. But Black had been a cop for thirty-five years, and I realized his position was deliberate.

The thought made me salty, so I said, "I'd love access to the original Lady Killer interview tapes, if you're feeling generous."

"The transcripts were leaked online."

Nice try. "Only sections were leaked. Not the entire tapes."

"True, but the leaked sections were pretty relevant."

"According to you," I countered. "The entire tapes would give a better idea of your interview technique."

"You mean mine and Detective Washington's."

I nodded. "It's too bad I'm too late to interview him, too."

He gave me a wry look. "You'd have to time-travel to early 1980 to do that." His tone said that he hadn't liked Washington very much.

"Tell me how you two started working together," I said.

Black's eyebrows rose. "You're warming me up," he stated. "Getting me talking before asking what you really want to know. It's a time-honored technique. You forget you're dealing with someone who has done this a lot."

For God's sake, was every single person involved in this case going to be difficult? "I can sit here all day," I said.

That caught me a ghost of a smile. "Now I can see why Beth likes you. Okay. I met Washington for the first time the day after Thomas Armstrong got two bullets to the face. I was one of the only detectives on the Claire Lake force, and I'd never worked a homicide before. We didn't have many murders. Mostly I worked assaults, robberies, and rapes. I was only thirty-one."

"So the Claire Lake PD brought in the state police," I said.

Black nodded. "Washington was a state detective. He'd never seen anything quite like the Armstrong case, either, even though he had more experience than me. The murder seemed random, but random murders had been done before. It was the note that threw us."

I nodded. *Am I bitter or am I sweet? Ladies can be either. Publish this or there will be more.* Everyone who was obsessed with this case knew that note by heart. "What did you and Washington think the note meant?"

Black's eyes were looking at something far away now, and the words came easily as he remembered. "Well, the Zodiac had done his business down in San Francisco," he said, "killing people at random and mailing notes to the newspapers. So we'd seen a similar MO before. But the Lady Killer note was in a woman's hand, a rounded cursive with flourishes that the handwriting experts said a man wouldn't make. The Armstrong murder was heartless and cruel, particularly brutal. Whoever had killed him had looked him in the eye as they shot him in the face. That isn't a woman's method."

"Are you going to tell me that poison is a woman's weapon?" I asked, stating the cliché. "Diane Downs shot her three kids point-blank, then drove slowly to the hospital, hoping they'd bleed out."

"That was a few years later," Black said. "Up in Washington, they had Bundy killing college coeds, and down in California they had Ed Kemper doing the same thing. Monsters, both of them, but they were men. We'd never seen anything like this."

I nodded. As every true-crime lover knows, the seventies were a banquet of particularly brutal serial killers. If you read enough true crime, you started to think that being a young woman back then was a pretty dangerous business. And it was amazing that anyone survived hitchhiking at all. "So what happened?" I asked.

"We gave the note to the press," Black said. "We had to take the chance. It hadn't worked with the Zodiac—they printed everything he told them to, but he kept killing anyway. But our hands were tied. There was a lot of arguing behind the scenes. Half the cops thought the note was a red herring and we were dealing with a man. The other half thought that the killer was probably a mistress of Armstrong's, though we couldn't find evidence of one. No one thought it was actually what it was."

"Which was?"

"A true, bona fide female serial killer." Black put his glass of water on the counter and stared at it, unseeing. "It's difficult to explain how hard that was to process for us in 1977. It's still hard now. We had no context, no idea what we were dealing with, no idea what to expect. None of us had the slightest bit of training or education in serial murder, let alone female serial murder. It was so unusual that we haven't had another case like the Lady Killer in forty years. A woman driving around shooting people for fun. We live in a very different society than we did in 1977, but that part hasn't changed."

"And then Paul Veerhoever was killed," I said.

Black nodded, seeming to remember I was there. "Veerhoever had two kids," he said. "He'd served six years in the military before an honorable discharge. His wife had had three miscarriages, and he'd been by her side for all of them. The first bullet didn't kill him—only hit him in the jaw. He was in unimaginable agony until the Lady Killer put a second bullet in his temple and left him by the side of the road."

My mouth was dry. This was what they thought Beth had done. It was this murder that a witness had said he'd seen Beth drive away from.

Detective Black walked to the only chair, on the other side of the coffee table, and sat down. Outside, I could hear birds calling over the ocean. The boat rocked gently, and I felt like I was a little drunk. I couldn't see how anyone could live here—too many ways for someone to break in, too many strangers walking by, no alarm system that I could see—but I had to assume he liked it. Cops, even former cops, could live in places I couldn't and not worry about it.

"The first time I met Beth was at our first interview," he said, though I hadn't asked a question. "The day after Veerhoever was killed. We had a witness identification by then. I knew who Beth Greer was, though I'd never met her. I knew who her parents were. I knew she lived in Arlen Heights. It seemed unlikely that she was a killer, but, like I say, we had no idea what we were looking for. We didn't know what a female Zodiac was supposed to look like. And Beth wasn't like any woman any of us had met."

"She was young and sexy and smart," I said. "Rich. So that made her a murderer?"

Detective Black leaned forward, put his elbows on his knees. "Aside from the witness identification, think about this," he said. "This killer, whoever they are, can get away scot-free. There's no connection to the victim, no fingerprints, no hair or fiber evidence, no blood or DNA. No witnesses. This person has just literally gotten away with murder. And she *decides to leave a note with her handwriting on it.* Paper that could be traced, handwriting that could be analyzed, possibly even fingerprints. Who would do that? Someone with an ego. Someone who thinks she's smarter than the cops. Someone who thinks she'll never be caught."

"Someone who wants to be caught," I countered. "Deep down, even if she can't admit it. She wants to be stopped."

"Psychopaths don't want to be stopped," Black said. "They want to keep doing what they're doing for as long as it gets them off. But they want to laugh at everyone at the same time. They can't help it. They're certain that no one will catch them, and a lot of times, they're right."

"The second note said 'Catch me.'"

"The second note wasn't a plea; it was a taunt. Because the writer didn't believe we could do it. Her ego didn't let her think it."

I thought of Beth's commanding rich-girl voice, the way she gave orders like someone who has had money and confidence all her life, and I didn't answer.

"Beth was like an unknown species of bird," Black said. "She wasn't a wife or a mother or a daughter, or even a true wild child, despite what the rumors said. She wasn't anything, which meant she *could* be anything. She wasn't man-hungry or money-hungry or any other kind of hungry. She drank too much, but she wasn't on drugs and she didn't gamble. She was beautiful, she was smart, and she was cold. Self-contained, impossible to crack, at only twenty-three. She had the means and the opportunity. A car and no alibi. And then we ran the ballistics."

The ballistics tests had showed that the gun used to kill Armstrong and Veerhoever had also been used in the home invasion that killed Beth's father, Julian, when Beth was nineteen.

The only time they took me seriously was when they thought I might blow their brains out, Beth had told me. *That was the only time I had them scared.*

"She didn't have a motive for any of it," I said.

"You don't always get a motive," Black replied. "That's something you learn in police work. You don't always get the why, especially with stranger killings. I had a long career after the Lady Killer case, and I worked a lot of cases I didn't fully understand. But I still closed them."

I thought of the fact that he had worked the Sherry Haines case, and I dropped my gaze to the coffee table. Black had a cop's knack for reading people, and I didn't want him to read me.

Then I went over what he'd said, ran through the words in my mind. Detective Black had been very careful. He'd talked about the Lady Killer and he'd talked about Beth. But he hadn't put the two of them into the same sentence.

"You don't think she did it," I said, realizing as I spoke that it was true.

I looked up to see those cop's eyes watching me, and I had the feeling they missed nothing. "I was a detective," he said. "I saw things that no one ever wants to see. I was there that first night, when we were called to Thomas Armstrong's body at the side of the road. I dedicated my career to fighting evil. Do you honestly think I would take Beth Greer's phone calls, her requests, if I thought she had killed those men? Do you think I would have any kind of relationship with a serial killer?"

He had such conviction, even now, all these years later. "No," I said. "I don't."

"I spent months investigating Beth," Black said. "I dug up every part of her life, because someone shot Julian Greer, then used the same gun to commit two more murders. After the ballistics report came back, Washington and I found everything we could find on Julian Greer, looking for the connection. Greer's murder had looked like a straightforward home invasion—the back door of the house was broken open and Greer was shot in the kitchen, his wallet and cash stolen. It was eleven o'clock on a Saturday morning. Mariana was with her bridge club, and Beth said she was out shopping. No one even double-checked her alibi." He shook his head. "I tried every way possible to believe that a nineteen-year-old girl shot her own father, then made it look like a break-in. That would have taken planning, cold blood, and the kind of hate that burns for years."

"Maybe her father was abusive," I said.

"That's just it. Washington and I went over everything about the man. He was clean. His marriage was unhappy, by all accounts, but that was all we could find. He didn't have any enemies, personal or professional. His former secretary sobbed when we interviewed her. She still wasn't over his death. She said that Julian was a wonderful man, but she hated Mariana. She said Mariana had ruined Julian's life."

I thought that over. I knew almost nothing about Beth's parents, except that both had had their lives cut short. Beth had told me she didn't want to end up like her mother—no, she'd said she was *terrified* of ending up like her mother. She'd said that Mariana was trapped. That sounded pitiful, and it didn't line up with the secretary's description.

"So you never figured it out," I said.

"Some detective I am, right?" He actually sounded regretful, as if he hadn't solved cases and saved people's lives for thirty-five years. "The only connection I ever found between the two cases was Beth. Beth lived in that house, and a witness said he saw Beth at Veerhoever's crime scene. This case outsmarted me in the end. Or maybe Beth did."

"And yet you don't think she's a serial killer." My mind was spinning. "My head hurts."

"Welcome to the Lady Killer case," Black said wryly.

There was a moment of quiet as I rubbed my eyes and thought things over. Black was right—the ballistics match meant that Julian Greer was a part of this somehow. He was, in a way, the first Lady Killer victim. "Is the secretary still alive?" I asked, my eyes still closed.

"I have no idea," Black said. "She was a young woman then."

"What was her name?"

"Sylvia Bledsoe."

Of course he remembered a name from forty years ago off the top of his head. He was that kind of cop. I dropped my hands and opened my eyes again to find him looking at me. The expression on his face was quietly happy, paternal. My own father had never looked at me like that. When my father looked at me, his expression was either bewildered or tensely pained.

"You're going to interview her, aren't you?" he said.

"If she's still alive, I may as well try."

He turned to a kitchen drawer, riffled through it for a notepad and a pen. He wrote something down and handed it to me. It was his phone number. "I can't give you the case file, because that would be breaking the rules," he said. "But if you have questions, or you need me, then call me anytime. I'll tell you everything I can."

I took the number. "Why are you helping me? Is it because of Beth?" I didn't like that idea—that Beth was hovering over every aspect of what I was doing, jerking all of the strings.

For the first time, Black's expression went a little hard, and I glimpsed the man who had faced down some of the worst of humanity without fear. "I agreed to this meeting because I wanted to meet the only person my top suspect has ever called me about," he said. "But that's not why I'm helping you. I'm helping you because you're Girl A."

My heart hammered in my chest. "I'm what?"

"We couldn't identify you by name in our analysis of the Sherry Haines case," Black said. "You were too young, and your identity was protected. But the murder file, the file I worked on, contained your name. I knew your name because I met you. I'm giving you the best chance to finally solve this case because you're Girl A. Because in forty years, you're the only one Beth has decided to talk to. If anyone can find what the truth is, I think it's you."

CHAPTER FOURTEEN

September 2017

SHEA

All that week, I had strange dreams. I'd see the Greer mansion sitting in the rainy gloom, dark and silent, framed by the black-branched trees. I'd see the bleak view out the back windows, looking over the edge of the rise to the ocean, and I'd see the imprints of footprints in the grass. As if someone wanted in—or could already come and go at will—and nothing I could do would stop them.

I'd see someone falling over that cliff. A pair of feet leaving the edge, sailing into the cold air above the ocean. I'd feel a cold gust of air from a broken-in door, and I'd see blood spiraling in that sink, red turning pinkish in the water.

I'd wake up certain that the taps in my bathroom were turned on, that the curtains on my window had changed position. Then I'd lie awake, alone in the dark, listening for sounds. Was that a footstep? A tap on the roof, as if someone were walking there? Was there someone in my living room right now, prowling quietly? If there was, how stupid was I to get out of bed and go look?

By day, I'd sit at the reception desk and wonder if the file cabinets behind me were opening while my back was turned, if the papers were moving from one side of the desk to the other. By night, I waded into the Book of Cold Cases and used my online searching skills to find Sylvia Bledsoe, the woman who had once worked as Julian Greer's secretary. Because there had to be answers out there somewhere. Anywhere.

"Come to dinner," Esther said to me on the phone one night after work.

"I don't think I can," I said. "I'm kind of busy."

"Doing what?"

I hadn't told Esther about my meetings with Beth Greer. She wouldn't know who Beth was, and once I told her, she would probably have an anxiety attack. "My usual stuff."

"Shea, I'm playing my sister card. You know I don't do it often. Come to dinner."

I caved. I really was tired of sitting here alone, wondering what those sounds were. "Okay. Tomorrow. I'll come after work."

"Yay!" She actually said that, unironically, as a thirty-three-year-old woman. "I'll make chicken tetrazzini."

"You don't have to do that." She knew that was my favorite meal, but it wasn't simple to make. Esther made the sauce from scratch, which immediately made me feel bad. "We'll order in. You don't have to cook. It's fine."

"I'd like to do it. Besides, we eat out all the time anyway. Will is going to be overjoyed."

I sighed. They were going to make a fuss, or at least Esther was.

"You know, Will has a cute coworker," Esther was saying. "He's single. Maybe I'll invite him, too."

Oh God. "Please don't. I'm begging you."

"I just think—"

"Esther, I don't want to be set up."

"It isn't a setup exactly. It's just dinner. You can't be single forever."

"I can. I literally can. That's a thing." No one understood single people. If you didn't have a partner and babies, how were you spending your time? I'd tried the marriage thing, and I'd still been me. Except an unhappy version of me.

"Okay," Esther said, "but being a spinster isn't healthy. This guy is a junior lawyer. He's really nice."

"Did you know that Ted Bundy was executed in 1989, but they didn't type his DNA until 2011?" I said.

Esther paused. I'd surprised her. "What?"

"No one actually knows how many women he murdered," I said. "With DNA, they can try and close old cold cases. But it's taking them years. We could find out about Bundy victims we didn't even know about."

"Shea," my sister said.

"Did you know that Gary Ridgway's coworkers called him Green River Gary?" I said. "They teased him about secretly being the Green River Killer. None of them knew that he actually was. He killed almost fifty women. That must have been pretty weird for those guys, reading in the paper that he was arrested, don't you think?"

"Shea."

"Esther, if you bring a date to this dinner, I swear *I will say those exact things* as dinner conversation. Is that what you want?"

"Okay, okay, I surrender. You win. It will be just us and the tetrazzini, okay? Come tomorrow."

I opened my mouth to agree, but there was a *thump* in the hallway outside my door, the sound of something shifting. Then the sound of the stairwell door opening and closing. I wasn't imagining it this time.

"I have to go," I said to Esther. "Someone's at the door."

"Oh, good. Maybe it's a neighbor coming to say hi. Maybe he's single and good-looking."

"Maybe it's someone here to murder me. If it is, I leave you my worldly possessions."

"Shea."

"Talk soon, sis," I said, and hung up. I let the joke fall away as I sat in silence, listening. Nothing for a long minute, and then a faint shifting sound, as if someone really was outside the door. I thought I could hear breathing.

I stood up, keeping the phone awake in my hand, ready to dial 911. I walked softly to the door, moving quietly so whoever it was wouldn't hear me approach. I looked out my peephole but saw only the wall across the hallway.

Packages were left in the mail room, so it wasn't UPS or FedEx. Who had a code to the front door of my building? I heard another soft sound. Someone was definitely there.

"I'm calling the police," I said loudly. "You need to go away now."

Silence.

"I'm not opening this door," I said. "You can't get in here. The police will be on their way in thirty seconds. Leave."

Still silence, but I knew there was a presence in the hallway. I dialed nine, waited a beat, then dialed one.

Finally, there was a sound. Whiny and growly, rather pissed-off. A cat's meow.

I blinked. Canceled the call. Then I opened the door.

In front of my door was a plastic pet carrier and two large shopping bags. As I watched, the cat carrier shifted, as if the cat inside was turning in circles, tired of being trapped.

Taped to the top of one of the bags was a note:

You were right. I decided not to come to my senses. I'm going to live with my mother for a while.

I agree he shouldn't get the cat. Mom is allergic, so the cat is yours now. Sorry to do this to you, but he's fixed and he doesn't bite. I guess you can drop him at a shelter if you have to, but I couldn't do it. If you keep him, let him sleep on the bed, because he loves it. He'll do anything you want for tuna treats.

Sorry again,

Alison

P.S. His name is Winston Purrchill.

He was a gray tabby. Big and sleek, his markings dark, with a white expanse on his throat and chest. His face wasn't pretty, and one of his ears was slightly bent near the top. When I opened his carrier in my condo, he walked out slowly, looking at me disdainfully from his muddy green eyes.

The shopping bags contained food, a litter box, a container of litter, and three packets of the promised tuna treats. I'd never owned a cat before, never had a pet of any kind. I'd never asked for this. What the hell was I supposed to do?

For the first time, I called Michael about something that wasn't murder-related. I'd already had a lecture from Esther, and I didn't know who else to call. "What do you know about cats?" I asked when he answered.

"I like them, even though most of them are assholes," he replied. "Why? Does this have to do with something you're working on?"

"No. It has to do with a cat." I explained what had happened. As I talked, Winston Purrchill sauntered around the perimeter of my condo like he was inspecting it, his gait unconcerned. Then he hopped up to my kitchen table and sat, placing himself directly on top of the file I'd made of the Lady Killer case, where it rested in its permanent place on the table. From there, he regarded me silently, his tail wrapped just so around his feet.

"Hold on. I'm getting a beer from the fridge," Michael said. I heard the sound of a fridge door opening, and the hiss of a beer cap being removed. The sound made me think he was wearing flannel. Plaid flannel. And the thought came into my head, as clear as if someone had spoken it: *I really need to meet this guy in person, because I think I like him.*

Michael came back on the line while I was still thinking that over. "Are you going to take this cat to a shelter?" he asked.

"I don't know." I looked into Winston's unblinking eyes, lined precisely with black. He seemed to be waiting for an answer, like Michael was. "No," I said. "It's too cruel. I'll keep him for a while."

"Maybe it'll be good for you," Michael said. "I'd like a pet, but I'm away from the house too much."

"It's just for a while," I told Winston, so we were both clear. "If I had a pet, I'd rather have a dog. A dog can ward off intruders."

Winston blinked at me in disbelief.

"It's easy, Shea," Michael said. "Just feed him and give him somewhere to sleep. A window to look out of. Cats don't ask for much."

"Okay." I reached a hand out. Winston sniffed it, running his nose along my skin. I relaxed my fingers and tried stroking his cheek, then the top of his head. He didn't object, so I kept going, curling my fingers into a scratching position. Winston tilted his head so my fingers were behind his ear, so I obediently moved them. He closed his eyes. "You're sitting on my file," I told him.

"Me, or the cat?" Michael said.

"The cat. He's parked himself on my Greer file, and now I don't want to shoo him off."

"Welcome to pet ownership. And I don't think you need to go through it again anyway. You know it by heart."

I did. Since my interview with Detective Black, I'd gone over my Greer papers again and again. The last time through, I'd read over the newspaper clippings that were the only public record of Beth Greer's young life: her parents' wedding announcement, her own birth announcement, and the brief and respectful notices of her parents' deaths. Based on the wedding photo, Julian Greer had been tall and handsome, while Mariana was petite and blond, her face much like Beth's except for a devastating sweetness in her features.

They both looked so formal in their wedding photo, and neither of them looked happy. It was unsettling to look at their faces and think of the fact that their marriage would be unhappy and then their lives would end, the groom killed in a home invasion, the bride dead in a car accident two years later.

"Have you talked to Beth again?" Michael asked me.

"No." The interview with Detective Black had left my head spinning, and I wasn't in a hurry to go back to the Greer mansion after what I'd seen—or what I thought I'd seen there. Aside from that, I wasn't ready to be in Beth's orbit again. When I saw her next, I wanted to be ready. "I think I want to find Sylvia Bledsoe first."

"You mean Sylvia O'Hare, or Sylvia Simpson."

"Right." Sylvia Bledsoe, the weeping secretary Detective Black had interviewed about Beth's father, had been married three times. Mr. Bledsoe, her husband when Julian died, was only husband number one. It had taken Michael and me a bit of digging to track her last names through husbands number two and number three. We'd found several Sylvia Simpsons, and I'd either phoned them—when I could find a number—or messaged them through Facebook, hoping to get an interview with the right one.

"I don't even know why I'm spending so much time on this," I said, scratching Winston behind his other ear as his eyes drifted closed in bliss. "It's probably a dead end. What do I think I'm going to learn from her?"

"You won't know until you talk to her," Michael said. "I'm here to help, Shea. Just say the word and I'll come to the meeting with you."

Meet Michael in person, face-to-face? Panic twisted through my stomach. The stupid reaction I always had. Now, on top of my usual day-to-day paranoia, I had the fear that Michael in person wouldn't live up to my imagination of him—and that I would disappoint him, too. Yet part of me wanted to see him at last, and part of me really did want his help. "I'll think about it." I looked Winston in the eyes as I said it, getting confidence from the calm way he watched me. *Of course you can do it*, his expression said to me. *What's the big deal?*

"You think about it, Shea," Michael said. "In the meantime, I'll get back to work."

CHAPTER FIFTEEN

September 2017

BETH

Sometimes, even now, Beth got the idea that she could leave. Why not? She had money, a car. There was nothing stopping her. She could simply go.

So she would get in her car and drive. She'd put her foot on the gas and form a plan in her mind, and yet somehow, no matter where she thought she was going, she always ended up at the lake. She'd find herself standing next to her parked car, looking out over the still water.

Not many people went to the lake. There were only a few spots where cars could park and people could come to enjoy the water. A sparse group of residents lived at the west end of the lake, but the east end, farther inland, was still thick and wild, the land cut only by small back roads. Beth would find herself in a stand of brush, her skin scratched and mosquitoes attacking her as she stared at the water, with no clear memory of exactly how she'd gotten here. She only knew that she'd simply showed up.

The fact that she couldn't remember always made her queasy, so she'd get back in her car and go home.

And it was comforting, in a way. She had been honest when she'd told Shea about some places holding you like a fist. What she hadn't said was that sometimes, when that fist was the only thing you knew, you didn't really want it to let you go.

This time, it was raining. She hadn't slept again, and she wanted a drink badly, and she was tired, so tired. She'd taken a garbage bag and thrown her parents' belongings into it—her mother's cold cream, the ashtray she hated so much, her father's ties, the stack of magazines on the living room credenza. She'd put the trash at the curb and driven off in the rain.

She'd ended up at the lake, as always.

But something was changing. The last time she'd come here, she'd felt it, and now she felt it again. It wasn't something she could grasp, but it was like a scent in the air or a breeze on the back of her neck. She wasn't imagining it. Not this time. Change was coming, and she couldn't stop it.

You're not leaving.

You're not talking.

She needed to talk to Shea again.

She got back into her car and drove home. At first, when she turned off the ignition in the driveway and stared at the curb where the garbage bag had vanished, she sagged in defeat. Then she got angry—that old ice-cold anger she'd had all her life, that had gotten her in so much trouble and still made her feel alive.

She got out of the car and started toward the house in the rain. She stared at the house as she walked, letting it see her gaze roaming over all of its ugly lines, hating it. She nearly snarled as she and the house stared each other down. Then she walked through the front door, which was open, and into the hushed darkness inside.

The first thing she saw was the magazines stacked on the credenza again. She knew that when she went upstairs, she'd see her mother's cold cream and her father's ties exactly where they'd been, as if she'd never put them in the trash. And the ashtray . . . that damned ashtray would be on the bedside table. How many times over the years had she tried to throw that fucking cold cream out? Too many to remember.

So Beth and the house would go another round, then. She'd expected it. But this wasn't going to go on forever. She knew that now.

She'd almost let her anger drain—almost—when she saw the wine bottle on the coffee table.

Red wine, her favorite. Though, of course, any wine would do. Beth would drink anything at all, given the chance. And the house knew it.

She stared at that bottle, gleaming in the half-light of the drawn curtains, and for a minute she wanted that wine so badly she would have done anything for it. She could practically taste it on her tongue, could feel the slide of it down her throat. She would have sold her soul for that bottle.

She closed her eyes. *Things are changing*, she told herself.

She walked to the table and grabbed the bottle, willing her hand not to shake. In the kitchen, she ignored the blood on the floor, tracking through it in her nice shoes. She ignored the breeze from the broken door and the huddled shape that she knew was her father's body against the lower cupboards. She flinched away from it and stood at the sink, yanking the cork from the bottle and upending it over the drain.

The wine gurgled down the sink. It looked like blood. From the corner of her eye, Beth saw that her father's body was gone.

"Fuck you," she said to the house, to her memories, to all of it.

She stood there until all of the wine had been drained from the bottle. Until the blood was gone from the floor, her tracks vanished like they'd never been. Until the door shut and the breeze stopped. Until it was over.

Then she put the bottle down and put her head in her hands, because she was alone all over again.

CHAPTER SIXTEEN

October 1977

BETH

The cops didn't like that she had a lawyer with her this time. Ransom seemed to fill the tiny interview room, his big frame taking up all the space. Detective Black looked uncomfortable, and Detective Washington looked furious. Beth sat silent, letting the men go at each other's throats.

"We want a handwriting sample," Washington said.

"No," Ransom replied.

"We'll get a warrant."

"When you have one, please present it. Until then, we decline."

Washington looked at her. This was the tactic, Ransom had warned her: address her directly, bypassing her lawyer, and get her to react. "We can get your handwriting, you know," he said. "Your checks at the bank, any letter you've written to a boyfriend. Your lawyer is just delaying."

"I defer to him," Beth said. "He's so very wise."

Washington looked like she'd cussed at him, and even Ransom glanced at her, his eyes narrowed.

"We've already searched the house," Washington said. "We're processing everything we found. We're going over the car inch by inch, too. Whatever we find there will indict you. Do you understand?"

"Don't answer that," Ransom said. "Don't answer anything."

Beth stayed still. She couldn't think of anything they would find in the house, aside from her mother's family china and her father's old papers, which she had never had the guts to read or throw out. Still, it had been a violation, the cops emptying drawers and flipping mattresses. They'd bagged and cleared her empty wine bottles as if they were evidence of something. Evidence that she drank too much. Was that going to be used against her, too? Probably.

Detective Black cleared his throat. He was wearing navy blue today, a suit that wasn't new but looked well taken care of. Beth wondered if he pressed his own suits, since he didn't wear a wedding ring. Or maybe he had a girlfriend who did it for him. If she *was* pressing his suits, he should definitely marry her.

There was something wrong with her, thinking these thoughts while she was being questioned for murder. Then again, the fact that there was something wrong with her wasn't news.

"I think we should back up," Detective Black said reasonably. "We're all here for a discussion. To clear some things up. Arguing won't get us anywhere."

"This entire discussion is egregious," Ransom said, bringing out his big lawyer words. "There's nothing connecting my client to this crime, or to the previous murder, or to either of these victims. You're wasting everyone's time when you should be finding a killer."

"We have the notes," Washington said, his gaze hostile on Ransom. If it were possible, or legal, for Washington to throw Beth's lawyer out the window, it was clear he would gladly do it. "We could easily eliminate your client as a suspect if she gave a voluntary handwriting sample. And we'd like a psychological analysis."

They went back and forth, playing their masculine game of one-upmanship as Beth tuned out. She looked at Black, and his eyes caught hers. He sighed a little, letting her see it, waiting for his partner to run low on steam. In return, she shrugged: *There's nothing we can do about either of them.* She liked that he didn't fidget, didn't smoke or pace; he had no theater about him. His gaze didn't travel down her body, but it stayed on her long enough that she felt the urge to twitch. Was it lascivious? She couldn't tell. Maybe, faced with the option of looking at either her or Washington and Ransom, he'd decided that she was the one in the room he'd rather look at.

When there was a break in Washington and Ransom's arguing, Black leaned toward Beth and said, "Tell me about your father's death."

Her world tilted. For a second it was tempting, even easy, to pretend it was just the two of them, talking privately with no one else around. Just her and this sympathetic man, asking her about the day her father died. She could open her mouth and tell him everything that was inside her, all the bad things that she kept locked away.

Then she glanced at the tape recorder, whirring quietly on the table. She looked at Washington, standing with his arms crossed, and Ransom, sitting in the folding chair next to hers. She could smell old coffee and stale cigarette smoke and something stuffy and rancid, like bad breath. And she remembered that day. She remembered the feeling of drowning, of sinking deeper and looking up, knowing she would never swim to the surface.

She turned back to Detective Black, her voice mechanical. "Someone robbed my father and killed him."

Black was still leaning forward, his upper body angled toward her, as if they were alone. "Whoever did it used the same gun for these murders," he said. "The ballistics will prove it."

Beth held still, not looking away. This was another game. They didn't have the ballistics report, not yet.

"Beth, tell the truth," Black said. "We're trying to help you."

That was where he made a mistake, because she knew he was lying. She looked him in the eyes. "You don't want to help me," she said. "No one wants to help me. No one ever has."

There was a second of quiet, the tape recorder the only sound. Detective Black actually looked surprised. He'd had a good life, she realized. Parents, maybe even grandparents, who loved him. A sibling or two. She could see it all: track team, stern but loving teachers, kisses behind the bleachers with a pretty girl. A few silly drunken experiences that were written off to high spirits, then losing his virginity to another pretty girl. Eventually, the police academy and making detective when he was barely thirty. He had the lean physique of a man who exercised instead of growing a paunch, and he didn't smoke. He saw bad things, sure, but he was saving people and putting the bad guys away. Saving the world.

This case was a problem for him, but it was one he would solve. Because in the end, the world always turned out the way he wanted it to.

Beth thought of her empty house, quiet now that her parents weren't screaming at each other anymore. She thought of the hours sitting alone in her room as a child, her hands over her ears, trying to make it all go away inside her head. She thought of her father's blood all over the kitchen floor. A lake of blood, deep and red, because it had gurgled out of him as he died. It had taken a cleaning crew three days to remove it. Ransom had made the arrangements while Beth and her mother stayed at a hotel.

And when it was cleaned up, Beth and her mother moved back in.

She always thought the house smelled coppery after that. She saw shadows in the kitchen, smelled her father's cologne mixed with blood. She was thought to be an improper young lady, because she couldn't cook, could barely make toast that she washed down with wine. No one had considered that she simply hated the kitchen at the Greer mansion and couldn't stand to be inside it.

Tell the truth. We're trying to help you.

Detective Black had never been as angry as Beth was right now.

"Do you own a gun?" Detective Washington asked for the hundredth time. He hated her, but at least his anger was something she understood. When she didn't answer, he said, "We know your father owned one."

Under the table, Ransom touched Beth's knee. Just the side of his pinky finger tapping her once—his keep-quiet signal.

Beth looked at Washington. "Fuck you," she said, her voice icy-calm.

Washington looked like she'd slapped him, and Ransom sighed. "We're leaving now," he said. "This interview is over."

Outside the police station, there were two photographers this time, plus a reporter shouting questions. Ransom looked unimpressed as he took Beth's elbow and led her to his car.

"Damn the papers," he said. "Some hack is writing a line about a 'lady killer' right this minute. I swear to God I'd like the world to surprise me, just once."

Beth got in the passenger seat. "You have nothing to say about what I said back there?"

Ransom got in, the car bouncing with his weight. His seat was set as far back as it would go to accommodate his long legs. "It would have been better if you were a little more ingratiating, I admit," he said, "but that was a low blow, so I'm not one to lecture."

That was almost amusing. Ransom was very much one to lecture.

"They're going to hate me no matter what I do," Beth said. "Don't you see that? I could be sweet, and those 'lady killer' articles are still going to get written."

Ransom looked thoughtful as he pulled out of the lot, narrowly missing one of the photographers. Beth thought it was probably an intentional near miss. "I do see that," he said. "People need someone to take their problems out on. You see that a lot when you're a law-yer. Since you're young and rich and lovely, you're as good a target as any. It's only going to get worse from here." He signaled and made a turn, heading up the hill to Arlen Heights. "All I ask is that you don't employ your sailor mouth when talking to the media, and definitely not if you ever talk to a judge."

"You think they're going to arrest me," Beth said.

"They very much want to arrest you. Two men are dead, and you're their only lead. The ballistics report might convince a judge to sign a warrant, and it might not. That's the gamble they have to take."

Beth pressed her lips together, looking out the window. "They're going to get my handwriting," she said.

"Sure, but not today. Just stay home, Beth, and don't let this make you crazy. That's all you have to do."

"I can't stay home," Beth snapped. "I have things to do."

"All of that driving around you do? Going nowhere? It needs to stop. Unless you want the press following you."

Don't let this make you crazy. Easy for him to say. "What if they're right?" she asked, Ransom's holier-than-thou wisdom getting on her nerves. "What if I really shot those men, and by defending me you're setting me loose to do it again?"

Ransom didn't even blink. "If you did it, they can damn well prove it, and not by getting you in an interview room and throwing Julian's murder in your face, trying to make you cry. That was pure bullying back there, so I'm going to remind you, Beth—don't ever talk to the police without me. That goes for reporters, too, but it goes ten times over for cops. If you talk to them alone, even your money won't save you."

There was more lecturing as Ransom drove her home, his version of fatherly advice: Don't date. Don't talk to strangers of any kind, because strangers will repeat everything you say to the nearest reporter. Don't write letters, because they could be intercepted. Be careful what you say on the phone.

Beth listened in silence, watching out the window. The words flowed over her, because she was stuck on one thing he'd already said.

In the interview room, they'd been trying to make her cry about her father's murder. But she hadn't felt like crying at all.

CHAPTER SEVENTEEN

September 2017

SHEA

Sylvia Simpson worked at a law firm in downtown Claire Lake. Even though she was past retirement age by now, she was listed on the firm's website as the assistant to one of the senior partners. But I definitely had the right Sylvia, which she confirmed when she replied to my Facebook message.

We met on a weekday afternoon. Our offices were only a few blocks apart, and I managed to take a break and slip from behind my desk. "Ten minutes," Sylvia had written to me on Facebook. "That's all I'll give you. Meet me outside my office at three."

Her firm was one of the nicest in town, the offices in a restored two-story Victorian house close to the ocean. At three o'clock, I stood on the front walk in my scrub top, wondering if I should go inside, when the front door opened and a woman of possibly seventy came out. She was wide and hard as a block of concrete, her white hair pulled back and her eyebrows drawn on in dramatic arches. She wore a gray wool skirt and jacket that were likely very expensive and still managed to look unflattering. She took a pack of cigarettes from her purse and motioned me around the corner of the house without a word.

"Surprised?" she asked me as she pulled out a chair on a small patio. She lowered herself into the chair and pulled out a cigarette and a pack of matches. Her voice was husky and low, intimidating. "An old woman like me, working. Caught you off guard."

She hadn't offered an introduction or a handshake. I pulled out a chair for myself and sat, feeling the cool, damp breeze from the ocean breathe past us. "Not really," I said.

"Huh." Sylvia lit a cigarette, inhaled, then exhaled, not bothering to blow the smoke away from me. "You're bluffing, but it's fine. If you think I'm old, you should see my boss. He's even older than I am. I've been his assistant for thirty-five years, and when he goes, I go. I'm the only person he trusts."

"That's nice," I said, pulling my phone from my bag. "Do you mind—"

"Put that thing away." Her voice was flat, hostile. I put the phone back. "How old are you, anyway?"

"Twenty-nine."

"A baby," she said, almost angrily. "Julian Greer was already dead by the time I was twenty-nine, and I was looking for a new job. I was looking for a new husband, too, because the first one had pushed me down the stairs one too many times." She gestured at me with the lit end of her cigarette to make her point. "Record *that*, why don't you?"

This was going to be a fun ten minutes, I could tell. "I want to ask you about Julian," I said.

"Such a nice man. Handsome, too." Sylvia took another drag on her cigarette and shook her head. "I worked for him for four years. I saw everything—everything. You're lucky, because you're talking to

the only person who knew what was really going on. Even those police who came to me after Mr. Greer died didn't know their asses from
a hole in the wall, and they didn't bother to ask. Because who cares
what the secretary knows, right? Well, let me tell you, we know everything. So listen up, Miss Twenty-Nine."

"My name is Shea," I said.

"Are you going to listen, or are you going to talk?"

I sighed. "Listen. I'm going to listen."

"Good. The first thing you need to know is that nothing was Mr.
Greer's fault. It was all because of that woman he married."

I blinked. "Mariana Greer?"

"She was the worst thing that ever happened to him. Everyone
knew it. Sure, she had money, and I suppose she was beautiful, but she
didn't have class. He used to come to work exhausted because they'd
had a fight and he didn't get any sleep. I'd put calls through from her,
and she would be in tears, yelling at him about something. At work.
It was a damned disgrace."

I watched her. Beneath her gruff exterior, Sylvia was lit up and
righteous. This was her cause, the thing she'd waited decades to talk
about. I decided to play into it.

"What was the wife's problem?" I said.

It was exactly the right question. Sylvia glanced at me and took
another drag of her cigarette, drawing out the drama. When she spoke,
she relished the words. "Oh, she had problems, all right. When Mrs.
Greer's mother died, she didn't leave her fortune to her daughter. She
left it to Mr. Greer, her daughter's husband. What does that tell you?"

To me it sounded sad, but I kept my face blank with confusion.
Sylvia scoffed at me and tapped her temple with her fingertip.

"Mariana Greer was crazy?" I asked.

"Why else would her own mother leave her inheritance to her
husband instead of her? She wasn't competent. Mr. Greer had a file of
papers the mother had left to him. I didn't see all of it, but some of the

papers had to do with his wife being sent away somewhere when she was eighteen." Sylvia made air quotes with her fingers at the words "sent away somewhere," her cigarette waggling in the air. "He didn't know about that before the wedding—I can guarantee it. It was only after they were married and her mother died that he learned his wife had been a mental patient. A damned mental patient—can you imagine? I felt sorry for that man."

I itched to go home to my laptop, or to call Michael. I'd never seen evidence that Mariana Greer had been mentally ill. "What happened to those papers?" I asked.

"Mr. Greer got rid of them sometime before he died. Burned them probably. The shame."

"What about the daughter? Did you ever meet her?"

"No. But we all know what happened with her, don't we?" Sylvia said smugly. "And we all know why."

"You think she committed those murders."

Sylvia stubbed out her cigarette in the plastic ashtray on the table. "With bad blood like hers, who else do you think did it? Santa Claus?"

I couldn't say why she made me angry exactly. Certainly, I was no defender of Beth, and Beth didn't need or want my help. For all I knew, Sylvia Simpson was absolutely right.

Still, I said, "You went through his papers, didn't you? Julian Greer's private file from his mother-in-law. He never showed that to you. You snooped."

Sylvia didn't even blink. "And you should thank me for it, because now you know the truth." Her voice was calm, but her cheeks were flushed and the chair made a loud noise as she pushed it back. "I know I'm an old battle-axe, but I was a good secretary to Mr. Greer. They say his own daughter shot him in cold blood. She's just as crazy as her mother was. She should have gotten the death penalty as far as I'm concerned. Now I'm going back to work."

"Which mental hospital was it?" I called to her retreating back as I stood. "I'd like to go through the records."

Sylvia was done with me, but she couldn't resist one parting shot. "Do you think her rich family would send her to one of the public ones?" she said scornfully over her shoulder. "Of course they didn't. It was a private place. I don't remember the name of it, but it was on Linwood Street. I don't know why she matters, but good luck."

Fifteen minutes later, I was back behind the reception desk at work, feeling strangely exhausted. Sylvia's grievances, held for decade after decade, were heavy. I couldn't imagine carrying that weight all the time.

Still, when no one was looking, I took a second to pull out my phone and text Michael: *I'm going to need some help pulling property records for Linwood Street. Specifically from the 1950s.*

This was my only bit of luck: Linwood Street was one of the now-gentrified streets downtown, and it wasn't very long. It definitely didn't have a hospital building on it. My recall of it was that it was mostly stately homes. One of those homes might, in the fifties, have been the discreet kind of place where a rich family could send their teenage daughter to have a mental breakdown.

I don't know why she matters, Sylvia had said.

I didn't, either. I wasn't sure why I was doing this. It was some kind of instinct. Beth's father had been murdered by the Lady Killer; Beth's mother was possibly mentally ill. All of this was part of the woman who fascinated me, the woman who—I could admit it—scared me, not least because some cold part of me actually liked her. What that said about me, I didn't even want to think about.

I split the property records on Linwood Street with Michael—he took half and I took half. I spent most of that evening sorting through online records while lying in bed with my laptop, Winston by my side. By one in the morning, I hadn't found what I wanted and my eyes could barely focus, but I wasn't ready to sleep.

I clicked open the digital file I had of the 1981 TV movie made about the Lady Killer case. It was called *Deadly Woman*, and I watched Jaclyn Smith, as Beth, face off against a soap actor who looked at least forty-five and was supposed to be playing Detective Black.

"I'm telling the truth," Jaclyn said. Her hair had been dyed red for the role, and her eye makeup was frosty, her lashes clumped and dark.

"We'll see about that, Beth," the soap actor said as dramatic music soared behind his lines.

Jaclyn leaned forward, the camera going into dewy soft focus on her beautiful face, the music swelling higher. "You've got to believe me!" she cried. She was wearing a cream blouse with ruffles at the neck and the cuffs; red blush had been dabbed on her cheekbones. Her voice went up a notch as she shouted: "You've just got to!"

"Listen, Beth," said the soap actor. "I'd like to believe you, but nothing you say adds up. You wrote those notes. You know you did. You're lying so much you don't even know what's the truth anymore. But I do. And the truth is, you shot those men!"

I sighed and paused it, freezing on a frame of Jaclyn Smith's face right before she got angry. In *Deadly Woman*, Beth was a manipulator, a heartless killer, a siren, trying to work her wiles on poor Detective Black and failing in the face of his moral superiority. It was all right there in the title.

I smoothed my fingertips over the top of Winston's head, then rolled over in bed and picked up my other early-eighties artifact, a book called *Who Was the Female Zodiac?* It was written in 1984 by a journalist named Henderson Metterick, and it was the only book ever written about the Lady Killer case. It had been out of print for decades, but I'd found a hardcover copy on eBay a year ago, the pages yellowed and fragrant with over thirty years of age. The book was a hack job of useless speculation, overwriting, and almost comically offensive misogyny, filled with words like *she-devil* and phrases like *Beth Greer's exotic, overpowering allure.*

This, I realized, was where it got tricky. Because the Beth I knew was possibly a murderer, a liar, a sociopath. But there was no other way to put it—everything that had been written about Beth for the last forty years was infuriating. I wasn't an angry person, but *Who Was the Female Zodiac?* made me want to kick Henderson Metterick in the balls, even though he'd been dead since 1991.

"Fuck you, Henderson," I said out loud, because it felt good. On the bed next to me, Winston Purrchill's ears swiveled toward me, but he was too lazy to open his eyes.

With the laptop still frozen on Jaclyn's face, I flipped through the book again, opening the photo section in the middle. Henderson might be a terrible writer and a woman hater, but he'd somehow gotten hold of good photographs. There was Beth as a little girl, posed on a chair, wearing her school uniform. The caption said she was age six.

I turned the pages, looking at more photographs. There was a photo of the Greer mansion, with a predictable caption about how rich and miserable the Greers were. Here was the first victim, Thomas Armstrong, posing with his family, dressed in a suit with a wide collar, sideburns on his cheeks. Then the second victim, Paul Veerhoever, a man with a round face and pale blond hair. He was standing next to his wife, a beautiful woman with curly brown hair tumbling past her shoulders. They were at a party somewhere, each of them holding a glass of wine and smiling awkwardly. I wondered what had happened to the wives of those men, what kind of lives they'd gone on to have. Both of them had left town, I knew. I hadn't been able to track down either of them.

And here, again, was Beth. This picture was taken the day she was arrested in December 1977; it was a shot of Beth being led down the front steps of the Greer mansion, her hands cuffed behind her back.

Detective Washington, frowning through his mustache, had her by one arm, while Detective Black, looking serious and troubled, walked at her other shoulder. His posture was almost protective, like he was shielding Beth from everything around her. Beth was wearing a belted trench coat that ended at midthigh, her red hair down, hoops in her ears. She had a solemn expression on her face, but there was no other way to describe her but radiant. Her skin was pale and flawless, her eyes large and dark, her mouth slashed with a shock of sexy red lipstick, her hair in a sensual cloud around her face. She looked like a goddess, and she was utterly, almost unnaturally calm.

I could see Beth's resemblance to Mariana in that photo. Mariana, who Sylvia Simpson said had been crazy.

I stared at the photo for a long time, taking in the faces. I felt like I'd been there that day, like I could smell the cold damp of the winter air and see the flashing of the police lights. Behind Beth and the two detectives were uniformed officers, young men who looked stern and excited. That must have been quite a day.

I reached to my bedside table and picked up my phone. I hadn't relistened to the recording of my interview with Beth. If I couldn't sleep, I may as well transcribe it. I pulled up the recording app, found the recording, and played it.

MY VOICE: Okay. Let's talk about the Lady Killer murders.
BETH'S VOICE: Let's.
ME: I don't suppose there's any point in me asking you if you committed them or not?
BETH: You'll form your own conclusions. Everyone does.

Winston lifted his head, his ears swiveling and his eyes blinking open. "Sorry, buddy," I said as the voices kept talking. "I know it's late."

But the cat wasn't just annoyed. He tensed, got his feet under him, and crouched low, his sleek body pressed down in terror. His tail bloomed wide as the fur on it stood up. He hissed, gave a low growl, and bolted off the bed and out of the room.

"Winston?" I said, and then I heard it. Something on the recording.

I picked my phone up and put it closer to my ear. Beth and I were talking—about my parents, about her parents. But in the background was a shushing sound. I turned up the volume and pressed the phone to my ear, wondering if the recording had picked up wind, or had created noise because of a technical problem.

But it wasn't the wind, or white noise on the recording. It was a whisper.

With an ice-cold finger, I rewound.

My mother never wanted to get married, Beth's voice said. *But it was the fifties, and my grandparents were rich. They expected her to marry well. She met my father, and that was that. More of a business deal than anything else. And a year later, she had me. She was trapped.*

There was a pause, and then I heard it clearly. A woman's voice as if whispered into the phone's speaker.

I'm still here.

I dropped the phone. It landed on the bed without a sound. From the recording playback came my voice: *Where's your bathroom?*

I took a breath, picked the phone up again. Played it again. Heard it again. *I'm still here.* I remembered what came next: the bathroom taps turning on, the kitchen cupboards opening, the blood. But at that moment, the phone had been on the table between Beth and me, in plain sight of both of us.

Whatever had been in the house that day had been waiting, watching, while we talked. Waiting to be heard.

I rewound the clip again, thinking to save it off my phone. Make copies. Send one to Michael, with his theories of levers and pulleys. Play it for Detective Black. Play it for Beth and see what her reaction was.

But while my finger was still on the slider, my phone went blank. It had turned itself off, the battery suddenly empty, even though I had charged it an hour ago. I scrambled to find my charger, plug the phone in, and power it up again.

When I finally did, the entire interview was gone. Deleted from the phone, from the cloud, everywhere, as if it had never been.

Whatever it was, whoever it was, it had said what it wanted to say. And now it had gone quiet again.

CHAPTER EIGHTEEN

October 2017

SHEA

I was sitting behind the Plexiglas at work, hanging up the phone, when I heard a familiar voice: "I'm here to see Shea."

I looked up to see Beth Greer standing at the counter, looking past Karen to me. She was wearing a dark gray wool wrap wound stylishly over her shoulders and neck. Beneath it, she wore elegant black pants. Her reading glasses were perched on top of her head. She looked amazing, as usual.

"You are?" I asked her, surprised. We didn't have an agreement to meet. I hadn't heard from her since before I'd met with Detective Black.

She gave me one of her subtle smiles, the one that barely brushed her lips. "I'm taking you to lunch," she said. "Let's go."

I blinked and glanced at Karen. She had a surprised frown on her face. Doubtless, she was remembering our conversation, when I'd wondered whether Beth was famous. She probably wasn't sure whether to risk being impolite to a famous person.

Beth raised a finger and pointed with understated command to the hinged door that would let me out of my cubicle. "Shea, I'm waiting."

I reached down and grabbed my purse from under the desk before I formed a conscious thought. I pushed back my chair and said to Karen, "See you later."

"We'll be back in an hour," Beth said, and Karen nodded as she turned away.

"Does that always work for you?" I asked her as we got in the elevator, my purse tucked under my arm.

"Does what always work for me?"

"Ordering people around."

One of Beth's eyebrows rose. "Shea, is it lunchtime?"

"Yes."

"Are you hungry?"

"I guess."

"Then we'll have lunch. I don't see where the confusion is."

The elevator doors slid open on the ground floor. "You don't have very many friends, do you?" I asked her.

"I don't have any friends," Beth said, her tone blunt. "You know the reason."

"It's been forty years."

"Not in this town, it hasn't."

I followed her out onto the street, then down toward the piers. Beth led me into one of the high-end cafés that the tourists frequented. "I'm wearing scrubs," I said self-consciously as we stepped inside.

Beth swept her gaze down me and up again, assessing. "I don't see a problem."

There wasn't. We were seated immediately in a corner booth and given glasses of water in seconds. I couldn't tell whether we were favored because Beth was infamous or because she was obviously rich. It certainly wasn't because of me.

"What?" she asked me, looking at me from above the rims of her reading glasses as she perused the menu.

"I can't figure out whether to like you, to feel sorry for you, or be annoyed by you," I replied.

"Try all three," she said, as if the answer were simple. Then she looked at her menu again. "I think you'd like the lobster bisque."

Of course she'd order for me. "Okay." I closed my menu.

Beth closed her menu, too, and pushed back her reading glasses again. "You haven't called me."

No, I hadn't called her. After the interview with the whisper was deleted from my phone, I'd plunged back into real-world research, the kind that was based on verifiable facts. And I had no desire to go back to that house. "I've been busy."

"I thought you wanted to interview me."

"I do."

"Well, here I am." She took a sip of her water. "I suppose Joshua told you a few things about me."

She was fishing, I realized. Even though Beth was the one who had set up the interview, she wasn't entirely sure what Detective Black had told me. I hadn't called her to fill her in, and she wanted to know.

The idea was surprising. I hadn't thought Beth had any weaknesses. I thought of Black's bitter voice as he said, *We aren't friends*, and I wondered if he was one of them. I also wondered why she called him Joshua.

"It was a good meeting, I guess," I said lamely.

Beth's gaze narrowed at me across the table. The waitress appeared, and Beth gave our order. I wasn't ready for this. I wasn't prepared to fence with Beth Greer in the middle of my workday. When

I'd gone to the Greer mansion, I'd built up to it, gone in prepared. This time, she'd ambushed me. My instincts told me that if I thought that wasn't deliberate, I was probably a fool.

But I'd lost our first interview without the chance to transcribe it, and now I had another opportunity. I wanted to know about Mariana. About Julian's murder. About the Lady Killer murders. The source of all of those answers was sitting across from me. I figured I may as well not let it go to waste.

As the waitress walked away, I pulled my cell phone from my purse and put it on the table between us. "I'm going to record this," I said. Beth said nothing as I tapped the screen.

When it was recording, I said, "Let's talk about your childhood."

She looked at the red light on my recording app for a moment, then shrugged. "Sure."

"You were an only child, and your parents didn't have a happy marriage. I think that must have been lonely."

Beth's voice was cool. "That's like saying Mount Everest is tall, but yes."

"I'm curious about your parents. Tell me about them."

Beth looked down at my phone again, and when she looked up she had a coldness in her expression that was as blank as stone. "It's dangerous to ask old people about their childhoods, Shea. Our buried things have been buried for a long time."

I met her eyes, and then the waitress came back with two bowls of lobster bisque. When she had gone away again, Beth said to me, "I've never asked. Are you married? My background check didn't cover your love life."

I picked up my spoon, trying to shake off the cold feeling from a minute before. "Divorced."

"Smart girl," Beth said. "If my parents had had the guts to get divorced, everything would be different."

"You said your mother was trapped."

"She was, and so was my father. Men can get trapped in their own ways."

"Did your mother have mental-illness issues?"

Beth frowned. "Excuse me?"

"It's something I heard. That your mother may have spent time in a private hospital when she was a teenager."

Beth blinked and put down her spoon. "Shea, please elaborate."

They were simple words, polite even, but my stomach went cold. Beth's inflection was lifeless, dead, her expression blank. She was waiting for an answer, and I had the feeling that if I didn't provide it, I would be very, very sorry. Which was crazy, because she was an over-sixty woman having lunch in a trendy restaurant.

I cleared my throat. "I found a source who said—"

"Who? Who said that?"

For a second, I didn't want to tell her. Then again, why was I protecting Sylvia Simpson and her forty years of judgment? "She was your father's secretary," I said.

"My father's secretary told you that my mother was insane?" Now her tone was incredulous.

"Well, she said—"

"That's bullshit. My mother wasn't crazy. My mother was a victim. She lived her entire life in shame."

"Who was she a victim of? Your father?"

"My parents fought, but my father was never abusive. He was good, in his way." Beth leaned back in her chair and picked up her spoon, stirring her bisque as if she had just remembered it was there. "I would have loved my father more if he had noticed me. But we never had much to say to each other. I don't think I've ever been very good with men."

I gaped at her. She'd been accused of murdering two men in cold blood, so no, maybe she wasn't very good with men. "Well," I managed, "I guess I know the feeling."

"You're not the type that's very good with men, either," Beth said, letting her judgment drop without a second's concern for my feelings. "You're attractive enough, but I'm going to guess you don't have a boyfriend." She pondered me. "Does your family try to set you up with dates? I bet they do. And because of what happened when you were a child, you're too messed-up to say yes."

My blood pounded in my ears. How did she *know* everything? How did she see me so clearly when no one else did? "There's only one man I'm actually interested in," I said, "and I've never met him in person."

She raised her eyebrows at that, the topic of her parents forgotten. "I'm intrigued. Tell me."

And for some reason, I did. I told her about Michael, about our strange setup.

Beth listened carefully, as if this was of keen interest to her. God knew why. But she narrowed her eyes as I talked, paying close attention. Like the last time I'd confessed to Beth, it was intrusive and freeing at the same time. When I'd finished, she spoke.

"Your problem is a simple power imbalance," she said.

"What does that mean?"

"It means this man knows everything about you, and you know nothing about him. He knows where you live, where you work, the fact that you're single. Has he told you if he's married?"

"He says he's divorced."

"Which could be a lie." She paused. "If he's a former cop, he might know about what happened to you as a child. Or he can easily find out."

The thought gave me chills. "I've never told him about that."

Beth shrugged. "In return, all you know is what he's told you over the phone. You have to believe what he says, because you don't know anything else. That's a power imbalance, and you know it."

I shook my head. "Michael's personal life is none of my business. We have a professional relationship."

"Except for the fact that you'd like to screw him."

"Beth, I *pay* him."

"Obviously, you wouldn't pay him for that part," she said. "That part would be volunteer."

With horror, I realized that my cell phone was still recording. I reached out and stabbed the recording off.

Beth watched me do it. "Apparently, you don't want to talk about sex," she said.

"I'd prefer to talk about *your* sex life," I shot back.

"We're not at that part of the interview yet," she replied, unfazed. "Maybe later. In the meantime, we're talking about you."

"I really wish we weren't."

She looked at me. Her eyes were mesmerizing, so large and deep, easy to get lost in, even now. She must have been impossible to resist when she was twenty-three. "For the record, I think this detective is probably exactly what he says he is," she said. "He's probably even nice. And actually single. But you're never going to know if you let him stay a mystery because it's more comfortable that way. That's my advice." She shrugged. "It's your call. Make it."

It wasn't until hours later, when the lobster bisque was finished, the bill paid, and I was sitting at my desk at the end of the day, that I realized four things about that lunch with Beth:

One, she really *had* come to find out what had happened in the interview with Detective Black. And because I hadn't called her. So she had at least one weakness.

Two, she'd said her mother had lived her whole life in shame. Why?

Three, she had deftly turned the subject away from her childhood, then made me turn the recorder off by embarrassing me.

And four, when I'd mentioned Mariana's possible mental illness, Beth had been angry. That was what that cold expression of hers was, the dead voice that gave me the chills. Beth hadn't been bemused or dismissive at the suggestion that her mother had been crazy. She'd been suddenly, icily angry.

When Beth was that angry, she was terrifying.

I was on the right track, which meant the answers were there. I just had to figure out where they were.

CHAPTER NINETEEN

October 2017

SHEA

My sister was the executive assistant to a bank CEO, which was where she met her husband, one of the bank's lawyers. She and Will lived in one of the new low-rise condo buildings downtown, not far from the waterfront, in a neighborhood that had been built for well-to-do people like them. When I arrived for dinner, Esther answered the door in linen pants and a blouse that would have cost a month of our father's salary growing up. By contrast, I was wearing dark jeans, a black tee, sneakers, and a stretched-out black hoodie, my hair in a ponytail. I looked like I'd just finished prowling the neighborhood, staring into everyone's windows, but Esther made no comment.

We probably shouldn't have liked each other, Esther and me. We were so different, even though we had the same black hair and dark eyes. Esther wore her hair in a fashionable layered cut that ended at her chin and looked amazing on her, and I left mine long and usually tied back. We probably should have hated each other, but we'd never quite managed it. We'd been through too much together.

Will gave me a hug in greeting. He smelled like aftershave and men's deodorant, scents I wasn't familiar with anymore. "It's so good to see you," he said.

I handed him the bottle of wine I'd brought, warm from my lap, where I'd held it on the bus. "It's good to see you, too."

In her early twenties, before Will, Esther had dated a man who hit her. I'd helped her leave him, packing a U-Haul in the middle of the day while her boyfriend was at work, shoving garbage bags of her belongings into the trailer as fast as we could. We may be very different now, years later—Esther successful and put-together, me a divorced wreck—but we still had the experience of the garbage bags in the U-Haul, of me sleeping with her those first nights in her rented apartment, eating Pringles out of a tube for dinner. When you share something like that with your sister, it never leaves you, for better or for worse.

Will went to the dining room to set the table, and I followed Esther into the kitchen, where she put my bottle of wine in her fridge and pulled an already-chilled bottle from an ice bucket. "Thank you for actually coming," she said.

"Thank you for not setting me up with Will's coworker."

She gave me a tight smile. "You scared me off that one," she said. "Well done. How was your day?"

I had gone to lunch with an infamous possible serial killer, but I looked at my sister and I couldn't bring that up. For once, I didn't want to talk about murder. "It was fine," I said. "Same old, really."

She wrinkled her nose. "You should get a promotion in that job. You've been there long enough. Supervisor or manager of the office. Or better yet, get out of there entirely. It's a dead end. You don't need some high-powered career, but you could definitely do better than that place."

Extra money would be nice, I agreed, but the thought of moving up and managing other people gave me hives. "If something promising comes up, I'll let you know."

"You're humoring me." Esther scooped tetrazzini into bowls and chopped a garnish to put on top of it. "You don't want to argue, so you're saying what I want to hear."

I was doing exactly that, but I didn't want to fight. "Have you heard from Mom and Dad?"

"I talked to them yesterday. You should visit them. It's nice in Florida this time of year."

"Esther, it's literally hurricane season."

I got another tight smile, because despite her lecturing, my sister had a sense of humor. "Okay, then, you could call them more often. Or ever."

I took a deep sip of wine. She was exactly right—I could call my parents more often. The Incident, when I was nine, had affected my relationship with my parents, even though none of us wanted it to. My parents had felt guilty that they hadn't somehow protected me from my abductor, though logically they had done nothing wrong. Their guilt, in turn, made nine-year-old me feel guilty for causing trouble and making my parents feel bad. Esther felt both guilty for not being there to protect me and resentful that for a long time I got more attention than she did, followed by guilt about the resentment. And the cycle went round and round, among four loving, well-meaning people who had no idea what else to do, and it was still going round twenty years later.

Sometimes, I thought I might like the cycle to stop. But my parents were in Florida now, and things were bumbling along well enough. There was no reason to dig up old bodies.

I watched Esther sprinkle garnish on our dinners with her beautiful, manicured hands as we stood in her beautiful kitchen. I shouldn't be here, in my circle of darkness, making things harder for her. She should probably have a better sister. But she was stuck with me.

Will appeared in the kitchen doorway and leaned on the doorframe. "I waited long enough," he said to Esther. "Did you tell her?"

I went still, my glass in my hand. "Tell me what?"

"I'm working up to it," Esther said, still looking at her garnishes and not at me.

"You said you'd tell her," Will said.

I looked at my sister, at the tense lines at the corners of her eyes, and my stomach turned. Was something wrong? "Tell me what?" I said again.

"It isn't a big deal," Esther said.

"It's a big deal," Will replied, his voice calm. "It's been a big deal for two years."

"Tell me," I said, trying not to panic. "Please tell me."

Esther sighed, the breath coming out of her from so deep that it changed the shape of her shoulders. Emotions flitted across her expression one by one: fear, stress, tense excitement, a hollow sort of sadness. She stopped fidgeting with the garnishes and turned to look at me. "We're starting IVF next week," she said.

I tried to compute this. "IVF? As in having a baby?"

"Yes."

I looked back and forth from Esther to Will, trying to read their expressions. "Okay," I said slowly. "Why IVF? Is there some kind of complication?"

"We don't know," Will said. He looked tense, too, though he didn't look as tense as my sister, who was practically vibrating like a piano wire. "We just know we haven't been able to get pregnant. We've been trying for two years."

I put my wineglass down on the counter. "Two years?" I looked at Esther. She was leaning against the counter, staring down at her hands. I noticed for the first time that she hadn't poured herself any wine. "You've been trying to have a baby for two years, and you didn't tell me?" I said.

"She wanted to tell you," Will explained. "I've been begging her to do it. It's just been difficult for us. We actually conceived twice but lost the baby very early."

I rubbed my cheek, feeling my numb skin. Pregnant? Esther had been pregnant twice, and she hadn't told me anything? "Esther?" I said.

My sister stared at her palms. "You've been going through a tough time," she said. "Your marriage wasn't working, and then you were going through the divorce. I didn't feel like I could burden you with it. And I didn't think I could talk to you about it. All of this murder stuff . . ." She shook her head. "You're so far away."

If she had shoved a knife in my gut, I couldn't have been more hurt. Or more surprised. I'd always thought I was close to Esther. No, I *was* close to Esther. We lived in the same town, and we talked every other day. We saw each other at Christmas. We did Sunday breakfast every other month. I'd had dinner here at least a dozen times in the last two years.

We had shoved garbage bags into that U-Haul together, stayed awake until it felt like our eyes were filled with sand. When Esther had called me and asked me to pack that truck, I'd dropped everything. And before that . . . before that, she'd been my big sister when I'd been through the worst thing that had ever happened to me.

You're so far away.

Will stepped into our pained silence, as he was so good at doing. "We've told you now," he said gently to me. "It's gone on long enough. Now you know. Let's have dinner, okay?"

"Sure," I said stupidly. "Sure." I looked at Esther. "I hope it works for you."

"Thanks," she said, and we took our bowls and went into the dining room.

"I think that went pretty well," Will said. The awkward night was over, and he was walking me to the bus stop in the dark. He would have gladly driven me home, but he knew better than to offer, because there was no way I would say yes.

I knew the stats—bus stops weren't any safer than cars. But I rarely took the bus at night, and I kept to populated, well-lit areas. Walking through a dark parking lot or parking garage wouldn't have been any safer. And besides, I'd never claimed that my hang-ups made any sense.

I huddled deeper into my hoodie in the cool, damp air. Esther's neighborhood was quiet, all of the families curled into sleep. There was no one on the street but us. "Sure," I said.

Will sighed as he walked beside me. "I'm sorry she didn't tell you, but you know how Esther is. She has to be handling everything, and she has to be the best at it. If she isn't pulling something off, she's so damn hard on herself. And part of her feels like she should be taking care of you, too."

"She doesn't have to take care of me." The protest was automatic.

"Well, she kind of does," he said bluntly. "And that isn't an insult, Shea. It isn't shameful to need someone to take care of you. You take care of her, too."

"She has you for that," I said. "At least, now she does."

"And you'd like to hate me for it, but you don't," he replied. "Besides, she still needs you. You know she does. And if we have a baby, she'll need you even more."

It would have been nice to hate Will—it really would have. But the truth was, he honestly was the best of men. Esther had won the marriage lottery, and she deserved it.

But tonight I felt the gulf between us as a large black hole. I'd been meeting for weeks with an acquitted murderer, and I hadn't told my sister about it. She thought I was already too far into the darkness, and she had no idea how much further I'd gone. How far I was willing to go. Just as I'd had no idea when she'd lost a baby, twice.

She had hurt, really hurt, when that happened. I knew my sister. She put on a competent show, but underneath she could hurt, and deeply. This had hurt most of all, which was why she hadn't told me about it.

You're so far away.

"I'll take care of my own life," I said to Will. "I promise."

"Shea, that isn't what this is about."

But it was. It was about the fact that my brother-in-law had to walk me to the bus stop because I couldn't accept a ride. It was about the fact that when I got home, I would yet again check my locks and my security before turning on my laptop and delving into the Book of Cold Cases. Same as ever. The only difference was that tonight I would have the company of Winston Purrchill.

Will waited with me as I got on the bus. Just in case. And I knew he was standing there for a long moment as it pulled away, disappearing down the street and into the darkness.

When I had turned the corner and could no longer see him, I pulled out my phone and called Michael.

"Where are you right now?" I asked when he answered.

"At home, going through property records until my eyes cross," he said. "Why?"

I looked out the window at the city going by. "Are you really divorced?"

"Considering how bad my marriage was, I sure as hell hope so. What is this about, Shea?"

I read the street signs as they passed. I could see the ocean from here, inky black in the darkness beyond the lights of Claire Lake.

"I'm on the bus," I said. "I just passed Sixth Avenue and Harbor Street. If I get off at the next stop, will you come and have a drink with me?"

There was a brief pause of surprise.

"Give me fifteen minutes," Michael said. "Yes, I'll have a drink with you. I'm on my way."

CHAPTER TWENTY

October 1977

BETH

The bar was called Watertown's, a big, high-ceilinged room with dim lighting and loud music coming from a jukebox. It was twenty-five miles outside the Claire Lake city limits, which was why Beth went there to drink.

They hadn't arrested her yet. It was going to happen; she could feel it the way you can feel electricity in the air when a thunderstorm is coming, when you see the lowering clouds on the horizon and feel the wind kick up. She didn't sleep much. Her life as she knew it would be over soon.

The Claire Lake papers had already convicted her: LOCAL HEIRESS SUSPECTED OF MURDERS and DID SHE KILL THEM? No one came forward to say they didn't believe it, that Beth would never do something like that. Except for Ransom—who was paid to defend her. Other than maybe her father, who was dead, Beth couldn't think of anyone else who would say that.

Instead there was a long line of people—the neighbors, girls Beth had gone to school with, grocery clerks, a few of the people who had gotten drunk at Beth's parties—who wanted to tell the press that Beth was strange, that she was frightening, that she had fits of anger. Stories were surfacing about noises at the Greer mansion while her parents were alive—shouting, furniture overturned, china broken. And of course they all said that Beth lived alone now, that she had no friends or husband, that she spent most of her time as a hermit except when she was partying. "She doesn't seem to *like* people," a girl who had known Beth briefly in seventh grade told the press. "I think she hates everyone."

Hating people in seventh grade made her a killer. Living alone because both of her parents were dead made her a killer. The pieces fit so nicely together. Beth had gone driving a few more times, but when she noticed a car following her, she turned around and went home. Was it the press? The police? It didn't matter.

Now Beth stayed home like Ransom had told her to, the curtains on the floor-to-ceiling windows closed, the TV on. She lay on her sofa and drank and thought about what had happened to her and why. About how neat it all was.

About how angry she was. People were right about that, at least.

She was sick of drinking alone on the sofa, so tonight she broke Ransom's commandment. She got dressed, got in her car—a Cadillac, because the police had impounded the Buick—and drove to a bar to drink.

It was second nature. Both of her parents had drunk from morning to night, and Beth had snuck her first drink at eleven. Now she sat at the dim bar, wearing a ringer T-shirt and high-waisted jeans, her hair twisted back. She started with vodka and stuck with it. Men came on to her, which she'd expected. She turned them down. All she cared about was that no one recognized her, or at least that none of them would let on.

She wanted to get blind drunk, but three-quarters of the way there an alarm went off deep in her belly, warning her to stop. She couldn't afford to lose control around strangers, couldn't afford to end up crawling all over a man in the back seat of his car and telling him everything. No mistakes, at least not big ones. At one o'clock, she paid her tab and walked outside to the parking lot, trying to keep her steps in a convincingly steady line.

There was a figure leaning against her car, waiting for her.

Beth stopped, her heart hammering in her chest. Some of the drunkenness drained away, absorbed by adrenaline. Then she recognized him.

"You have got to be kidding me," she said.

"You're not driving home," Detective Black said.

Beth closed her fingers around the keys in her hand. "What's it to you?"

"I'm the police," he said. "I'm not letting you get in an accident."

Incredibly, he was wearing a suit, or parts of one. He had no jacket, and his tie was loosened past his clavicle, his shirt unbuttoned at the top. But his dress pants were barely wrinkled and his shoes were shiny. His face was tired and his hair was slightly mussed, but he watched her with cop's eyes.

"Fuck off," Beth said, because she was tired and drunk and couldn't think of anything else to say. "Go away and leave me alone."

"I'm not going to do that," he said stoically. "My car is just over there. I'll drive you home."

"How did you know I was here?"

He didn't answer, but she knew. With the suspicious instincts of the drunk, she knew.

"You were following me," she said.

Black didn't answer. He looked away, unable to meet her gaze. Even in a parking lot at one in the morning, he was handsome.

"Well, screw it," Beth said. He was leaning against the driver's door, blocking her way, so she walked around the car to the passenger side. She'd climb over the gearshift and drive off, leaving his nice-looking ass to fall to the concrete. But Black rounded the car the other way and blocked her again, putting his hand over hers as she reached out with her key.

"Nice Cadillac," he said.

It was. It was big and black. It was a nice car if you were a man, a big stupid man who cared about idiotic cars. It had been her father's—he had bought it because a man as rich as he was, as high up in the world as he was, should own a Cadillac. But he'd never loved this car, just like he never loved his expensive house or his expensive wife. His expensive daughter, even. This big, shiny car hadn't prevented her father from ending up dead on the kitchen floor.

Beth pushed the words out at Detective Black like venom. "I have to drive it because I don't have my other car. You do."

Ransom had said that meant the cops were going to look for fingerprints, blood, hair. It was a waste of time. Beth wondered if they'd find her father's fingerprints in that car, a shadow of him left over from when he was alive.

"You'll get it back," Detective Black said.

"Don't bother."

"Beth, get in my car. I'm not letting you drive."

"Who shines your shoes?"

He looked surprised. "Pardon?"

"Your shoes are shiny," Beth said. "Your clothes are pressed. You don't wear a wedding ring. So who does it?"

The detective blinked. "I do it myself."

"The shining and the pressing?"

"Yes."

Beth had never known a man who did that. "Don't you have a girlfriend?"

"Actually, yes, I do. I'm engaged."

"Then why doesn't she press your shirts?"

"If you were engaged, would you press your fiancé's shirts?"

"I'd rather die, but I'm never going to be engaged."

"Okay, then, we have that settled. Get in my car."

She let him lead her to his car and let her into the passenger side. She was so tired, and she probably was too drunk to drive. Especially with a cop watching. She had enough trouble with the police as it was.

"What does she do?" she asked Black as he got in the driver's side and slammed the door.

"What does who do?"

"Your fiancée."

"Oh." He turned the key in the ignition. "She's a teacher."

Beth leaned back in her seat and watched him. It was fun to interrogate him for once, instead of the other way around. "What does she teach?"

"Kindergarten."

Beth laughed. "You're dating a kindergarten teacher?"

He stiffened as he pulled out of the parking lot. "What's wrong with that?"

"Do you actually think that's going to work?"

"Why wouldn't it work? We love each other."

Beth wasn't convinced, but then again, she knew absolutely nothing about what love looked like. She only had her parents' example. "She's a teacher, and you're a detective," she said.

"I believe we've established that."

"You work long hours. Your business is dead people. You can't even tell her about anything you do. Did you see those dead men?"

Black stiffened, and she knew he had, both at the crime scenes and later, when the bodies were on slabs in a cold room somewhere. "Jesus, Beth, you're something else," he said, and it wasn't a compliment.

Beth licked her lips, tasting the last of the vodka on them. No one liked her. She was used to that. She had beauty and money and sex appeal, and she slept alone every night while everyone she'd ever met told the press she was likely a murderer.

"Do you drink?" she asked him.

"I have the occasional beer."

"A glass of wine at Christmas," she said, thinking of her parents' liquor cabinet, which was stocked from floor to ceiling. All those bottles had seemed rich to her as a child, their deep blacks and browns and greens, their jewel-colored labels. Her mother had always liked to drink, but the drinking had been out of control after Julian died— she'd started every morning and she never stopped. She'd made a run at emptying that cabinet, and Beth had done the same. And the pills . . . Her mother had been taking those pills.

Black made a turn, heading up the hill to Arlen Heights in the darkness. Here, outside the city, there were no streetlights, no headlights behind them, barely any light at all. "You know," Detective Black said, his voice calm, "we're alone together in this car, and anything you say is off the record. Is there anything you'd like to tell me?"

Suddenly, she was enraged. Absolutely enraged. That he thought she would fall for all of this: his handsomeness, his offer of a ride, his white-knight act when she was alone in the middle of the night. How stupid he thought she was. And then she realized. "You weren't following me at all," she said, rage making her voice tight. "Someone else was following me—one of the lesser cops. And when he saw me go into that bar, he called you."

Detective Black was silent.

"You came out and took over and told him to go home," Beth said, "because you wanted to talk to me alone. You thought it was a good opportunity, because I'm drunk and lonely. You could charm me, make me feel special. Make me feel like we're friends. Get me to talk to you."

"It isn't what you think," Black said.

"It is," Beth said, still angry at him, but also at herself for falling for it, even for a minute. Ransom would kill her if he could see her right now. He'd told her a hundred times never to talk to cops alone, that they were dangerous. He was right. Why was she too stupid to listen? "Let me out of the car," she said.

Detective Black's voice was tight. "Beth, I'm not letting you out of the car."

"Do it!" she shouted, grabbing the door handle. She wasn't going to jump out of a moving car—at least, she didn't think she was. But she was just drunk enough that her emotions were out of control, ping-ponging through her head, making her crazy.

"It's pitch-black out there and dangerous." Black's jaw was tight; he was angry now, too, though he didn't even slow his driving. "We're in the middle of nowhere. I'm not pulling over and letting you out. I'm taking you home."

"Fuck," Beth said, just to shock him. Then she said it a dozen more times, filling the car with the word. Men hated it when she said "fuck." Women hated it, too, but it was more fun to shock men, watch the expressions on their faces as their opinion of her changed. And it always changed. Even the good-looking ones, the ones who'd started out looking at her with appreciation—their opinions changed just like everyone else's did.

Detective Black waited it out, grimly driving the car as Beth finished her tantrum. When she finally slumped silent into her seat, he said, "I told you, it isn't what you think. I didn't do this to entrap you. I did it to warn you."

Beth didn't feel drunk anymore. She felt painfully sober, her head throbbing, her throat sore from all of the shouting she'd done. She wanted to be drunk again. She was drained and tired and she didn't want to look at him anymore, because the more she looked at him, the more she was tempted to ask him to come inside the house with her, just to see if he'd say yes. She could feel the thin thread of possibility, the razor's edge that she could ask him and he'd come, even though everything about it was wrong, even though he had his kindergarten teacher. Maybe, just maybe, he'd ruin himself for her. She could taste that on her tongue, and she wanted to spit it out.

"Listen," he said when she didn't speak, oblivious to the turmoil in her exhausted brain. "It looks bad for you. I'm telling you this in my professional capacity. Do you understand?"

She tried to bring her mind around. "They're going to arrest me."

"It looks likely. You're their only suspect, and they have to arrest someone. The public has to see someone blamed for this."

That made Beth angry again, because she saw the meaning of what he was saying. "You don't believe I did it."

He was silent for a second. "I've lain awake every night for a week, trying to figure it out." He sounded almost as if he were talking to himself instead of her. They were in Arlen Heights now, winding through her darkened neighborhood. "I can't understand why you would suddenly kill two random people. Why it feels wrong to me, yet it feels right at the same time. When I look at you, I see a dangerous killer, and I also see a girl who was left alone to wander lost after her parents died. I see both of those things at the same time, and it drives me crazy."

Beth sat silent, her eyes burning. She couldn't remember the last time she'd cried.

"Then I finally got it," Black said. There was quiet wonder in his voice. "Damn it, the answer finally came to me, and it's worse than I thought. You're very clever, Beth, and I hate to say it, but you're also goddamned brave. What I still don't know is why you would do it."

He pulled into her driveway now, his headlights illuminating the mansion that she hated so much. "Why I would do what?" she asked, her voice dull, her stomach turning. Maybe whatever he thought he knew was wrong, but hope was dying in her by the minute. It had been dying since she got in the car.

"Why you'd cover for someone else's murders," he said.

That did it.

Beth pushed the car door open, leaned out, and threw up onto the driveway.

CHAPTER TWENTY-ONE

October 2017

SHEA

It had started to rain as I sat in the corner bar. I could see the drops rolling down the windows. It wasn't even late; I'd left Esther's right after dinner. Then I'd sent myself straight from that awkward evening into this one.

My hands were clammy where they curled around my glass of soda with lemon, but otherwise I was surprisingly calm. Even though I'd only seen one photograph of him, I was sure I'd recognize Michael De Vos when I saw him. And I did.

He was wearing jeans, a white shirt, and a dark brown blazer that matched the dark brown of his hair. His brows were furrowed as he came through the door and scanned the dim room, and then he saw me. We stared at each other.

Michael came toward me. His brows were still furrowed, like he was trying to figure something out, which he probably was. As he got closer, I realized he was bigger than I'd thought—over six feet tall. He looked nothing like my ex-husband, Van, who had his name because his parents were Van Morrison fans. Van was slender and occasionally grew a patchy beard. He was the kind of guy who looked ridiculous in baseball caps. Michael's shoulders filled out his jacket, and even though he was clean-shaven and clean-cut—except for the fact that his hair was an inch too long—he had shadows under his eyes. Still, the photo I'd seen hadn't done justice to what he was like in person.

He pulled out the chair across from me at my little table and sat on it. "This is a surprise," he said.

It was his voice, the voice I knew so well from the phone. "Thanks for meeting me," I said.

"Are you kidding me?" His eyebrows rose. "You're my most mysterious client by far. I couldn't pass up the chance to finally meet you in person."

I wondered if he was teasing me, but he wasn't. He actually thought I was mysterious. I glanced down at my jeans and hoodie, thought about my dark hair in its ponytail and my lack of makeup except for a few swipes of mascara. I didn't look anything like Beth, with her expensive slacks and beautiful turtlenecks. She was the epitome of the mysterious woman, the siren who walks into the detective's office and begs him to take the case of protecting her, sending him straight into trouble.

That wasn't me. Still, I could channel a little of Beth right now. What would she do in this situation?

Your problem is a simple power imbalance. It's your call. Make it.

"Why aren't you a cop anymore?" I asked him.

The waitress drifted by, and Michael ordered a beer. Then he turned back to me. "I joined for the most cliché of reasons," he said.

"To please my father and my uncle, who were both cops. To get their approval. That was important to me, and I tried. I really did."

"And you didn't like it?" I asked.

"I hated it. It took years for me to admit it. Being a beat cop was absolutely the wrong job for me. I'm not the guy who can haul a two-hundred-pound drunk out of a bar or pull a child's corpse out of a wrecked car. I'm not knocking it. It just wasn't me."

"What kind of guy are you, then?" I asked him.

"I'm a desk guy, a research guy. A puzzle guy." It should be incongruous for a man over six feet tall, but when I looked at Michael, somehow it fit. He had depths of intelligence behind his expression, and I knew he was adept at researching, writing, theorizing. Despite his size and muscle, deep down he was a nerd like me. "You have to do a lot of years and be really good to make detective, if they'll even take you," he said. "I didn't have the patience or the talent. So I weathered the disappointment from my family and my then wife, who thought she was marrying a cop, and I quit. Now I do this instead."

"You do stakeouts and follow mysterious people," I said.

He smiled a little. "It was fun making you curious about my cases, but the fact is that I mostly do insurance work, taking pictures of people who claim they're in chronic pain while they lift furniture or go waterskiing. It isn't very glamorous. That's why I like taking your assignments—because it feels the most like real detective work. And working on the Lady Killer case is a dream for me. Does that answer your question?"

"Yes," I said. "You put up with a lot from me. I'm sorry I'm so weird."

Michael shrugged as the waitress put his pint of beer in front of him. "It's okay. You probably have your reasons."

I didn't want to talk about my reasons. Not tonight. "Were your father and uncle cops in Claire Lake?"

"Yes, they were. If you're asking if they worked the Lady Killer case, my father was in uniform at the time. He did things like canvass-ing neighborhoods looking for witnesses, that sort of thing."

"Your father worked the Lady Killer case, and you didn't think to tell me?" I said, incredulous. I thought of the photo of Beth's arrest, the uniformed cops in the background. "Was he there the day Beth Greer was arrested?"

Michael's voice was tight. "Most of the Claire Lake PD was there that day. And, yes, my father was there as well."

"Are you kidding me? Can I interview him? I think his memories would be valuable."

His expression had gone carefully blank, though his posture stayed casual. "You can't interview my father, since he was an alco-holic who died at age forty-eight."

I was such an idiot. "I'm sorry."

"It's fine. Even if my father was still alive, you wouldn't find it very pleasant to interview him. Not about this."

"Why?" I read his expression. "Your father thought Beth Greer was guilty."

"That's one way of phrasing it. To the day he died, he referred to Beth Greer as 'a murdering whore.'"

I blinked. The words shouldn't have shocked me, but they did. "What about your uncle?" I asked. "What did he think?"

"My uncle Mike, who I'm named after, fell off a ladder in 1977 and needed back surgery. He was off the job for six months, then confined to a desk for eight months after that. So he didn't work the Lady Killer case at the height of it. That always bothered him, because when the murders were happening, everyone in Claire Lake was afraid and it was all hands on deck. He hated that he wasn't part of the hunt. He died last year."

I glanced at my drink, which was warm now, the ice in it melting to slivers. "Did your uncle think Beth was a lying whore?"

"Mike was more soft-spoken than my father, but he thought Beth

Greer was guilty. He thought she got away with murder." Michael frowned, thinking back. "He always said that it was difficult to understand unless you were in her presence, but Beth was hard. She didn't care about any of the victims, any of the deaths. She wasn't even surprised when they arrested her. And through the arrest, the trial, all of it, she always knew more than she let on. Mike said that if Beth Greer didn't do it, she sure as hell knew who did."

I thought about that. About Beth coming to my office to buy me lunch unexpectedly, assuming I would go with her. About how she had wanted something, and how she'd shaped the conversation to avoid the pitfalls she didn't want to get into. About how she had never once mentioned the Lady Killer victims in any of our conversations, as if they didn't matter to her. "It's an interesting theory," I said, "and Beth gives me the chills sometimes. But hard people, who don't care about others, don't cover for other people's crimes. They don't go to trial in a capital case for someone else. That doesn't add up."

"I agree, but Uncle Mike wasn't stupid. He had good cop's instincts. So does Joshua Black."

"Black doesn't think Beth is the Lady Killer. He told me so."

"He doesn't think she's completely innocent, either." Michael smiled. "And so we come around to the beginning again. Over and over."

"How far did you get in the Linwood Street property records?" I asked him.

He took a deep sip of his beer. "You don't give out easy assignments, do you? Trying to figure out what was in every building on Linwood in 1951, when Mariana Greer was nineteen, looking for something that could have been a private mental hospital—it's a challenge, even for a research geek like me."

I slumped in my chair. "I'm wasting your time, aren't I? I'm sorry." He had other jobs, other clients, and I was asking him to work on this because of something a bitter old woman had told me. "I don't even know why I'm pursuing this. I'm not a cop, or a journalist, or an investigator."

"I've read the Book of Cold Cases." Michael's voice was quiet. "You're a writer, Shea. Haven't you figured that out yet?"

I swallowed hard, my cheeks heating. I'd never thought of myself as a writer—just as a blogger with a strange hobby. But Michael thought I could do this. Detective Black thought I could do this. Maybe the only person who needed convincing was me.

"At least send me an invoice," I said.

Michael shook his head. "I told you, the chance to crack the Lady Killer case after forty years is payment enough for me."

He paused, and there was that moment—that one moment, perfect and still, when I could have told him everything. Michael had told me so much, given me so much. I could tell him about me. The reason I had so many hang-ups that he didn't understand. The reason I'd been afraid to meet him. The reason I was alone. I could tell Michael that I was Girl A.

Hi there. Are you cold?

The blood in my mouth when the man hit me that day, my hands scrabbling on the car door handle as I tried to jump out into the snow.

The shocking impact when I hit the snowy pavement and the dry crunch as I got my boots beneath me and started to run.

The plumes of my breath in the air as I ran and hid, certain that the man was circling the block, getting out of his car, coming after me. The creeping cold as I ran into a garden shed and stayed still, trying not to make a sound.

I could tell Michael all of that, because for better or for worse, it was the truth about me. But we were sitting here face-to-face at last. He was handsome, and he understood me—at least part of me—and we were trying something new. It wasn't the time to tell him.

It didn't escape me that I could talk about any number of gruesome murders, but I couldn't talk about the murder that had almost been mine. Actually, I could talk about those other murders *because* I couldn't talk about the one that had almost been mine.

Besides, Michael wasn't telling me everything about himself, either. No one did. Everyone kept secrets, at least for a little while.

CHAPTER TWENTY-TWO

October 2017

SHEA

"Let's talk about the evidence," I said, turning on the recorder on my phone.

It was Saturday, we were at the Greer mansion, and Beth was sitting on the sofa. She was wearing black full-length yoga pants and a black tee, her feet bare. She was lithe and elegant, ageless. She looked like a movie star—Meryl Streep, perhaps—graciously submitting to an interview. "Why?" she asked me. "I think you've read the trial transcripts."

"More than once," I said. The house was silent around us—no pipes or electric hums, no far-off barking dogs. Except for the sound of a clock ticking on the wall, the Greer mansion was the quietest place I had ever been. My eyes kept traveling to the shadows in the corners, and my ears kept straining for any kind of sound.

I hadn't wanted to come back here; I'd dreaded it. But after seeking me out for lunch, Beth wouldn't meet me anywhere else. It was either come, or give up the chance to talk to her. In the end, I couldn't stay away.

At least I was rested. I had started to sleep properly for the first time in ages—Winston Purrchill liked to take half the bed, and I spent every night with his warm, solid presence beside me. I woke every morning with his calm face looking into mine as he pawed my cheek, insisting on breakfast. I'd never been as comfortable sleeping beside my own husband as I was sleeping beside that cat. I had no idea what that said about me.

"Then you know what the evidence was," Beth said.

"There was enough evidence to bring an indictment," I said. "It wasn't nothing."

Beth shrugged.

I glanced down at my notes, though I didn't need to. I knew everything by heart. "There was the handwriting analysis. Comparing your handwriting to the Lady Killer notes."

"That wasn't a match," Beth said.

"Actually, the results were inconclusive."

She jangled the ice in her glass. "Which isn't a match."

I nodded. Handwriting analysis had been seen as gospel in 1977, but these days it had come under a lot of scientific fire. "What if I offered to pay for a new analysis?"

"It still wouldn't be a match," Beth said.

She was unreadable. I was far out of my league, dealing with someone who had been believed a killer for forty years. Still, I said, "The witness, Alan Parks, saw you leaving the second scene." Parks lived in Alaska now, and he'd refused every one of my attempts to talk to him.

"He saw the back of a head with red hair," Beth said. "For all we know, it was Ransom in a wig. And Alan Parks was drunk."

"But he identified your photo. He admitted that he'd had two whiskey sours before leaving the house to walk his dog. It wasn't exactly the kind of intoxication that would make someone hallucinate."

"As an alcoholic myself, I think I can give expert testimony on this one. Two whiskey sours isn't sober."

"So if he didn't see you that night, then what did he see?"

"I have no idea what he saw. It was forty years ago." Beth's voice went softer as she watched me. "Do you think you're scaring me with this line of questioning, Shea? I don't scare easily."

"I'm not trying to scare you."

"Then what are you trying to do?"

"Get your perspective on things. Like I said when we first met, I want to know what it's like to be you."

"All right, then. Do you want to know the most exciting day of my life? It was the day they arrested me." She looked at my expression and said, "I'm being serious. I didn't say it was a *good* day. I said it was exciting. You can't read an accurate account of that day in any of the newspapers of the time, because none of them printed the real story. They only said I'd been arrested, and they ran that photo, the one with my tits in it."

Her description was crude, but not entirely off base. She was talking about the photo of her in front of this very mansion, being led down the driveway with Detective Black on one arm and Detective Washington on the other. The photo in *Who Was the Female Zodiac?* in which she leaned toward the camera, her lips parted as if she were speaking. The pose and the angle, with her hands bound so tightly behind her, outlined the curves of her body, even beneath the trench coat. If she was a killer, she was the most sexual killer anyone had ever seen.

"It's kind of a famous photo," I said.

"Nothing about that photo is as it seems," Beth said. "But then again, it made me look like a bitch. It played into the narrative that I was a serial killer. And it sold papers."

"The gun," I said, trying to stick to the topic of evidence. "There was the ballistics report that said the same gun killed your father and the two Lady Killer victims. How do you explain that?"

Beth looked at me evenly. "Do you think I killed my father?"

I stared back at her. "The truth?"

"Of course."

I bit my lip, thinking. "I think it's unlikely. You were nineteen, and it was a very violent crime. You didn't need his money—you were already his heiress, and you had all the money you wanted. You told me Julian wasn't abusive."

Beth took a sip of her drink, listening. She looked tense, but if I had to guess, I thought part of her was enjoying this.

"The thing is, though, it's possible," I went on. "Your childhood wasn't happy—you admit that. You were left alone a lot. You had no close friends. Most serial killers who have been studied can trace their tendencies back to childhood, and yours was definitely isolated. You've never been psychologically examined by court order, so no one knows if you're a sociopath or not."

"Gosh, you're a charming date," Beth said dryly.

I gave her a shrug that was pure Beth, the one that said, *Maybe you have a point, but probably not.* "You asked. What I come back to when I think about it is that if it *was* you, then it was almost the perfect crime. Because who was going to suspect the grieving teenage daughter?"

There was a moment of silence, both of us watching each other in the silent living room.

"The person who committed those murders," Beth said, her voice low and calm, "was dangerous. Someone with no conscience and no fear. Someone who wanted to see people die. Someone who wouldn't have stopped." Her eyes met mine. "You've been asking about my parents, my childhood. Why don't you go upstairs and see my childhood for yourself?"

"Upstairs?"

"Yes. The second door on the left was my childhood room. It's been left as it was, so you can see what I saw as a little girl. My father's study is up there—his papers are still there if you want to read them. My parents' bedroom—now my bedroom—is at the end of the hall. My mother's clothes are still in the closet. Look at anything you like."

Sick dread settled in my stomach. "You still have your mother's clothes?"

"I can never quite seem to get rid of them," Beth said. "I get so far, and then . . . well. Not all of the answers you want so desperately are going to come from me. Some of them are going to come from this house."

The air was still, as if the house were listening, waiting. I didn't want to go upstairs, but I'd made a decision when I came here in the first place. I'd decided that despite whatever I'd seen the last time, despite the voice I'd heard on my phone, I wanted to risk it. I was tired of being so safe all the time. I was tired of being so afraid that I never lived my life.

I wanted to see what was upstairs.

I picked up my phone from the coffee table and turned off the recording. I was going to bring it with me and take pictures. I didn't ask Beth's permission.

I stood and walked to the stairs. They were worn hardwood, with a runner placed down the middle that was well cared for but obviously as old as the rest of the house. I put my hand on the hardwood banister and climbed.

The Greer mansion looked large from the outside, but the upstairs was a single hallway with a row of doorways on each side. The air was still, and there was carpet, a thin nap of dusty roses. There was no artwork on the walls, no family photos lining the hall. The boards beneath the flowers creaked softly under my feet.

The doors lining the corridor were all closed. I opened the second door on the left.

It was a small room, tidy, with a single twin bed made up with a gray blanket. An ornate desk sat against the other wall, the kind of desk a young girl might use. Next to it were bookshelves, empty. There was a rug in the middle of the floor. A wooden clock ticked on the wall.

Beth Greer had been born in 1954. Which meant this room, her little-girl room, had sat here unchanged for some sixty years.

Some families didn't change their children's rooms. They kept their kids' beds, their bookshelves, long after the child in question had grown up and moved out. My own mother had kept my and Esther's room intact until my parents moved to Florida. But that was a pattern born of love, of nostalgia, and the thought that maybe grandchildren would want to use the room someday.

That wasn't what this was. This little girl's room had never been changed because the space wasn't needed in a house with so many rooms and only three people. It was unchanged because Mariana Greer couldn't be bothered. And then it stayed unchanged because both Julian and Mariana were dead, and Beth had let it sit for another forty years.

What the hell was wrong with this place?

I moved past the bedroom and farther down the hall. The air was still, even stuffier than it was downstairs. Like fresh air was alien to this place. The next door I tried opened to a bathroom, but the one after that was a room with a heavy wood desk with a blotter on it and a leather chair. Julian Greer's study.

I stepped inside. I felt like an intruder in this room, as if the man who owned it would walk back in at any minute. *He's been dead for over forty years*, I reminded myself as I approached the desk and put my hand on one of the drawer handles. After a brief pause to inhale a breath, I yanked the drawer open.

Inside was a pack of cigarettes. Winstons, in the distinctive red and white package. Next to it was a heavy metal lighter. There was an empty ashtray on the desk.

I pushed aside the cigarettes, left here by a man dead for decades, and picked up a piece of paper from the stack beneath it. It was a phone bill dated January 3, 1972, listing the calls in and out of the house.

My God. Had Beth thrown nothing away in all these years? This was some kind of mental illness, maybe even a psychosis. How was it possible that she looked so modern and fashionable when she lived in this museum? How could she be mentally stable when for forty years her life had been lived in a shrine to her parents?

Beneath the phone bill was another, and another. On the third bill, I thought I saw the ghost of dark handwriting on the back of the paper. I turned it over and saw three words scrawled in ink:

I'm still here

The breath left my throat. Those were the words I'd heard whispered into my phone. I turned over the other two phone bills and saw the same three words written on the back. Suddenly, I'd hazard a guess that I'd see those words written on every piece of paper in this desk.

I grabbed my phone out of my back pocket with numb fingers and snapped photos of the scrawled words. Thinking of the way the last interview had vanished from my phone, I immediately texted the pictures to Michael. I didn't even bother with a message. He knew I was at the Greer mansion right now.

I hit SEND, and then I noticed that the air was cold. And there was the soft sound of someone breathing right outside the open door of the study.

"Beth?" I called out.

The air grew colder, and there was a soft *shh*. I looked down and saw that all of the desk drawers were open.

I took a clumsy step back, then rounded the desk to bolt for the door. It slammed closed, and I saw the shadow of something moving in the crack beneath the bottom of the door and the floor. Not feet—something sliding smoothly across the door, from one side to the other and back.

I lifted my hand to the doorknob, and something pounded on the other side of the door. *Bang. Bang.* I stumbled back in shock, and my phone fell from my hand, spinning across the floor and under the desk. I dropped to my knees as the banging continued, heavy and rhythmic, almost a human sound but not quite. Flinching with each *bang*, I groped under the desk until my fingers found my phone. I glanced back over my shoulder and saw the smooth shadow still moving back and forth. It definitely wasn't human feet.

I pulled my phone toward me. There was a crack across the screen. The banging stopped, and the room rang with silence. I rose to my knees and glanced beneath the door again. The shadow was gone.

In my hand, my phone lit up, and a voice came from the recorder. A harsh whisper, like I'd heard before.

"I'm still here," the voice said.

That was when I got to my feet and ran.

Beth wasn't downstairs. She wasn't in the living room. Her empty glass with its melting ice was sitting on the table.

"Beth!" I shouted.

Upstairs, I heard footsteps in the hallway, heading for the stairs.

I grabbed my bag from the sofa and put it under my arm. The curtains in the living room were drawn, but I could see a shadow of something beyond them, out there on the grass.

In my hand, my phone lit up again. The recorder played, and this time it sounded like an old recording, or maybe an old answering machine.

"What do you think?" a woman said through my cracked screen.

"Is she bitter, or is she sweet? I could never decide. Sometimes she was so sweet, but other times . . . Well, I don't like to think about it."

I wanted to run, but something drew me to the window instead. I stepped forward and yanked the curtain open.

There was the dead expanse of lawn outside, the empty ocean. A girl stood at the edge of the drop, her back to me. She was blond, slender, and young—a teenager, wearing jeans and a flowered blouse. Her feet were bare. Her hair lifted in the wind. She stood for a moment, and then she tipped forward and vanished over the edge in a whisper of fabric.

I shouted and pounded the glass.

"She can get so angry," the voice on my dead phone said. "She loses control. But I think you should look behind you. She's coming down the stairs."

There were footsteps behind me. I turned from the window and bolted from the house, down the front steps to the driveway. The cool, damp air hit my face like a slap. I was almost at the sidewalk when I sank to the ground, frozen in panic, my breath heaving and my stomach turning. I stared at the grass as the moisture soaked through the knees of my jeans and a bird called overhead. In the distance, a car went by. The world going about its business.

Footsteps came toward me on the sidewalk. It was Beth. She had put on ballet flats and a trench coat—not the old coat from the seventies, but a newer one, dark blue, expensive Burberry. It was belted at the waist, and the hem fell past her knees. In the cloudy light, she looked like the woman in the YouTube videos and the photographs, and also like the woman I knew. Her eyes were unreadable.

When she came to my side, she lowered herself down to a crouch. She touched my cheek with her fingertip, dragging it lightly across my skin, tucking a loose strand of hair behind my ear.

"For someone so paranoid, you should choose your friends more carefully," she said.

I was starting to breathe again. The fear was still there, but my stomach had slowed its nauseated turning. "Who is she?" I asked Beth.

"You're so close," Beth said. "You have so many questions, so many things you want to know. You've come closer than anyone else ever has. You've almost finished the game, Shea. You've almost won. Just use your brain and figure out the last part."

Then she stood and walked to the Greer mansion. When she got to the steps, the front door swung open.

Then Beth went inside, and the door closed behind her with a *click*. And she was gone.

PART II

CHAPTER TWENTY-THREE

December 1977

BETH

She tried going out at night. She crept out of her own house like a criminal, getting in her car and driving around Claire Lake as it slept. But even at night she was noticeable, her big Cadillac gliding through the silent streets. Ever since the night with Detective Black, the police had almost always been on her tail, and even during her night drives, she'd see headlights behind her. So she gave up and went home.

She'd gone last night, not getting home until almost four. The tension was going to kill her; alcohol was the only thing that killed it. She was lying on the sofa, halfway through a bottle of wine and blearily watching TV with all of the curtains closed at two in the afternoon when the phone rang. She reached a hand to the end table and picked it up. "Hello?"

There was the sound of breathing on the other end of the line. In the background, wind and traffic, as if the call was coming from a roadside phone booth.

And just like that, she knew who it was. She knew what voice would be on the other end, even though she hadn't heard it in two years. The voice she'd been searching for. The voice she hated. The haziness of the wine started to drain away.

"Lily," Beth said.

The voice on the other end was beloved and terrifying, strange and also as familiar as her own. "They're coming for you," Lily said.

The police. She was talking about the police. "They're coming now?"

"Yes, they are."

"How do you know?"

"They think they're so discreet." The voice was disgusted. "Honestly. I could see them from the road."

Beth sat up. If Lily was talking about the road, then she was near the house.

No, she couldn't be. But she'd driven past. While Beth had been sitting on this sofa, drinking and waiting, Lily had driven past before finding a phone booth. How many times had she done that, when Beth had been looking for her for so many days?

"You bitch," Beth said.

"Maybe, but I'm sitting here while you're about to be arrested. This is all your fault, Beth. You could have stopped it."

She wasn't drunk now, not at all. Panic tried to climb up her throat. "I didn't do all of this. You did."

"Only because you made me." Lily sighed into the phone. "I even left a note. Did you read it?"

Of course she had. The note had been in all the papers. *Am I bitter or am I sweet? Ladies can be either.*

Which one are you today? Mariana would say when they were little girls. *Are you bitter, or are you sweet?*

And the girls would have to choose. Lily always chose bitter, which would make Mariana laugh and shake her head.

Beth would say she was sweet. Mariana never laughed at that. She'd just nod and say, "How nice."

"Why are you calling?" Beth asked Lily now, listening to her breathe on the other end of the line.

"I want to know what you'll do," Lily said. "Whether you'll run. Whether you'll break. Whether you'll talk."

"I could tell them everything."

"Will you tell them how you could have stopped it?" Lily asked. "You've been looking for me, haven't you? Driving the streets, searching. Too bad you didn't find me. You should have looked harder."

She should have. She knew that now. She'd been panicked and half-drunk, and for some reason she'd thought she'd have more time. But now she was out of time.

Was that the crunch of gravel, the low hum of a motor? More than one? There wasn't a lot of traffic in Arlen Heights, especially in the middle of the day. The police were coming, and Beth's time was up.

Lily's voice was clear, unhurried, as if she knew Beth would obey even as the police closed in. "You're not leaving, Beth," she said. "You're not talking."

"I hate you," Beth said, her throat choking and her eyes burning with unshed tears.

"No, you don't," Lily said. "You really don't."

Beth put down the phone, her breath sawing in her throat. Her palms tingled with sweat. She needed to call Ransom.

There was the sound of another car outside. Lily was a liar, but she wasn't lying about this. Beth was about to be arrested for murder.

This is all your fault, Beth.

You're not leaving. You're not talking.

And just like it had during the police interview, the fear snapped and the anger took over. That cold, comforting rage.

Beth went upstairs, changed her clothes. Put on dark high-waisted jeans, a cream blouse with a pattern of brown diamonds on it, her favorite shirt. Red lipstick. Hoops in her ears. There were more sounds now, low voices at the side of the house. Did they think they were being stealthy? Lily was right; it was ridiculous. Did they think she would run? Where did they think she would go?

Beth put on heeled boots, and then as a final gesture she put on her trench coat, belting it at the waist. She picked up her purse. She walked to the windows in the living room and dragged open the curtains.

There were men outside. Uniformed cops, bracing in position. They looked startled at the sight of her.

Beth gave them a wave.

She walked calmly to the front door and opened it. There were cops here, too, on the lawn. A brown Pontiac at the end of the drive-way, pulled up behind her Cadillac. Marked cruisers parked farther down the street. A crowd of neighbors was gathering, and the press was already here, two reporters and two photographers flashing pictures of Beth standing in her doorway. As she watched, a van pulled up two doors down and a female reporter got out, followed by a TV camera-man. The woman left the cameraman behind with his heavy equip-ment and jogged up the street in her high heels when she saw Beth.

Beth watched the chaos building in front of her house, feeling oddly calm. She wondered if Lily would drive by again, just to see the scene she'd created. It would be a crazy move, but you never knew what Lily would do.

The doors of the brown Pontiac opened, and Detectives Black and Washington got out. They were wearing suits, and both of them looked unhappy. This circus wasn't what they'd wanted; someone somewhere must have leaked information to the press. Beth took a grim satisfaction in the frowns on their faces, the angry displeasure in Washington's eyes. What did Beth care about a few photographs if this mess embarrassed them?

As the detectives came up the driveway, yet another car pulled up to the curb. Ransom got out, his hair a little disheveled and his tie askew. He saw her on the front porch and pointed at her. "Don't say anything, Beth!" he shouted. "Not a word!"

"Miss Greer!" the female reporter called to her, jogging up the driveway behind the detectives, flanking them. A flashbulb went off. "Miss Greer, do you have anything to say on the day of your arrest for the Lady Killer murders?"

"Get out of here," Detective Washington growled. The reporter fell back a step but didn't leave.

Beth put her hands in the pockets of her trench coat and watched. Ransom started across her lawn toward her, his expensive shoes sinking into the damp grass.

"Detective Black!" one of the other reporters shouted. "What evidence do you have that Beth Greer is the Lady Killer? Was she having an affair with the victims?"

"What the hell is going on?" shouted the man who lived two doors down, his face going red as he stood in the street. "This is a good neighborhood!"

As if in response, another police cruiser came around the corner, this one flashing its lights and blaring its siren. Someone in Arlen Heights had called the police—on the police. The uniformed cops on the lawn shouted, and Black and Washington turned and waved their arms at the cruiser, signaling it to shut up. It, too, pulled over, and the siren went quiet, though the lights still flashed, flickering over the sunny day. Another reporter showed up, and another camera flashed. The TV cameraman had gotten his bulky equipment up and running and was now shooting the whole scene.

Washington gestured to one of the uniforms. "Help us out over here." The uniform hurried over, and Washington said, "We need you to handcuff her."

"We don't need handcuffs, for God's sake," Detective Black said.

"It's a goddamned murder arrest!" Washington barked at him. "I don't care what she looks like, we're handcuffing her!"

"You will not!" Ransom was climbing the front porch steps now. He was out of breath and his shoes were wet, but Beth could see instantly that he was in his element, that this kind of moment was the thing he lived for. He elevated his voice to a theatrical boom so the reporters could hear it. "The police will not mistreat my client!"

"Get out of the way, Wells!" Washington shouted. "And someone turn those fucking cherry lights off!"

Beth looked at the reporters' faces and knew they'd all heard the profanity, that it had been caught on record on the TV camera.

"No handcuffs," Black said as the uniformed cop took his handcuffs out. Beth kept her hands in the pockets of her trench coat. Ransom was standing beside her now. Flashbulbs were going off, mixing with the lights from the police car, and more reporters were shouting questions.

"We're doing this," Washington said. He grabbed the cuffs from the uniform and strode up the porch steps, reaching out to grasp Beth's arm. His grip was hard and painful as he jerked her hand from her pocket.

"Elizabeth Greer, you're under arrest," he said, beginning to drone on about courts of law and rights to remain silent.

"Hands off my client!" Ransom shouted. "She is offering no resistance! Are you getting this on the tape? Did you get that?"

Beth let Washington spin her, yank her other hand out of her pocket. She let herself go limp, like a doll, as his grip bruised her. He cuffed one wrist, then pulled the other behind her back. Beth caught the wince of shocked disgust on Detective Black's face and realized Washington was going far off the script. He wasn't supposed to use handcuffs, and if he used them he was probably supposed to cuff her hands in front. With her hands cuffed in the back, she looked like a common criminal, like someone caught breaking windows or fondling children. Even though she was accused of two murders, Black didn't think Beth was a common criminal. She could see it on his face.

The cuffs were cold, and they bit into her wrists. Beth didn't wince. She rolled her shoulders, shifted her weight so the cuffs didn't pull as hard.

This is all your fault, Beth. You could have stopped it.

"I want the record to show that my client is cooperating," Ransom was bellowing. "We have here on the footage that the police are assaulting her. My client may file charges."

Washington was pulling Beth down the steps now, and Black quickly took her other side as reporters crowded in. There were more flashes mixing with the police lights, microphones shoved in her face.

"Beth!" one reporter shouted. "Beth, do you have anything to say? Anything at all?"

She could feel Ransom's wrath from three feet away, could feel Detective Black stiffen against her right side. Telegraphing to her to be quiet.

This was the moment, she realized. She wasn't just a rumor anymore. She wasn't just a headline. Now she was a murderer.

Lily had made her a murderer.

Beth leaned away from Washington, angling her body toward the microphone. The pose, with her hands behind her back, outlined her figure for the cameras, even with the trench coat on. She knew it as well as she knew her own body in the mirror. She kept her voice calm, as if she were talking to someone boring at a cocktail party. "The police can manhandle me all they want, but it still doesn't make me guilty," she said.

There was a murmur of reaction, more shouted questions, and then Washington was putting her into the back seat of the brown Pontiac, his hand on her head. "Watch it," she heard Black say to him.

"Beth, I'll follow you," Ransom shouted. "Don't say anything." He turned and hurried back to his car, shaking his head as reporters followed him, trying to get him to comment.

It was awkward sitting in the car with her hands cuffed behind her back. Beth shifted on the seat, trying to brace herself without pinning her arms and twisting her shoulders as the detectives got in front and Washington put the car into gear.

"We need to switch her cuffs," Black said as the car inched down the driveway, crowded with people.

"No, we don't." Washington shot back. "She'll live. We're not getting her back out of the car now."

Black was silent as they finally pulled free of the crowd of people, which was starting to disperse. From the window, Beth could see reporters running back to their cars, the TV cameraman getting a last shot of the car backing out before lowering his camera and turning back to his van.

"Beth, are you all right?" Detective Black asked her.

She ignored him. The neighbors were talking, and thanks to the reporters her arrest would be all over the news by six o'clock. She had been arrested for murder, a catastrophe that meant life as she knew it was over. Everyone thought she was the Lady Killer. She was on her way to jail, and then to a trial, which she could very well lose. She had just been publicly humiliated, dragged from her front porch and pushed into a police car in a spectacle of an arrest. It was all because of Lily, who by now was probably on the road out of town, the pay phone she'd called from sitting empty.

And still, as Arlen Heights receded in the background, Beth could only think one thing:

That was goddamned fun.

CHAPTER TWENTY-FOUR

October 2017

SHEA

In the first days after my last visit to the Greer mansion, I was afraid.

I kept my cracked phone in the bottom of my purse, unable to look at it. I went to work and back in silence, sitting alone on the bus with my bag in my lap. I stopped listening to audiobooks, because I didn't want to hear about death anymore. Instead I sat with a roaring in my ears, as if something were going to happen any second and I had to be ready.

I forced myself to concentrate at work. I never went out after dark. I checked my security system multiple times before going to bed. And when I finally slept, my dreams were full of blood and a familiar voice, saying: *Hi there. Are you cold?*

No matter how many times I awoke thrashing and sweating, Winston Purrchill was always on the bed next to me, regarding me with his sleepy eyes, drowsily wondering what was wrong. I fell asleep over and over with my hand on his soft fur or my face next to the solid curve of his back, watching the rise and fall of his breathing, listening as the low, uncouth rumble of his purr drifted off into sleep. I would have lost my sanity without my cat that week. If Alison or her ex-husband ever showed up to take him back, they would do it over my dead body.

And then something changed. Maybe I got tired of the fear; maybe it just lost its grip. But instead of being afraid, I got mad.

I thought about those blows against the door of Julian's study, and instead of terror I only felt anger. I couldn't explain it, and I couldn't even trace it to a source—I was suddenly furious at everything. At Beth. At the man who had tried to abduct me when I was a child. At whoever had killed Thomas Armstrong and Paul Veerhoever and left them by the side of the road like trash. At all of the murderers—so many of them—who got away with it and left the victims to end up on the Book of Cold Cases, one after another. It all tumbled together in my mind. I'd never been this angry, and now I started to see what I'd been missing.

After I got home from work one day, I got a text from Michael. I had to pull my cracked phone from the bottom of my bag to read it. *There's some missing information in the online property records. We'll have to try the records office downtown to see if they have the archive.*

Okay, I texted back.

Sending you an email now, he wrote. *There are two addresses that are missing records prior to 1960. I'm sending you everything I have.*

Okay, I wrote again.

His next text came back right away: *Are you all right?*

Of course Michael knew something was wrong. I stared at the words, wondering what the answer was. Based on what was going on in my head, I seemed to be going crazy. But to tell the truth, I wasn't so sure.

I looked at the crack on my phone screen. I'd dropped my phone when something—maybe something dead—had banged on the door of Julian's study. I'd thought about getting my phone fixed or replaced, but I hadn't done it yet. Suddenly I wasn't sure I was going to.

I opened a drawer in my desk, pulled out the number Detective Joshua Black had given me, and dialed it before I could lose my nerve. "It's Shea Collins," I said when he answered.

"Shea." His voice sounded pleased. "What can I help you with?"

There were a hundred questions I could have asked him, but that wasn't why I called. Instead I said, "Have you ever hated Beth?"

"On and off for forty years." He said it without missing a beat, and I immediately knew I had called the right person. "Are you in that phase right now?"

"I'm so angry," I admitted as I gripped my cracked phone. "I can't stop. I don't know what to do about it."

Detective Black was quiet for a long minute, his breaths somehow soothing on the other end of the line. Then he said, "Shea, I'm going to say something, and you're not going to like it. But it's my job to tell the truth."

I swallowed. "Go ahead."

"Anton Anders has a parole hearing coming up."

It was my turn to be silent, the emotions churning in my gut robbing me of words.

"You don't want to go," Black said. "I've seen it so many times with victims. And for some of them, it's the wrong thing to go. But you need to go to that hearing."

"No." The word was automatic. The letter from the parole board was still buried in a pile of mail. I hadn't touched it.

I also hadn't thrown it out.

"Think about it," Detective Black said. "Because the truth is, you don't have to sit home, afraid. And you can hate Beth—God knows, I have. But even if you hate her, you have to keep going. Because the truth is going to come out."

I thanked him and hung up a few moments later. I was calmer now. I woke up my laptop and checked my email.

The first email that came up was a Google alert. I had a few alerts set up for various true-crime cases I'd written about, in case there were any updates. This one was my alert for crimes in Claire Lake. I would read that one later.

The second email that came in was from Michael—the property records on Linwood Street. All I had to do was open the email and start the work of filling in the missing parts.

Instead of being angry or afraid, I could get to work.

I looked again at Michael's text on my phone: *Are you all right?*

I let out a breath and texted back: *I am now.*

The next day, I left work an hour early. Still wearing my scrub top and jeans, my purse over my shoulder, I hurried four blocks from the office to the city courthouse, getting to the records office half an hour before it closed. The records office sent me to the archives office— apparently a different thing entirely—so I lost an extra five minutes wandering the basement hallways, looking for the right sign.

I finally found the archives office and stepped inside. Except for the clerk, I was the only one there.

"I'm looking for the records for these two addresses," I said, sliding a piece of paper with the Linwood Street addresses on it. "I need the pre-1960 records, and they aren't online."

The clerk behind the counter, a fortyish woman with bobbed hair, slid on her reading glasses and scanned it. "That's over forty years ago. Anything over forty years is kept in a different room. That takes longer."

That would be my third room in a row. "You can't get them now?"

She glanced at the clock, not bothering to hide it. "Submit a request form, and someone will contact you in the next few days."

She was trying to be firm, but I sensed an opening. "We can do this in the next ten minutes," I said. "I'll go with you, read the files, and you'll still go home on time. I promise."

"Ten minutes?" She looked at the clock again, then looked at me, this time curiously. "Why do you need this so urgently, anyway?"

"I'm a writer." When she looked at my scrub top, I added, "In the evenings. I'm writing a book."

Her eyes went wide. "Oh. A mystery?"

"Yes, a mystery."

"I love Lee Child."

"So do I," I said, which was actually true. "I'm writing something a little like that, and I have a great story idea. I just want to have a quick look at the file to settle a research point." To juice the story up, I added, "I think one of these buildings might have been a private psychiatric hospital."

"An old psychiatric hospital, huh? That's a pretty good setting." Her expression softened. There was no one in line behind me, no one else in the room. "Okay, put the 'Closed' sign on the door behind you and we'll go quick. I want to be out of here at five minutes to five."

Thank you, Lee Child, I thought as she let me behind the counter and admitted me to the file room.

It was a dim, dry place, windowless and claustrophobic, lit with fluorescent light and lined with file boxes. The clerk, who now told me her name was Carole, pulled two boxes and opened them. "There won't be much," she warned, "for buildings that old."

I flipped through the file for the first address, scanning as fast as I could. Normally I would have taken Carole's advice, filled out the form, and taken my time researching what I needed, but my gut told me I was running low on time. Either there was something here, or there wasn't. I needed to know.

I didn't find anything interesting in the first building's history, and with five minutes to go, I went to the second box. While Carole gave me an impatient sigh in warning, I flipped back in time for the building at 120 Linwood.

And there it was: The original building was built in 1940, and ownership was transferred to something called the Elizabeth Trevor House for Women in 1949. I had never heard of the Elizabeth Trevor House for Women, but I sensed that it could be a lead. I pulled out my phone and took a photo of the records page, then another of a property tax report. There was a record of sale back to a private family in 1956, and I photographed that, too.

"Hey," Carole said. "No photos allowed."

"Just one more minute." I tried to text the photos to Michael, but there was no signal inside the records room. I tried pulling up my phone's browser to search the Elizabeth Trevor House for Women, but nothing would load.

"Okay, I have to go home," Carole said. She was exasperated with me. I didn't blame her. "Did you find what you were looking for?"

"I don't know." I looked for anything else in the file that would give me a clue; there was nothing. I put the file back in the box and helped Carole put the boxes back, feeling foolish. I'd barged in and derailed the last fifteen minutes of her day like I was doing something important, but it was probably a dead end. I bet this never happened to Lee Child.

"So it wasn't a psychiatric hospital?" Carole asked as we walked back out of the archives room and she locked the door with a key from the ring in her hand. I tried my phone again, but there was still no signal. We were too deep in the basement.

"I don't know. It was something called the Elizabeth Trevor House for Women. There's no signal down here, so I can't tell you what that was."

Carole had paused and was looking at me with a bemused look on her face. "The Elizabeth Trevor House? I've never heard of it, but that wouldn't have been a psychiatric institution. You're barking up the wrong tree."

"What do you mean?"

"Elizabeth Trevor wasn't crazy, at least that I know of, so they wouldn't have put her name on a mental hospital."

"What?" I blinked at her. "Who was Elizabeth Trevor?"

Carole tutted at me with the pleasure of someone who knows an obscure piece of trivia that has finally become useful. "You should brush up on your Claire Lake history," she said, "especially your feminist history. Elizabeth Trevor was a factory worker who got fired because she got pregnant when she wasn't married. She campaigned for rights for unwed mothers. In those days, single mothers were discriminated against by employers, landlords, doctors, everyone. Elizabeth Trevor tried to change all that. She was a badass." Carole nodded. "You're not looking for a psychiatric hospital; you're looking for a home for unwed mothers. Are we done here? I'm going home."

CHAPTER TWENTY-FIVE

October 2017

SHEA

"Jesus, Shea, what is it? I got here as fast as I could." Michael slid into the booth opposite me, brushing his hair back from his forehead. "I've never heard you sound like that."

Panicked—that was how I must have sounded. Excited. Alive.

I cupped my hands around my hot coffee cup. We were in a diner around the corner from the courthouse. People were coming to grab takeout on their way home from work. I was still in my scrub top under my jacket and was finding it hard to keep warm. The shock was starting to get to me.

"I'm sorry," I said to Michael. "I know you were probably busy."

He shrugged and motioned to the waitress for a coffee. He was wearing a gray T-shirt under a dark brown blazer, a look that was just formal enough that I knew he had been working when I called. "It sounded important. I wanted to hear what it is."

I let out a breath. "This is going to sound insane," I said. "Completely insane."

"Okay. I'm ready."

"I may have just cracked the Lady Killer case."

The waitress brought Michael's coffee, and I watched her give him a once-over before she walked away. Michael didn't notice. He also didn't touch the cup. "What did you find?" he asked, his gaze fixed on me.

"Beth's mother wasn't mentally ill," I said. "Sylvia got it wrong. The place Mariana went before she was married, the papers Julian had—she wasn't admitted to a mental hospital. She was in a home for unwed mothers."

I watched it hit him, the way it had hit me. The way it was still hitting me, almost an hour later.

"I found it in the file for 120 Linwood," I said, pulling out my phone and calling up the photos I'd taken of the file. I turned the phone so he could see the photos on my cracked screen. "From 1949 to 1956, it was the Elizabeth Trevor House for Women. There are no records of the place online, but there are articles about Elizabeth herself. She was an activist for the rights of unwed mothers."

"You're kidding." Michael peered closer at my photo, trying to read. "I'm going to send myself this," he said.

"Go ahead." I watched as he texted himself the photos. "The timeline adds up," I said. "Mariana is at the Elizabeth Trevor House before her wedding to Julian. It's kept a secret. After they're married, Julian and Mariana have Beth. Then, a few years later, Mariana's mother dies, and her will leaves everything to Julian instead of Mariana. Including her secret papers."

"Julian would learn of the secret for the first time," Michael said. "We have to assume the premarital baby wasn't Julian's, then."

"Probably not, but who knows?" I took my phone back. "Either way, he'd be angry, but especially if the baby wasn't his."

"So Beth Greer has a half sibling." Michael picked up his forgotten coffee and sipped it, thinking.

"A half sister," I said.

His eyebrows rose. "How do you know the baby was a girl?"

Because I saw her standing at the edge of the drop behind the Greer mansion, her blond hair blowing in the wind. I saw her go over. I've heard her voice on my phone, telling me she's still here. "Think about it," I said. "The woman's handwriting on the murder notes. The woman seen at the crime scene who resembles Beth. The fact that no physical evidence ever tied Beth to the crimes. Because it wasn't her, but it was the next best thing. It was her sister."

"We need documents." Michael rubbed his temple. "A birth certificate. Patient records from the unwed mothers' home. Some type of ID so we can track this woman and find out where she is, what her life has been, if she's still alive."

"She isn't still alive," I said.

"You don't know that."

I did. There were some things I knew better than Michael did. The woman who had pounded on the door of Julian's study had definitely not been alive.

"I've been working on the handwriting samples you sent me," Michael was saying, making rapid notes on his phone. "The Claire Lake PD never released a photo of the original notes, but I'm sure I can find something. A photo we can compare to the handwriting you saw in Julian Greer's study." He continued typing, his coffee forgotten again. "It's possible that Mariana's first baby died and we're completely off track, which is why we need records. But to track down this lead—Jesus, Shea, we have so much work to do."

He was right. We had a lot of work to do, and all of it was important. And it was possible I was wrong.

But I wasn't wrong. I had heard Mariana's voice. *Is she bitter, or is she sweet?*

Sometimes she was so sweet, but other times . . . Well, I don't like to think about it.

When my phone rang hours later, at one o'clock in the morning, I wasn't sleeping. I knew who was calling. I picked up the receiver and said, "Beth?"

"I can never sleep," Beth said. "Can you?"

I sat up, wide awake. "I won the game," I said.

"Did you?" Her voice didn't have its usual fight. She sounded tired, so tired.

Still, I pushed on. "Your mother had a child before she married your father. You have a sister. I'm going to find her."

Beth sighed. "You're going to regret that. But, then, it's too late. You've already met Lily."

Lily. "Is that her real name?"

"What a curious question," Beth said. "It's the only name I've ever known her by. And I've known her a long, long time."

"She's dead, isn't she?"

"If you already know the answer, why are you asking the question?"

My spine tensed. Next to me on the bed, Winston Purrchill gave me a look of displeasure as I disturbed his sleep. "I saw her," I said. "Standing behind the house. She was blond. Pretty, I think. She went over the edge. Is that what happened, Beth? Did she jump?"

There was a short, bitter laugh on the other end of the line. "Lily would never have killed herself. That would have been too easy. She was showing off, trying to scare you. You're lucky. You should see what she does to the people she *doesn't* like."

And there it was—the crux of everything. When you looked beneath the files and the records and the search for proof, this meant that the pretty girl I'd seen with her blond hair blowing in the wind had been the deadliest serial killer in Claire Lake history. She had shot two men point-blank in the face. She had killed Julian Greer and left him to bleed on the floor.

"Who was she?" I asked Beth.

"There are so many answers to that question." Beth's voice was slurring a little. She sounded drunk, but she didn't drink. She must have taken a pill. "She was the shame of my mother's life. She was the person who ruined mine."

"And yet you covered for her crimes. You went to trial for her. You nearly went to death row."

"I had my reasons," Beth said. "If you knew Lily, you'd understand." She paused, and then her voice lowered to a slurred hush. "I think I hear her now."

"Beth?"

There was quiet on the line, rustling. Then Beth said, "Come tomorrow, and I'll tell you. It's time. This is all going to be over soon, and I'm so damned tired."

I felt a bolt of alarm at the idea. "Beth, I don't want to come to that house."

"No, but you will." Despite the drugged tone of her voice, she still had that imperious way of talking. "You will. Here she comes."

She hung up. I stared into the darkness, thinking about Beth spending the night alone in that house, with whatever lived there. About spending every night there for forty years.

Tomorrow—today, technically—was Saturday. I could get up in a few hours, get on the bus, and go to the Greer mansion to hear everything.

Or I could stay home, and avoid whatever waited in that house for me.

I lay back on the bed, stared at the ceiling, and wondered which one I would do.

CHAPTER TWENTY-SIX

November 1960

BETH

At age six, they told Beth she was lucky. She was living in a big house high above the ocean, with a backyard that looked over the water. She had a room all to herself and no siblings to argue with. She had all of her parents' attention and never had to share it. She went to private school, where she wore a uniform of a navy blue skirt and a dark green sweater that was very becoming against her red hair. *Beth is pretty and extremely bright,* her teachers told her parents, *though it puzzles us why she doesn't talk much in school.*

Oh, don't worry about that, her mother told the teachers. *Beth is just lonely. It's how she's always been.*

In the evenings after school, Beth would sit in her room and study a little—everything was so easy—but mostly she'd look out the window. Her parents didn't want her company; children were to be seen, not heard or really spoken to. Her parents didn't want each other's company, either, and most nights one or the other of them was out. That didn't bother Beth, because she believed that was the way everyone's parents were.

So Beth would sit alone in her window seat, looking over the darkened back lawn, which sloped down to the ocean. The lawn was vast and green and empty. It did not have a swing set or even a patio. The house ended, and there was just green and then endless water, as if the world were waiting to swallow the house whole.

Beth did not play on the lawn. She didn't practice cartwheels on the grass or go down to the ocean and put her toes in the cold water, balancing in her bare feet on the wet rocks. She didn't take her dolls out there to have tea or pretend she was an explorer with her stuffed animals as her assistants. She wasn't expressly forbidden to do those things—her parents paid little attention to what she did, even when they were home—but the fact was, she didn't want to. The lawn wasn't a good place.

There was no part of this house that was a good place, really.

But still, people said she was lucky. She was. The house so beautiful, so big. The fact that it wasn't good didn't seem to matter to the people who told her she was lucky. Those people didn't have to live here.

If someone had asked her—which no one did—what exactly was wrong about the house, she couldn't have said. There weren't creaks or cobwebs or groaning ghosts. It was something about the high ceilings, the elaborate moldings, the slightly off angles of the rooms when you walked down the corridors. There was an older house that had been partly torn down and remodeled into a newer one, and the old house didn't like it. It was still in pain. It was a silly, childish thing to believe, and yet when she lay in bed at night, she imagined it was true.

Her father, in some before-Beth-was-born renovation, had had plate glass windows put in the living room, overlooking the lawn, and then had floor-to-ceiling curtains installed over them, as if he found that he couldn't quite bring himself to look out the windows he'd bought. Beth never asked him why, because she didn't like looking out those windows, either. When she peeked behind the curtains during the rain—and it rained much of the time—the water flattened on the glass and made shapes in the wind, reminding her of palms and fingers running down the glass. The lawn beyond was as empty as if all of humanity had vanished, and the dark gray ocean in the distance looked angry. There was something about the view that made it feel like the house was a ship sailing over the edge of the world.

In the living room the sofa, low and squat and square, didn't match the intricately carved fireplace mantel that looked like it was from a century ago. None of the art—modern splashes of paint on canvas that were expensive and were supposed to represent something or other—looked right on the walls. The house was her father's; the attempt at decorating was her mother's. Much like her parents' marriage, none of it went together. And none of it was Beth's. Her room was girlish, but it was subdued. There were no play areas or places for a little girl to run around in the Greer mansion. Another thing Beth assumed was normal.

From her bedroom window upstairs, she could see trees at the edges of the lawn and the roofs of the houses on either side. Upstairs felt less like drowning, and her room was her own. With no one to talk to but her dolls, she had no idea she was lonely, because she had never known anything else. Until the day she saw the footprints.

It was an early morning, sometime around Thanksgiving. Beth woke early; maybe she'd heard a sound, unusual in the silent house. The sky was chalky gray, and for once it wasn't raining. Pulling herself out of bed, Beth went to her bedroom window.

The lawn was laced with dew, wet and silver. Marring the dew, a set of footprints crossed the grass.

The prints were made by small feet, maybe a little larger than her own. Barefoot. A child not much older than herself had come from the left side of the lawn, approached the plate glass windows. Walked along them, as if looking in. And then, as if frustrated by the curtains, the prints circled back the way they had come and vanished.

Beth stared at the footprints in silence. Against the carpet of her bedroom, her bare toes curled. The dew would be cold this time of year, just barely liquid, almost icy frost. It would be numbing on bare feet. There were no children in the neighboring houses on either side. Where had a child come from?

She left her room and went downstairs, moving quietly through the silent house. Her father had left last night, but her mother was home. Her mother was an insomniac who regularly slept until eleven o'clock or noon, and the house had no servants. In her pink and white nightgown, her hair down her back, Beth walked through the gloom to the plate glass windows in the living room.

She pulled back the edge of the heavy curtains. The footprints were still there in the dew, just outside the glass. And at eye level, as if the child who made the prints had blown hot breath on the glass and written in the fog, were the words:

I WAS HERE

It took Beth a moment to realize that for the words to be readable, the child outside would have had to write them backward. Which she had done, flawlessly.

How she knew the other child was a girl, she couldn't have said. She just knew.

A pulse began to beat in Beth's neck. The house around her was dark and silent, her mother still asleep. There was no one around, no one to talk to, probably for hours. Just Beth and her dolls.

She leaned forward and blew on the glass until a patch of fog came up. Then, writing carefully backward herself, she wrote her own message:

COME IN.

CHAPTER TWENTY-SEVEN

December 1960

BETH

Christmas, for the other kids on the school bus, was exciting. It meant presents and sweets and, most importantly, school break. Today was the last day before the Christmas holiday, and they were on their way home.

Beth sat alone, looking out the window and listening to the boisterous shouts and laughter of the other children. Though she had a thick wool coat and an expensive pair of shoes, a fine wool scarf wound around her neck and matching mittens, she was cold. The damp chill seeped up from her feet and shivered through her body. Her fingertips were numb.

There was no snow outside, but it was still Christmassy. Downtown, the stores were lit up with shopping displays, and the school was decorated with the kids' drawings. In January, the damp paint-soaked papers would be drooping from the walls, and they'd be sent home with the kids for their parents to put away. Beth would throw hers in the garbage. But today, on the last day of school before Christmas, even the cold chill of the school had felt almost festive.

The dark was setting in, clouds covering what little light the sun gave off before it quickly set. The houses in the neighborhood had their Christmas lights up, the red, green, and blue winking as the bus passed by. Beth sat in silence, watching. None of the other kids spoke to her, which was how she liked it. At the beginning of the school year, two of the older girls had bullied her, calling her "rich girl"—a stupid insult, since there were no poor children at their school. But the older girls were determined to pick on Beth, and eventually there was a fight, and Beth got a bloody nose. The school called her mother, who took over an hour to come and take Beth home. She had smelled like she did after her "day drinks," as she called them, and she shouted slurred abuse at the teachers, the principal, and the girls in the yard, calling them profane words. No one bullied Beth after that. No one wanted to be her friend, either.

Today there were no Christmas lights on the Greer house, but the windows were lit up, which was a surprise. Often Beth got off the bus to an empty house, which she entered using the key on a chain around her neck. Sometimes one parent or the other was home—rarely both. But it looked like they were both home today, early for them on a Friday afternoon, and even as Beth got off the bus and approached the house, she could tell that something was going on.

The thought didn't give her any feeling of anticipation. She didn't expect a party or any holiday cheer. There had been something wrong over the past week. Her grandmother had died, and Beth had heard her parents arguing downstairs late into the night, their voices tight and angry. She'd heard her mother crying, and her father saying, *Jesus Christ, Mariana, what a goddamned mess you've made.* Her mother's teary, furious answer was: *I want to see her. Just once. I want to see her.*

Beth didn't know what that meant. The housekeepers came once a week and the house was as neat as ever, so there was no mess. And her mother could see Beth anytime she wanted.

Looking at the lit-up windows in the lowering dark, she had the feeling she was about to learn what the goddamned mess was.

She walked into the front hall on cold, numb feet. In the living room, the lights and the lamps were on. The curtains were closed. Beth unwound her scarf and walked into the room. Her mother was sitting in one of the orange-upholstered chairs, while her father stood by the window, a drink in his hand, his back to the curtains. As Beth walked into the room, neither parent looked at her.

In the corner of the room was a Christmas tree, a real one, giving off a cold, pungent pine scent. It had been delivered today, set up by someone hired to do so, and it wasn't yet decorated. There were no gifts beneath it. The tree sat in shadow, out of place and a little sinister.

Sitting on the sofa, the one that matched her mother's chair, was a girl.

She was a year or two older than Beth, perhaps. She had blond hair, long and straight, combed neatly down her back. She wore a navy blue skirt and a blue and white checked blouse, dark knee socks, black oxfords on her feet. Her hands were folded politely in her lap. She looked at Beth and smiled.

"Hi there," the girl said.

"Beth." Her mother turned in her chair, smiling, as if she'd just realized Beth was there. The smile was tenuous, mostly sober but not quite. Mariana had put her hair up, and she wore a string of pearls around her neck. Beth had not seen that string of pearls since the last time her mother had tried to go to church, at Easter. She had put them on with her dress and then gone back to bed and fallen asleep when whatever pill she'd taken that morning kicked in. "Hi there, honey. I'm so glad you're home. This is your cousin Lillian."

Beth stared in shock. She didn't have a cousin Lillian; she didn't have any cousins at all. Her father was an only child—hence the large inheritance—and her mother had a sister who was dead. Lillian was Beth's middle name. But she could see no hint of a lie in her mother's fragile smile, her father's blank face. She looked back at the girl.

"Hello," she said obediently.

"It's nice to meet you," Lillian said.

"She's come to stay for Christmas." This was her mother again, her fingertips rubbing the pearls around her neck. "Isn't that nice? You'll have a little playmate. Two sweet, matching girls. The two of you can be friends."

By the window, her father made a disgusted sound and took a sip of his drink.

"I like dolls," Lillian said. "Do you like dolls?"

Beth looked at her, and for a long moment nothing else existed. Her parents, with all of their terrible grown-up problems and confusing undercurrents, were gone. The half-lit room in this uneasy house was gone. Even the chill in her feet, in her bones, was gone. There was only her and Lillian.

"I like dolls," she said.

Lillian slid off the sofa, as if she agreed that the two adults in the room didn't exist. "Good," she said. "Let's play."

"How old are you?" Beth asked Lillian when they were in her room. Now that they were alone, surrounded by Beth's actual dolls, the new girl seemed to have lost interest in playing. Instead she looked around Beth's room, touching the bed and the pillow, looking in her drawers. Beth sat on the edge of the bed, watching in fascination.

"Eight," Lillian said. Her blond hair was so perfect it shimmered in the gloomy light. She picked up one of Beth's books—an old Dick and Jane from when she was learning to read, which suddenly made her feel like a baby—and flipped through the pages. "Are all of these things yours?"

"Yes."

"Why are you here by yourself?" Lillian put the book back and picked up a teddy bear, turning it over, pressing her fingers into its neck as if she thought something might be inside. "Don't you have any friends?"

Beth blinked. She watched Lillian's pale, elegant hands pressing into her teddy bear's fur. She couldn't even be offended at the intrusion; she felt, as Lillian obviously did, like Lillian had a right to be here. "No, I don't have any friends."

"Why not?"

"I got beat up at school by bigger girls, and my mother came."

She didn't explain the rest of the story, and it seemed that she didn't need to. Lillian nodded as if she knew what the rest of the story was already. "That's because you didn't take care of it yourself," she said.

"How?" Beth asked.

"You make them afraid of you." Lillian squeezed the teddy bear's neck briefly, then put it down. "Then they won't pick on you anymore. It's easy. I'll show you how."

"No one is afraid of me," Beth said.

"They will be." Lillian picked up Beth's most precious ornament, a jewelry box with a ballerina on the top. "I'm going to help you," she said matter-of-factly, looking closely at the ballerina. "You're very lucky."

Beth swallowed. She had the sudden feeling that Lillian was going to throw the jewelry box to the floor, smash it just because she could. She could almost picture it, the shards of pretty china, the broken ballerina skidding in pieces beneath the bed. She thought it might have something to do with the lesson of making people afraid. But still she didn't stand up and grab the box away.

"Where did you come from?" Beth asked.

"Nowhere," Lillian said, still holding the box. "I live with some

people who don't care about me. I don't live in a nice house like this."
She didn't sound happy about it.

"Why are you here?"

Lillian looked at her. Her eyes, Beth noticed, were gray-green,
her lashes dark. "I wanted to come here," she said. "I've been here
before."

And suddenly Beth remembered. The footprints in the dew, the
words on the window: *I WAS HERE.* She hadn't seen the girl who'd
made those words, but suddenly she was sure. "That was you?" she
asked, her voice a whisper.

Lillian frowned, for the first time looking a little uncertain. "I
knew about this house," she said. "I wanted to come here. And one
night, I thought about it as I went to sleep, and . . . I think I dreamed it."

Beth was excited now. "Yes," she said. "I saw you. Your footprints."

"My feet were so cold," Lillian said. "I couldn't find a way in. I
couldn't see in the windows. I had to give up and go back to the trees.
And then I saw you." She looked at Beth. "Sometimes I imagine things
that aren't real. But you saw me that night, and I saw you. You told me
to come in." She smiled. "And here I am. Now we can be sisters."

Beth's heart was pumping hard in her chest. This was wonderful
and terrible at the same time. It was going to be a nightmare, and it
was also going to be the best thing that ever happened to her. She
knew that already. Her life was starting.

"Who are you?" she asked the strange girl.

"I'm Lillian," the girl replied. "That's your name, too, isn't it?"

"It's my middle name," Beth said. She was Elizabeth Lillian Greer.

"Like you were named after me," Lillian said. "I think that's nice,
but no one ever calls me Lillian. Everyone calls me Lily."

CHAPTER TWENTY-EIGHT

December 1960

BETH

That first year, when Lily came to stay, there was no real Christmas. Beth's parents usually made an attempt at the holidays, with a lot of spiked eggnog, a few expensive presents for Beth, and a meal cooked on the twenty-fourth by the housekeeping staff and eaten the next day. It wasn't fun, but it was something.

But that year, the tree sat in its shadowy corner, pungent and undecorated. No presents ever appeared. The girls played in Beth's room while Beth's parents had some kind of awful fight downstairs, carried out in angry, snarled tones. Sometime in the middle of the night two days before Christmas, her father left the house, the door slamming behind him. Lying in her bed, squeezed next to Lily, Beth listened to his car start up and drive away.

In the silent dark, Lily spoke. "We don't need him," she said. "Go to sleep."

The next morning, Beth's mother found them in the kitchen. Her hair was done, and she had makeup on, though her eyes were red. She was wearing a red sweater and a plaid skirt that fell below the knee, as if she thought she might go to a Christmas party. "I'm going shopping," she said, her voice dull. She put on her coat, picked up her purse, and left the house.

She was gone for three days.

No one had told the housekeeping staff to cook a Christmas meal, so there wasn't one. The girls were left alone in the house as the wet snow fell outside and melted on the cold grass. The first day, they raided the kitchen, eating cookies and drinking chocolate milk. They watched TV until late and went to bed after midnight. Beth jumped at every sound, expecting one or both of her parents back any minute to shout at them for being bad, but they never came.

On Christmas morning, the girls ate more chocolate and played dolls and dress-up. They raced each other around the yard, churning up the wet snow as the ocean roared at the bottom of the cliff. Beth thought of the other kids from school, and she knew that she wasn't having the right kind of Christmas, a normal kind of Christmas. She didn't unwrap gifts or leave cookies for Santa. She didn't have turkey. It felt sad, but then she and Lily popped popcorn six times, smothering it with butter and eating it all day until they went to bed.

I should miss them, she thought as she and Lily jumped from the coffee table with their arms outstretched, seeing which one of them could touch the ceiling first. And she did miss her parents, a little. But she didn't miss the watchfulness, the waiting for the moment when her parents started politely snapping at each other, forgetting that she was in the room. She didn't miss having to tiptoe everywhere, remembering never to touch anything or ask for anything or make any noise, because she was supposed to be seen and not heard. She didn't miss lying alone in bed in this strange house, wondering why she was so afraid of it, of beams and roofs and windows, as if she and the house hated each other.

"You're not really my cousin, are you?" Beth asked that night as they wound the bedcovers around themselves and ate the last of the candy they'd found in the pantry.

"No, I'm not." Lily's profile was perfect as she snapped off a small bite of chocolate. "You don't have a cousin."

"Then who are your parents?"

"I live with foster parents," Lily said. "This is the second family I've lived with. I'll probably live with a different one next year."

Beth had never imagined meeting a real-life orphan instead of reading about them in books. "Where are your real parents?" she asked.

Lily thought this over. "My mother is alive," she said. "My father, I don't know. Maybe he's dead. If he isn't, I plan to find him someday."

"What about your mother? Do you plan to find her?"

Lily thought about this again. "My mother doesn't want me," she said. "But maybe she has no choice."

The next day, they ran out of cookies, so they tried baking cookies themselves from a recipe book that was stacked under the sink, the pages stuck together with disuse. Beth singed a finger when she opened the hot oven, so the girls turned the oven off and ate the uncooked batter instead. There was a brief fight that day, when Lily took a doll Beth wanted to play with. Lily won.

Beth's mother came home, still wearing the red sweater and the plaid skirt. Her hair had been taken down and put up again, and her mascara had dribbled into raccoon bruises beneath her eyes. She looked around the mess of the house, at the two girls sitting on the living room sofa, surrounded by blankets they'd pulled off the bed.

"How sweet," she said. "It looks like you two had fun. I'm sorry . . . I'm sorry I wasn't home for Christmas."

"It's okay," Beth said. Her mother had been so sad ever since Beth's grandmother died. She'd probably just gone off to be sad somewhere, Beth decided, since Lily was here to keep her company. It wouldn't be much of a Christmas if your mother had just died.

Beth had explained this to Lily, who had given her a blank look. Beth had to remember that Lily didn't understand anything about mothers.

Her mother looked past Beth at Lily and said her name, the word seeming to twist in her throat. "Lillian . . ."

"Yes, Mrs. Greer?" Lillian asked sweetly.

Mariana just looked at her. Beth noticed that Lily and her mother had the same color hair, the same pretty blond.

"Nothing," Mariana said after a moment. "You two sweet girls have fun." She went upstairs, and Beth heard her parents' bedroom door click shut.

Beth's father came home the next day, ragged, tired. He looked at Beth and said, "Housekeeping will be here in an hour. Have them clean up this mess." Then he turned to Lily. "Pack your bags. You're going home."

"No!" Beth cried.

"Shut up," her father said, and even though he wasn't a very warm father, even though he expected her to be neat and quiet and never play, he'd never said those words to her before. He turned to Lily again and said, "You have five minutes. I'll have a taxi at the door to take you to wherever you're going."

Lily looked up at him with wide, sweet eyes. "Yes, Mr. Greer," she said.

Beth followed Lily upstairs to pack. She felt like crying, but Lily was unperturbed. She didn't even seem concerned that she was being sent out into the world, into a taxi, alone, at age eight. Beth didn't want to cry in front of her, didn't want to seem like a baby.

"Will you come back?" she asked as Lily slung her single cloth bag, filled with only a few clothes and a toothbrush, over her shoulder.

"Yes," Lily said. "They can't keep me from this house. No one can."

Over dinner one night a week later, Beth asked her mother and father who Lily's parents were.

Mariana glanced at Julian, then looked back at Beth. "I'm glad you two are such good friends," she said, touching Beth's hair. "And Lily doesn't have parents. Isn't that sad?"

"Everyone has parents," Beth said. "Kids don't come from storks. I know that now."

"Well, no, she didn't come from a stork," Mariana said, picking up her fork and studying the silver tines. "Goodness. I don't know who you've been talking to about babies. I'll have to call the school and ask what they're teaching these days. I meant that Lillian's parents are dead."

"But who are they?" Beth said. "Did you know them? Is that why she came to visit?"

Mariana looked uncertain. "Yes," she said. "I knew them. Lillian's mother was a friend of mine, but she's dead now, and I feel bad for that little girl. She's practically your cousin. Okay?"

At the other side of the table, Beth's father put his fork down and pushed his chair back. He walked out of the dining room without a word.

Beth knew her mother was lying to her, because Lily had said that her mother wasn't dead at all. Her father knew she was lying, too.

But Mariana pretended that nothing was wrong, even though everything was wrong, just like she always did. "He's just angry," she said of Julian, smiling and touching Beth's hair again. "He doesn't like little girls the way I do."

CHAPTER TWENTY-NINE

December 1961

BETH

Lily was as good as her word. She came back to the Greer mansion the next Christmas. And the next.

At first, every year for months and months, life went on as usual and Lily wasn't mentioned. Then, as the darkness of winter set in, Mariana's mood would begin to spiral down and she'd drink more. There would be more day drinks, which would start earlier and earlier, more arguments that Beth could hear as she lay in bed at night, because her parents thought that if they argued after she went to bed, she wouldn't hear them. As if they could fool her into thinking they had a happy family if they only argued after she was supposedly asleep.

Then, like clockwork, Mariana would get excited about Christmas. She'd decide that Christmas was going to be wonderful this year and it was going to solve all of her problems. She'd go shopping and buy stacks of decorations that she never put up. She'd go looking for the biggest, most expensive Christmas tree. And she'd invite Lily to visit. If Lily's foster family had any objections—which was unlikely—their objections would vanish at Mariana's influence and her money. Mostly her money.

Lily always came, sleek and beautiful as a cat, her blond hair brushed soft and shining. She'd be polite and talk about how grateful she was, but as she spoke she'd lock eyes with Julian, and the two of them would stare each other down. Then Julian would pack a bag, say he was going to visit friends, and he'd leave the house.

Beth learned early that Lily and Julian hated each other. She had to learn it. The undercurrents in the house at Christmas were too deep, too important, and she needed both Julian and Lily for survival. She couldn't afford to lose either one, so she made strategies to appease both of them. She didn't talk about Lily in Julian's presence, because if she did he'd simply get up and leave the room. She made one attempt to win Lily over to Julian's side by telling her that her father was actually very nice, that once you got to know him he was kind.

Lily only looked at Beth with dead, flat eyes. "Your father would let me die in the street like a stray dog," she said. "But he can't, so that's too bad for him."

Beth didn't talk to her about Julian after that.

Some Christmases, Mariana left the house after her husband did, and the two girls played alone. A TV was installed in the living room one year, and that Christmas, Beth and Lily watched *My Three Sons* and *Bonanza* and *Bewitched*. There were cartwheel competitions on the back lawn, but Lily always got closer to the edge of the drop than Beth did. No matter how close Beth got—it was part of the competition—Lily always got so close it was scary, her sneakers sliding almost over the precipice when she landed. Every competition they had went the same way, with Lily pushing and Beth sick with fear, until Beth learned, over and over, not to let the fear bother her.

Other years, Mariana stayed home at Christmas. She tried playing board games and baking cookies with them, things she never did when Beth was here alone. She pretended that Christmas was cheerful and that everything was fun. She read them stories, most of which were for little girls, younger than Beth and Lily, but they listened anyway. She played made-up games with them.

"Once upon a time, there were two little girls," she'd say. "They were kidnapped by an evil witch who wanted to eat them, but one of them was bitter and one of them was sweet. Which girl is which, do you think?"

Beth always wanted to be the sweet girl, of course. But no matter how sweet she was, Mariana never played these games when Lily wasn't here. Besides, even though Mariana never told the end of the story, Beth knew the sweet girl was the one who got eaten. The bitter girl was the one who survived.

Lily was Beth's best friend. Her only friend, really. Beth didn't need anyone else, because Lily knew everything. Lily knew what sex was before Beth did; she knew what death was; she knew which adults were stupid and which were even remotely worth listening to. She knew how to handle the other kids at school. She taught Beth when to fight, when to suck up, and when to flirt, even with other girls. "She's easy," Lily said when Beth described one particular classmate. "Pretend you like her, and you'll get what you want."

"I don't like her," Beth said.

"For thirty seconds, you do. Smile at her like you would a boy." Lily snapped her fingers. "Now she'll do what you say."

It worked. Everything Lily told Beth to do worked.

When Beth was ten, a group of boys in her class noticed her. Beth was tall by then, with long red hair and wide eyes. The boys would corner her in the playground, pinch her and poke her, call her names. Try to push her down.

"It's because you're pretty," Lily, who was twelve, said when Beth complained about this problem. "Get used to it."

"I *hate* being a girl," Beth said, throwing her favorite doll across her bedroom. She'd boxed up most of her dolls the year before but had kept this one out because she loved it so much. Now she'd get rid of it. "I hate it. Being a girl is awful."

Lily only looked at her with that flat, dead expression she sometimes had in her eyes, as if she felt absolutely nothing—good, bad, nothing at all. "Being a girl is the best," she said, "because no one ever believes you'd do something bad. People think you'll do nothing, which means you can do anything. I'll show you."

That night, they snuck out at midnight and went to the school, their boots crunching in the snow. With Beth's hopscotch chalk, they wrote bad words on the wall of the school—words that Beth knew in theory but had never said aloud. They wrote them in blocky letters that didn't look like loopy, girlish letters. When Beth got back to school after the break, she found that the boys had been questioned about the swear words, and two of them had gotten in trouble for it. No one ever asked questions of the girls.

Beth felt a little bit bad about that. But she knew what Lily would say: that the boys shouldn't have bullied her in the first place. And really, Lily was right. Beth was a fast learner.

The Christmas Beth was twelve and Lily was fourteen, Mariana stayed home. They played Snakes and Ladders, which the girls were too old for, and Mariana drank through the entire game. By the end, she was slurring her words, tilted over on the sofa, drunk. The girls helped her upstairs to her bed, where she promptly fell asleep.

In the dim light of the bedroom, as half-frozen rain pelted the window, Lily looked down at Mariana, sprawled on the pillow. Beth watched Lily's face, her eyes, as Lily watched the woman on the bed. Beth stared at the shape of Lily's nose and chin, which were so like Mariana's.

She had always known, deep down. Even when she didn't understand how babies were made, when she didn't understand anything about her own mother or her parents' angry and complicated relationship, she had known. She still didn't understand everything, but she'd guessed enough. "Your parents aren't dead, are they?" she asked Lily, her voice soft, so as not to wake Mariana.

"No," Lily said, still looking down. "They're not. That's just a lie your mother told you."

"*Our* mother."

The words hung there, meaning everything, changing everything. Beth's feelings were enormous, too big for her to contain: excitement, dread, guilt, shame. But when Lily looked up at her, she saw no answering emotions in Lily's eyes. She simply looked blank again.

"She doesn't want you to know," Lily said. "She brings me here every Christmas because she feels bad for abandoning me. It's always too much for her. Then she does it all over again."

Beth made the words come out, the ones that were harder to say. "And my father?"

"He isn't my father," Lily said bluntly. "I don't know who my father is. I don't know where he is. I don't think he's dead. I don't know what happened between them or why. I plan to find out."

"Maybe she'll tell us someday," Beth said. But they both looked down at the sleeping woman, her sprayed hair stiff on the pillow, and they knew it wouldn't happen. Whatever had occurred was so deep inside Mariana that maybe she'd made herself forget it was there.

"She isn't his," Lily said, talking about Julian and Mariana. "She's mine."

No, *she's mine*, Beth thought. *I'm the real daughter, the one she had after she was married, the good girl. The sweet one.* But she already knew she had lost that battle. There was no question about Mariana belonging to Beth. She belonged to the bitter girl, the one who wouldn't be eaten.

"So what do we do?" she asked Lily—who was her half sister, and not her cousin or a distant family friend, which was how Mariana referred to her whenever she spoke about her to other adults. If any of the other adults suspected the truth, they were too polite to say anything. "Do we just keep pretending we don't know?"

Lily reached out and traced a finger down the side of Mariana's face. Beth fought off the instinct to punch her hand away, to prevent Lily from ever touching her mother. "For now," she said, answering Beth's question. "It doesn't matter, really. I'm going to get what I want. Everything I want."

"What do you want?" Was it to live here? To be a real daughter? Beth didn't know if that was possible, or if Lily even would. Living here would mean living with Julian.

"I want lots of things," Lily said. She looked around. "This house, for one."

Beth had no idea how fourteen-year-old Lily would get this house, but she said, "I hate this house."

"That's because you don't understand it."

"It's ugly."

"It's an abomination that shouldn't exist," Lily said, "and it knows it. That's why I like it. It's exactly like me."

"You can't own a house," Beth said, tentative because she didn't want Lily to get angry. "You're too young."

"Not for long." Lily looked at Beth, really looked at her for the first time in a long time. "What do *you* want?"

I want you to get away from my mother, she thought. *I want you to leave and never come back.* But, no, she didn't mean that. Beth was just afraid. She'd be lonely and desolate if she didn't have Lily.

She needed Lily. Just like she needed Julian and Mariana. Beth had to get through another day, and another year, and she needed all three of them to get there. But she needed Lily most of all.

So she said the one thing she knew would work, the one thing that Lily was susceptible to. The one thing that would keep Lily on her side. "I want to be like you," she said.

There was a moment when she wasn't quite sure Lily believed it. And then her sister smiled.

CHAPTER THIRTY

December 1968

BETH

The Christmas Beth was fourteen, Lily came to the Greer house with a bruise on her temple and faded yellowy green marks under the skin of her cheekbone. Mariana pretended not to notice, but later that night both of the girls could hear her sobbing in her bedroom as Julian told her to stop, please stop. *It's my fault*, Mariana said. *All my fault.*

Lily didn't want to talk about it, but Beth knew that something had happened at her foster home. Lily wasn't above faking bruises to get sympathy, but she wasn't faking this. That year, she was quieter than usual and her eyes were hollow, her mouth set tight.

Surprisingly, Julian stayed home that year, the first Christmas he'd done so since Lily had first visited. Something about seeing Lily bruised and angry must have made him feel more comfortable having her around, as if she'd lost a round in their endless contest. They avoided each other and barely spoke, but Beth saw Lily's gaze follow Julian whenever she saw him, and she didn't like the look in Lily's eyes.

That was the year David disappeared.

David was a groundskeeper. In the summer, there was a small crew of men who came to maintain the lawns and the gardens, but in the winter there was only David. He came at the end of every month and spent a few hours cutting out dead annuals, removing any snow and ice on the ground, and raking old leaves. He was supposed to come the day after Christmas, but he never showed. As days passed, it became clear that he was gone, and no one knew what had happened to him. Maybe he had suddenly left town. He was just a grounds-keeper, though, so it was considered a minor mystery, shrugged off by Julian and Mariana and never spoken of again.

Lily went home on the twenty-eighth, and for once Beth was glad to see her go, glad to be free of the flat look in Lily's eyes.

They didn't find David until late April, his broken body on the rocks below the cliff. They couldn't pinpoint how long he'd been there, but it had been months. It was declared a suicide, but Beth had an uneasy feeling in her stomach. Lily . . . But she had never seen Lily anywhere near David, never seen her look at him or talk to him. So, no, it wasn't possible. What would be the reason? There wasn't one.

Beth put her suspicions away and didn't think about them anymore.

The next year, Lily's bruises were gone and she was thinner, her cheekbones sharper, her hipbones as hard as diamonds. She was seventeen, a year from aging out of the foster system. "My new family barely pays any attention to me," she said. "They let me do whatever I want."

"What happened to your old family?" Beth asked.

"Bad things," Lily said, and for the first time in months, Beth thought of David again.

"What bad things?" she asked as fear curled into the pit of her stomach.

Lily only shook her head. "It doesn't matter. People do bad things to themselves. It's their own fault. Let's go do a cartwheel race on the lawn."

They hadn't done cartwheel races for a few years, and Beth didn't really want to go near the edge of the drop right now, when she was thinking of David down there, his bones broken. But she went, and she cartwheeled close to the edge, the cold air and the excitement making her breath come short. After a while, she forgot about David again.

That night, the half sisters sat in Beth's new room—she'd graduated a few years ago from her little-girl room to a teenager's room down the hall, though the little-girl room was still intact—and listened to records on Beth's record player. Lily sat cross-legged on Beth's newer, bigger bed, her legs slim and flawless in her tight jeans, her breasts obvious beneath the fabric of her striped turtleneck, making the black and blue stripes bend into wonky shapes. "I've got something for you," she said.

Beth looked up from the Neil Diamond record she was putting on the player—Lily said she had atrocious taste in music, but Beth disagreed—and saw that Lily was holding her hand out, and there was a small white pill in her palm.

"Take it," she said.

Beth looked at it warily. She and Lily regularly stole from Julian and Mariana's well-stocked liquor cabinet, and had for years, but Beth had no experience with pills. "What does it do?"

"It makes you high, silly," Lily said. "Like really high. It's better than anything else I've tried."

Beth didn't want to get high. She wanted to play records and get drunk when her parents weren't guarding the liquor cabinet. Being high with Lily sounded like something that wasn't terribly fun. "I don't know."

Lily's gaze went darker, flatter. "Take it."

Saying no to Lily was always a tricky proposition. You had to do it the right way. "It would probably destroy me," Beth said. "Obliterate me completely. You know what a lightweight I am."

Lily laughed—she was susceptible to compliments, but you had to use the right tone so she didn't suspect you were lying. "You are," she said. "You'd probably be halfway to California before you came down." She put the pill away, and Beth breathed a silent sigh of relief.

She didn't think Lily should be taking the pills, either, whatever they were. But she wasn't going to start nagging her half sister. That would be pushing things too far. With Lily, it was all about balance.

A few hours later, they took Beth's bicycle out of the garage in the middle of the night. They went to a neighbor's house, where the girl who lived there had just left for college, and broke into the unlocked garage. Lily took the absent girl's bicycle, and they went for a ride, pumping up the hills and coasting down in the wet, freezing-cold neighborhood, flying by the dark houses while the rich people inside slept.

Each girl had brought a bottle of wine—Lily red, Beth white. "Which girl is bitter, and which girl is sweet?" Lily said, mimicking Mariana's old game when she saw the wine Beth had picked. "Little girls can't be both, you know. They have to be one or the other."

"We also have to be eaten, apparently," Beth said. "It's all we're good for."

The wind was cold on Beth's cheeks as they rode, cold enough to hurt and make her eyes water, but she loved it. She loved that the drizzle soaked her wool hat and the ends of her hair, and that her fingers went numb on the handlebars right through her mittens. In those hours in the middle of the night at Christmas, the girls had the world to themselves. They could be anything, do anything, and there was no one to stop them.

"What do you want to be?" Lily asked her when they paused, leaning their bikes on a wet park bench so they could take swigs of wine. "An actress? A singer? What?"

Beth shrugged. Her future was a blank. She was pretty enough, but she had no particular talent in one thing or another. She couldn't sing or dance or write. Hollywood had exploded with movies like *Butch Cassidy and the Sundance Kid* and *Easy Rider*, but those movies were about men. She'd read a copy of *On the Road* that she'd swiped from the library, looking for the glamour and forbidden excitement, but all she could see in it was a bunch of boys driving around, showing up at their girlfriends' when they needed a place to stay. Beth didn't want to be a girlfriend who took in a broke boy and fed him, gave him money, and had sex with him before he went off to other adventures and other women. That didn't sound like freedom, like free love. It sounded like a bore.

"You need to be *something*," Lily said.

"Why?"

"Because otherwise your parents are going to marry you off by the time you're nineteen, and you'll have a baby by twenty. And that will be it." She gave Beth a flat stare. "Then again, maybe that's what you want."

That made Beth briefly furious, a flash of anger that made her see red. "I won't," she said. "I won't end up like our mother. And I won't get pregnant like she did, either."

"Yes, you will. You'll even get a husband, a man who makes a lot of money and will take your virginity for you, though I guarantee you won't enjoy it. It won't be any fun at all."

There were no words to describe how terrifying that thought was, how it made a black hole of panic open up in the pit of her stomach. She had so many feelings for Mariana—love, desperation, disdain, anger—but she did not want to end up like her. Repeating Mariana's life was the worst thing that could happen.

But Lily wasn't completely wrong. Beth took a long swig of wine, hoping it would dampen the terror.

"We need to talk about money," Lily said.

Beth frowned. "What?"

"Money," Lily said again. She took a sip of her wine, but she didn't seem drunk, while Beth felt her head start to spin. "I'll be eighteen soon, and I'll be out of the foster system. How much money will Mariana give me, do you think?"

Beth wasn't following. "Mariana is going to give you money?"

"Of course she is," Beth said. "She has to. She feels bad about me, remember? I'll have to figure out how much I'll need. She has plenty."

"Mariana doesn't have money," Beth said.

"Sure, she does. She goes shopping all the time and her wallet is always full of cash."

That was true. They'd seen the money come out of the wallet plenty of times. "That's my father's money," Beth said. "He gives her an allowance."

For the first time in a long time, Lily actually looked surprised, and the surprise wasn't pleasant. "Beth, what are you talking about? Mariana's family is just as rich as Julian's."

Beth took another drink of wine. "That's true, but Mariana is the only one left. And her mother left all of her money to Julian."

"To *Julian*?"

Beth nodded. "I heard them talking about it. Our grandmother thought it was best that her husband look after all of it because our mother doesn't know how to handle money. So he got all the money, and he gives Mariana an allowance." She had never really thought about this before; her parents had never argued about it, both of them accepting it as the natural order of things. But she could tell by Lily's face that something was wrong. "What is it?"

Lily looked off into the darkness, her breath pluming, her skin pale against the night. "Damn it," she said softly to herself. "I'd laugh if it wasn't so fucking tragic."

Beth felt her jaw drop at the word. Lily had no problem swearing, but even she rarely used the f-word. "Lily?"

"God damn it," Lily said.

Beth was starting to get scared—drunk and scared—so she said, "Can we talk about something else now?"

Lily's eyes had that cold look that made Beth want to get back on her bike and flee. "Of course you don't want to talk about money," she said. "You have all the money. From Julian, from Mariana. I bet you have a trust fund, don't you?"

"Not until I'm twenty-one," Beth said. "And it isn't a lot. I still have to get an allowance from my father."

"An allowance," Lily said. She took a step toward Beth, pulled a glove off. "You're going to get an allowance and marry a rich man, and someday when Julian is dead you'll get that, too. And me? I'll just disappear."

Beth watched Lily's bare hand. Something about it disturbed her. She was so drunk, and she knew now that she shouldn't have talked about this, shouldn't have told Lily those things, but she couldn't say why. "You won't disappear," Beth argued. "You'll stay here. You'll have Mariana and me."

"Will you let me visit at Christmas?" Lily asked. Her hand touched Beth's hair where it came out from beneath her wool hat, stroked down the silky red strands. "Will I be allowed to sit on a chair in the living room if I stay quiet and wear my best dress?"

"What are you talking about?" She didn't like Lily touching her hair. Lily wasn't a toucher; she didn't like to be hugged, held, or even to hold hands. She found the touch of other people repugnant, but now she was running her fingertips down Beth's hair.

"Do you know what I think?" Lily said. "I think you'll marry some rich, boring man and decide you feel guilty about me. And you'll invite me over for Christmas, and when I get there you won't be able to think of a single thing to say."

Tears stung Beth's eyes, because that hurt. "You know that isn't true. I don't want to marry anyone."

"You will, though, and I'll be no one. I'll take more pills, and then I'll take the wrong pill and I won't be able to stop, and one day I'll take enough of them that I'll never wake up again. Because no one is coming to save us, Beth. We aren't little girls anymore, and it's time to face the fact that no one is coming to figure things out for us and make them better. We have to decide for ourselves or disappear into nothingness. Sometimes I think the only way to be someone is to do something bad."

Her fingers were still touching Beth's hair. Beth's hands were numb inside her gloves, and she didn't want the wine anymore. In this moment—despite the absurdity of it, despite the fact that there was no evidence and no reason—she could see Lily pushing David off that edge. In this mood, Lily was capable of anything. When she'd been home last year, when David disappeared, Lily had been seething with anger. And this year was worse. "Lily, you're scaring me."

"Women don't even get to do that, do we?" Lily said. "The really bad things. We get to be the girlfriend." Her voice rose, shrill. "'Oh, he seemed so nice. He seemed so charming. I never believed he could hurt anyone.' Why don't you ever hear of a woman in a clock tower?"

Beth was confused now. "Why would you want to go into a clock tower?"

The fingers stopped their stroking, and Lily put her hand back into her glove. "I wouldn't," she said. "I'd have no reason. Why don't we go home now? I think you're tired."

Beth *was* tired. And after Lily was gone yet again, that entire night, that strange conversation, seemed like a dream. Lily was a teenage girl, not a—whatever Beth had thought she was. It was ridiculous, really. No one would believe a pretty blond teenage girl was capable of truly bad things.

No one would believe that at all.

CHAPTER THIRTY-ONE

December 1970

BETH

The Christmas Beth was sixteen, Lily didn't visit. Mariana said that Lily was "busy," but Beth knew the truth: Lily wasn't invited. This year, Julian and Mariana took Beth to a Christmas party instead.

Mariana bought Beth a dress to wear. It was high-necked, sleeveless, dark green, belted at the waist, the hem falling to the floor. When Beth put it on, she looked like what she was: the daughter of Claire Lake's richest and most prestigious couple, a debutante with all the money in the world. She felt like a fraud, and she snuck a bottle of schnapps from her father's liquor cabinet and drank as much of it as she could before they left for the party.

She was worried sick about Lily. Lily had turned eighteen—a legal adult who didn't live with foster parents anymore. Had she moved out already? Where was she living? Beth would sneak Lily money if she knew where she was, how to reach her. But in the periods between Christmases, the girls had never had any contact. Part of this was Julian's rule, because he hated Lily and didn't want Beth to talk to her. But part of it was Lily herself. "You don't want anything to do with those people," she'd say about whatever foster family she was living with. "I don't want them talking to you on the phone or reading my letters. It's better for me that way."

Beth had respected that, even though she longed to talk to Lily sometimes. But now Lily was gone, and no one knew where. She hadn't even left a forwarding address. It hurt.

Julian drove to the party. He was wearing a tuxedo, his longish hair neatly combed, his face freshly shaved. Beth's father was handsome, but the creases around his eyes and the soft sag beginning in his jaw hinted at the truth: Life wasn't always easy on him. He spent more and more time at work, or golfing in summer, or "meeting with clients." Beth was old enough to wonder now if he had a girlfriend, or more than one. She was old enough to wonder where he went when he'd "visited friends" every Christmas of her childhood. She was old enough to wonder where her mother went, too, since she had no family to stay with, only "bridge friends," who didn't seem very friendly. She was also old enough to know that neither of them would ever tell her. Silence was a great talent of the Greer family.

Mariana had ironed her blond hair smooth and sprayed it into a perfect formation, rising from her hairline and sweeping back and down to her shoulders. Her dress was gold lamé; her coat, mink. Her eyes were made up so heavily she looked like she was in disguise, though the effect was also strangely sexual. Her elegant, narrow hands fidgeted in her lap, grasping for a cigarette as she stared silently out the passenger window.

Beth wished, for the first time, that she had one of Lily's little white pills. Maybe that would make her forget whatever was about to happen tonight.

"Remember your manners," Mariana said into the silence of the car, as if a conversation had just been happening. "These are people from your father's company. You have our reputation to maintain."

At the wheel, Julian snorted. Beth agreed with him. She couldn't imagine what kind of reputation Mariana thought they had.

"Just be nice," Mariana said, her voice thin with exasperation, like she was on the edge of tears. "Be *nice*. For once. That's all I ask."

In the back seat, Beth stared out the window, unable to look at her mother anymore. She'd skipped school for two weeks before the school finally called her mother and reported it. She hadn't had any reason to do it, except that school was boring and she was curious how long it would take for the school to get up its courage and call home. The result was predictable: Mariana showed up at the school, wearing her mink at eleven o'clock in the morning, demanding answers about where her daughter was. Claire Lake didn't have any private high schools, so Beth went to the public school, which made the scene even more exciting.

Beth knew that she should probably be embarrassed, but instead she'd felt a detached curiosity, because the whole thing was theater. No one, including Mariana, actually cared where Beth was. The school cared about pleasing the wealthiest family in town, and Mariana cared that Beth wasn't nice. It was all a drama, like on TV.

Lily was the only one who really cared about Beth, about whether Beth was happy, about whether she would get what she wanted. And now Lily wasn't coming. Most likely, now that she was an adult and not a helpless little girl, she would never be invited over again.

Beth wondered where Lily was right now.

The party was at another house in Arlen Heights, this one a large old-fashioned mansion with a circular drive. The house was lit from every window, and Beth could hear classical music as they pulled up.

"It's lovely," Mariana said as they got out of the car, an automatic compliment.

Julian snorted and said nothing. Beth agreed with her father again.

"Tom Fenegan will be here," Julian said. "I need to talk to him about a few things. I expect we'll spend part of the night in the study."

"Of course," Mariana said. "I haven't seen Helen in a long time. We'll need to catch up."

This was her parents' code: *I won't be spending the evening anywhere near you. Fine with me.* Beth blinked hard and followed her parents up the drive, trying not to wobble drunkenly on her high heels.

The air inside at the party was stiff, as if everyone had dressed up but no one actually wanted to be there. Beth spent half an hour with a glass of champagne in her hand, painfully drunk, sweating in her green dress, and wondering why she was here before the answer to the puzzle presented itself in front of her. He looked about nineteen, he was handsome, he was wearing a tux, and he was the son of the house. He introduced himself as Gray.

Beth shook his hand, aware that hers was ice-cold.

"I've been told to introduce myself," Gray admitted amiably as he stood next to her. "I can't say I mind, because you're pretty. Also, we're the youngest people here. Pretty boring, huh?"

He had the easy manner of a boy who had known from birth that he'd own everything—knowledge that flowed in his blood. No one had ever told him no. No one had ever wanted to. *Just like me*, Beth thought.

Beth knew he was the reason she'd been brought here, because she wasn't supposed to say no to him, either. She knew that they looked very nice together, him in his tux and her in her green dress, and that the older adults were watching them. She thought of Lily saying, *Your parents are going to marry you off by the time you're nineteen, and you'll have a baby by twenty.* She already wanted another drink as the schnapps wore off.

Beth listened to Gray's relaxed chatter as he filled in the gaps of her silence. He probably thought she was so quiet because she was shy. The truth was that her stomach was turning and she was sick with horror, with realization: *I'm sixteen, and this is the map of the rest of my life. This is all of it. Unless I do something.*

She wondered if she could find Lily. She could tell Lily this was happening to her . . . And then what? What did she think Lily would do? Swoop in and save her? She glanced at Gray, who was shaking the hand of an older man. She glanced around at the house—big, ugly, ostentatious, down the street from her parents. *No one is coming*, she reminded herself. *No one is coming.*

She had looked up clock towers after Lily had mentioned them that night on the park bench. That comment had made no sense, and Lily always made sense. Lily didn't ramble about things she didn't mean. It had taken an actual trip to the library, a place Beth never went, and after wandering helplessly and feeling like an idiot she'd broken down and told the librarian that she was doing a school paper, and was there anything about people in clock towers?

The librarian had looked bemused. "Clock towers? Do you mean Charles Whitman? What a strange thing to be doing a paper on."

But she showed Beth a few newspaper clippings and magazine articles about the man who had taken guns into a clock tower in Texas in 1966 and started shooting people. There wasn't a lot to read, but it was still too much. Beth was shaking when she left the library.

Lily had known about that. She'd thought about it. *Why don't you ever hear of a woman in a clock tower?*

Beth drank more champagne, then excused herself to one of the huge marble bathrooms to throw up.

"You could have been nicer to him," Mariana said to her when they left, as they were getting in the car and her father was starting it. "You could have laughed more. You can be charming when you want to be."

Beth sat in the back seat, feeling the welcome cold air on her overheated skin. She wasn't drunk anymore, and she found herself wondering how she could steal the bottle of red wine from the liquor cabinet. "Lily should be here," she said.

"This isn't the time for little girls to play together," Mariana said sharply. "You have more important things to do."

"Like what? Get married? I'm sixteen."

"You need to be seen by important people," Mariana said. "You're old enough now. You can start planning your future."

"You're unbelievable," Julian said to his wife. "You're setting her up to be you, aren't you? Is that what you want? Did you start at sixteen?"

"Stop it!" Mariana's voice was cracked and shrill. "*Stop it!*"

The car was silent, the cold night gliding by outside.

"I want to talk to Lily," Beth said. "I want to talk to her on the phone or send her a letter. I want to tell her that she should have been here."

"You have no need to do that," Mariana said.

Beth felt her jaw flex. She was grown-up enough to be introduced to boys named Gray, but not grown-up enough to send her own letters. "Where is she?" she insisted. "Where did she go?"

"She moved out of her foster parents' house," Mariana said. "She didn't leave an address that I know of."

"We have to find her!" Beth felt panic rise in her throat.

Julian chimed in as he pulled into the driveway of the Greer mansion. "For God's sake, what for? I'm sure she's fine."

Beth stared at the back of his head. There was something about the confident tone of his voice—for a second, she was certain that Julian knew where Lily was, even if Mariana didn't. Lily was Julian's enemy, and Julian was far from stupid. He wouldn't let Lily drop out of his sight.

Even so, he didn't get it. Julian had thought Lily would ask for money or something. But no one knew how David the groundskeeper had gone over the edge or what had happened to the foster family that gave her bruises. Lily was an adult now, wandering somewhere alone. She looked like a pretty blond eighteen-year-old, but she was actually a loaded gun. No one understood that except Beth.

Everyone assumed Lily was just another girl who would disappear into obscurity.

Why don't you ever hear of a woman in a clock tower?

No one would ever think it was possible. Beth herself hadn't thought it possible—she hadn't wanted to. But really she knew.

She'd send a letter. She didn't need her parents for that. Late that night, when they were asleep, Beth went into her father's study and rifled through his desk. She found a piece of paper in his handwriting with Lily's address on it, a house in Portland that was likely a board-inghouse, because her hunch had been right—Julian did know where Lily was.

Beth wrote Lily a letter in her neat, well-schooled handwriting, a letter that was full of panicked pleas:

> *I wanted you here this Christmas. It wasn't my idea not to invite you. They made me go to a party and meet a man named Gray, because everything you said is true. Help me. Write me and I'll find a way to give you money. I'll do anything. Just please write me, and come visit, and don't do anything stupid. Please, please.*

She mailed the letter and waited. She never got a reply. But she never got the letter back, either, so she knew it had been delivered.

Maybe Lily didn't write because she was angry. Maybe she wasn't talking to Beth anymore. Maybe she was finished with the Greers and starting a new life.

Or maybe everything Beth wrote in her letter, Lily already knew.

CHAPTER THIRTY-TWO

October 2017

SHEA

"Stop," I said. "Stop."

Beth stopped talking, and silence fell. We were in the living room of the Greer mansion, surrounded by its musty vintage furniture. Outside the curtains, darkness had fallen. The dinner hour was long over, but neither of us had eaten. Beth had been talking for hours.

The house was still, as if the entire place was listening to Beth. There was no movement past the curtains on the lawn outside. The ceramic mermaid and shepherdess sat unseeing on the shelf behind the sofa, their glassy eyes blank. On the coffee table next to Beth's elbow was a glass ashtray the size of a baby's head. I hadn't noticed it before. It likely hadn't been used in decades, and yet it was still there, gleaming in the dim light.

"Yes, Shea?" Beth said. "Did you get all of that?"

I grabbed my phone, which was still recording, and jabbed it with my thumb. Then I picked up my papers, though I knew all of the dates by heart. "You're talking about Christmas 1970," I said. "Your father died in March 1973."

Beth's face was still, pale and beautiful. "Yes," she said softly.

"What happened in those two years? Where was Lily?"

"Seattle for a while," Beth said. "Salt Lake City. There were a few months in San Francisco, then Arizona. Those are the places I know of because those are the places I sent money when she eventually wrote me and asked."

"You sent her money?"

Beth's smile was bitter. "I didn't have much money of my own at sixteen, but I sent her whatever I could beg, borrow, or steal. I thought I was helping my poor half sister who had been treated so badly. I was stupid in those days. All I can say for myself is that it was the last time she fooled me."

"How did she fool you?"

"Because my father was sending her money, too. She'd blackmailed him with threats that she'd start telling the truth about whose daughter she was. My father hated Lily, but it was easier to shut her up than to fight her. At least at first. I think he figured if he just paid her, she'd stay away forever. But I didn't know about that until after he died. I just stupidly thought the money I sent her was the only money she had." Beth looked away from me, at the windows, seeing nothing as she spoke. "What you don't understand, Shea, is that everything is my fault. All of it. I didn't pull the trigger, but I might as well have. Everything is on me."

The air in the room was cold now, oppressive, hard to breathe. I felt beads of sweat start along my hairline. "Why?" I asked.

"Because I could have stopped her," Beth said, still not looking at me. "I knew what she was, even then. I didn't want to admit it to anyone, but I knew. I was the only one who suspected about David. But

Lily left town, and I chose to believe it was over. I finished high school and stopped thinking about it, except when I sent her money. I made the same mistake Julian did, but the difference was that I knew better. I knew Lily, and he didn't. So while I was worried about math tests and the fact that my parents wanted me to marry Gray, Lily was . . ."

I was leaning forward, entranced despite the cold sweat running down my skin. "Lily was what?"

"She never told me," Beth said. "But I'll bet there are deaths in those cities, when Lily was there, that no one could ever explain. Unsolved murders, even. They'd be buried under decades of other murders by now, forgotten. But they're there, like David's death. Like whatever happened to her foster family."

The silence was a heavy weight in the room. This was the crux of it, then; this was what Beth wanted me to believe. She wanted me to believe that at eighteen, her sister had become a serial killer.

It wasn't so strange, was it? After all, I'd been willing to believe that Beth was one herself.

"I should have looked for her," Beth said. "I should have found a way. She'd given me addresses to send money to. She was using assumed names—Veronica Jenshak, one or two others. I should have taken my money, gotten in my car, and gone to find her. Tried to stop her. Done whatever it took. I think part of her wanted me to do it—to defy my parents, leave town, and go look for her, even if it was only to have her locked up. Part of her wanted me to *care*. She called me and begged me once. It was the only time in my life I ever heard her distressed."

My mouth was dry. I was on the knife-edge, listening to her words. "What did she beg you for?"

But Beth shook her head. "That was later—years later. I'd stopped giving her money by then. But before my father died, I was young and scared and stupid. I thought maybe Lily would just behave, be nice, if

I gave her the money she wanted. I stayed home, and people died because of it. I don't have to know who they were to know they died. I just know."

I wondered if it was possible to find any murders that might be Lily's. Without an exact timeline, it was nearly impossible. "And then what?" I asked.

"And then two things happened." Beth ran a hand through her hair and turned back to me. "The first is that I finished high school. It was understood by everyone that I would marry Gray, but I had to finish high school first. After that, it was simply a matter of waiting for him to propose. That was all I was good for—marrying rich. College was out of the question; my parents would never have sent me, I didn't have my own money, and my grades weren't good enough for even a small scholarship. So that was that. I was going to be a wife."

It sounded terrible. "And the second thing?"

"The second thing that happened was that Julian decided that with Lily gone so long and my future all but settled, he was done paying Lily her blackmail money. And he stopped."

My muscles were tense, aching, my mind racing. "March 1973," I said.

Down the hall, there was the *shush* of a tap being turned on in the bathroom.

"I had written to Lily about Gray over the years," Beth said. "I told her I didn't want to marry him, to marry anyone. She never answered me about that. Her letters were always short and to the point: how much money she needed and where I should send it. She never even signed her real name. She'd only sign her letters with 'See you soon.'" She glanced at me. "Before you ask, I burned every letter after I got it, so, no, you can't see them."

I sagged in my seat. She knew me so well.

Beth swallowed, her jaw tight. "Even though Lily never said anything, I knew she was reading my letters. I was selfish. I wouldn't go find her, but in a way I wanted her to come back and find me. Then one Saturday, I went shopping and my mother went to her bridge club and my father got shot in the face, right in the kitchen over there." She motioned toward the hall, toward the sound of the taps. I felt queasy, wondering if there was blood running in that sink right now. What I would see if I went in there.

"Lily," I said.

"I got what I wanted, didn't I? Lily came back. It changed everything," Beth said. "Everything. My mother fell apart. Gray's family got cold feet, because my father was the prestigious one in our family, the CEO. Without him, we were just a silly girl with nice tits and her sad, broken mother. We were an embarrassment, as if murder was contagious. It was easy for Gray and me to break it off—Mariana was so drunk she didn't even notice. And as an added benefit, all of Julian's money came to Mariana. And to me."

"Beth, you don't know," I said. "Maybe it wasn't Lily. Maybe—"

"It was Lily," Beth said. "I knew she had killed my father, and I never said anything, because I was nineteen and no one would have believed me. I never said anything because I was afraid of her. I never said anything because it was my fault. I'd told Lily about the way the inheritance worked, about Gray. I'd set everything in motion."

"This is insane," I said. "All of this is insane."

"But it's true," Beth said. "I caused everything. I knew what my sister was and I didn't stop it. And six weeks after Julian died, Lily came home."

An hour later, I stumbled out of the Greer mansion and down the front walk. I was sweaty, gasping for air, as dizzy as if I were sick. I dropped my messenger bag on the sidewalk and stood for a minute with my hands on my knees.

It was full dark now. I hadn't intended to stay this late; I never stayed out after dark unless it was with my sister and Will. Now I was stranded in Arlen Heights in the dark, alone.

I closed my eyes and tried to catch my breath. *That house.* How did Beth live in that house? Something had been in the kitchen right before I left—something that thumped heavily as it moved around, something that hit the floor hard enough to feel it. I hadn't had the guts to go look at whatever it was, whatever Beth had awakened by telling the story of Lily. Whatever she had perhaps made angry.

"Why?" I asked no one, letting the word whisper out into the dark air. Why was Beth telling me this after all these years? Why me?

It wasn't a whim, I knew that. Beth Greer didn't have whims. She did things according to plan.

Maybe her plan was to drive me over the edge, give me a nervous breakdown. If so, it was working.

I pulled out my phone. My pulse was pounding in my throat. I was alone at night, far from home. I could call a taxi or an Uber. I could call Michael to come get me. I could call Esther and Will. I could go to the nearest bus stop and wait in the darkness, alone.

My thumb hovered over Michael's number. He'd come for me, I knew. If I called, he'd come.

I took another breath, and another. I didn't dial his number.

Face your fears, Shea. It's time.

Was that Beth's voice I heard in my head? I wiped my forehead, stood up straight. I looked up and down the quiet street. There were no cars, no one walking at this hour. The bus into Arlen Heights didn't run this late. I'd have to walk to the bottom of the road, over a mile downhill, to catch the bus downtown.

Somewhere far off, a door slammed. The wind rustled in the trees.

Behind me, the lights went off in the Greer mansion, leaving me in even deeper darkness. I turned and looked back at the house, my sneakers crunching against the gravel of the sidewalk.

The Greer mansion was still and silent. In an upstairs window was a foggy handprint, as if someone had just pressed their palm against the glass. While watching me.

I took a step back, and then another. Then I put my phone in my pocket and started the long walk down the hill.

CHAPTER THIRTY-THREE

October 2017

SHEA

The ocean was tame at the piers, where the houseboats bobbed in the water, but it was still the ocean. When the wind kicked up and the weather got stormy on the horizon, the boats shifted and clanked, groaning as the water tried to pull them free of their moorings. Spray slapped up on the edges of the old boards that made up the piers, and the smell was deep and fishy, salty and a little rotten. On the park bench where I sat at seven thirty in the morning, I could see the houseboats rocking, the last remnants of their flower boxes moving in the wind. Some of the boats had lights on, yellow in the dark as their occupants started their mornings. I wrapped my coat and my sweater more tightly around me.

"It isn't going to storm," the man next to me on the bench said. "It looks like it is, but it isn't. It's going to blow over."

The man next to me was in his late seventies, but he looked much older. He was tall and too thin, his clothes hanging off him. His skin was splotchy, his eyes sunken. He looked very unwell, and he was well aware of it. A cane leaned against the bench next to him. But a few feet away, in the tiny parking lot, a sleek Mercedes waited for the man, with a hired driver inside. The man was Ransom Wells.

He had phoned me over an hour ago as I lay sleepless in bed. "This is Ransom Wells," he said when I answered, as if it weren't six o'clock in the morning. "Beth Greer wishes for me to speak to you, and I happen to agree. I understand you work downtown, and I don't wish to interrupt your schedule. If you meet me at the bench in Langland Park, near the piers, I will be there at seven thirty, and I'll say all I wish to say."

"Okay," I said, and hung up. Then I got up, got dressed, and took the bus to the piers.

Ransom, I knew, had been a big man, florid and exciting, his presence electric. The Lady Killer case was only one of the many cases in his legendary career; he had gone on to defend celebrity clients in other high-profile cases, always making a splash in the press. But the Lady Killer case, his brilliant victory defending Beth Greer, was the one that launched him.

He had retired only ten years ago, and those years had not been kind. He had lost most of his famous bulk, as if something was eating him from the inside. He looked tired. But his posture was upright as he sat on the bench next to me, and his hands, though the veins were blue and the knuckles prominent, were large and strong, the last vital thing about him.

"I suppose I've shocked you with my appearance," he said.

"A little," I admitted. "But I'll get used to it."

"Then that makes one of us." He sighed. "Shea Collins. You are a blogger, I understand, and you work at a doctor's office. Where you need to be in just over an hour."

"Yes." I had my scrub top on under my sweater and my coat.

"You are also Girl A."

A few weeks ago, I would have been beside myself with excitement to get an interview with Ransom Wells; he was my version of a rock star. Now, I only felt tired and a little sad. "So much for my hidden identity," I said. "It seems everyone knows."

"Actually, the secrecy was taken very seriously at the time," Ransom said. "You were only a little girl, and no one wanted the publicity to ruin your life. I just happen to know everything and everyone. I always have." He glanced at me. "Though you no doubt know, I did not defend Anton Anders. I didn't work that case at all."

"I know," I said. If he had, I wouldn't be talking to him now. I would never have come.

"The Anton Anders case was a very big deal in this town," Ransom said. "I realize you can turn on the TV or surf the internet and read about murders that were even more horrible, killers that killed a hundred people. But in Claire Lake, especially among the police and the investigators, the Anders case was a lightning rod. It shaped how the police do business. As tragic as it was, it's seen as a model of perfect police work, how an investigation can remove evil from society when it's done right from beginning to end. It's still discussed, still taught twenty years later. And Girl A is a part of that. That's your legacy, like it or not."

I thought about how scared I had been, at twenty-nine, when I'd realized I was alone in the dark outside the Greer mansion. How the simple idea of getting home had seemed insurmountable. I shook my head. I didn't really care about police training. "I never chose that legacy. I never chose any legacy."

"That's because we don't always get to choose. In fact, we rarely do."

I looked at the houseboats, moving in the gray light. I wondered if Detective Joshua Black was in his boat right now, getting up. The man who had caught my would-be killer, living the later part of his life alone.

"I take it you've met him," Ransom said, watching my gaze and reading my mind. "Joshua."

"Yes."

"How happy he must have been," Ransom said. "To see you, alive and well and so lovely, twenty years later. He wouldn't have let on, of course. But that meeting would have warmed his heart. He's that kind of man."

"Why is he alone?" I asked.

"He was married for fifteen years or so, but it didn't work out. It never does with cops. They're an ornery bunch, married to work, and most of them are uncouth and hard to stomach for long periods of time. Joshua was the exception, but even he couldn't make it work. Dealing with death for a living is lonely. And there were no children."

"He has some kind of friendship with Beth," I said.

"That's because he never truly believed she killed those men. And he was right."

I looked away from the houseboats and at Ransom, taking in his sallow profile. "But he doesn't know who really did it," I said. "Beth has never told him. And neither have you."

Ransom was silent, looking out at the water.

"Is that why she called you now?" I asked him. "Because I learned about Lily? I wonder how much you knew about her." I watched his profile. "You knew everything, didn't you? And you didn't tell Detective Black, or anyone."

"It's true," Ransom said. "We let it dangle as a mystery for forty years now. We didn't do it to be cruel. We did it because when a man like Joshua Black is given too much of the correct information, he'll run himself into the ground chasing it down. And then he'll find things that he doesn't want to know. There was no good in giving

Joshua the answers, Shea. It would only have caused him pain, and it didn't matter anyway. Because everything was already over."

"That *is* cruel," I said.

Ransom nodded. "Yes, it is. But everything about this story is cruel. The beginning, the middle, the end. All of it." He sighed. "I was the Greer family lawyer in the years before I went into defense work full time. Julian came to me the year I took over my father's practice. Lily had been coming to the house for some years by then. Mariana always passed her off as a distant relative, but of course Julian knew the truth. He found out about Lily when Mariana's mother died and left him all of her papers. When the secret came out, Mariana wanted the little girl to visit for Christmas. It destroyed the marriage for him. He never forgave her."

"I guess it's unsettling, to learn that your wife had a child before you met her," I said.

Ransom gave me a disgusted look. "An eighteen-year-old girl from a good family, completely sheltered from the facts of life, doesn't get pregnant because she decides to," he said. "Have you ever felt shame?"

The question was so startling that I could think of nothing to say.

Ransom's watery, intelligent gaze was fixed on me. "You have," he said, reading my face. "We all have. Shame is corrosive and draining, and it never lets go. Mariana's father was gone—he walked out on the family shortly after he came home from the war. Her sister died in a drowning accident. Mariana was taken advantage of, pure and simple. She was practically a child. And then she was ashamed, and she paid with that shame for her entire life. Over and over, every day, she paid."

I was watching his face as he spoke, and I could see it. It was so easy to see when you knew what you were looking for. "You loved her," I said.

The wind blew and lifted his thinning white hair. "I suppose it doesn't matter now," he said. "She's been dead for over forty years. But, yes, if Mariana had even lifted a finger at me, I would have left my wife for her. But she never did. Don't worry, there is no torrid affair you need to write about after all this time. Mariana had no idea how I felt, and I never told her. It was strangely innocent, in its way."

Innocent, and sad. I couldn't think of anything to say but "I'm sorry."

Ransom shrugged. "Time passes, and these things cease to matter. They're just thoughts that float away on the wind. I don't need you to pass on my silly emotions to the next generation. I have information I need you to pass on instead."

I felt my spine stiffen, some of the old excitement moving into my veins. It was a part of me, that excitement, and it always would be. "What information?"

"I'll give it to you in my own good time. You're here at my invitation, and I'll do this the way I want to. What I was trying to say was that Julian came to me about his wife's illegitimate child. He wanted to know if the girl had a legal claim on his money. The answer was no, and I told him so. We both laughed at that idea. I remember it very clearly." He tapped his fingers on his cane, then stilled them again. "Lily was an embarrassment, but she was just a little girl. Frankly, I put her out of my mind. I barely thought about her again until she found me in the law library six weeks after Julian died. She just walked in and sat down opposite me at the table I was reading at."

"Lily came to find you?" I said.

"Oh, yes. God knew how she knew where I was, but she did. She was lovely by then, and very sensual in a strange way. But when I saw her face-to-face for the first time in my life, she wasn't lovely at all. She radiated something . . . repellent. A coldness. It's hard to explain when you haven't been in its presence. I know that Beth loved Lily, that they were sisters, but I have loved Beth for nearly fifty years, and Lily made me want to crawl out of my skin. She made me check the room, looking for the exits, wondering how quickly I could get to one. She made me want to call my children, make sure I knew where they were. She could fool a lot of people with her pretty, young exterior. But she couldn't fool me."

"'I know pure evil when I see it,'" I said, quoting what Ransom had said in that interview all those years ago.

"That was a slip," Ransom said. "The reporter was asking me about the Lady Killer. I was thinking about Lily when I said that. The reporter assumed I was talking about Beth. And of course, once it ran I couldn't correct him, so that quote went down in history."

"Was Beth angry about it?"

"No. 'At least it's dramatic,' she said. 'You always had a flair for drama, Ransom.'" He glanced at me. "Beth has a great many flaws, as I'm sure you've noticed. She has her own coldness and selfishness, which come from the terrible conditions she grew up in. She can be egotistical and secretive, argumentative, blunt. I understand all of those things, and I will still defend Beth Greer until I shuffle off this mortal coil. Which won't be a long wait now."

"What did Lily want?" I asked. "When she came to you in the law library?"

"She wanted money. She'd had both Beth and Julian sending her money for a while, but Julian had cut her off, and Lily wanted more. Now Julian was dead, so she knew the money should be Mariana's. Lily wanted to know if she could get Mariana to sign something to access it. Not just guilt money—something permanent. 'You know who I am,' she said, and I had to admit that yes, I knew. She said she'd go to the press, tell them who she was. She wanted money for the promise to stay quiet. Just like she'd done with Julian."

I tried to imagine myself at twenty-one cornering Ransom Wells, ordering him to set me up for life. Lily may have been a psychopath, but she was also pretty ballsy. "What did you tell her?" I asked.

"I told her to go to hell," Ransom said. "Incidentally, I hope she's there now. Because I meant it. I told her that some silly blond chit wasn't going to scare me. She said, 'That's what Julian thought until I shot him in the face.'"

Jesus. "Did you believe her?"

"Did I?" Ransom thought about it. "I had to do a quick recalculation when she said that. Because if she'd done it, then I was in danger. And, yes, I believed her. I had the same preconceptions and prejudices of any man my age in 1973, but I've always been more willing to face the truth than other people are. And the truth was, this girl had killed my client, my friend, for his money, and it was nothing to her. She let me see the truth of herself in that moment. I don't think she did that very often."

I was engrossed now. The sun was up, and I didn't know if I would be late for work, but I didn't care. "What did you do?"

"I told her I didn't believe her. I told her that Julian had been murdered by a robber in a random home invasion. I told her that if she had killed Julian in hopes of getting his money, it would have been an awfully foolish move. Mariana had a nervous breakdown after Julian's death and signed all of her affairs over to me. And I had no intention of submitting to blackmail, so Julian's death would be for nothing—if, of course, she had actually killed him. Which, I said, I doubted." He folded his hands over his cane. "It was a risky move, talking to her like that, but I've made risky moves all my life. I insulted her, but at the same time I gave her an out. She took it. She left, and I never saw her in person again."

"But that wasn't the last you heard of her."

"No. But I don't want to think about Lily anymore. She's your problem now." He pulled a sealed envelope from his leather satchel and handed it to me. "Here are some papers, the few that are left. Julian destroyed most of them. There are also some other things of my own that you need to read. Ask yourself why Beth has decided to tell everything now, after all of these years."

"Why?" I asked, taking the envelope.

"There's a reason behind everything Beth does," Ransom said. "She hasn't told me what the reason is, but I know there is one. I haven't asked her about it. There are a lot of things I haven't asked Beth about. I've survived this long and I've been as successful as I have, because I don't ask about things I'd rather not know."

I looked down at the envelope in my hand. "I don't think I have that talent. Maybe I'd be better off if I did."

"It's time for it all to come out, I think," Ransom said. "I don't know why the time is now, but it is. Whatever you find, Shea, do me a favor and don't tell me a damn thing."

CHAPTER THIRTY-FOUR

May 1973

BETH

Six weeks after Julian died, Beth did something she'd almost never done: She spent the day shopping with her mother.

Mariana had always been a shopper. It was her job: Buy nice things, then buy more nice things. Sometimes, like at Christmas, she'd be briefly excited about what she bought, but the rest of the time she shopped with a curious blankness, often forgetting about her purchases and leaving them piled in a corner, still in the shopping bags. Shopping certainly wasn't a joyous mother-daughter activity, and as soon as Beth could drive she would take one of the family cars and go shopping for herself.

Since Julian's death, things had spun out of control. Mariana drank nonstop; Beth drank almost as much. The two women wandered the house like ghosts, sometimes sleeping until noon, sometimes awake at four in the morning. Beth alternated between telling herself Lily hadn't really killed Julian and freezing, mind-numbing fear. She wanted so badly to fix things for her mother, to make things right again. But already Beth knew that she wasn't the one who made things right in bad situations; she was the one who somehow made things worse.

She had finished high school, which was meaningless. Why had she bothered? She wasn't going to college. She wasn't going to be a teacher or a nurse or a normal person. Her father's business partners would take over his company, Greer Pharmaceuticals, though Beth would get a share of the profits for life.

She was supposed to marry Gray and be a society wife, but that was over, too. For six weeks, Beth stared at the nothingness of her future with helpless numbness, tempered with flashes of anger that only eased when she raided Mariana's liquor cabinet again.

I should do something, Beth thought to herself over and over. But she couldn't make herself do anything.

And then one day in May, the sun was shining and Mariana was temporarily sober. She put her hair up, put her makeup on, and said to Beth, "Let's go shopping!"

Beth said yes.

They drove to the Edengate Plaza, a brand-new shopping center on the outskirts of Claire Lake. Mariana wore a long, draped dress and had tied a paisley scarf into her blond hair. Beth wore a ringer tee and high-waisted jeans, flip-flops, her hair down. The air was tinged with the first promise of summer, warmth edging into the cool dampness, almost hot under the direct sun and in the enclosed car. Beth felt her hangover drain away in the sunshine. Neil Diamond played on the radio as they drove.

"This is going to be so fun!" Mariana said, her voice bright.

Beth smiled tentatively at her mother, and she thought maybe it *would* be fun. The Edengate Plaza was new, still an exciting place to go. It was a long building of dusty brown brick, with a colonnade along one side roofed by dark brown siding. It was built for Claire Lake's richer clientele, with fashion shoe stores, dress stores, and jewelry stores lining the colonnade. The sign in front showed a drawing of three hourglass women, in Chanel dresses and pillbox hats, strolling the colonnade in high heels, with the slogan THE ONLY SHOPPING EXPERIENCE YOU NEED!

"Look, honey," Mariana said, pointing at the sign as they parked. "It's the only shopping experience we need!"

Beth laughed, more excited that Mariana had used the term of endearment than about the joke. She couldn't remember the last time Mariana had called her that.

They joined the shoppers on the colonnade. They tried on shoes, dresses. Mariana bought a lipstick in deep, vibrant red, the kind of color you'd see on Marilyn Monroe or Hedy Lamarr. When Beth found a silk shawl that was the same red, Mariana cried out in excitement.

"You should buy that," she said. "It's perfect for you."

"Do you think?" Beth asked.

"Oh, yes." Mariana took the shawl, wound it over Beth's shoulders, and stood back. "It's beautiful. You look like a woman who can conquer anything."

Beth didn't feel like a woman who could conquer anything, but in that moment it didn't matter. That was what Mariana saw when she looked at her, and it made her feel better than she had in weeks, maybe ever. She bought the shawl.

The few men at the Edengate Plaza looked at them that day. They looked at Mariana, beautiful and blond and pale, the scarf wound in her hair. They looked at Beth, nineteen and sultry without even trying. For once, Beth didn't mind. It was nice to be looked at, to be admired. They ate hamburgers at the nearby burger place, and they shopped some more before finally going home.

And then, as they pulled into the driveway, Mariana cried out in joy: "Lily!"

Beth looked, and the coldness came back, the darkness starting to lower again. Because Lily was sitting on the front steps of the Greer mansion, wearing jeans and a poncho, waiting for them to come home. And Mariana's joy wasn't forced or false anymore. It was genuine.

Lily stood as Mariana got out of the car, closing the door behind her, forgetting her packages, forgetting Beth. She nearly ran toward her first daughter, and her expression lit up. She stopped a few feet short of Lily, unwilling to hug her, though clearly wishing to. Hugs repulsed Lily, so Mariana touched her lightly instead, brushing her fingertips over Lily's shoulders, her face.

"You're so thin," Mariana said as Beth slowly got out of the car. Lily had lost weight. Her face was thin, and she wasn't wearing any makeup. The poncho was worn and had holes at the seams, and Beth knew that part wasn't a put-on; Lily must be broke. She herself hadn't sent Lily any money in months.

"Where have you been?" Mariana was asking, too excited to wait for an answer. "You'll have to tell me everything. Are you okay? I've been so worried about you. When did you get back?"

"This morning." As Lily spoke, she looked past their mother at Beth, a smile in her eyes. *We know a secret*, that smile said.

She was ruining everything, everything. She was a monster. "Mother," Beth said, holding Lily's gaze.

"Beth, please." Mariana barely glanced at her. To Lily she said, "Why don't you come in? I'll make you a lemonade."

"Mother," Beth said, louder.

Mariana turned and snapped at her, her good mood from their outing gone. "Beth, you're being rude."

"No, please," Lily said. She put her hand on Mariana's arm, and Mariana stared at the contact, stunned. "I want to hear what she has to say. What is it you'd like to tell us, Beth?"

Beth stared at them. At Lily, so thin and waifish under her poncho after years on the road. At Mariana, beaming at this one small touch from her daughter, her firstborn. The bitter girl, not the sweet.

She killed Julian. Beth was supposed to say the words. *She broke into the house and shot him in the face. She shot your husband and left him dead on the kitchen floor. Don't you care? Doesn't anyone care?*

No one would believe her. And if she could ever prove it was true, it would kill Mariana. It would crush her forever.

It was over. This nice day, her mother's attention, the possibility that anything good could start to happen. Beth had been a fool to enjoy herself, even for a few hours, but she couldn't bring herself to regret it. She could still feel the warming sun in her hair, still hear Neil Diamond on the radio, still hear Mariana say "honey." She could still feel that echo of the moment when she looked like she could conquer anything.

She still liked the illusion, even though she knew the truth. She couldn't conquer anything at all.

"Welcome back, Lily," she said. "How long will you stay?"

CHAPTER THIRTY-FIVE

_____

December 1977

BETH

Jail wasn't as bad as Beth had thought it would be.

She didn't have to talk to people, for one. She didn't have to argue or justify herself or make good impressions on people. She didn't even have to make decisions anymore—Ransom, out there somewhere in the freedom of the real world, made most of her decisions for her. She didn't have to plan a schedule or decide what to wear or what to eat. She didn't have to wake up every day in the Greer mansion, breathing its stuffy air and looking at the reminders of her parents in every room. She didn't have to see the kitchen floor, picture the way the blood had looked pooled on it. She didn't have to see Mariana's beautiful clothes in her closet, never to be worn again. She didn't have to think about anything at all.

Not that Beth wasn't thinking—she was. Her memories were sharp and detailed, tormenting in their precision. It should have been an overwhelming blur, too much to take in, but for once Beth's brain wouldn't shut down, wouldn't disappear into panic or numbness. She was awake now, maybe for the first time in her life.

Ransom told her the arrest had happened because of the gun. The ballistics had matched the gun from Julian's murder to the two Lady Killer murders. They didn't have the gun itself, but they had someone who had seen Beth at the second murder scene. So they'd taken their gamble.

Beth was angry—she knew that. Buried deep down, somewhere beneath the endless buzzing and thinking in her brain, were the hot coals of fury, powering everything. It was sobriety that made things clearer—the forced sobriety of being incarcerated with no access to alcohol. It wasn't until a few days had passed in her cell that Beth realized her hangover had completely cleared up, that for once she wasn't a little bit drunk or a lot drunk or living the aftereffects of being drunk. She slept deeply despite her surroundings, and she ate every bite of jail food. She could think for the first time in years. It wasn't pleasant—if someone had handed her a bottle of wine, she would have upended it and drunk the whole thing, no questions asked—but it was unavoidable. If Beth was going to be forced to think clearly, she may as well try to come up with a plan.

Besides, while she was in the depths of this jail cell, she was safe from Lily.

Beth knew she wasn't acting the way a terrified, wrongly accused woman was supposed to act—eating, sleeping, not weeping or falling apart. She knew that every guard who saw into her cell, every person she spoke to, was making and spreading a scathing impression of her. *She's cold. She doesn't talk, doesn't cry. She doesn't even look worried. She isn't sorry those men are dead.*

Detective Washington hated Beth, especially after the circus of the arrest. He was furious, as if the whole thing were Beth's fault. Ransom was high on a wave of outrage, working at his most expansive decibel level. The uniformed cops treated her with a mix of salaciousness and callousness, like she wasn't a person at all but a pinup photo in a magazine. And Detective Black was miserable, painfully unhappy about the indignities Beth was subjected to, uncomfortable around his partner and the other cops, unable to do anything about it. He was so twisted up Beth almost felt bad for him. Almost.

She couldn't afford to feel bad for anyone right now. Not even herself.

Her refusal to talk galled Detective Black, she knew. He thought that now that the worst had happened—now that Beth was sitting in a jail cell wearing an oversized jumpsuit—she should finally be a proper woman and fold under pressure. Beth sat in her cell and knew that Detective Black was bound to be disappointed in her. Being behind bars, eating crappy food, being called a murdering cunt—these weren't the worst things that could happen. The worst things had already happened years ago.

She looked up one day to see Black being let through the door of her cell, the uniformed female guard closing the door behind him. Beth had been given no notice he was coming.

He was wearing a dark blue suit. She wondered if his kindergarten-teacher girlfriend had helped him pick it out. He was clean-shaven, his hair neatly combed, though he wore it a little long for a cop. Beth had caught the faintest whiff of aftershave when he'd walked next to her during the arrest, and she knew that if she could lean in and smell his neck, the scent would be pungent and male. Aftershave, Beth thought, was one of the most important scents in any girl's world. It was the smell of fathers, or uncles, or teachers, or priests, or husbands. Beth's own father had worn aftershave, but the smell would be different on

Detective Black, because sometimes aftershave was the smell of a man who wasn't, and would never be, yours.

He looked at her for a long moment as she sat on the edge of the cot in her cell, wearing her denim blue jail jumpsuit. It was cold in here, but Beth didn't cross her arms. She kept her hands at the edge of the bed, beside her hips, holding on as she looked him in the eye.

"Where's the gun?" he asked her.

"I don't know," Beth said. The truth, for once.

"Why were you at the second murder scene?"

"I wasn't." So much for the truth, then.

Ransom would have a panic attack if he could hear her right now.

Detective Black scrubbed a hand over his face. "You're covering for someone," he said. "You know I know it. You know it's the only answer that makes sense. The question is who. And why."

Beth said nothing.

"I'll find the answer, you know. I'll find who you're covering for."

She'll kill you if you do. "You won't."

"You don't have much faith in me. I'm very good at my job."

"If I'm convicted, you won't have to bother."

Was she going to be convicted? Ransom was her only hope. She had told him to get her out of this, and she knew he was going to use every trick in his book. He did it because she paid him, so she had no sentimental attachment to Ransom. But still, right now he was all she had.

"You have to tell me," Detective Black said, still a few moves behind. "Beth, you're not stupid. You know how serious this is. Everyone, and I mean everyone, believes this was you. I'm the only one who sees what's really happening. You're going to be convicted, do you understand? You're going to spend the rest of your life in prison. I'm the only one who can help you."

It was a good speech, but Lily had taught Beth well. Everyone wants what they want: That was one of Lily's lessons. Detective Black wanted to help her, yes. But he also wanted to solve this case. He wanted to be the one to uncover the truth. He wanted justice. He wanted Lily.

No. No one got to have Lily. No one except Beth.

"The Hamlet act is getting old," Beth told Detective Black. "You're so torn, aren't you? You think I didn't do it, but you also think I'm a lying bitch."

He looked like she'd suddenly spit on him. "I don't think that."

"Yes, you do. I didn't kill those men, but I could have. I could have shot them while I looked in their faces, watched them die, and felt nothing. That's what you think, yet you know I didn't actually do it. It's driving you crazy, and it's so *boring*."

Black shook his head. There were splotches of red on his cheekbones. "You're trying to piss me off. But, Beth, I'm trying to help you."

"No one," Beth said clearly, slowly, letting the words ring through the cold cell, "no one is trying to help me. No one is coming for me." Black opened his mouth, but Beth talked over him. She was so sick of people talking over her, of men interrupting her and speaking on her behalf. As if they knew even a fraction of what went on in her mind, as if they knew what it was like to be her, for a day, for an hour. Sometimes she was so angry she wished she'd shot those men herself, which was exactly what Lily understood about her.

"I can help myself," Beth told him. "I don't need you. Go home to your kindergarten teacher. Go marry her and make your conventional little life. And don't ever come back here."

Now Black had his own flare of anger, rare and welcome, at least to Beth. "You're being a fucking idiot. I'm the only one who wants to get you out of this—not because you're paying me a fee, but because I actually want to. If you're convicted, your life is over."

"So what? I'm nothing to you. Get out."

He held steady. "I'm not giving up. If you didn't do this, then whoever did goes free to do it again. Whoever has that gun. Whoever wrote those notes and shot those men. It's a woman, isn't it? You know it is. If she isn't you, Beth, then she's going to kill more people until she's stopped. Are you going to be a part of that?"

"Get out," Beth said.

"Beth—"

"Get out."

He left. Beth watched him go as a door closed inside her and another part of her died. She gripped the cold, thin mattress of her jail-cell cot, and she thought, *I am not going to live the rest of my life in here. He's wrong about that. And Lily isn't going to kill anyone else, either, ever again.*

Beth would make sure of it.

She was in jail, arrested for two murders, her lawyer home with his wife and kids. She was alone, at the bottom of a life that had had a lot of bottoms, looking at the rest of her life in prison. It was, by any measure, the worst moment of her life.

And for the first time, Beth Greer finally knew exactly what to do.

Six days later, Beth was taken from her cell to a room lined with folding tables, each framed with dirty glass. On each table was a phone, large and black, screwed to the table, the cord contained under a plastic shield so it couldn't be used as a weapon. A few of the other booths had women in them, wearing inmate clothes and hunched over their phones, talking to lawyers or husbands or children. The voices in the room were low, sharp, and tense, and the air—like the air everywhere in here—smelled like sweat.

Everyone expected life in jail would break her. Even Ransom, who knew her so well, had his doubts. When he'd finished blustering, he'd asked if he could bring her anything: books, a pillow, an extra blanket. "Don't let this get to you," he'd said, worried. "People are watching. That's what they want. And for God's sake, don't talk to your fellow inmates."

There was no chance of that. Beth had asked Ransom for a sweater and the copy of *Moby-Dick* she'd always meant to read. The book had always seemed too dense and boring for her, which made it the perfect jail-time read. She spent days in her cell trying to decode the impenetrable prose about whales, ignoring everything around her. The only thing she missed, hard and long like other women missed their babies, was alcohol.

There were few phone calls for Beth in jail. Ransom always came in person, and she had no one else in the world except for Lily. She'd had two calls before this one, both of them hang-ups as soon as she came to the phone, so she knew Lily was afoot. She was playing her game.

This time, when Beth answered, Lily's familiar voice was on the other end, though she sounded muffled and far away, as if they were talking through a two-way radio. "I bet you're not sweet anymore," she said.

Beth had thought she was ready for this—she knew that Lily wouldn't be able to resist calling. But the first thing she thought of when she heard her sister's voice was that last day with Mariana, the day they went shopping at the Edengate Plaza. Beth had been alive for twenty-three years, but that was the only day in any one of them that she would get back if she could. The thought choked her, made pain and anger rise up from her stomach into her throat. It was the first time she'd let herself feel furiously angry since the arrest.

"What do you want?" she said.

"What's it like?" Lily asked. She sounded cheerful, unconcerned. "I admit I'm curious about prison. It's probably not so bad. Is it full of dykes?"

"Turn yourself in and find out," Beth said.

Lily laughed. "Are you scared in there? You always were such a coward, Beth."

Once, before so many people had died, those words coming from

Lily would have been hurtful. But Beth wasn't six years old anymore. She didn't feel stung. She only felt icy calm, and the certainty that Lily was underestimating her.

Lily's weakness—maybe her only one—was that she thought she was smarter than everyone. Especially Beth.

"I've had a lot of time to think," Beth said. As if they were having a normal conversation. Because in Lily's world, everything was just fine.

"Do tell," Lily said.

"I've been remembering the night our mother died."

There was silence on the other end of the line.

"Which one of us killed her, do you think?" Beth asked her half sister. "You, or me?"

More silence.

They had never talked about this. There had never been time. After that day when Lily came home, she had stayed at the Greer mansion on and off for two years. She'd show up when she needed money, stay until she and Mariana had a fight, and then she'd take off again. Over and over. When Lily was gone, Mariana would be sick with worry. When Lily came home, Mariana always welcomed her back.

Beth watched all of it, helpless. Mariana never wanted to hear the truth about Lily: that she was a user, a manipulator. That she didn't love Mariana the way Beth did. That in the stretches when she was away, out of sight, Beth was certain that people were dying. She could never prove it, could never find Lily when she truly wanted to be lost. But Beth knew her half sister, and she knew that when Lily was in one of her cold, angry moods, someone somewhere was going to die.

"She's just lonely," Mariana would say in Lily's defense, over and over. "All those foster homes. She's starved for a mother's love."

I'm *starved for a mother's love*, Beth wanted to shout, her inner six-year-old still in pain. But it would have made no difference; Mariana wouldn't hear it. She had only now edged into the territory in which she could admit, even obliquely, that she was Lily's mother. She was too fragile for anything more.

Beth stayed silent to keep her mother safe. But when Lily was home, she always hurt her mother, cutting her with words, punching her with accusations: *Look at you. What's wrong with you? You don't care about me. You never cared. That's why you sent me away every year.*

One night, Lily and Mariana screamed at each other, Mariana with tears streaming down her face. *You failed me*, Lily shouted while Beth stood in the living room doorway, unable to stop either of them. *You never loved me. I hate you. Everything that's happened to me is your fault.*

And Mariana: *I didn't know what else to do. I loved you so much, Lily. I loved you more than anything. I didn't know what else to do.*

It ended, as it always did, with Lily leaving, slamming the door behind her. Mariana, already half-drunk, drank more. But Mariana was on those pills: What were they? Uppers? Downers? Where had she gotten them? She was always so secretive, especially with Beth.

Maybe Beth could have stopped her mother from drinking so much and taking pills. Maybe she should have. But she looked at Mariana's bleary eyes and her tearstained face, and the words rang in her head: *I loved you more than anything.* And Beth went to bed.

When she heard her mother leave her bedroom in the middle of the night, mumbling to herself as she walked down the corridor to the stairs, Beth got up and followed her. She watched as Mariana, clutched in some paranoid delusion that only she could see, went out the front door and got into her car. Beth listened to the car drive away, and she did nothing.

I loved you more than anything. The words went around in Beth's head as she stood there.

Within an hour, Mariana was dead. Lily didn't call or come home, and Beth was completely alone.

"Sometimes I think it was me who killed her," Beth said now, twisting the knife into her half sister. "But then, she wouldn't have mixed the pills with the alcohol if you hadn't told her she failed you. That you hated her."

"That's a lie," Lily said.

"Tell yourself that if you want." Beth's hand on the receiver was slick with cold sweat. "You're the crazy one, not me."

"Does it make you feel better to think of me as crazy?" Lily's voice was sharp. "Does it make you feel smug? Are you sure you're the sane one, Beth?"

It was so hypnotic, that voice. So convincing. Beth rubbed her forehead. Yes, she was the sane one. She had never killed anyone. Except Mariana, that night she stood and watched her leave.

Except everyone who came after, because she didn't stop Lily when she'd had the chance.

"How long was it before you knew she was dead?" Beth asked. "You were gone. When did you finally know?"

There was another brief pause, and then Lily gave her the truth for once. "Three months. But part of me knew. I'd been living like she was already dead. Then I looked for her obituary in old copies of the paper, and I found it. I knew. That's why I'd started looking at obituaries."

For one moment, crackling over the phone line from jail, Beth felt her own pain and her sister's pain mix together. It was still so raw, even now. Mariana, for all her faults, had been the only thing that both of them had ever wanted. Had they loved her? Did either of them even know what love was? For that matter, had Mariana ever known?

Yes, Mariana had known what love was. *I loved you more than anything.*

Did Beth love Lily? Maybe. But her feelings for Lily were too much like her feelings toward herself. Hate, pity, fear—and anger. So much anger.

And Lily . . . She wasn't sure Lily knew how to love anyone.

Still, she opened her mouth to speak. *Our mother is still in the house*, she wanted to tell her sister. *I hear her sometimes. She wants to open the bedroom door.* Maybe Beth *was* the crazy one. Still, it was possible Lily would understand.

But Lily spoke first. "It's your fault," she said, and the moment of shared grief was over as she brought out her old weapons, anger and blame. "You let her die that night. You know you did."

Beth went cold, and she put her confession away. "I'm going to get out of here. You know that, right?"

"You probably will. You weasel out of everything bad. You always have. I suppose I should say sorry that they arrested you instead of me, but I'm not sorry at all. It's nice to see you suffer for once."

Beth knew that tone. Lily was feeling victorious, untouchable. This was when she was at her weakest. "When I get out, I'm giving you enough money to go away forever. And then we're never seeing each other again."

Now Lily sounded interested. "I'm finally getting my half?"

"Anything," Beth said, a note of desperation in her voice. "Anything you want. Anything to end this."

"Then get out quick, dummy. I'm waiting."

"When I get out, how do I find you?"

"You don't," Lily said. "I'll find you."

When Beth stood to go back to her cell, she knew her expression was hard. She knew the guard was watching her, that she'd go home and tell her husband that Beth Greer, the infamous Lady Killer, was the coldest woman she'd ever seen. She knew that in some ways, even if she won this game with Lily, she was damaged forever.

But it didn't matter now, if it ever had. Since that November morning so long ago when she'd seen the writing on the window, this was always going to happen. She could see that now. They had been locked in this together, she and Lily, for all these years. And now they were coming to the end. At last.

Beth went back to her cell in silence and started reading *Moby-Dick* again.

CHAPTER THIRTY-SIX

October 2017

SHEA

The envelope from Ransom Wells was a treasure trove of information. Michael and I couldn't process it all sitting at the table at the diner where I'd met him after work.

"I need my laptop," Michael had said. "I have to verify this."

That was how we ended up here, at his apartment. Just the two of us, alone. I was breaking another one of my rules, but it didn't matter. I had to be here, going through this file.

Everything about Michael's apartment said *divorced guy who moved out in a hurry*. The sofa was secondhand, definitely bought after the move, but the TV was big and new—he'd brought that with him. His fridge was full, but he didn't have very many dishes. There were unopened boxes stacked against one wall, but there was artwork that he'd chosen over the sofa, a large framed print of the ocean taken from the top of the bluffs, the seabirds wheeling in the sky, the whitecaps breaking in an endless beautiful pattern. On one of the end tables was a framed photo of Michael in police uniform, standing with two men who looked almost exactly like him, obviously his father and his uncle.

"Ignore the mess," he said sheepishly when he saw me looking around. He walked to a crowded, well-used desk in the corner—Ikea, likely bought and put together in haste—and picked up a laptop, bringing it over to the sofa.

"It's fine," I said, meaning it. "I've lived this mess."

His eyebrows rose. "Meaning?"

"You brought your favorite things when you moved out," I said. I pointed. "The family photos, the TV, the ocean print. Your work computer. You left everything else."

"She picked out our sofa, and I always hated it," he said, speaking my language. "So now I have this. The ocean print is a photo I took myself. I'm no photographer, and I don't even have the best camera, but I lucked out that day. I've always just really liked that picture. My ex never understood why I spent the money getting it enlarged and framed. So, yeah, I took it with me."

I got that. There was a lot of talk about the psychological effects of divorce, about the emotions and the heartbreak, but no one ever talked about the things. How you had to go through every item you owned, even in your head, and figure out whether it was really something that was yours or not. How you had to pack your things, move your things, haul your things. Throw out your things. Van and I had sold our house, which meant we'd had to empty every closet, every room, one by one, decide what was going to happen to every potted plant and picture frame. It had been excruciating, so exquisitely painful and drawn-out that I never wanted to do it again.

I was living with Winston Purrchill, and that was enough for me.

Still, I was very aware that I was alone with Michael. He was wearing dark jeans, a T-shirt that had a faded Rolling Stones logo on it, and a long leather jacket in a style that at one time had been referred to as a car coat. I'd always pictured him in my mind with a retro look, and it turned out he really had it. And—I had to admit it—I liked it.

"Do you want a drink?" he asked, oblivious to how tongue-tied I was. He put his laptop on the coffee table and took his coat off.

"No, thanks." I sat on the sofa, next to him but with a few feet of space between us. I was still wearing my scrub top and my sweater, though I slid my coat off. "Let's start with the birth certificate," I said.

That was the first gift Ransom Wells had given us: Lily's birth certificate. According to the certificate, Lily's name was Lillian Knowles, and she was born in January of 1952. Her mother was Mariana Pattinson, age nineteen. Her father was unknown.

"Knowles," Michael said, waking up his laptop and beginning to work. "That's the name they gave Mariana's baby. They didn't give Lily Mariana's maiden name, likely because they didn't want her publicly connected to the family. But where did Knowles come from?"

We found the name further back in the family tree; it was Mariana's grandmother's maiden name. So Lily started life without being given her mother's name, or her father's, either.

Lily had spent her life in foster care. The records were sealed—even to Ransom Wells—but there was a one-page summary from a report made in 1969, when Lily was moved from one family to another. *Hostile behavior,* the report listed laconically under the heading "Notes." The reason for the transfer was only listed as *suicide of family member.*

I wanted to shake the truth out of whoever had written those four words and nothing else. Suicide of family member? Lily would have been seventeen in 1969—the year after she'd come to visit Beth with bruises on her face. The next year, when Beth had asked what happened to her foster family, Lily had said, *Bad things.*

Maybe those bad things had really been suicide. Maybe they had been murder. If murder, was this unnamed family member Lily's first victim? Or was the first victim David, the groundskeeper?

"I have more questions than answers," I said to Michael as I handed him the paper. "This is going to drive me crazy."

"Tell me about it," Michael said. "Read this."

It was a newspaper clipping from 1975. A man named Lawrence Gage had been shot in his bedroom in Phoenix, Arizona, in an apparent home invasion. Gage was divorced, and he was in bed alone. The intruder came through a screen door, killed Gage, and took some cash and valuables. No one could think of any enemies Gage, a retiree, could have had. The crime was especially distressing because Gage was shot in the face.

"Another victim," I said.

"Read the last part," Michael said.

The final paragraph stated that Gage had lived in Phoenix for four years, ever since he retired. He had moved from Claire Lake, Oregon, where he had spent all of his career running a department store.

If Gage was from Claire Lake, and Lily had killed him in Phoenix—if she was his killer, which Ransom seemed to think—then it wasn't random. Lily had tracked Gage to a different city. She had targeted him. Why?

Ransom Wells had kept this article in his file all these years. Why?

I looked up. My eyes locked with Michael's, and we asked each other the question silently before I said it aloud. "Lily's father?"

"I checked the dates," Michael said. "Mariana was nineteen when Lily was born. Lawrence Gage lived in Arlen Heights then. He would have been forty-three."

I thought of Ransom saying, *Mariana was taken advantage of, pure and simple. She was practically a child. And then she was ashamed.*

"He could have known Mariana's family," Michael said. "He was wealthy and ran a department store. They would have moved in the same circles."

He could have been a friend of the family, which meant he could have met teenage Mariana. Perhaps he had assaulted her; perhaps he had only fooled her. The result was the same either way. Lawrence Gage went on with his life as if nothing had happened, and Mariana was sent to the Elizabeth Trevor House for Women to have her baby in secret. A little girl.

And then, years later, had he woken to see that little girl grown into a woman, standing over him in bed with a gun to his face?

What had driven Lily to the extremes she'd gone to? It was convenient, and so modern, to simply say that mental illness had been the reason. When mental illness was combined with a neglectful and possibly abusive childhood, you had a recipe for a serial killer, or so the research said. You had someone you could put in a box, someone you could point to and say: *See? Look at that person. That person isn't me.*

But there was nothing in these papers that said Lily had ever been diagnosed by a professional. There was nothing to say she'd seen a psychiatrist at all. For all her love for Lily, Mariana had never taken her to a doctor or a social worker. There was nothing to show that either Mariana or Beth had ever tried to help her. There was nothing that spoke to how much Lily might have suffered. There was nothing to show that, after being born in secret to the wrong woman at the wrong time, Lily had had any chance at all.

"Lily's father isn't named on the birth certificate," I said. "If Lily found out who he was, it must have been from Mariana."

Michael looked at the date in the newspaper clipping. "Lawrence Gage was murdered three months after Mariana Greer died. If Mariana had told Lily that Gage was her father, Lily had known it for three months by then. I wonder what took her so long?"

I rubbed my forehead, trying to process everything. I was tired.

There were too many gaps in the timeline—too many months and years when Lily had just dropped off the map in a way you could still do in the midseventies, when there was no internet and there were no cell phones. In 1975, a simple fake ID and a crossing of state lines would allow you to start a new, anonymous life.

Michael, who was following my train of thought without realizing it, kept talking as he shuffled through the papers. "Between Gage's murder in 1975 and Thomas Armstrong's murder in 1977 is a complete blank. Where was Lily? What set her off to start the Lady Killer murders? And where is she now?"

"I told you, she's dead," I said.

Michael narrowed his eyes at me. If he suspected it was Lily I'd seen at the Greer mansion, the presence I had felt, he decided not to ask. Instead he said, "I'd like to see some proof of that."

"I'd like to see a lot of things," I replied. "Let's add it to the list."

The last pages Ransom Wells had given me were records of charitable trusts. One was a charity for orphaned girls; another was to support single mothers in poverty. Another was a charity to provide mental health services "for teenage girls at risk." Another was for victims of violence. All of the charities were run by numbered companies. And, according to Ransom's paperwork, all of the numbered companies were owned by Beth Greer.

I had wondered more than once what Beth had done with her time over the past forty years, since she'd never married or had children and she had no need to work. This was the answer.

"Why did he give us this, do you think?" Michael asked, reading over the papers. His laptop was sitting on the coffee table, and outside it had long ago gone dark.

"This is the story," I said, feeling bitterness as I looked at the records. I pointed to the newspaper article about Lawrence Gage. "Lily is the villain." I pointed to the charity records. "But not Beth. He wants us to see Beth as the heroine, the one who selflessly saves orphans and single mothers. She's the sweet one, not a killer like her sister."

I shouldn't be surprised. Ransom had told me he'd be loyal to Beth to the end.

Michael put the file down. "It's late."

I looked at the clock on my phone. It was nearly ten thirty. "I'm sorry," I said, getting up and grabbing my coat, my cheeks burning. "I've overstayed my welcome."

"Of course you haven't," Michael said, standing up. "I'm a night owl. I just don't want you to miss the last bus."

I zipped my coat, busily grabbed my bag, and started to put the papers in it.

"Because you're going to take the bus, aren't you?" Michael said into the silence. "You're not going to take me up on my offer of a ride."

"I know it's weird," I said. "I just . . ."

"I know." He put his car coat back on.

"What are you doing?"

"Walking you to the bus stop."

"You don't have to."

He looked amused. "You, of all people, are going to tell me that?"

It was cold out, the air full of the promise of oncoming winter, but for once it wasn't raining. I zipped my collar all the way up as we walked.

There was no one else at the bus stop. The lights of the houses and apartment buildings glowed yellow in the night, a reminder that although this was a lonely spot, there were people nearby. I had no desire to live outside the city, in the unbroken darkness, where there was no one around. I needed the lights and noise of people, even if I wasn't talking to them.

I turned to find Michael looking at me. How was he this hand-some? Even his jawline was nice. Since when did I ogle men's jawlines? That wasn't like me.

Then again, maybe it was.

I didn't think. For once, I didn't drive myself crazy. I just leaned up, put my hands on his shoulders, and kissed him.

His lips were soft, his skin faintly rough with stubble. He kissed me back, not even hesitating, before he put his arms around my waist and pulled me closer. He deepened the kiss, running his hands up my back, and my body started to hum in a way I hadn't felt in years, or maybe ever. Everything got warm, even in the damp cold of a fall night in Oregon. I was pressed up against him like it was the most natural thing in the world. Then, as we heard the bus pull up, he broke the kiss and stroked his fingers gently through my hair.

"Be careful," he said. "Be safe."

I nodded, pulled reluctantly away, and got on the bus. My skin was prickling, and my lips were still warm. I sat down and stared ahead, my bag in my lap. I could still taste him.

Slowly I came back to myself. I watched Claire Lake out the win-dow, the lights going by, and my phone pinged with a text.

It was from Beth Greer.

It was a photo. An old one, black and white, a picture of two teen-age girls sitting on the sofa in the Greer mansion—the exact same sofa where Beth had sat every time I interviewed her. One of the girls was Beth, aged around thirteen. The other girl was Lily.

Both girls were wearing sweaters and wool skirts. There was a Christmas tree out of focus behind them. Beth was easily recogniz-able, even though this photo was from so long ago—her cheekbones, her lips, her large dark eyes. She was leaned in toward her sister, a smile on her face that was tentative and yet so hopeful it was a little heartbreaking. This was Beth when she still thought that things might work out somehow. Beth when she still had two living—if unhappy—parents. Beth who was in the middle of the much-looked-forward-to yearly visit from her sister, who was obediently posing for a Christmas photo taken—obviously—by Mariana.

Lily, two years older, was blond. She sat upright, her hands folded on her lap, her shoulders straight, her chin angled just so. She looked straight at the camera with eyes that were dark like Mariana's. Her face was narrower than Beth's, her lips thinner, but the girls were so clearly related—it was in the set of their bodies, their cheekbones, their identical hands. But Lily sat more confidently, and her smile only played at the corners of her mouth. It didn't reach her eyes, which were curiously flat as she looked at the photographer—her mother.

Another text came after the photo. *I thought you might like this*, Beth wrote. *It's Christmas 1967.*

Sweet and bitter, I thought, looking at Lily and remembering the article about Lawrence Gage, shot in the face in his own home. Remembering that Julian Greer was about to die the same way a few years later. I wanted to reach back through the doorway of this photo and—what? Stop Lily? Change everything? Save Julian's and maybe Mariana's lives?

I put my phone away. I didn't answer Beth. I didn't have to. She knew I'd seen the picture, and she'd probably guessed every thought that went through my head as I stared at it. She knew she had me as obsessed as ever.

Be careful, Michael had said. *Be safe.*

The sweet girl in that photo had stood by and done nothing after her father was killed, after her mother somehow died in the fallout, after two men were shot point-blank on their way home from work. She had known who the killer was, and she had done nothing about it. She had even gone to trial for capital murder to cover her sister's crimes.

Why? I wondered. What was so compelling about Lily Knowles that would make Beth go to such lengths to protect her?

What if I found out Esther was a murderer? What would I do?

The right thing, of course. I'd do the right thing.

But I didn't know what that was anymore. Maybe I had never known.

CHAPTER THIRTY-SEVEN

**Excerpt from trial transcript,
People v. Elizabeth Greer, February 1978
Prosecution examination of
Dr. Oliver Da Sousa, psychiatrist**

CHARLES MANKOWSKI (prosecuting attorney): Dr. Da Sousa, did you examine the defendant, Miss Greer?

OLIVER DA SOUSA: I did not.

MANKOWSKI: But you have given advice on other cases similar to this one?

DA SOUSA: Yes, I have worked extensively with the criminally insane, including women who are criminally insane.

MANKOWSKI: What were your conclusions when presented with the facts of this case?

DA SOUSA: In my opinion, these murders were committed by a woman who is mentally ill, possibly delusional, and has a pathological hatred of men.

RANSOM WELLS (defense attorney): Objection.

JUDGE HEIDNIK: Overruled. I'll allow it for now. Dr. Da Sousa, please continue.

MANKOWSKI: Thank you, Your Honor. Dr. Da Sousa, you were saying that the murderer in this case is mentally ill.

DA SOUSA: Yes. It is my assessment that this person, this woman, has violent tendencies brought on by fantasies in her mind. She is dissociative, sociopathic, and possibly psychotic.

MANKOWSKI: How would such a person appear to the people around her? Would she appear as normal?

WELLS: Objection.

[Disruption in courtroom]

JUDGE HEIDNIK: Order.

WELLS: Objection.

[Disruption ceases]

JUDGE HEIDNIK: I will allow the question since it calls on the doctor's expertise. Dr. Da Sousa, please continue again.

DA SOUSA: Okay. Thank you. Yes, such a person can appear as normal to the people in their lives. They can even appear to be successful and charming when they choose to. It's a form of camouflage for them. But underneath the surface, this woman would be very angry, would feel out of control.

MANKOWSKI: Have you studied Miss Greer, and this case, even though you haven't examined her directly?

DA SOUSA: Yes, I have.

MANKOWSKI: And what is your conclusion?

DA SOUSA: Given that both of her parents died violently, Miss Greer, or such a person like her, could be dissociative. Possibly even sociopathic. It could have started from an early age.

WELLS: Objection.

JUDGE HEIDNIK: Sustained. The jury is asked to disregard that question and answer.

MANKOWSKI: Okay, we'll return to the woman who committed these murders. Dr. Da Sousa, you have said that it's your professional opinion that this murderer, whoever she is, could appear normal?

DA SOUSA: Yes. In fact, it's likely, since both of her victims found her harmless enough to approach her.

MANKOWSKI: Does such a woman feel remorse for what she's done?

DA SOUSA: No, she does not.

MANKOWSKI: So she may not stop killing, then. She may be dangerous to others.

DA SOUSA: It is very likely that she will continue to kill more people, yes. Such a woman is very dangerous.

Excerpt from cross-examination the following day:

RANSOM WELLS (defense attorney): Dr. Da Sousa, do you have an explanation for the fact that the notes found with the victims have been compared to Beth Greer's handwriting and have been found not to be a match?

DA SOUSA: I do not.

WELLS: Do you have an explanation for the fact that no physical evidence has been found to connect either of these crimes to Miss Greer?

DA SOUSA: I do not.

WELLS: Do you have an explanation for the fact that you told your colleague Dr. Anderson Jermyn that Beth Greer was, and I quote, "sexy as hell and probably a slut"?

[Disruption in courtroom]

JUDGE HEIDNIK: Order. Order.

MANKOWSKI: Your honor, I object and ask that that last question be struck from the record.

JUDGE HEIDNIK: Overruled. Order.

[Disruption ceases]

WELLS: I apologize for the crude language, Doctor, but it was a direct quote. Do you need me to repeat the question?

DA SOUSA: That was spoken in confidence.

WELLS: Please answer the question. Do you have an explanation?

DA SOUSA: No, I do not.

Prosecution examination of Detective Joshua Black, Claire Lake Police Department

CHARLES MANKOWSKI (prosecuting attorney): Detective Black, what would you say Miss Greer's demeanor was when you and Detective Washington first interviewed her?

BLACK: I'm not sure what you mean.

MANKOWSKI: For example, would you describe her as hysterical?

BLACK: No, I would not.

MANKOWSKI: Would you describe her as calm?

BLACK: I think that would describe it, yes. She was calm.

MANKOWSKI: When you and Detective Washington came to her door to request an interview, was Miss Greer surprised to see you?

RANSOM WELLS: Objection. The witness cannot judge the defendant's state of mind.

MANKOWSKI: It's a valid question, Your Honor. I am asking an experienced detective to give his expert impression of events.

JUDGE HEIDNIK: I'll allow it this once, but please stick to factual questions going forward, Mr. Mankowski.

MANKOWSKI: Thank you, Your Honor. Detective Black, please answer the question. Was Miss Greer surprised that the police had come to interview her?

BLACK: I don't know.

MANKOWSKI: You don't know what surprise looks like?

BLACK: I didn't ask her if she was surprised, so I can't answer that question.

MANKOWSKI: I see. I'll stick to factual observations, then. When you came to her door with Detective Washington and during that first interview, did Miss Greer weep?

BLACK: No, she did not.

MANKOWSKI: Did she struggle or act hysterical?

BLACK: No.

MANKOWSKI: Did she ask what this was about, what was going on?

BLACK: I think it was pretty clear what was going on. The police were asking to speak with her.

MANKOWSKI: Please answer the question. Did Beth Greer ask what was going on?

BLACK: No, she did not ask us that.

MANKOWSKI: Did she request a lawyer?

BLACK: In that first interview, no, she did not.

MANKOWSKI: Did Beth Greer comply and answer your questions in that first interview?

BLACK: Yes, for the first part.

MANKOWSKI: And what happened after the first part?

BLACK: It's in the recording and the transcript. She got up and left.

MANKOWSKI: Did Beth Greer seem like she was taking this seriously?

BLACK: I have no idea if she was taking it seriously. I assume she was.

RANSOM WELLS: Objection, Your Honor.

JUDGE HEIDNIK: Sustained. The jury is asked to disregard that question and answer.

MANKOWSKI: I'll ask one more factual question. Did Beth Greer use angry profanity in that first interview?

BLACK: It was a stressful situation.

MANKOWSKI: Please answer the question.

BLACK: I don't—

RANSOM WELLS: Objection, Your Honor.

JUDGE HEIDNIK: This is factual, so I'll allow it.

MANKOWSKI: Please answer the question, Detective. We can all hear the recording and read the transcript, but I'd like your answer. Did Beth Greer use profanity when you interviewed her?

BLACK: Yes, she did.

MANKOWSKI: Can you please read this line from the interview transcript? Right there.

BLACK: Here?

MANKOWSKI: Yes, you can see it clearly. This line here.

BLACK: "It wasn't me, you idiot. I wasn't in that fucking car."

CHAPTER THIRTY-EIGHT

February 1978

BETH

Beth sat in the courtroom for the whole thing, watching. By then, she was so numb that it didn't seem real. This was happening to someone else, on TV or in the movies. Ransom brought her clothes—blouses, skirts hemmed below the knee, pumps—and Beth wore them. She tied her hair at the back of her neck and wore makeup, but not too much.

Her job was to sit in silence and not speak. Ransom didn't put her on the stand. *No offense,* he'd said, *but that would be the height of idiocy. So no goddamned way are you getting up there.* Ransom rarely swore.

There was a motion from the press to have the trial televised. Ransom fought it and won. Beth was relieved, though not because she wanted privacy or had any fear of a media circus. Nothing could be said about her that was worse than what had been said already. No, what she was afraid of was Lily watching the entire thing on TV.

She'd absorb every word, every gesture, just like everyone else would. She would relish the chaos she'd caused. She'd make fun of Beth's outfits, laugh in front of the TV. Beth didn't want Lily to know exactly how confused everyone was, how incredibly wrong they had it. She didn't want to give Lily the satisfaction.

She didn't want Lily to see the testimony about the dangerous, psychotic woman who had done this, and possibly get angry.

And she didn't want Lily to see Detective Black.

He looked as handsome as ever on the stand, wearing a dark blue suit and a wide blue tie. He'd had a haircut, and she missed the slightly too-long look he usually had. With his hair cut short, he looked more like a cop, though there were faint lines around the edges of his eyes and he looked painfully uncomfortable. He kept his gaze trained on the prosecutor, Charles Mankowski, and never looked at her, but she could feel his awareness of her all the same.

Halfway through his testimony, Ransom shifted in his seat and wrote something on his notepad, angling it so she could see. *Hostile*, the note said. Black was supposed to be a witness for the prosecution, but he was deflecting Mankowski, not following the script. Beth had listened to enough of Ransom's wisdom by now to know that this was a problem for Mankowski, to have one of his own witnesses disagreeing with him. Sure enough, the next thing Ransom wrote was: *This is good*.

Beth raised her gaze back to the witness stand again. Black was answering about whether she had taken it seriously when she was questioned, and Ransom stood to object. The judge answered, and for a second Black turned her way and their eyes met. He looked and sounded cool when he answered questions, but in that brief look Beth could see that he was miserable and torn. *I have to say all of this*, that look told her. *I can't say anything else, because you didn't give me anything.* He knew she hadn't murdered anyone. He knew that whoever had shot those men in the face was still out there, maybe about to shoot someone else. But he had no proof, no evidence, no trail to follow, and it was killing him.

Mankowski went back to murdering Beth's character, asking whether she'd used profanity. It was so stupid she would have laughed if her life weren't on the line. Black answered, though he didn't want to. *It's okay*, she telegraphed to him, even though he wasn't looking at her. *I'm not mad.* She realized for the first time, watching him, that she was looking at probably the only good person she'd ever met in her life. A person who got up every morning actually wanting to right wrongs, a person who wasn't out to serve himself or get rich or check out with alcohol and drugs when things got too hard. Someone who was going to marry a kindergarten teacher and have nice kids and actually be a good father. The only person in her life who hadn't lied when he'd told her he was trying to help her. He really had tried.

If she'd given him Lily, handed her over to him, it would have been the best gift he'd ever been given. It would have put all of his questions and doubts to rest, and he would have known he was bringing a true murderer to justice. But if they had no evidence against Beth, then they had no evidence against Lily, either. No gun, no fingerprints, no way to prove she was there or even in town. If Beth could slip away from this, slide her neck out of the noose, then so could Lily. The difference was that once Lily was free again, she'd start to think about killing. She'd start planning something bad.

And if Beth made Detective Black Lily's enemy, he'd be dead before he could see what was coming. Even if she warned him.

No one would listen to her warnings about Lily. That, she already knew.

Black's testimony ended. Ransom declined to cross-examine him, not wanting to trample on Mankowski's disaster, wanting to leave the memory of that hostile witness in the jury's minds. Black was dismissed and left the stand as well as the courtroom.

Everyone was watching.

Beth kept her gaze ahead of her, on nothing, her expression blank and slightly bored, as if Detective Black meant nothing to her. She didn't have to watch him to know that he didn't look at her, either. There was nothing for anyone to see. Even Ransom was making quick notes to himself, not looking at Black leaving the room. Without anyone seeing, her knight had tilted at windmills for her as much as he could, and now it was over. She was alone.

Beth looked at nothing as the courtroom buzzed quietly around her, and thought, *What will I do if I get out of here?*

Two weeks later, she was acquitted. The jury had deliberated for four days.

They gave her her things back, had her sign papers. Made her wait in one room, then another. She knew this was a monumental moment, that everything was changing yet again, but all she could think was that she was incredibly hungry and she wanted a drink. She wondered if Ransom would give her money for a hamburger, or whether she had her own money again. She wondered where Lily was. There was no way her sister was missing this. She probably wasn't far.

Ransom eventually came to get her. This was a triumphant day for him. "There's a sea of media outside," he warned her. He looked her over. "You're wearing that?"

"Yes," Beth said, adjusting the red shawl around her shoulders that she'd bought at the Edengate Mall. She'd had Ransom bring it to her in a suitcase, along with a list of other clothes. It was over. She never had to go back to her jail cell, never had to eat that food or talk on that awful phone. There was a liquor cabinet at the Greer mansion that had been fully stocked the day she'd been arrested.

She knew it wasn't possible, but if she inhaled the scent of the red shawl, if she concentrated on it, she thought she could smell her mother.

She put on Mariana's red lipstick, too. Then she left to face the reporters.

CHAPTER THIRTY-NINE

October 2017

SHEA

"The question is," the voice in my ear asked, "what makes a killer? Are killers born, or are they made? Can they be stopped, or are they simply a human anomaly, a genetic gamble? Maybe the killing itself is buried deep in his psyche, waiting for the chance to come out. Or maybe the would-be murderer can be saved, the course of his life changed. Maybe it's happened a million times, and because he never killed anyone, we never knew it was possible."

I pulled my earbuds out. I was listening to a podcast this time instead of an audiobook as I sat in the break room at work. The half-eaten remains of my sandwich sat on the table in front of me.

Karen poked her head around the door, an annoyed look on her face. "Lunch break is over, Shea."

"Right," I said, pushing my chair back. I was lost in a fog today, forgetting details, not listening. I had to keep it together, come out of the dark into my real life. I needed this job. I had bills to pay. I couldn't think about murder all the time.

I dumped my food into the garbage and came back out to the front of the doctor's office, taking my seat behind the Plexiglas. There were six people in the waiting room, reading or talking softly or, in one case, napping. It was quiet and stuffy. For the first time, I realized that Esther was right about this job: I was literally spending all of my life in a waiting room.

"It's quiet," Karen said. "The doctor was reviewing patient files this morning. You can put them away while I take my lunch." She nodded to a cart, then turned to grab her lunch bag and leave. As she did, the cart jostled and a stack of files fell to the ground.

I got off my chair and squatted, picking up the files as Karen walked away. I had one in my hand when I realized it was Beth's.

Karen had left, and there was no one who could see me. I was crouched on the floor behind the desk, out of sight of everyone, out of sight of the security cameras that kept watch on the waiting room. I had maybe ten seconds.

It was like the kiss with Michael—I didn't even think. I flipped open the file and looked at the top page, scanning it. I read the diagnosis, the notes from the doctor. The analysis of the test results.

Oh, Beth, I thought.

There's a reason behind everything Beth does, Ransom Wells had said. *Ask yourself why Beth has decided to tell everything now, after all of these years.*

I closed the file, stacked it with the others, and put them away, my mind circling over what I'd just read. When Karen came back from her lunch break, I said, "I don't feel well."

She looked me over. "You don't look so good."

"I think I'm feverish." I gathered my things, put on my sweater. This was a doctor's office; the last thing we were supposed to do was spread illness to the patients. "I'll go home and go to bed."

She shrugged and turned away as a patient came to the window.

I left the office and stood on the sidewalk. What I'd just read in the file was still going around in my mind, but it also seemed off. It had something to do with why Beth had agreed to talk to me, but it wasn't the only reason. There had to be something else.

I pulled out my phone and opened my email, scrolling back for the message from Michael about the Linwood Street property records. I had a gut feeling I was missing something, a detail that was an important piece of the puzzle. Maybe it was buried in the past, in the property records.

I stopped scrolling when I saw the Google alert that had come into my inbox days ago. It was an alert I'd had for years, set to deliver me anything to do with crime in Claire Lake, in case there was a juicy story I could use for the Book of Cold Cases. There was so little crime here that I didn't get an alert very often. I'd forgotten about this one almost as soon as it came in, and it was still unopened.

Feeling something strange in the pit of my gut, I opened it.

It was a news article scraped from the *Claire Lake Weekly Press*, one of the few newspapers—if you could call it that—left after the gutting of local media over the past twenty years. It usually focused on upcoming street festivals and farmers' markets, mixed with laconic paragraphs about the occasional break-in and bicycle theft. Any darker crimes that happened in Claire Lake—domestic violence, drug overdoses—were ignored, as if they never happened at all.

The *Weekly Press* had reported this story because its air of mystery was of the safe, cozy kind that wouldn't upset the tourists too much. The underpaid stringer who wrote it had done the usual bare minimum for his tiny fee:

UNIDENTIFIED REMAINS
WILL UNDERGO DNA TESTING

Human remains, possibly several decades old, were found near the east shore of Claire Lake by two children playing in the woods last month, according to the Claire Lake Police Department.

The remains were found on the uninhabited side of the lake in early September. They were in a state of advanced decomposition, and only a few parts were recovered. "We do not yet know who this person is," said Officer Martin Furlong of the Claire Lake PD in a statement. "There are no residences near where the body was found. It appears to be a hiker who possibly got lost, or it is a body that was left there by someone unknown." Asked if the body could be the victim of a crime, Officer Furlong replied, "We don't know yet, and given the state of the remains, we may never know. That's up to the coroner."

County coroner Tamara Li has stated that the remains are those of a Caucasian woman who has been dead anywhere from 25 to 45 years. She was in her mid-20s when she died. The coroner's office is not releasing any other details, but they have confirmed that the remains are being tested for DNA to help narrow down who the woman might be.

Asked for a cause of death for the unknown woman, the coroner's office declined to comment.

It's possible that no cause of death is able to be determined with remains that old. Police are trying to match the body to missing persons reports, and anyone who may have information on the unidentified woman is asked to call the Claire Lake Police Department.

It was right there, in my inbox: the reason Beth Greer had agreed to talk to me, to have the entire story come out right now.

Lily had been found.

I knew it as surely as I knew my own name. That was Lily, out there in the woods at the edge of the lake. They would run the DNA, and then—what? There had been no DNA testing in 1977, but Beth's blood and saliva could have been taken when she was arrested. Or maybe they'd find another connection through her family tree. They might not connect the body to Beth tomorrow, or next week, or next month, but they *would* connect it sooner or later. And Beth knew it.

I sent the article to Michael with the message: *I want to know everything about this.* I started for the bus stop, my feet moving slowly at first, then faster. It was starting to make sense now, this crazy story. But there were still pieces missing. Pieces I had no choice but to find.

I'd gone this far; it was time to go the rest of the way.

Before the bus arrived, I did one last thing: I called Esther's cell phone.

She answered on the second ring. "Shea? Is everything okay?"

"I'm sorry to bother you," I said. "I know you're working."

"It's okay. What's the matter?"

Because she knew something was the matter. She always knew.

"I just wanted to tell you," I said to my sister, "I met this woman. She was acquitted of murder forty years ago. No one has ever been sure if she's innocent. She agreed to do an interview with me. I've been talking to her for weeks now."

"Alone?" Esther sounded alarmed.

"Yes. I thought it would be fine. She's been telling me things. Some of it might be lies, but I think most of it is the truth. I don't think she did the murders, but I think what really happened might be worse. There are ghosts in her house that terrify me. And I met Michael, my private detective, face-to-face for the first time, and I kissed him. The second time, not the first time. And I got a cat by accident. His name is Winston Purrchill."

"Okay," Esther said.

"So I've had a lot going on, too," I said. "Things I haven't been telling you. You said I've been so far away, and I know that's true. I don't want to be far away anymore. I want to tell you everything. If you have a baby, I want to be part of it, as much as you'll let me. You're my best friend. If you called me and told me to get you a U-Haul and some garbage bags again, I'd do it. I'd do it as many times as you asked me to."

"Oh." There was a pause, and I knew Esther was crying. "Oh, Shea. Of course you'll be part of it. You're my best friend, too. But I worry about you. This thing you're involved with sounds dangerous. You need to walk away from it. You need to let it go."

"I can't." People were passing me on the sidewalk, ignoring me. The bus was coming. "I have to see it to the end."

"Don't. I don't like the sound of it. I can rescue you this time, Shea. Let me do it."

I shook my head, even though she couldn't see me. "I can finish this. I have to. And then I'm going to change things, Esther. I promise."

I hung up before I could change my mind and beg my big sister to come get me and fix everything. Right away, my phone rang. Michael.

I answered it. "Did you get my message?"

"Is this what I think it is?" He sounded excited.

"If you mean Lily, then yes. It's her."

The bus pulled up, and the doors opened. I got on, my phone still to my ear.

"I'll call my contacts," Michael said. "One of them will know something. The coroner likely has a theory about cause of death. She just didn't share it with the press."

"I want to know if Beth's blood or saliva was taken in 1977. If it wasn't, I can get you a sample." I thought about the glass Beth drank from, her grapefruit juice and soda. Maybe it was still sitting on the table.

"Wait a minute," Michael said. "Where are you right now?"

"I'm going to the Greer mansion."

"You're going to talk to her?"

"No. She isn't there." That had been in the file I'd read. "She's in Portland for a medical test. She won't be back until tomorrow."

"So you're going to—what? Break in? That isn't a good idea, Shea."

"It's the only way to get answers. I'd appreciate it if you didn't call the police. I don't plan to steal anything, I promise."

"Jesus, Shea—"

"She has an aneurysm," I said. I could lose my job for telling him, but I didn't care anymore. "It's dangerous, and it's inoperable. If it bursts, she dies. She could die tomorrow, or she could live another decade. There's no way to know."

"My God. So that's part of the reason she decided to talk now."

"But not why she chose me." I stared out the window of the bus as Claire Lake went by. "I still don't know why she chose me. I'll be fine, Michael. I'll call you when I'm out of there."

I didn't give him a chance to answer. I hung up the phone, turned it off, and watched Claire Lake recede beneath me as the bus climbed to Arlen Heights.

CHAPTER FORTY

October 1977

BETH

She was looking for Lily.

It wasn't the first time. Over the years, during the periods Lily had vanished, Beth had sometimes hired a private detective to look for her. She'd paid out of the money left to her after Julian died. But it was always fruitless, because when Lily wanted to vanish, she'd simply vanished.

Still, Beth had looked. When Lily vanished again after Mariana died, she'd looked. And when she felt that her sister was close—with the same dreamlike certainty she'd had years ago, looking at Lily's footprints in the dewy grass—she'd even get in her car and drive around Claire Lake, wondering if she'd see Lily at the next stoplight, around the next corner.

Lily was close now. Beth could feel it, but that wasn't why she was driving tonight. She was driving because Lily had killed a man.

He'd been left on the side of the road. Shot in the face, like Julian. But this man wasn't someone Lily knew. She'd chosen someone random, and she'd left a note: *Am I bitter or am I sweet? Ladies can be either.*

Lily had gone into her clock tower at last.

Beth had gotten a phone call four months ago, after Lily had been gone for well over a year. *I'm in a hospital*, Lily had said, the line crackling. *They don't know my real name. I don't have any identification. I want to get out of here, Beth. I need you to come and get me. Please. Please.*

Was it the truth? There was always that question with Lily, but Beth hadn't cared. She'd felt numb at the sound of Lily's voice, followed by scathing relief that wherever Lily was, she might be locked up in a hospital. *Thank God someone is looking after her so I don't have to,* Beth had thought. *Someone is keeping her from hurting people.*

It could have been a lie to get Beth's sympathy and, more importantly, her money, but something in Lily's voice told Beth it might not be. For the first time in Beth's life, Lily actually sounded worried about something. In fact, by the end of the call, as she heard the hopelessness in Beth's voice, she'd begged.

Get me out of here. Please, Beth. Please.

Beth drove downtown. Lily wouldn't have much money, so she would have to find a cheap room to rent. Beth started with Claire Lake's cheapest motels, then the YWCA. *Have you seen this woman?* She used one of the only photos she had of Lily, from their last Christmas together. It was ridiculously out-of-date, but Lily hated to have her picture taken, and Beth didn't have anything more recent.

Lily Knowles? she asked at place after place. *Veronica Jenshak? Amy McMaster?* She tried the aliases she knew, but no one recognized them, or the photo.

So Beth got back into her father's Buick and thought again. Lily was here; she was sure of it. She also knew that Lily expected Beth to be looking for her. The note left with that man's body had been so clear. Lily wanted Beth to panic, to find her, to stop her. To Lily, it was a game.

Get me out of here. Please, Beth. Please, Lily had said in that phone call four months ago.

And Beth had said, *No.*

She didn't know what had landed Lily in a mental hospital, and she hadn't asked. What had mattered was that Lily was locked up, looked after, unable to hurt anyone. Beth had hung up the phone with a sense of relief. Lily wasn't her problem anymore.

And for a while, she wasn't. But now this.

Wherever she'd been, Lily was free.

Beth rubbed the hangover from behind her eyes and tried to make herself think, but she was so tired. This was her fault. She should have found out what hospital Lily was in, made sure she stayed there forever so that no one else would die. She should have done . . . something. Anything.

Think, Beth, think. Where else would someone go when they had no money? Then she knew. The houseboats on the piers—the eyesore of Claire Lake. If there was a room to rent on one of those ratty old boats, it would be the perfect spot.

Beth drove the Buick to the piers and got out, tying her trench coat more tightly in the chill wind.

The third boat was the winner. Lily had used her Veronica Jenshak name and rented a room, an impossibly small sliver of space, for cash. She'd packed her bag and left only an hour ago.

Beth searched the empty room, flipping the mattress on the bunk and looking in the meager cupboard, swearing to herself because she already knew she'd find nothing.

The landlady could describe her sister's car, though: a blue Pinto with rust on the back bumper. *I'm coming for you, Lily,* Beth thought as she got into her father's expensive Buick and started it again. *Drive fast, because I'm coming.*

She knew her sister. Lily had left the houseboat for good—stiffing the landlady on part of the rent—and wasn't coming back to the piers. She was out cruising, hunting somewhere, but Beth didn't think Lily had left town yet. She bought a bottle of wine and kept driving.

The sun was setting. The dead man had been shot after leaving work. Would Lily try the same tactic again? Beth scanned the slowly emptying streets of downtown. She saw a blue Pinto and followed it for half a mile before she could catch a glimpse of the driver, who wasn't Lily. Then she circled back to downtown. The first bottle of wine was almost finished, so she bought a second one.

She ended up on the edge of Claire Lake, on a side road no one used. She got out of the car, listening to the silence over the water. Lily was here somewhere. Beth was half-drunk, and the wine flushed her with grief and anger, sadness and an almost unbearable ache. She was all-powerful, and she was a speck of insignificance. She knew everything and nothing at once. Alcohol always did this to her in the beginning—it was why she loved it so much.

There was a flash of headlights at the other end of the lake, through the trees.

Beth had gotten back into the car and was about to slam the door when she heard a *crack* echoing across the dark, empty water, like a firework. Or a gunshot.

She put the car into gear and reversed up the path to the main road.

She drove fast, the Buick slicing up and down over ruts. *Did I really hear that?* Her thoughts spun wildly. *Did I?*

She thought she heard another *crack*—or was that the car? She careened around one turn, then another, coming out onto Claire Lake Road. There was a car pulled over ahead, the engine running, the headlights on. A second car was pulling away as Beth turned the corner. It was a blue Pinto.

She made a snap decision and stopped next to the car that was pulled over. She opened her door and put one foot out to get out, to help whoever it was. She froze.

It was already over. A man was dead on the ground. And his face . . . his face . . .

Beth went cold. *I'm too late.*

I need to run. I need to catch her.

Beth got back in the Buick and put it into gear, speeding up onto the road, looking for the fading taillights of the Pinto.

And behind her, a man walking his dog came out of the trees and watched her go before he ran for the nearest phone.

CHAPTER FORTY-ONE

October 2017

SHEA

The Greer mansion stood in shades of gray and white, like a tinted photograph. The wind had kicked up, cold and wet, though the rain hadn't started yet. There was no one around as I got off the bus and walked up the street, no cars going by, no one walking their dog. Arlen Heights was hushed and quiet.

There was no car in the driveway. I stood facing the house, still wearing my work clothes and coat, my messenger bag strapped over my shoulder and across my chest. I took a minute to take in the swirling ugliness of the house, its pretension and clumsy lines and misery. An awful thing that was tolerated because it was made with money and pretended to have class. *It's an abomination that shouldn't exist*, Lily had said, according to Beth. *That's why I like it.*

I pulled out my phone and turned it on. I ignored all of the missed texts and messages from Michael, from my sister. I called Beth.

"I'm at your house," I said when she answered.

"I know," Beth said.

"How do you know when you're in Portland?"

"So you looked at my file," Beth said. "I wondered if you would. I admire you for it. It's what I would have done if I were you."

"How did you know I'm at your house?"

"I have a motion sensor that triggers whenever someone comes up the driveway. I'd like to know if someone is going to burn the house down. That way I can cheer them on."

I scanned the front of the house. "Are there cameras?"

"Lily smashed all the cameras a long time ago. I never tried again."

"She doesn't like her picture taken," I said.

"She never did. That photo I sent you is one of the only ones I have of her. Lily didn't like to see herself on camera."

"Maybe they can do a computer reconstruction of her face," I said. "That is, if they found her skull."

There was a long moment of silence on the other end of the line. "Oh, Shea," Beth said, and her voice was impossible to interpret. "I see you've been paying attention."

"What did you do?" I shouted into the phone.

"I stopped her."

In front of me, a light went on in the upstairs of the Greer mansion, where no one was home.

"You stopped her?" I said.

"Yes. No police with their burden of proof. No trials and no lawyers. No more hospitals that didn't fix her, then let her out again. I stopped her. Me. Because I was responsible, and I always had been. I was responsible for every single death, just like you've felt responsible ever since you escaped your abductor's car."

That was an unexpected punch to the gut. Because she was right—
I did feel responsible. It made no sense, but guilt doesn't have to. It
simply exists, weighing you down and choking you until you can't
breathe anymore.

Another light went on in the house, this one on the other side, the
light beaming out of the window and glowing on the leaves of the
trees. It should have been a comforting sight, but it wasn't.

I watched the light go on downstairs in the living room. The lights
in the house were getting brighter, the white glow blasting through
the windows and into the lowering gloom. My cheeks were numb now,
and so were my hands, the hand holding my phone so cold I couldn't
feel where my fingertips touched the plastic. The wind grew sharper,
and the first splatter of rain hit my skin, harsh and cold.

"How did you do it, Beth?" I asked. "How did you kill her?"

"You have so many questions," Beth said. "Go ask her. She'll
tell you."

Lily was in there, lighting up the windows and wandering the
halls. If I went in, it would just be her and me.

Then again, maybe that was what I'd come here for. To talk to
Lily alone.

As if someone knew what I was thinking, the front door of the
Greer mansion opened with a *click*. It swung wide, the light spilling
onto the front porch. She was inviting me in.

I knew I shouldn't go. I wondered if she'd kill me. I wondered if
she'd try.

I wouldn't let her. Lily didn't get to kill *everyone*.

"You may as well do it," Beth Greer said in my ear. "She wants you
to, and you know you aren't going to say no."

"Is that what you want?" I asked.

"What I want is for this to be over. I want to stop doing penance.
It's time for the real story to come out, and you're the one to tell it. If
you have the guts."

I looked at the house. What was I going to do? Go home? Lock my doors and hide, like I'd been doing for twenty years? Spend the rest of my life in hiding?

If I did that, what would I have to live for? What kind of life had I chosen since that cold winter day when I was nine?

"Screw it," I said to Beth, and I hung up the phone. I dropped it in my bag and walked to the front door, not giving myself time to think. I'd been thinking too long, too hard. I'd done nothing but think. Where had it gotten me?

I stepped through the door expecting to be blinded by the bright light inside, but the Greer mansion looked the same as always. It was dim and clean, untouched and faintly musty. I stepped into the corridor as the front door slammed shut behind me. "Lily?" I said.

There was no answer. I walked into the living room, taking in the burnt orange sofa, the squat coffee table with its angled legs, the shelf of awful figurines on the wall. The curtains on the windows were closed. The silence was oppressive, like someone was watching me.

I turned toward the corridor, the stairs. I could go into the kitchen, but I didn't want to. There was a bad, coppery smell coming from there, and it made my stomach turn. I had the feeling that if I went into the kitchen, I'd see something I didn't want to see. How had Beth ever come back into this house? Why didn't she tear it down, brick by brick?

The stairs creaked under the soles of my sneakers as I climbed. I reached the landing and looked down the corridor. The upstairs hall was dim and silent, the doors closed. The quiet was so heavy it was a living thing, pressing into my skin and trying to push down my throat.

I walked to the end of the hall to the last door—the master bedroom. I pushed open the door and saw a king-sized oak bed, matching nightstands, large dressers, a wardrobe. There were ashtrays on the nightstands, a yellowed book next to one of them, and through the half-open closet door I could see the sleeve of a red dress.

Beth sleeps here, I thought in horror. It was like a museum for a bygone era, for people who were long dead. The only sign that Beth lived in this room was the unmade bed and a tube of Sephora hand cream, the modern label jarring, like something in a dream.

I walked to the closet and opened it. I recognized some of the clothes as Beth's, but there were polyester dresses in here, leopard-print blouses and cork-soled shoes. Mariana's clothes.

Beth Greer lived like this, buried in her parents' belongings. She'd lived like this all these years.

This place was suffocating and dead. I could barely breathe in this closet; I had no idea why Beth had lived like this for so long. Why she'd wanted to.

Maybe she hadn't wanted to.

I grabbed a handful of hangers from the closet, then another, then another. I dumped a pile of dresses on the bed—silk, rayon, polyester. Gold, powder blue, fire-engine red. I opened a drawer in the dresser and found Mariana's old girdles and bras, her high-waisted under-wear. I threw all of those on the bed, too. If Beth couldn't get rid of all of these things, then I would.

I left the master bedroom and walked into the next room—Beth's teenage room. It had a narrow bed with a checkered blanket. There was an expensive 1970s stereo in a cabinet with glass doors, a record player on top of it and a stack of records leaning against it on the floor, as if someone had just been riffling through them, choosing what to play.

Gritting my teeth, I grabbed the records and threw them out into the hall, letting them crash to the floor. Peter Frampton, Neil Diamond, Fleetwood Mac. I opened the closet and found Beth's teenage clothes in here, jeans and wraparound flowered tops. I threw those into the hall with the records, letting them crumple off the hangers. It felt good to destroy this place, to rip open its wounds. It felt good to make the dust billow. If I could have drawn a deep breath, I would have screamed into the silence.

I finished wrecking Beth's teenage room and walked back out into the hall. The door to the master bedroom was open. I walked to it and looked in.

Everything I'd torn out of the closet was back in its place. The room looked like I'd never touched it.

Fear clenched my stomach, and I understood. This wasn't Beth's house; it was Lily's.

There was a cold breath on the back of my neck, and something smashed me into the wall. I hit the wall hard, the breath rushing out of me in surprise, and icy hands wound into my hair, pulling my head back.

I did scream then, the sound ripping out of me. I was staring at the ceiling, my head pulled back by a hand I couldn't see. Something was breathing on me, its breath so cold I shuddered in repulsion.

Look, it said.

Still gripping my hair, the hands pushed me down the hall. The door on my right flew open. The door to Beth's childhood room. I struggled and screamed again, trying to twist out of the thing's grip, but it was impossible. I was shoved to the doorway, then through it.

And as I stepped over the threshold, I wasn't in the Greer mansion anymore.

It was freezing. I was standing at the side of a road, looking around in the dark. Gravel crunched under my feet and the wind crept down my collar onto my neck. I could see the road, trees, and between the trees, the distant dark surface of a lake.

I was at the edge of Claire Lake. A few feet from me, a car was pulled over—a blue Pinto. The hood was popped open, and a woman stood in front of it, staring down into the guts of the car. Her blond hair obscured her face. Her hands were in the pockets of her wool coat.

And then I knew: It was the night of October 15, 1977, and Lily Knowles was about to kill someone.

"No," I said, but no one heard me. I wasn't here; I was in Beth's old bedroom. But then why could I taste the lake in the air, and why did I know exactly what was about to happen?

There was the sound of a motor, the sweep of headlights, and the crunch of gravel. A man's voice called out: "Need some help?"

"No," I said again, but even though I saw my breath plume into the night air, no one heard me. Lily looked up, and a smile flashed across her face as she saw the man. She was the girl from the Christmas photo, only now she was a grown woman, her face filled out and her body curved beneath her coat. Her blond hair was soft and gleaming, and her smile was on the edge of flirtatious. She was irresistible.

Ransom Wells had said Lily made him want to crawl out of his skin, and right now, I could see it. There was nothing behind Lily's eyes—nothing at all.

"Sure," Lily said. "I'd love some help."

I screamed, though still no one heard me. I lurched forward, trying to stop what was going to happen, but my hands hit glass. I banged on it, kicked it. Thomas Armstrong got out of his car and closed the door behind him, smiling at Lily.

"Let me help," he said.

I screamed and screamed, banging on the glass.

Lily turned toward him, her hands still in the pockets of her coat. She took a step on the roadside gravel in her black pumps. I could hear everything—the slam of his car door, the gravel under their feet, the drone of a far-off car on the two-lane highway that crossed several hundred feet away. I could see Lily's hair lift from her neck in the damp wind, could see the thick mascara on her lashes and the dusting of light blue eyeshadow. She had pinkish gloss on her lips and blush on her cheekbones. Above her smile, her eyes were dark and cold as she took another step toward Armstrong, who was walking forward. Then she took her gloved hand out of her pocket.

There were tears running down my face now. I banged my fists on the glass over and over, shouting "No," but I knew it would make no difference. It was October 15, 1977, and what was going to happen was going to happen. It was already done.

I was still screaming when the gun went off twice. Still screaming and banging on the glass when Lily stepped over the body and dropped a note on it. Still screaming as she slammed the hood of her car, got in, and drove away.

I leaned against the glass, my throat ragged. I was crying; I couldn't say why. Thomas Armstrong had been dead for forty years, and this was some kind of sick movie, a replay so Lily could torture me. I had to get out of here. I didn't want to be in this place, in this time.

I took a step back, and I was standing in Beth's old bedroom, my hands on the glass of the window that looked out over the yard. My skin was cold and clammy, and my face was wet. I blinked my burning eyes and lifted my hands off the glass.

"What was that for?" I shouted into the silence. "Why did you show me that? I already know the ending."

Behind me, footsteps came down the hall from the master bedroom, nearly at a run. A figure flashed past the doorway, and I glimpsed blond hair, much like Lily's. Except that wasn't Lily.

I stepped out the door as the footsteps rushed down the stairs. "No," a voice said in soft panic. "I'm sorry, Lily. I'm so sorry."

"Mariana?" I called.

I hurried down the stairs, following her. I didn't care that she'd been dead for decades, that I was chasing a ghost. Her voice sounded terrified, almost ragged with pain. I caught sight of her in the front hallway, which was ice-cold. I descended the last step with my breath pluming from my mouth.

Mariana Greer—it was definitely Mariana, the woman I recognized from her wedding photograph—was standing at the front door. She was in a silk negligee under a white bathrobe, her feet bare. Her hair was tied back with a headscarf, the kind women used to wear to bed to preserve their hairstyles, with her blond hair spilling out the back. In that moment, even though she had died in 1975, she was as real as I was. I could see the tears tracking down her face as she fumbled clumsily at the door.

"I'm so sorry," she said. "Where did you go, baby? Please don't leave. I'm so sorry."

What had happened? An argument? Had Lily left? Why was no one trying to stop Mariana from leaving in her nightgown in the state she was in?

"Don't go," I said, but she had figured out the lock now, and she was turning the knob. I lunged forward, thinking to hold the door closed, but nothing I did mattered. Mariana Greer opened the door and ran outside, heading for her car, trying to find her daughter. Heading for the accident that would kill her.

I ran out the front door after her, but Mariana was gone. The cold, wet air hit me in the face. The sky was bleak and gray, as if someone had bleached it; the clouds were inky black. What time was it? What day was it? How long had I been in the house?

I had to get out of here.

I took a shaky breath and stepped onto the porch, and then I looked down. There were wet footprints here, the impressions of rubber sneakers. Had Mariana been wearing sneakers, or had her feet been bare? Who had been standing on the porch with wet shoes? The tracks led into the grass, which was tamped down where someone had walked on it. The droplets of rain were disturbed in a path leading toward the trees and around the house.

Everything had been too strange for too long, and nothing mattered anymore. I stepped off the porch and walked onto the lawn, following the footprints through the trees.

In a moment, the wet, stark, black trees thinned and the vista behind the house opened up in front of me, the bare grass, the drop, the gray sky. It had the same effect it always had: It was awful and hypnotic at the same time, like the view looking down from a great height. I wanted to walk toward it; I felt the draw. I made my feet stay still, and I locked my gaze with Lily Knowles's at last.

She was standing in the middle of the lawn, her sneakered feet in the cold grass. She looked to be in her twenties; she had the narrow face I'd seen in the Christmas photo with a few more years passed, though in person—was this *in person*?—she was more beautiful. She was wearing jeans and a coat of army green, and both items hung off her frame, as if she'd either borrowed them from someone bigger or lost weight. Her blond hair was down around her shoulders, and it lifted in the wind as if she were really here.

"You're finally here," Lily said. Her voice was unreal, an echo. And yet I knew it was her real voice, coming from wherever she was.

And for a minute, I wasn't terrified. I was just standing on the lawn, looking at Lily Knowles, who was the reason I'd come. She was the reason I'd come from the beginning, though I hadn't known she existed at the time.

"You died," I said to her.

Lily, who wasn't real, who wasn't alive, shrugged in that way I instantly recognized from her half sister. It was the way I'd learned to shrug, too: *Maybe what you say is interesting, and maybe it isn't.* "Everyone dies," she said, her voice echoing.

"Why are you still here?"

"I'm waiting for Beth, and she knows it."

"Tell me why," I said, because I was looking at a serial killer, and I had no idea how much time I had. "Please, just tell me why."

"There's no why," Lily said. "There's only what happened. There's only what I did."

I shook my head. There had to be more. There had to be. "I don't understand."

The wind gusted up, hard and cold, and Lily held out her hand.

She was standing a few feet away, out of reach, but I still felt the fear begin to grip me again as I looked at that hand. There was no way I was going to take it. "What are you doing?" I asked her.

"You came back here for a reason," Lily said.

"No."

"Yes, you did." Her hand was still held out, and it held the same fascination and repulsion that the view over the drop had. I had the impulse to step toward it, and yet that was the last thing I wanted to do.

"Come with me," Lily said.

"No."

"It's too late. You're already here."

I knew I should run, but I couldn't. I moaned in terror as I tried to make my legs move, but they wouldn't obey me. "No," I said again.

"*Come with me.*" It was a hiss this time, harsh and furious, and then Lily's hand grabbed mine. I hadn't moved; I hadn't seen her move. But she had me, and her grip was icy and so hard, like concrete or bone. Her fingers crushed mine.

"Please," I begged her, wild with fear as she began to pull me slowly across the grass. "Please, Lily. Where are we going?"

"This is what you came for." I couldn't get free of her; she was holding me too hard, pulling me toward the drop to the ocean. "I'm going over, and you're going with me."

I started to scream, or at least I tried to. I didn't know if any sound came out of my throat or if it was all in my head. But I opened my mouth and tried, with everything I had, to scream as she yanked me forward.

I fought her. I really did. But I finally learned what Beth always knew about Lily: There was nothing to stop her when she wanted something. She took what she wanted. And now she was taking me.

She brought me to the edge. The toes of my sneakers went over, and I looked down. It wasn't a perfectly sheer drop; there were ledges, and brush, and rocks. And far below, the rocky shore and the ocean, the waves crawling up to the foot of the cliffs as the tide came in.

"Beautiful, isn't it?" Lily said.

I screamed.

But she had me in her grip, her icy chill moving all the way through me. My struggles were hopeless.

I tried to beg Lily for my life, but my breath was gone.

Her voice was in my ear, as intimate as a lover's. "Let's go," she said. And she pulled me down.

CHAPTER FORTY-TWO

March 1978

BETH

Snow had fallen the night before, and there were wet crystals on the ground, melting into the lawn. Beth's sneakers were damp, her feet icy as she turned the key in the door of the Greer mansion and stepped inside.

It was three o'clock in the morning. Since the day of her acquittal, Beth had been hiding in a motel for nearly a week while reporters camped on the street in front of her house. Courtesy of Ransom, she'd sat alone in a run-down room, sleeping and sometimes watching television. Thinking.

Eventually, her posh neighbors had had enough; they'd called the police, and now the press was gone. There had been nothing to see, anyway—no dramatic homecoming to report on. Just the same old headlines, day after day:

POSSIBLE "LADY KILLER" GOES FREE. BETH GREER UNREPENTANT. NOT GUILTY VERDICT ROCKS OREGON TOWN.

Whether Beth Greer killed those men in cold blood or someone else did, one of the newspaper editorials said, *the result is still the same: A killer is walking our streets right now, free.*

Tonight, with Arlen Heights quiet again, Beth had Ransom drop her off down the street so no one would see her come home. She was wearing jeans, an old dark sweater, a wool coat. Her hair was in a ponytail, and she wore no makeup. She had a single bag of belongings over her shoulder. The red shawl and the red lipstick were long gone.

She slipped silently into the house and locked the door behind her.

It was cold in here. Musty. Beth walked to the living room, and the first thing her gaze went to—even before she dropped her bag— was the liquor cabinet. She stared at the gleaming bottles, lined up just so. At the small fridge that contained chilled wine and ice. She could *taste* it, the cold vodka sliding down her throat, the decadent flavor of red wine. She could taste all of it.

She was out of jail now. She could drink. She could quit drinking forever and start a new life. She could do anything.

From upstairs came the sound of water running from a tap, and a footstep.

Beth closed her eyes. She had expected this. Those days sitting in the motel, waiting, she had known this would happen. It was time.

The cold air grew sharper, as if a door were open or a window broken somewhere, letting in a draft. Ignoring the running tap upstairs, Beth opened her eyes again and walked to the kitchen. She stood in the doorway, looking dully at the scene in front of her. The blood. The body.

Julian.

She hadn't been home the day he died, so she hadn't seen it, really. She hadn't felt the cold air or seen the blood, so this wasn't a memory. She and Mariana had come home after the cleaning crew that Ransom hired had left, though she imagined the kitchen always had a strange smell after that.

Still, she'd never seen it. She didn't know if she was seeing it now, whether this was real or she was losing her mind. She wasn't sure she cared.

After a while, she turned away from the kitchen and walked upstairs. The door to the master bedroom was open. Standing in front of Mariana's open closet, her back to Beth as she looked through the clothes, was Lily.

Beth was *definitely* seeing this. She knew that.

Lily was wearing a silk kimono that fell to her knees, the fabric covered in gaudy pink and purple flowers. Her blond hair flowed down her back. Her legs beneath the hem of the kimono were bare, and Beth could tell she was naked underneath it. In the en suite bathroom, the water ran in the tub. The kimono was one of Mariana's.

"Our mother had such beautiful clothes," Lily said to Beth without turning. "Most of them fit me, you know. I think I'm going to wear them."

"What are you doing?" Beth choked out. Even though she had known this would happen, had expected it—she'd baited Lily to come find her—it was still shocking to see Lily in this bedroom, wearing Mariana's clothes. *She really doesn't care*, Beth thought. *She really doesn't think I'll do anything.*

"I'm taking a bath." Lily turned and looked at her. Her face had that curious blank look that Beth had long ago learned to be afraid of. "I live in this house now."

The sight of Lily after all this time was hard to take. She looked like Mariana, like Beth, like herself. Beth knew every line of that face, from childhood to adulthood. She had loved that face and been terrified of it. She'd had nightmares over the years that Lily was dead, her body unidentified in a hospital somewhere. She'd also had nightmares about Lily coming home. She didn't know which was more frightening.

And now Lily was standing here, naked in Mariana's robe, and part of Beth wanted to scream and run, to forget everything she'd planned. Another part felt like all of her pieces were falling into place at last, like for the past months she'd been a doll who wasn't put together properly. She knew Lily like she knew her own heart.

There was only one way out of this. Only one way forward. She'd known it since she'd sat in a cell, watching Detective Black walk away.

"You can't live in my house," she said through numb lips.

"It'll be my house," Lily said. "You're out of prison now. You'll sign this place over to me, and it'll be mine."

"No."

Lily's voice was flat. "You have no choice, Beth."

Just do what she says. The instinct was so old it was automatic. *Do what Lily says, and she won't get mad.* But this time Beth fought it. "And where am I supposed to go?" She had a flash of leaving here, walking out the door. She could go anywhere, and she would be free. She could pretend, as she had so many times, that Lily didn't exist anymore.

And in the meantime, Lily would go back to killing. She always did.

"You're not going anywhere," Lily said. "You stay here with me. That murder trial bullshit is over—it was fun for a while, but now we can move on. You and me, in this house. Kind of like that first Christmas." She took a step toward Beth, and even though she was almost naked, it seemed threatening. Beth tried not to flinch. "We're sisters," Lily said. "Two halves of the same person."

We're not, Beth wanted to say, furious that what she'd just been through had been reduced to "murder trial bullshit." But the old instincts bubbled up again, persistent. When Lily was in this mood—when Lily was in most moods, honestly—it was best to placate her. But you had to do it so she wouldn't see through it. "I just got out," Beth said, putting a note of weakness in her voice. "I don't know what to do. I haven't thought about it."

"You'll do what I tell you," Lily said. "I'm done being half a person. I'm done being the girl who doesn't exist. This house is mine. And if you want to stay out of trouble, then you're mine, too."

Beth pictured spending the rest of her life here, doing whatever Lily wanted her to do. There would be blood on her hands sooner or later. Lily wouldn't want to keep doing her killings alone. "I know what you did," she said, trying not to panic. "Those two men. And before that—Lawrence Gage, was that his name? He was your father, and you killed him, too."

There was a quick second in which Lily was surprised, that unpleasant surprise that Beth had seen on her face only once before. Then she figured it out. "The lawyer," she said.

"He knows who your father was. Lawrence Gage's murder was in the papers, and Ransom showed me." She took a step closer to her sister, the words pouring out. "You broke in and shot him, just like you did to my father. To Julian." It was hard to say her father's name, and she shuddered, thinking of what she'd just seen in the kitchen. She made herself say it again. "You killed Julian."

Lily was utterly calm, watching her. "You wanted me to," she said. "He was going to make you marry that boy. He didn't love you like you wanted. When it was over, Beth, you never said a word. Not to Mariana, not even to your precious cop. You didn't tell anyone. Just like you did nothing that night when you watched Mariana get into her car."

Those words sliced her, the injury that went deepest and wouldn't heal. Lily had already stormed off that night. Yet she knew that Beth had stood there, watching their mother leave. Maybe they really were two halves of the same person, like Lily had said.

If Lily was a killer, then so was Beth. If they stayed here together, it was a matter of time before Lily made Beth do the next murder herself. And if Beth tried to go to the police, the first man on Lily's list would be Detective Black. The second one might be Ransom.

"Why?" Beth asked her sister. "Why do you do these things? Can you at least tell me why?"

Lily looked at her curiously. "Do you want a reason? I can pretend there is one, if you like. I can tell you it's because of my childhood, or the fact that my father raped my mother. I can tell you it's because of the foster homes. Or I can tell you I'm simply bad. Take your pick, Beth. I can tell you whatever you want."

"That's all?" Beth cried. "After everything, that's all you can say? Did you do it all just because you *wanted* to?"

"I don't know," Lily said. "I did want to. It was easy, you know. I thought it might be hard." She shook her head, frowning. "It's a high, killing someone. But sometimes . . . sometimes there's a moment where you have the power of life and death, and then you realize it doesn't make you any different than you were before." She rubbed her temple. "I'm going to take a bath. I don't want to talk about this anymore."

She turned her back, and just like that, everything died in Beth. Love, loyalty, even fear. She saw Mariana's face that last day they went shopping, the scarf in her blond hair. She saw Julian's face in the rear-view mirror as they drove to the Christmas party when Beth was sixteen, the crinkles at the edges of his unhappy eyes. She saw Paul Veerhoever crumpled at the side of the road, his face a bloody pulp in the darkness.

I loved you more than anything, she heard her mother say.

She felt nothing. Nothing.

No one is coming to save us.

We're two halves of the same person.

No one is coming.

She had known she would have to do this, no matter how hard it was. It was time.

She did it quickly. As the water ran in the bathtub, as Lily turned away, Beth grabbed her father's ashtray from the nightstand. The housekeepers had emptied the ashtray some long-ago day, but it still smelled like ashes, the smell that was Julian and Mariana. It was big and extremely heavy, made of solid thick glass. She swung it with every ounce of her strength at the back of Lily's head.

It was hard. *Hard.* Lily stumbled forward, but she didn't quite fall, and Beth had to hit her again. Again. Her hands were icy and numb. Her arm ached. Her brain had gone somewhere else, somewhere this wasn't happening, where time had no meaning. Maybe it had taken a few seconds to hit Lily with the ashtray; maybe it had taken hours. Beth would never know.

There was blood, and Lily was on the floor, but she wasn't dead. She twisted onto her back and hit Beth in the face, her fist smashing into Beth's cheek, and this time Beth had to hit Lily in the forehead. She thought she might be screaming.

When Lily went quiet, bleeding and moaning softly, Beth dragged her into the bathroom. The bathtub had started to overflow, water running onto the tiled floor. Beth pulled Lily's body to the tub and shoved her under the water, holding the back of her bloody head until her sister finally went still.

It was easy, you know, Lily said. *I thought it might be hard.*

There's a moment where you have the power of life and death, and then you realize it doesn't make you any different than you were before.

Beth wasn't crying now. She wasn't screaming. She wasn't making any sound at all.

She couldn't feel her hands in the warm water. Her knees were soaked. Her arms ached, and her stomach was hot and liquid. For a humiliating second, she thought she might shit herself, but somehow she didn't. Somehow she turned the water off and sat back, gasping breath after breath as if she'd been running.

The house was quiet, so quiet. If Beth had been screaming—she thought she might have been screaming—none of the neighbors would hear. She was alone.

No one was coming.

She breathed for a while, and then she thought about it, feeling strangely calm. There was the ashtray. Blood on the bedroom floor. The crumbs of old ashes. The water sloshing on the bathroom tile. The body.

She would need to clean up all of it.

She would need to put Lily somewhere no one could find her. She would have to do that alone.

But she thought maybe she could do it.

She looked at Lily's slumped body, still in the kimono, and she thought about crying. She thought about taking her sister's cold hand in hers, telling Lily she was sorry. She didn't do any of those things, because Lily would have hated it.

She reached out and touched her fingertips to the small of Lily's back, leaving them there for only a second before pulling them away again. Lily had always hated to be touched.

Beth got to her feet and got to work.

CHAPTER FORTY-THREE

October 2017

SHEA

I was drowning. I opened my mouth, and salt water rushed in, pushing its way down my throat. I couldn't breathe, couldn't open my eyes. Every part of my body was in pain.

I thrashed, and my hands scrabbled against rocks under the water, cold and slick. I clawed at them, trying to get my head above water. My head throbbed like it was going to explode. I was so disoriented I didn't know which way was up until the soles of my feet hit rock and I pushed off, screaming.

I broke the surface and screamed out loud into the air. I couldn't help it—pain was radiating from my knee up and down my leg, throbbing as my feet pressed against the rocks. The water was only waist-deep, but my legs wouldn't hold me. I sank again, resting on my good knee as I tried to wipe my hair out of my face and open my stinging eyes. I could only use my right arm; the left was useless, dangling in the water in a dead mass of agony.

I pushed my hair back, gasping and sputtering, blinking the salt into my eyes. I was at the bottom of the cliff, below the Greer mansion. I had fallen to the rocks where the tide was coming in. The freezing waves shoved at me, jerking at my useless arm and trying to unbalance me on my one good leg. I remembered Lily's hand gripping mine, the way she'd pulled me. *Let's go*, she'd said. But I didn't remember the fall itself. Was that a protective instinct in my brain, blocking out the fall? Or was that Lily?

Because as I'd fallen, she'd showed me everything.

The last night in the mansion. The confrontation with Beth. The ashtray. The bathtub.

How long had I fallen? Three seconds? Five? I'd seen all of it, the way you can dream a year's worth of dreams in a twenty-minute nap. Instead of seeing the rocks and the ocean rushing up at me, I'd seen Lily die.

The waves pushed harder at me as the tide continued to come in, and I tried to move myself toward the rocky shore. My knee and my arm screamed at me, even though both were under icy water. I glanced down and saw that my left arm was hanging at a crazy angle below the elbow, the elbow itself the wrong shape. I forced myself to look away as my teeth chattered. I must have hit the rocks at the bottom of the water when I landed, though I didn't remember it. I was probably lucky the tide was coming in, because if I'd hit the rocks without any water to break my fall, I'd be dead.

I moved my good leg and my good arm, pulling myself forward. I slipped and fell, then got purchase again. The pain was so bad I screamed, over and over, as I inched another step, and then another.

Did something touch the back of my neck?

I crawled faster, letting the pain wash over me. *This is it*, I thought grimly. *Drowning or hypothermia—that's how I'm going to go. Or maybe Lily will just grab me and finish me off.* She could push my head under the water, kill me the way Beth had killed her. If she bothered, I wouldn't be able to put up much resistance.

My body was shaking—adrenaline, fear, pain, shock, and cold taking over. My vision was blurred. I thought I saw a shape moving from the corner of my eye, but I couldn't be sure. I lurched to the left as my damaged knee buckled again, and reached out with my good hand to break my fall. I was emerging slowly out of the water now, into the shallower depths on the rocky shore, beating the incoming tide.

My elbow was broken. I knew it; the pain was too much, and I could feel bone grind against bone as I limped over the rocks. I blinked and realized that there was something red in my eyes. I touched my forehead and found a gash, open and salty and bleeding. I pressed my fingers to it, remembering some long-ago first-aid tip about stanching a wound. My neck was wrenched, and even my teeth hurt. Where was I going to go from here? Where was the nearest house? My bag and my phone were long gone, vanished into the ocean, and, despite my situation, I mourned all of those interviews, all of my notes, drifting away on the current somewhere.

I managed to get into knee-deep water, and then I turned course along the shore, parallel to the cliffs. With the blood slowing its flow into my eyes, I could see that I was heading in the direction of Claire Lake proper, away from Arlen Heights. Far in the distance, the cliffs tapered down, toward the inland lake that gave the town its name. To my right were the cliffs, and to my left was the ocean. The only way to go was forward.

I didn't know how long it would take me, and I didn't know if I would make it before the tide came all the way in. My feet had long ago gone numb in their sneakers.

But I sloshed one foot in front of the other, and I started to walk.

I didn't know how long I walked—it felt like hours. I was limping harder, barely able to put weight on my bad knee, and now that my arms were out of the water my left elbow was starting to swell. The sleeve of my shirt was tight and getting tighter, and the rising tide was up to my thighs.

I realized sluggishly that the wall of cliffs to my right had diminished. There was a path leading up the rise, and then a low wrought iron fence. I could glimpse something bright blue and bright yellow past the fence—a children's slide, I realized. It was a playground.

The sky was getting dark, though I still had no idea what time it was. I changed course, leaving the water and pulling myself painfully up the path. There was no one on the playground. I limped to the swing set and lowered myself to one of the swings, shaking with cold.

There was a *creak*, and then movement at the corner of my eye, and a little boy appeared. He was seven or eight years old, maybe, wearing rubber boots and a thick wool coat, a wool cap on his head. He had come around the corner from the monkey bars and stood looking at me with his big brown eyes, keeping a wary distance away.

"Hi," I managed to say, wondering how to sound unthreatening when sitting on a child's swing, shaking and shivering and bleeding, my arm twisted at the wrong angle. "I'm hurt. Can you help me?"

The boy rubbed his fingers together in a nervous gesture, watching me but not coming any closer. He didn't speak.

"Where's your mother?" I asked him.

He pointed behind him, though I could only see the monkey bars and the other side of the fence.

"What's your name?" I asked him as pain throbbed in my feet, which were no longer as numb as they had been in the ocean. My knee was seizing up, too; there was no way I was ever getting off this swing.

The boy spoke softly at first, and then he repeated himself: "Toby."

"Toby," I said. And then it hit me—this lonely place, this little boy, the absence of any other kids or parents. "Are you real?"

His eyes went wide. "Are you?"

Would a ghost ask me that? I didn't know. Maybe not. "Yes," I said. "I'm real, and my name is Shea. I need help. Can you find your mother for me?"

Toby took a step back, but he was still staring at me.

"Please," I said to him, my voice thin with pain.

"Toby!"

A woman came through the gate, running. She was wearing jeans, a thick sweater, and a thick coat. She resembled her son, her hair in short twists, and she looked alarmed. "Toby, I told you not to go to the monkey bars! Get away from that lady!" She stopped when she got to the boy and looked at me. "Oh my God."

The world faded out for a second, then came back into focus. "I had an accident," I managed as the woman pulled her cell phone from her back pocket. "Can you call an ambulance, please?"

Stay awake, I thought as the woman dialed 911. Another half-forgotten piece of wisdom—weren't you supposed to avoid passing out? Was that for a concussion or hypothermia? I couldn't remember. I gripped the cold chain of the swing and tried to stay upright. I looked at Toby, whose back was pressed into his mother's legs now. He was still watching me.

"Why didn't you ask the lady?" he said as his mother spoke into the phone.

"What?" I said.

"The lady behind you. Why didn't you ask her? Didn't she want to help?"

I stared at him. I didn't want to turn around. I couldn't. "There's a lady behind me?" I asked the boy, my voice almost a whisper.

He shook his head. "Not now. Before." He pointed to a spot right behind the swing set. "She was right there."

I could hear a siren, far away now but getting closer. Toby's mother held the phone to her ear with one hand, and she dropped her other absently to her son's shoulder, keeping him close.

Everything spun, and I gripped the swing chain tighter. "Toby," I said, "I want you to promise me something. If you ever see that lady again, don't talk to her. Run."

I thought maybe he nodded. But I couldn't be sure, because the world faded and I closed my eyes.   .

CHAPTER FORTY-FOUR

October 2017

SHEA

When I awoke, the first thing I saw was Michael.

He was sitting next to my hospital bed, absorbed in reading something I couldn't see. He was wearing a black zip-up hoodie, and he had several days' worth of dark stubble on his jaw. He had a frown of concentration between his eyebrows, but when he heard me move it disappeared as he looked at me.

"The drugs are wearing off," he said in a gentle voice.

They'd been wearing off for a while. I'd opened my eyes once before, though I had no idea how long ago. That time, no one had been in the room. I saw the empty coffee cup next to Michael and guessed why he'd been gone last time.

"I can't move," I said, my voice a croak.

Michael reached to a table out of my line of sight and brought a cup of water with a straw, putting the straw to my lips. "Your elbow is broken," he said as I drank. "So is your knee. Two fractured ribs, the gash on your forehead got ten stitches, and you were halfway to hypothermia. Still you walked three miles. No one knows how you did it."

Lily, I thought as I let the straw go. But no, that wasn't right. Lily had been there somewhere as I walked, but she hadn't done it for me. I'd done it myself.

Lily might have pushed me over the edge, but everything after that had been me.

"Your sister was here," Michael said as he put the cup of water away. "She wanted to take leave from work, but I told her to go and I'd call her if you woke up. Which I'm going to do shortly."

Esther would be worried. Really, really worried. What she wouldn't know yet was that now, at what looked like my lowest point, it was finally time for her to stop worrying about me. "I have to tell you something," I said to Michael.

"Yes, you do," he said. He was calm, confident, and sure, concerned without being rattled, and I knew to my bones that I'd picked the right man. That he'd be what I needed him to be. "I hope it's a story about how you fell over the cliff behind the Greer mansion and ended up in the ocean."

"How did you know that's where I went over?"

"Because Beth Greer says her motion sensors went off and you told her you were at her house."

I felt my first pulse of trepidation. "Beth is here?"

Michael gave me a look. "Of course not. She called someone, though it wasn't me, and told them. I heard it through official channels."

That sounded like Beth: manipulating as much as she could without getting directly involved. I felt the fire of something burn deep in my belly. Revenge, maybe. "Listen," I said to Michael.

He turned his dark eyes to me. "I'm listening."

I took a breath, organizing my thoughts, and then I started. "When I was nine, I was walking home from school. A man pulled up beside me in his car."

This wasn't the story he was expecting. I saw a flicker of recognition cross his eyes, but he didn't interrupt.

"He asked if I was cold, and then he told me my parents were waiting for me and he had to take me to them. He told me to get into his car, and I did." I lay back against the pillows. The painkillers were definitely wearing off, and everything was starting to hurt, but I was used to pain now. I had to get this out before they gave me pills that put me to sleep again. "I knew something was wrong almost right away," I told Michael. "It was a gut feeling, even though I was only a kid. We weren't heading in the direction of my house. I asked if I could get out, and the man said no. Then he put his hand on my leg, trying to push it under my uniform skirt."

There was silence in the room except for the busy murmur of the hospital outside. Michael looked tense, but still he didn't interrupt, and again I knew I'd picked the right man. "I won't go into details," I said. "We struggled. He didn't manage to sexually assault me, because he was still driving the car. He did hit me hard enough to make me bleed. The car slowed down and I got the door open. I jumped out and ran."

Michael closed his eyes. His breathing was a little harsh.

"I was sure the man was chasing me," I said. "I thought he would get out of the car and run after me, or that he'd circle the block, looking to grab me again. I didn't think he'd just let me run." Pain throbbed up from my broken elbow, and I tried not to wince. "I ran into a stranger's backyard and hid in the garden shed. I crouched in there, barely daring to breathe, jumping at every sound. I had no idea how long I stayed in there, but I found out later it was three hours. It was winter, and by the time I got home it was fully dark and I couldn't feel my hands or my feet."

Michael opened his eyes again, his jaw working as he bit back whatever he wanted to say.

"My parents were frantic," I said. "There were police at my house. My father was crying. I'd never seen my father cry. I didn't think it was possible. They were in a panic because I hadn't come home from school, and when my parents called the police about it, the police had showed up in minutes. They were alarmed because a girl had been found dead fifteen miles away, and they wanted to be sure it wasn't me."

Finally, Michael spoke, and though his voice was tense, he kept it low. "Anton Anders," he said.

"He didn't chase me," I said. The words were harder to get out, because I was gritting my teeth through the growing pain. "He didn't come after me at all. When I ran, he drove to a different neighborhood and waited near a schoolyard. He picked up a girl named Sherry Haines. She was nine, just like I was. He raped and murdered her and dumped her body by the side of a two-lane highway. He did all that in the three hours while I was hiding in the shed." I looked at Michael. "You know the Anton Anders case, I assume, since you were a cop, and so were your father and uncle." When he nodded, I said, "I was Girl A. I *am* Girl A. She's me."

"I wondered about it," Michael admitted. "The way you reacted when I said that Joshua Black solved the Sherry Haines case. It seemed personal somehow. You're the right age to be Girl A. I could have gotten access to the files, found your name for myself. But I didn't."

"You're supposed to be nosy," I said.

He looked at me and saw that I was trying, however weakly, for humor. A smile touched the corners of his handsome mouth. "Professionally nosy," he corrected me. "If you wanted to tell me, I figured you would."

He was right. "If I hadn't hidden in the shed," I said, "if I'd gone straight home and my parents had called the police, maybe Sherry Haines would still be alive."

"Or maybe not," Michael said. "Maybe he would have found a different victim on a different day. They've never been able to tie Anton Anders to any other cases, but no one who looks at the Sherry Haines case believes she was his first victim. He was too practiced. You were a terrified nine-year-old girl who had just been assaulted, Shea. Nothing was your fault. Nothing at all."

"I know," I said. "I've thought about every angle for the past twenty years. I know I'm not to blame. But I'm not a little girl this time around." I shifted in the bed as the pain got fiercer. "Don't call a nurse yet," I said when Michael reached for the call button. "Just listen. Beth Greer murdered her half sister, Lily, in 1978. She hit Lily over the head with an ashtray in the master bedroom of the Greer mansion, then drowned her in the bathtub. Then she dumped Lily's body in the thick of the woods at the end of Claire Lake. Lily has been there all this time, until her remains were found a few weeks ago."

"Jesus Christ, Shea," Michael said, shocked. "Did Beth confess?"

"Of course not."

"Then how do you know this?"

I shook my head. "It doesn't matter." Behind Michael, the door opened and a nurse came in. She pulled a wheeled tray with her: a blood pressure cuff, pills in a small paper cup. I ignored her and put my good hand on Michael's arm. "Call your cop friends," I said. "And call Joshua Black. Tell all of them that Beth killed Lily Knowles because Lily was the Lady Killer. It's her remains that were found, that I messaged you about. DNA will prove it if they do a test. For all I know, Beth is going to try and find some way to stop all of this from happening. Call them *now*."

"You're awake," the nurse said, coming along the other side of my bed. "We need a moment, please," she said to Michael.

"Shea, this is crazy. If Beth didn't confess, there's no way you can know this."

"Lily killed all of them, including Julian," I said. "We'll give them everything Ransom gave us. We have to re-create the timeline and look for murders we didn't know about before. Mariana was an accident. She drank too much, or maybe took medication, after a fight with Lily. She thought she was going to find Lily, to apologize to her, when she got in that car."

"Um," the nurse said, probably shocked. But I wasn't looking at her. I was looking at Michael.

His gaze held mine. He guessed how I knew, maybe. I had too many details. I had seen it.

But like he'd said before, if I wanted to tell him, I would.

"This is it, isn't it?" he said. "This is the end after all these years."

"This is the beginning," I said as the nurse lifted my arm. "Call them. Now."

CHAPTER FORTY-FIVE

From the *Claire Lake News Online*, October 2017:

POLICE INVESTIGATION IN ARLEN HEIGHTS SPARKS QUESTIONS

Police were recently seen entering the Arlen Heights home of Beth Greer, who was acquitted of a series of murders in 1978. They were inside the home for several hours, apparently with the authority of a warrant.

Carl Contreras, chief of police with the Claire Lake Police Department, declined to give a statement except to say, "I cannot comment on any ongoing investigation."

Greer was arrested and tried for the murders of Thomas Armstrong, 31, and Paul Veerhoever, 36, in 1977. She was found not guilty. The murders have never been solved.

"She's quiet," a neighbor, Winifred Platts, said of Greer, who has lived in her childhood home since the acquittal. "The press used to hang around after the trial, but they went away and it's been quiet ever since. We don't see her much, just at the store or whatnot. She doesn't seem to have any friends. We're not happy to have a murderer in the neighborhood, but she had her day in court. If she didn't do it, then I guess she didn't. But I don't like this police search at all."

Claire Lake Police will not comment on whether the warrant is connected to the so-called Lady Killer murders. Because of double jeopardy laws, Greer cannot be charged with those murders a second time.

"So what does it mean, then?" asks Timothy Garge, another neighbor who was busy raking his lawn. "Did she kill someone else? That's just great. If she doesn't sell, we might have to."

From the *Oregon News*, October 2017:

"There's nothing to find at my house," Beth Greer said.

... The law of double jeopardy would apply to the murders of Armstrong and Veerhoever, though it would not apply to any other crimes Miss Greer might be accused of that arise from the investigation at her home.

Miss Greer issued a statement through the office of her attorney, Ransom Wells: "The search of my home was legal persecution, pure and simple." The statement was not given personally by Wells, who his staff say is in declining health, but sent by email to local media outlets. "I have lived a quiet life for forty years, ever since my acquittal at trial. I have harmed no one. This has been brought on by a blogger named Shea Collins, who is seeking fame based on lies about crimes she claims I've committed. All of it is categorically false, and I'm considering legal action to protect myself."

Collins apparently runs a website called the Book of Cold Cases, which contains several articles about the Lady

Killer murders along with articles about other famous unsolved crimes. Collins appears to be a Claire Lake resident,
though attempts to reach her for comment were met with
silence . . .

"She's messing with me," I said.

I was fully dressed in my hospital room, sitting in a wheelchair,
talking on the phone as the nurse put my bag in my lap. I was being
discharged after a monthlong stay that included surgeries on both my
elbow and my knee. My arm was in a sling and I'd be on crutches for
a few months at least, but I was finally going home. It should have
been an exciting moment, but I was too busy talking to Joshua Black
to notice.

"Messing with you?" he said. "She just seems angry to me."

Of course Beth was angry. The full force of the Claire Lake PD
had come down on her. What Joshua Black had to do with any of it, I
could only guess; for a man who had been retired for a decade, he
seemed to be central. No one in the department held more respect or
more sway.

"She's screwing with my head," I said as the nurse started pushing
my chair down the hallway. "She's gone to the media to tell everyone
who I am, and that she's planning to sue me. She's sent so much traffic to my website that the server crashed. I have over two hundred
emails in my inbox, and my phone won't stop ringing with requests
for interviews. She's just made me famous."

"Sounds terrible to me," Black said.

"It is terrible. I haven't talked to my bosses yet, but I could easily
get fired over the publicity. And I've never wanted to be in the public
eye." Even now, all I wanted was to go home to my condo and get
Winston Purrchill back from Esther, who had taken him in while I'd
been in the hospital. I wanted one of my quiet nights with my laptop,
my cat, and my familiar anxieties, and I had the feeling I was never

going to have one of those nights again. "And at the same time," I said to Joshua, "I called my health insurance company this morning. I assumed I was going to be in debt for the rest of my life, but guess what? I'm not. Everything is paid for."

"Wow," Joshua said. "And you think that was Beth?"

"She's the only rich person I know." I'd had two surgeries, including titanium pieces inserted into my crushed left elbow. I'd had drugs and antibiotics and physical therapy, which I was going to continue for months as an outpatient. Even with the insurance from my job, I'd thought I'd be underwater forever. The bill for the deductibles alone was probably more than my annual salary. And yet I didn't owe a penny.

I could practically hear Beth's voice, dry and a little impatient: *Well, my dead sister* did *try to kill you. I suppose I'm somewhat responsible.*

She'd paid my hospital bill, and then she'd made a statement that threatened to sue me, and threw me to the publicity wolves. *Game on, Beth.*

"God only knows what she's thinking," Joshua said. "I've never known."

He was angry, too. Since my accident, he'd visited me in the hospital a few times and we'd talked on the phone. I liked him so much it was a little scary, and I felt for him. He'd spent forty years believing that Beth wasn't a murderer, and now he wasn't so sure. I knew that his original intuition was right—Beth wasn't a murderer, at least while she was accused and on trial. The murder had come after. But I couldn't explain to him how I knew that, because Joshua Black didn't seem like the type to believe in ghosts.

What I had given him was everything I knew about the existence of Lily Knowles, starting with her birth certificate. Lily Knowles, who had left no legal trace behind since aging out of the foster system at eighteen. It had taken Black maybe half a minute to ask himself if Beth's missing half sister was connected to the remains found by the lake. Now he and the Claire Lake PD had taken over.

"I don't know what she's thinking, either," I said, though that was a lie. I knew exactly what Beth was thinking. She wanted me off-balance, wondering what she was going to do next. She wanted me to understand how much power she had. And she wanted a fight. "Are you going to tell me what they found in the master bedroom?" I asked him. "The police will only say that any evidence they find will be sent for testing. It's frustratingly vague."

"You know I can't tell you that," he said, though I had no doubt that Joshua knew every detail of the investigation. "I will ask *you* again, though, how you knew exactly where to look and what we might find. You seem to know a lot about something that happened before you were born."

"Beth told me," I said. The nurse had pushed me into the elevator, and we were descending. "She told me about Lily Knowles in our interviews, and Ransom Wells gave me the documentation, including the birth certificate. According to Beth, Lily is responsible for the murders of Julian Greer, Thomas Armstrong, Paul Veerhoever, and Lawrence Gage. And there are likely others, too, including a grounds-keeper. We just have to find the others."

There was a moment of silence on the other end of the line. Joshua was playing it close to the vest, which he was so good at. How he'd felt when he'd learned, after forty years, that Beth had a half sister, he hadn't told me. He was all business when he talked to me about the case. I suspected that maybe, for the first time in a long time, the legendary Detective Black was mad. Really mad.

"So you went to the Greer mansion alone," he said to me on the phone now as the elevator doors opened and the nurse pushed me down the busy hallway.

"Yes," I said.

"And you fell over the cliff."

We'd gone over this before, more than once, but a cop is always a cop. "Yes. I fell."

"And Beth wasn't home at the time."

"You know she wasn't. She was getting a medical scan done. It's an ironclad alibi. Beth didn't push me, I swear."

"It just seems odd that you would fall over a dangerous cliff on your own. You're certain you weren't intoxicated?"

"I'm certain. It was an accident, okay? I stood in the wrong place and leaned the wrong way, and over I went. They really should put a fence up there. It's dangerous. Now, how about you tell me what the lab is testing and how long it will take?"

The change of subject worked. "I never said there was any lab testing."

"It was in the statement in the news."

"No, it said that anything that was collected *would* be sent for lab testing. You're as bad as those reporters. There's nothing to report."

"No? Then why am I hearing that the DNA tests on the body that was found by the lake are being expedited?"

"Where are you hearing that?"

"Some of those emails in my inbox are from people who hear things. Is it true?"

"I'm hanging up now. Please be careful, Shea. That's all I ask."

I thanked him and hung up, thinking *Of course I'll be careful, but I've already survived Anton Anders and Lily Knowles, two of Claire Lake's worst murderers. I can survive Beth Greer.*

The nurse pushed me through the front doors of the hospital, and I inhaled the fresh air, taking it in deep even though it was cloudy and cold. The bite of fall felt good in my throat and my lungs. An SUV had pulled up to the curb, and a familiar figure got out.

I thanked the nurse as Michael De Vos took the crutches from her and helped me out of the wheelchair. He was bundled in a wool coat against the chill, and he'd left the stubble on his jaw at my request. He looked woodsy and masculine and all-over good. He smiled at me and kissed me sweetly as I leaned on the crutches.

"Ready?" he asked.

"Yes," I said.

He opened the passenger door of the SUV. I hesitated for a moment, my gaze on the darkness of the passenger seat.

I glanced at Michael to see him watching me. He looked like he wasn't in a hurry, as if he could wait all day. "You can do this," he said.

"I know," I replied.

I limped to the passenger seat and got in. I handed Michael the crutches as I swung my bad leg into the SUV. Then I took a breath and closed the door, ready to go home.

CHAPTER FORTY-SIX

Five Months Later
April 2018

From the popular podcast *Listening to True Crime*, episode 109, released April 13, 2018:

> **PAULA WATTS (LTC host):** I've done a deep dive into this. The Lady Killer case has been an obsession of mine for years—I know I'm not the only one. There are a million details, a million theories. And I mean, Beth Greer! You just look at her, and it's like, "Could she have done it? Maybe she could. Maybe she shot two random men just because she was rich and bored and crazy." You can see it, in a way. And then you wonder, am I thinking that because that's what society has programmed me to think? That any woman who doesn't fit inside a neat little box, any woman who has sexuality as blatant and unapologetic as Beth Greer's, maybe that woman is

dangerous. Maybe she should be shunned and put in a jail cell. For us as women, I think, we look at that case and it brings up so many questions.

SHEA COLLINS: I know. I agree. I've been obsessed with the case myself for a long time, which you can see from the articles on my site.

PAULA: But this is crazy, isn't it? This is nuts. I read that they reopened the Julian Greer case. Jesus, they reopened it! Because now we know that Beth Greer's mother had a baby out of wedlock, and Lily Knowles existed, and she, at the very least— We don't know much, but we know she was a foster child in the system and that as an adult she was a psychiatric patient. And I'm not saying anything about people with mental illness, because they can't help that, but this was the seventies, and the treatment Lily probably got was to get thrown in a room somewhere with some screwed-up antipsychotic drugs, and that's it. She was a mess.

SHEA: They've found some of her psychiatric records and released them, though not all of them. They've also reopened the Lawrence Gage case in Arizona. Did you know they lost the bullet in that case? It's just gone. Apparently there was a fire in one of their evidence storage spaces and some evidence was lost, including that bullet. So we'll never know if the ballistics match the other murders. But I've heard they're pursuing the case with DNA.

PAULA: There was DNA left at that crime scene?

SHEA: They found a couple of hairs, I think. And if they can get the DNA from the hairs, they can match it to—

PAULA: They might match it to Beth Greer, right? Because Lily was Beth's sister.

SHEA: Yeah, I think that could happen. Or they can match it to the DNA from the body they found, which we think is Lily's body.

PAULA: So have they matched the DNA from that body to Beth's?

SHEA: I don't know. No one will tell me.

PAULA: Come on! You're the expert on this case. You know everything!

SHEA: There are lots of things the cops won't tell me, though believe me, I ask. I'm a big pain in their asses. They pretty much hate me, but that's fine.

PAULA: You're so freaking brave it blows me away. Beth Greer must hate you, too. And maybe she isn't the Lady Killer, but she's a pretty intimidating person, even now.

SHEA: I don't think she hates me. She agreed to have me interview her in the first place, and she told me about Lily. No one knew about Lily until she pointed me in the right direction.

PAULA: But because of you, she could be looking at new murder charges. Aren't you a bit scared of her?

SHEA: I've been researching this case. I've seen some things. I had an accident it took months to recover from. Honestly, not much scares me anymore. I want the truth to come out.

PAULA: Does Beth Greer ever call you? Do you guys, like, hang out? Be honest. What's she like?

SHEA: We don't hang out. We have talked—I'll say that she knows my number, and I know hers. We don't shoot the shit or anything. As for what she's like, I don't really know how to describe it. I think the Beth you see in the media, in the photos, a lot of that is the real Beth. It isn't like she's at home baking cookies or something. She's hard to figure out, and she likes it that way.

PAULA: If you guys have wine parties or start a book club or something, call me. I'll move to Oregon for that.

SHEA: If we do that, I'll definitely call.

The doctor's office fired me.

I couldn't blame them. I'd left work one day a nobody, and then I'd been in the hospital for a month and I'd come back famous—or maybe I was infamous. I never really knew which it was.

It didn't matter. I was busy. Traffic and memberships on the Book of Cold Cases skyrocketed. I got a lot of interview requests, though I didn't accept many of them. I started work on an article about my interviews with Beth, the amazing story she'd spun. The article was long, and it was by far the best thing I'd ever written, and, to my amazement, *Rolling Stone* bought it. After that came more requests—for more articles about the Lady Killer case, and for articles about the other cases I'd researched. I was a guest on a few podcasts, and then, with Michael's help, I tried the unthinkable: I started a podcast myself. The numbers started out good, and then they got better.

I'd never planned to be this person, talking all the time in the spotlight. I'd never chased fame, and I wouldn't have chased it now except for the fact that my fame served one important purpose: It kept the spotlight on Beth.

Michael's private detective business started to climb, too, and he took on better and better cases. Our relationship was serious, and it was the best thing in my life—I was crazy about him, and I thought he felt the same about me. We worked together on a lot of projects, both mine and his, and we spent a lot of nights at either his place or mine. But we mutually agreed that we weren't living together yet, and we made no mention of marriage. We were both too burned. It was one of the things we understood instinctively about each other without having to talk it to death. There were a lot of things like that with me and Michael.

"I like him," Esther said when we had lunch together one Saturday in a diner in downtown Claire Lake. "He's ultraserious, like you are. He's smart. He likes you. And as the girls say today, he's a snack."

I flinched. "Please don't say things like that. You're an embarrassing mom already, and the baby isn't even here yet."

My sister smiled and sipped her sparkling water with a twist of lime. She and Will had been scheduled for their first round of IVF when they found out she was already pregnant. Now she was quietly happy in a way I'd never seen her, though of course she was still Esther the overachiever. Everything about this baby was being organized to the smallest detail. I wouldn't be surprised if it had a 401(k) already. "You can be the cool aunt," Esther said. "I'll be the awkward mom. It works for me. How is the physio going?"

I shrugged and speared a piece of roasted potato—using my right hand, because my left elbow ached almost constantly. "I go as often as I can."

"Shea. You're working too much. You had a terrible trauma. You have to take care of yourself."

"I am," I argued. "I will. Just as soon as all of this is over."

Esther frowned. "I know that Beth is over sixty, but she looks pretty healthy to me. You're exposing her as a murderer. Maybe you should be careful in dark parking lots."

"I never go into dark parking lots," I said. "And Beth talks a big game about suing me, but that's bluster. She doesn't actually care about murder charges. If she did, she would never have agreed to talk to me at all."

"I don't get this," Esther said. "There's no such thing as someone who doesn't care about murder charges."

"That's because you haven't met Beth."

I didn't tell her about Beth's aneurysm. Beth thought her time was limited, and she didn't care about how the last part—whether weeks or months or possibly years—played out. She'd been tied to that house, to Lily and Mariana and Julian, for forty years. She was done.

At one in the morning that night, my cell phone rang. I was alone in bed—Michael had an early flight to San Francisco in the morning—and I was halfway between waking and sleeping. Winston was curled against my chest, kneading imaginary biscuits on my T-shirt, and he flattened his ears in annoyance when I reached over him and answered the phone.

"Hi, Beth," I said. She only ever called me at one in the morning.

"'An anonymous source'?" she said, not bothering with hello. "Did they actually buy that? I don't know whether to be insulted or amused."

"Try both," I said, using one of Beth's own lines. She was talking about an article that had just run on CNN's website, in which I said that "an anonymous source" had tipped me off to the possibility of Beth murdering her half sister in 1978.

"Whatever," Beth said, sounding more like the twenty-three-year-old she'd been in the seventies instead of a woman who was over sixty. "I also saw the *60 Minutes* thing. Were you trying to pull at my heartstrings?"

The *60 Minutes* piece was an interview with the wives and grown children of Thomas Armstrong and Paul Veerhoever about the devastation the murders had left in their lives. "No, that was all Michael," I said to Beth. "I know better. You don't have a heart."

"Neither do you."

I smiled, stroking Winston Purrchill's grumpy head. "I have a heart, Beth. I just don't let you see it. How's Lily? I haven't seen her since she pushed me off a cliff."

"What a bitch you are," Beth said mildly. "I knew it when I first saw you in that park, thinking you could follow me. I knew you'd be a pain in my elderly ass."

I leaned back against my pillows. "If I'm such a pain in your ass, then why are you calling me?"

"Because Ransom is dead."

I went quiet, staring into the darkness. I wondered what to feel. Sadness, anger, pity? Try all of them. "I'm sorry," I said, the phrase we all use when we can't think of what to say, one that provides no comfort at all.

Beth was quiet for a long moment, and I realized she was collecting herself. I'd never known her to have any kind of strong emotion, let alone one that made her speechless. I was witnessing it now. I waited.

"Well," Beth said at last, her voice tight. "Don't think this means anything. There are other lawyers. He left me in the hands of his successor, in fact. I've still got some fight in me. So what's your next move?"

"Your DNA," I said.

"You must have been so disappointed to find out they didn't take samples in 1977," Beth said. "It was blood type they looked at back then, not DNA. But they never even asked for my blood, because they had nothing to compare it to."

"They'll get it now," I said.

"My lawyer is fighting that."

"He'll lose."

The first time we'd had one of these middle-of-the night conversations, it had felt utterly strange. Beth and I were supposed to be enemies. I was trying to get her put away for murdering Lily. But she'd call me, and we'd spar like we had in her living room in the Greer mansion.

I didn't know why we did this. I just knew it was instinctive for me. Beth understood my obsession with this case because she was the center of it and was as obsessed as I was. And, of course, there was Lily. No one knew Lily the way Beth and I did. No one had seen her, felt her presence, the way we had. It was impossible to explain, which made it so simple when I talked to someone I didn't have to explain it to.

"Is Joshua talking to you?" I asked her.

"Joshua will never talk to me again," Beth said, "but you knew that already. How is he, by the way?"

"He's fine," I said. "Angry and determined, but fine. He doesn't act like he's retired."

"That's because he isn't. On paper, yes, but otherwise, no. I'm glad I've given him a new cause so he can do his white-knight act again. He was always happiest when he had a crusade."

"What did you do with the ashtray?" I asked her.

"It's still in the house. I've tried to throw it away a dozen times, but Lily won't let me. It always comes back, and she moves it around the house. It was in the living room one day when you were here. You saw it."

I remembered the ashtray I'd seen, big and heavy. I'd thought at the time it was the size of a child's head. Strange, because Beth didn't smoke. She had hit Lily with it so hard—so hard. They must have found the marks on Lily's skull. "You never left town in all this time," I said.

"You think I didn't try?" Beth laughed without humor. "I'd pack my suitcase, and she would unpack it. I'd throw things out, and she'd bring them back. I got in the car a dozen times without any belongings except the clothes on my back, trying to run. I always ended up back at this house. You can believe me or not, but it's true." She paused. "I didn't want to do any of this, Shea. I know I'm the villain here, and I accept that. But I've paid and paid and paid. Prison might even be refreshing at this point. Do you know why I call you at one in the morning? Because despite everything, you're the only person I can talk to."

I had just been thinking the same thing about her, but I wasn't about to admit it. "Giving my name to the press was a nice touch," I said. "Have I mentioned that you got me fired?"

"Being fired isn't the only thing you should thank me for."

I sat up against my pillows. "Thank you? For what?"

"For waking you up—all the way up. It's amazing what you can do when you stop sleepwalking through your own life, isn't it?"

I thought about my life now—my writing career, my relationship with Michael, my new relationship with Esther. I was starting the process of getting my driver's license, and I had stopped hiding in my condo all the time. Still, I couldn't let Beth Greer take all the credit. "You didn't change my life, Beth. I did."

"Do you know what's interesting?" Beth said, her tone imperious again, as if I hadn't spoken. "Joshua Black won't speak to me, but I saved his life. To this day, I think Lily would have killed him if she got the chance. Because Lily disappeared, he got to spend thirty years on the job catching criminals. Catching murderers. Like the man who tried to murder you."

There was silence on the line. I couldn't think of anything to say.

"Good night, Shea," Beth said, and then the line went dead.

CHAPTER FORTY-SEVEN

Eight Months Later
Christmas Eve 2018

SHEA

The day the story ended, I was standing in line at CVS, waiting to buy aspirin.

It was raining. They said it was a winter storm, the rain ice-cold, the streets dangerous. The advice on the news was to stay home for Christmas, tuck in with your family, and don't leave the house. I had planned to do that—I was about to spend the next two days with Michael, sipping wine and watching TV with Winston Purrchill on my lap. I'd only leave to visit Esther and Will and my new nephew, Zach. It had been a wild, stressful, wonderful year, and I was going to unwind. I just needed some aspirin first, because no matter how much time passed, my knee and my elbow still ached.

The line was six people deep, and I stared at nothing as I waited, thinking about the book I was writing. An agent had contacted me after the *Rolling Stone* article ran, and we'd shopped a proposal to publishers. Four months later we had a deal, and now I had to write the rest of the book. Once this book about the Lady Killer case was finished, the publisher was already interested in hearing a pitch from me for another book, about a different case. Apparently, I was a true-crime writer and podcaster now instead of a doctor's receptionist. I still wasn't sure how that had happened.

Everyone in line moved up, and my phone started buzzing silently in my purse. Whoever it was, I didn't feel like talking right now. My knee and my elbow were throbbing, and I wanted to go home. But my phone buzzed, then buzzed again. On the TV mounted on the wall, the man talking about the terrible weather was interrupted, and I heard the words "Beth Greer."

I looked up at the screen. A news anchor was talking. Beneath him was the headline: BETH GREER DEAD.

". . . died suddenly and shockingly," the anchor said. "Miss Greer's car was seen driving erratically on Claire Lake Road. When the car stopped and medics arrived, Miss Greer had already passed away. It's thought she had some kind of medical emergency, possibly a heart attack or a stroke, while driving. Beth Greer first came to fame here in Claire Lake when she was accused of being the so-called Lady Killer—"

Everything went cold. My head spun. In my purse, my phone buzzed and buzzed.

"Excuse me," said the woman behind me in line. "It's your turn."

I walked to the counter. I put the box of aspirin down. Then I turned and left.

Damn it, Beth, I thought as I walked unseeingly out of the store and into the parking lot. *You and your goddamned aneurysm.* I got soaked as I walked to my car, a sensible little Honda I'd bought when I got my driver's license. The safest car I could buy, because no matter how much I vanquished her, deep down, part of me was still that terrified nine-year-old girl.

Only yesterday I'd gotten the news: The DNA from the body found at Claire Lake was a familial match to Beth. The woman's body, with violent blows to its skull, was Beth's relative. Beth had used every delay tactic her lawyer could come up with to put off giving a sample of her blood, but in the end she'd given it. She had been buying time.

The noose had been closing in on Beth. It was almost completely closed, in fact. But in the last moment, she'd slipped away, this time for good.

I got soaked by the rain as I fumbled for my keys. I dropped them, and I bent to the concrete, feeling for them with numb fingers. My hair was wet in my eyes, water dripping into my coat down the back of my neck. My broken elbow and my broken knee pulsed with old, unhealed pain. A headache pounded in my temples. I picked up the keys and mopped the water off my face as the rain came down harder and my teeth started to chatter.

I finally opened the car and got in, slamming the door and sitting in silence as the rain pounded the roof. Where had Beth been going when it happened? The news said she'd been on Claire Lake Road, which wound inland by the lake at the base of the cliffs. What was she doing there? Was she going to the place where she had left Lily's body?

Had she been trying to escape again? *I got in the car a dozen times without any belongings except the clothes on my back, trying to run.*

Had she known when it started happening, or had it all been too fast? Had there been pain?

On the passenger seat next to me, my phone buzzed and buzzed. I could see the display where the phone had half slid from my purse: Michael. Esther. Joshua Black. Michael again.

Beth Greer was dead.

Months ago, I'd gone to Anton Anders's parole hearing. Michael had gone with me. I didn't have to face Anders himself, but I'd read my prepared statement to the parole board. I'd told them that Anton Anders was a rapist and a murderer who had tried to kill me. The fact that it was over twenty years ago now didn't matter; what mattered was that I'd almost died. What mattered was that if he went free now, I would never feel safe. I would go back to hiding in my condo, back to taking the bus. I'd go back to living half a life, when the only thing I'd done "wrong" was walk home from school. I'd told them I didn't think that was justice. I'd said that true fairness in the world wasn't possible, but letting Anton Anders have his freedom wasn't even close. I'd said that it was a pretty simple decision to at least be more fair than that.

They'd denied his parole. The first person I wanted to call when I heard the news was Beth. It didn't make any sense, but there it was.

I didn't call her, but she heard the news anyway. The next week, I got a package in the mail: a red shawl, old and well cared for, folded neatly in tissue paper. It took me a minute to realize it was the shawl Beth had worn the day she was acquitted, when she stood next to Ransom in front of all those reporters. The shawl from the photo that had gone on the cover of *Life*.

Beth hadn't put a note with the shawl, but she didn't have to. She was telling me that she knew what victory felt like, especially when it was hard-won. I put the shawl in the closet, neatly tucked into its tissue paper, and I didn't tell anyone about it.

Beth Greer was dead.

She was a murderer. A bitch. A cipher. A lonely girl raised by a broken family. She was brave and manipulative and selfish, and I owed her. I hated that, but I did.

I wondered if she'd seen Lily at the end. Because when I drifted off to sleep at night, I still felt Lily's hands on me, and I still heard her voice, icy with death, in my ear:

Let's go.

I pushed my wet hair out of my eyes, started the car, and headed home.

CHAPTER FORTY-EIGHT

February 2019

Someone new had bought the Greer mansion.

Why not? It was a beautiful structure on a piece of Arlen Heights' prime real estate. It was a piece of Claire Lake history, now that Beth Greer was dead. The rumors that it was haunted only added to the mystique, and no one really believed that, anyway. It was true that Julian Greer had been murdered in the house, but that was in 1973—too far back to seem real to the family that was moving in. It was rumored that Beth Greer had killed her own sister in the master bedroom, and she'd died before they could prove it. But it didn't matter much. The couple who bought the place were in their thirties, their kids eight and ten. The seventies were a bygone era to them.

The family had money—lots of it. They had plans. All of Beth's dusty midcentury furniture was cleared out, sent to high-end consignment services to be sold to collectors. The old magazines and old ashtrays, Mariana's jar of cold cream and Julian's ties, were disposed of. Walls were going to be knocked out, and the living room and kitchen would become an open space. The old kitchen cupboards would come down, and stainless-steel appliances would make an appearance. A fence went up along the cliff to the ocean, and in spring a landscaping company would start digging to make a sleek stone patio for entertaining, with a retractable roof to keep out the rain. People would sip drinks and look out over the ocean in summer, making boisterous conversation as the kids ran in the yard.

For a while, there were only workers coming and going in the house, handling everything: paint, pot lights, hardwood flooring. But once the house was livable—and once the all-important fence went up—the family moved in. For the first time in decades, the Greer mansion had life in it.

Cars came and went. The kids went to school; the parents went to work. Friends and family visited. Weekends were nonstop, as the kids went to their friends' homes or had them over, and the adults ran errands. There were dinner parties and birthday parties and outings with grandparents.

But at night, after the exhausted kids were asleep and the parents were drifting off, thinking about tomorrow's to-do list, there was a light in the window of a room upstairs. A soft light that moved, as if someone were pacing. Watching. Someone who never slept.

Sometimes, there were two lights.

The family never talked about the cold spots in the hallways, or the strange dreams they sometimes had about someone walking through the house. They never talked about the doors left open, or the feeling you often got, especially when you were home alone, that someone was just behind you. The little girl never told anyone about the footprints she saw in the dewy grass some mornings, as if someone had come to the living room windows and looked in. The little boy never told anyone about the time he woke up to find someone— something—holding his hand, holding it in an icy grip as he lay paralyzed on the bed. He always told himself he'd dreamed that hand, though he never quite believed it.

No one ever talked about why they never went near the cliffs, even when there was a fence protecting them, or why they preferred to keep the curtains over the floor-to-ceiling windows closed.

They went about their lives without talking about the unnerving things, the dark things, about the house.

And at night, while they slept, two strange lights burned in the darkness.

ACKNOWLEDGMENTS

With every book, I owe thanks to my editor, Danielle Perez. With this book, gratitude doesn't cover it. She worked tirelessly to make this book the best it could be. It's possible she has read it as many times as I have by now, which is an incredible feat. I owe her an unending debt for her patience, expertise, and willingness to always dig a little deeper. Thank you so much, Danielle.

Thanks to my agent, Pam Hopkins, who as always is a voice of reason in a crazy business. She is my rock.

Thanks to my husband, Adam, who helps me with plot problems, makes sure I always have the time and space to write, and does a million small things for me. I would never have written my first book, or any book after it, without your partnership and support.

Thanks to my sister, Nicole, and my brother, David. We had to lean on each other this year. I would be a wreck without both of you.

Thanks to the marketing and publicity team at Berkley, including Fareeda Bullert, Jin Yu, Danielle Keir, Tara O'Connor, and many others who do so much hard work putting my books into people's hands (or in front of their eyeballs). I appreciate everything you do.

Thanks to the art department at Berkley, who go above and beyond to give me amazing covers.

Thanks to the librarians and booksellers who recommend my books—you are magic. Thanks to the bloggers and everyday readers who tell a friend, "You've gotta read this." Thanks to the readers who write me nice notes, which always tend to hit my inbox on my lowest days.

Thanks to Molly and Stephanie, who talk me off the ledge over and over again, with every book. I'm always happy when I can return the favor.

Lastly, thank you to my mother, Suellen, who made me the woman I am and who passed in November 2020. I gave her an early copy of each of my books, but on release day she'd still go to her local bookstore, buy a copy, and tell the sales clerk excitedly that she was buying her daughter's book. I was beyond lucky to have a mother so brilliant, brave, and loving. Thank you for everything, Mom. Rest well.